CATARACT

CITY

CRAIG DAVIDSON

CATARACT CITY

a Novel

GRAYWOLF PRESS

First published in Canada by Doubleday Canada,
a division of Random House of Canada Limited

This publication is made possible, in part, by the voters of
Minnesota through a Minnesota State Arts Board Operating Support grant,
thanks to a legislative appropriation from the arts and cultural heritage fund, and
through a grant from the Wells Fargo Foundation Minnesota. Significant support
has also been provided by Target, the McKnight Foundation, Amazon.com, and
other generous contributions from foundations, corporations, and individuals.
To these organizations and individuals we offer our heartfelt thanks.

Published by Graywolf Press
250 Third Avenue North, Suite 600
Minneapolis, Minnesota 55401

www.graywolfpress.org

Published in the United States of America

ISBN 978-1-55597-674-3

2 4 6 8 9 7 5 3 1
First Graywolf Printing, 2014

Library of Congress Control Number: 2013958012

Cover design: Kapo Ng

For Colleen

"My city's still breathing (but barely, it's true)
through buildings gone missing like teeth.
The sidewalks are watching me think about you,
sparkled with broken glass.
I'm back with scars to show,
Back with the streets I know
Will never take me anywhere but here."

— The Weakerthans, from "Left and Leaving"

CONTENTS

CATARACT

CITY

PROLOGUE

STONY LONESOME

DUNCAN DIGGS

O f the 2,912 nights I spent in prison, two were the longest: the first and the last. But then, most cons would tell you the same. That first was endless, even more so than those long-ago nights in the woods with Owen when the wind hissed along the earth and the darkness was full of howling. In the woods an animal might rip you to shreds, sure, but it had no goal other than to protect itself and its offspring. The Kingston Pen housed animals who'd flatline you for looking at them cockeyed or breathing their air.

My cot felt no thicker than a communion wafer, coils corkscrewing into my spine. Penitentiary darkness was different than the outside-the-walls variety. A prison never achieves full black: security lamps forever burning behind mesh screens in the high corners of the cellblock, hourly flashlight sweeps. Your eyes become starved for true night—anything is better than granular, gummy semi-dark where shapes shift, half glimpsed, at the edges of your sight.

Still, you get used to it, in time. You get used to everything. Then comes that last night. We'd talk all about it, you know?

Some guys had been in and out a few times; it didn't mean as much to them. But for most of us it was . . . listen, it's like my buddy Silas Garrow says: *We all owe, and we're all paying.* What else is prison but the repayment? Then they set you loose. But some part of you figures you haven't quite paid enough. You've paid what the law demands, sure, but some debts exist beyond that. Blood dues, you could say. And those aren't collected in the usual way, are they? Those ones tiptoe up behind you like a sneak-thief.

That last night I lay in my cot—a new one, still prickly—thinking I'd die. The dread certainty entombed itself in my skull. It wouldn't be anything crazy, nobody was going to stab me in the neck with a sharpened toothbrush or anything like that. No, it'd be a boring and commonplace kind of death. An itty-bitty shred of plaque might detach from an artery wall, surf through my bloodstream, lodge in a ventricle and kill me dead. That would be fair and right, too, because I'd killed a man myself. A fair one-to-one transaction, blood cancelling blood. Fairer still that it should happen in the hours before my release. You've got to figure that's just the way such debts get repaid: with a gotcha.

I must've sweated off half my body weight that night. You could've wrung my cot like a sponge. When the first wave of sunlight washed across the cell floor . . . to be honest, I didn't know what to make of it. I could still die two steps outside the gates, I guess. That'd meet the accepted terms just as well.

And so it happened that one afternoon, nearly eight years after I'd scrubbed with delousing powder and donned an orange jumpsuit, my prison term ended. I collected the items I'd been admitted with: $2.32 in change, half a roll of cherry Life Savers stuck with pocket lint. I shook a few quarters out of the manila envelope and slid them into the prison's pay phone.

It was a surprise to everyone who I called. Truth? I surprised myself.

Exiting the penitentiary was a shocking experience. Maybe it's meant to be.

Two guards led me down a tight hallway, hands cuffed. A steel door emptied into a small yard, its clipped grass shadowed by the high wall. Jesus, *grass*.

One guard removed the cuffs while the other stood with a shotgun at port arms. I rubbed my wrists—not because the cuffs were tight but because I'd seen it done in films when the jailers took the cuffs off a criminal. Which I was. The fact cold-cocked me. For the past eight years I'd been a red fish swimming in a tank with other red fish. But I'd be freed into a sea of blue fish, law-abiding fish, and I was fearful I'd stick out—the prison bars permanently shadowing my face, even in clean sunshine.

The guards opened another door set into the grey wall. I walked between them. No tearful goodbyes. The door locked softly behind me. I stood in an archway ten feet from a main road. The Saint Lawrence Seaway was a strip of endless blue to the south. Cars motored up and down the hill, entering and exiting my sightline with strange suddenness. I hadn't seen anything move so fast in eight years; my eyes needed to adjust.

I took a few tentative steps. A tight group of onlookers clustered on the far sidewalk, gawking at me. I'd heard about these people; they hung around the gates hoping for this exact sight—the first fumbling steps of a long con as he squinted into the new sunlight, his legs trembling like a newborn foal's.

Ghouls. I ought to flip them the bird! But the idea of doing so filled me with shapeless fear—I pictured one of them making a call, then the prison doors opening to swallow me up again.

What charge? A red fish failing to swim submissively amongst the blue fish?

Owen leaned on the hood of his Lincoln, his right knee—the bad one—slightly bent to take the weight off.

"Thanks for coming," I said.

His face tilted upwards, smiling at the sun. "Hop in, man."

The Kingston Pen stood atop a hill, a monstrosity of conical turrets and razorwire. I'd forgotten how beastly it looked from the outside. I unrolled the car window. Wind curled over the earth, pulling up the smell of springtime grass. I inhaled deep, dizzying breaths.

Owen drove down a switchback and hit the highway. My breath came in a shallow rush—I was nearly hyperventilating. Stands of Jack pine blurred into a green wall topped by a limitless sky. I hadn't seen unbroken sky in so long. It's too easy to forget the sheer size of the world. We didn't speak at all until we hit Cataract City limits. It wasn't uncomfortable.

"So," Owen said, "do I need to watch my ass?"

"Well, old buddy, it's like this. Every night for the past eight years I've lain in bed with a three-hundred-pound schizo squealing in his sleep underneath me. You figure I'd want to wrongfoot you if it meant winding up back with all that?"

Owen said: "Fair enough."

We reached our old street, driving past the house Owe used to live in. Not much had changed. The cars were rustier. I got out, then leaned in through the open window. "There's something I'll want to talk to you about."

"I thought we just settled that."

"Yeah, we did. Dead issue. This is something else."

"Remember what side of the law I'm on, Dunk."

I cocked my head. "Aren't we on the same side?"

He gave me a quick half-smile. "Of course, same side. Run it by me any time."

The front door to my parents' house was locked but the key was hidden under a chunk of pinkish granite in the flowerbed, where it'd always been. The house was untouched: same photos in their familiar frames, floorboards squeaking in the same spots they had when as a teenager I'd sneak out to watch the stock-car races. The TV was new but the fridge was the same faded green number my folks had owned since Moses wore diapers, running on a compressor my dad scrounged from the Humberstone dump. A note sat on the kitchen table, written in Mom's neat cursive.

Sorry not to be home, Duncan. Both at work. Make yourself at home— and this IS your home, for however long you need it. Love, Mom & Dad.

My room was pretty much as I'd left it. The poster on the wall of Bruiser Mahoney was yellowed and curling at its edges, but the sheets on my bed were fresh.

I knelt at the closet door as I'd done so many times as a boy and peeled back a flap of carpeting. Pried up the loose floorboard and took out the cigar box my father had given me: *Sancho Panza*, it said. My dad had passed it around the waiting room after my birth, back when smoking in hospitals wasn't a crime.

I sat on the floor cross-legged, opened the lid and pulled out an old Polaroid: Me and Owe and Bruiser Mahoney, snapped in the change room of the Memorial Arena. I turned it over, read the words on the back.

To Duncan and Dutchie, two warriors in the Bruiser Mahoney armada. Yours, BM.

I lifted out the box's final item. It had remained in my backpack next to my hospital bed when I was twelve. Nobody had bothered to poke through the pack: not the cops, not my folks, nobody. When my parents drove me home from the hospital I'd placed the item in the box under the floorboards, where it'd sat now for . . . how long? Over twenty years.

The silver finish was tarnished but the weight was true. I cracked the cylinder, spun it, spellbound by the perfect coin of light that glinted through each empty chamber.

PART ONE

DOGS IN SPACE

OWEN STUCKEY

─

After dropping Duncan at his folks' house, I drove south, stopping at a lookout a few miles upriver from the Falls. A spit of land arrowed into the river; the ground closest to shore was overhung with willows whose ripening buds perfumed the evening air. In the summer families would colonize the picnic tables, stoking fires in old tire rims, grilling tube steaks and corn on the cob. Children would splash in the river under the watchful gaze of their folks; the wild boys who swam from the shallows would earn a cuff on the ear from their fathers—the Niagara turned black and snaky twenty yards from shore, and the river basin was littered with the bones of men and boys who'd pitted their will against it.

Was this where Bruiser Mahoney had regaled us with the tale of Giant Kichi? If not, Dunk and I had surely been here before. As boys, we'd investigated every crest and dip in this city. No place was unknown to us.

I remembered the still pools behind the gutted warehouses on Stillwell Road teeming with bullfrogs—Dunk and I would watch tadpoles push themselves out of translucent egg sacs, their iridescent bodies glittering like fish scales. Bizarre to realize that a creature so large, carbuncled and fucking *ugly* could begin its life so tiny, so radiant.

The oxbow lake we visited must be west of here, but its exact location was lost to me now . . . it struck me that a man inevitably surrenders his boyhood sense of direction, as if it were a necessary toll of adulthood. Boys weren't dependent on atlases or cross streets—a boy's interests lay off the city grid, his world unmapped by cartographers. Boys navigated by primitive means, their compass points determined by scent and taste and touch and sense-memory, an unsophisticated yet terribly precise method of echolocation.

If I couldn't find that oxbow now, I could still remember how afternoon sunshine would fill the slack water, which was bathwater-warm on high August afternoons. A car was submerged at the bottom of the lake; local legend held it was haunted: its occupants, a family from out of town, had been driving through a snowstorm and crashed through the ice. In the schoolyard it was whispered that at the stroke of midnight, three apparitions would hover over the water: the car's damned occupants, who were rumoured to have been atheists—a filthy word in Cataract City—and probably vegetarians to boot. Having never received a godly Christian burial, their forlorn ghosts were damned to haunt the lake.

There was the starlit field behind Land of Oceans, a marine mammal park where the corpses of whales and sea lions and dolphins were heaped into mass graves. One night Dunk and I hopped the chain-link fence and kicked through dry scrub to the graveyard, finding nothing untoward apart from the smell wafting from the ground, earthy and fungal like certain exotic cheeses you couldn't buy at the local *Pack N' Save*. Duncan led us up what we both believed to be an isolated hummock until we were perched perilously at its lip, staring into a hole. At the bottom, curled like a smelt in a bowl, was Peetka, the performing bottlenose dolphin. Her body was stiffening with rigor mortis—I'd imagined the sly creak of floorboards in an abandoned house—a bloody hole in her head eight inches from the crusted blowhole where a veterinarian had excised a twitching nugget of brain. A dusting of quicklime ate into the milky blue of her eyes. When headlights bloomed over the curve of the earth we'd fled into the long grass, blood booming in our ears, not stopping until we were in the sheltering woods, where we'd collapsed in hysterical, adrenalized giggles—the only way to dispel that terrible pressure.

The two of us had barely spoken on the ride home from prison. My eyes kept skating off Dunk. Prison had reduced him in some unfathomable way. You wouldn't know to look at him—he was freakishly muscular, a condom stuffed with walnuts—but a distance had settled into his eyes. He'd been banged up eight years. Ten percent of the average human lifespan. Ten percent he'd never reclaim. Ten percent that I'd stolen from him?

I drove back to the Niagara Parkway, swinging around the city hub and turning onto Sodom Road, motoring between grape fields in the alluvial shadow of the escarpment. My department-issued .38 dug under my armpit. I'd carved an X into the soft lead of each bullet, fashioning dumdum rounds. A year ago I'd barrelled through the cheap pressboard door in a lowrise apartment off Kaler to find some fucko smashed on bath salts pressing a carpet knife to his girlfriend's neck. I shot him three times—textbook centre of mass, a neat isosceles in his chest—yet he'd still managed to nearly saw her head off. From then on I told myself I'd have stopping power, whether or not the department condoned it.

I pulled into a weedy cut-off. The land rolled away from me in swathes of deepening darkness; I spotted a trembling finger of flame burning someplace in the trees. I'd been here before—this exact spot, always at night. Some nights I'd lie in bed listening to my fingernails grow until I couldn't stand the sound, then get up and drive through the heart of Cataract City. Past the Memorial Arena and down Clifton Hill, skirting the Falls that threw up their endless spray. I didn't need that primitive boyhood sonar to guide me anymore.

Presently I stepped from the car and flexed my knee; it always throbbed in the springtime and lately it'd been acting up in the winter, too. The clean smell of the forest: cut-potato scent of earth, dry leaves leaving a taste of cinnamon on the tongue.

"Home again, home again, jiggedy jig."

The wind curled under my trouser cuffs. Worried for no reason I could pinpoint, I glanced over my shoulder and saw the distant glimmer of Clifton Hill. The city makes you; in a million little ways it makes you, and you can't unmake yourself from it.

When I was twelve I spent three nights in these woods with my best friend—Duncan Diggs. It wasn't that we were assing around after dark and got waylaid far from our safe streetlit world—lost someplace in the lovely woods, dark and deep, like Frost wrote in that old poem. We were kidnapped: that's what the papers would write and that was what happened, strictly speaking. But it didn't feel that way. The man who did it . . . looking back, I can say he was thoughtless. His actions put us in danger; we could've died. But I wouldn't say he was evil. He was just broken in the way some men can become broken, and failed to see how it might also break those around him.

Was I scared? Shit, yeah. We were lost and cold and hungry and terrified that we'd be torn apart by the makers of those soft, sinister noises that rebounded within the night pines. But I wasn't scared of the man who'd brought us there. If you were to ask Dunk he'd say the same.

But all this happened a long time ago, when we were kids. If there's one time in your life you want to remember fondly, it's those years.

The man who took us into the woods was our hero, back when we were young enough to believe in those. *Big* heroes, you know? Larger than life. As you grow up you find most heroes are the same size as anyone else; their heroics are small, selfless and continual. Back then we believed in the ruddy breed of heroism depicted in the G.I. Joe comics we'd read on rainy afternoons in my basement, water trickling through the downspouts like clicking marbles. We believed heroes like that existed because the world seemed huge enough to hold them. The world still seems huge now, but in a sometimes depressing way that I can't quite explain. As boys, it was only hugely unknown. Just because we'd never met such men wasn't proof that they didn't exist.

Then we met our first hero in the flesh. He was the sort of creature who didn't seem like a man at all. He gave no sense of being made out of the same ever-failing parts that other men—our own *fathers*—were cobbled together from. He looked every inch the superhero, with muscles where there shouldn't rightly *be* muscles. He inhaled the same air as we did, but I wouldn't have been surprised to find out he had gill-flaps on his neck that helped him breathe under water or microscopic barbs on his fingertips that let him climb the tallest buildings without fear. He was perfection in the raw. A perfection that was undisciplined and maybe even unwanted: he'd occasionally frown during a match—a fleeting frown as if to say the expectations his perfection created were a small burden. But surely now and then even Superman wished he could ditch the red cape and settle down in the suburbs, right?

On the first Saturday of every month the two of us would head to the old Memorial Arena with our fathers. Our hero would high-step through a blistering fan of fireworks wearing a fur-edged robe, dark hair whipping round his face like a lion's mane. You couldn't have convinced me he was anything less than a minor god who, having disrupted the order of Olympus, had been cast down to earth for a thousand years of penance amongst the fallen.

His name was Bruiser Mahoney. Dade was the name his mother gave him. Rathburn is the name on his tombstone. But he told us to call him Bruiser.

It was Bruiser Mahoney who took us into these very woods. We went willingly. That's what we mortals do with our heroes: we follow.

A bat flashed across the headlights, wings spread from its black walnut body, chittering on its way to the hunting grounds.

"Behold zee creatures of zee night," I said, a bad Bela Lugosi. "Vhat bee-ootiful music zey make."

My voice was a croak; I laughed, and the sound travelled past the headlights, hit a wall of darkness and echoed back at me. I sat back inside the car and cranked the heater against the chill that had settled into my flesh. The antenna pulled in a station south of Buffalo; the DJ cued up "Who'll Stop the Rain." The heat made me sluggish; I shut my eyes to the sound of Fogerty's wounded baritone, letting it carry me back.

———

THE NAME ON MY BIRTH CERTIFICATE reads Owen Gregory Stuckey, but as a kid everyone called me Dutchie. Later it would become Dutch, but for the early years of my life there was always that extra *ie*.

People used to ask if I got the nickname because my family was from Holland, but that wasn't it. Before I was even a year old I had a brown mop that grew straight down. Mom chopped it below my ears, so the thick ends looked like the bristles of a broom. Mom thought I looked like the little Dutch Boy on the cans of paint.

On the first day of school Mom introduced me to the kindergarten teacher: "This is my son, Owen, but everyone calls him Dutchie." Never mind the fact that maybe I didn't dig the nickname. I was five years old. It's not like I cut my own hair or insisted it be styled into a horrible Prince Valiant, right?

The teacher called me Dutchie. Kids called me Dutchie. The die was cast. In the end, I didn't really mind; it's not like Dutchie was so much worse than Owen, which is kind of a nelly name. A few years later Mom named our new puppy Kyle. Our dog got a human name while mine was more suited to a dog.

Duncan was the one kid who called me Owen. But usually he shortened it to Owe. I called him Dunk, same as everybody else.

We grew up in Niagara Falls, also known as Cataract City—a nickname based on the Latin word for waterfall, I learned in class. But my mother, a nurse, said there was an above-average rate of actual cataracts in the city, the eye kind, which often led to glaucoma. For this reason Mom was in favour of legalizing medical marijuana. She'd never smoked pot herself but hated to see people in pain.

"The worst they'd get is a bad case of the munchies after smoking those doobs," she once said, earning a raised eyebrow from Dad.

As a kid, I found it tough to get a grip on my hometown's place in the world. What could I compare it to? New York, Paris, Rome? It wasn't even a dot on the globe. The nearest city, Toronto, was just a hazy smear across Lake Ontario, downtown skyscrapers like values on a bar graph. I figured most places must be a lot like where I lived: dominated by rowhouses with tarpaper roofs, squat apartment blocks painted the colour of boiled meat, rusted playgrounds, butcher shops and cramped corner stores where you could buy loose cigarettes for a dime apiece.

When I was seven or so, riding the bus with my mom, I heard an old geezer rattling on about our city. He had webs of shattered veins in his nose and carried his anger like a pebble in his shoe. Later I'd discover that my city was full of men like him, haunting the Legion Halls and barbershops. I recall what he said verbatim—partly because of the weird mix of venom and resignation in his voice, and partly because of his inventive use of cuss words.

"You want to know how Niagara Falls came to be?" he said. "America swept all its shit north, Canada swept all its shit south, and the dregs of the dregs washed up in a string of diddly-ass border towns, of which Cataract City is undoubtedly the diddliest. Who else takes one of the seven wonders of the world—the *numero uno* wonder, the Grand Canyon can kiss my pimpled ass—and surrounds it with discount T-shirt shops and goddamn waxwork museums? May as well mount the Hope Diamond in a setting of dog turds. Can't hack it in Toronto? Come to Cataract City. Can't hack it in Buffalo? Cataract City's waiting. Jumped-up Jesus Kee-*rist*! Can it get much sadder? It's like finding out you can't hack it in purgatory and getting your ass shipped straight to hell."

He'd stared out the bus window, lip curling to touch his nose. "Welcome to hell, suckers."

I remember, too, how nobody on that bus rose to the city's defence.

My father worked at the Nabisco factory on Grand Avenue. The Bisk, as it was known. If you grew up in Cataract City and earned a university degree, chances are you left town. If you grew up in Cataract City and managed to finish high school, chances are you took a job at the dry docks, Redpath Sugar, the General Motors plant in St. Catharines or the Bisk. Plenty of the jobs were simple enough that any half-competent person could master them by the end of their first shift. One of my schoolmates' dads filled sacks of iced tea mix. Another drilled holes in ignition-collar locks. The only question was whether you could do that same task eight hours a day for the next forty years.

The first seven years of my life, my father worked on the Nilla Wafers line. I don't know what he did beyond that. When you're a kid all you know is that your dad puts on his suit or overalls and vanishes from your life until nightfall. Sometimes my pops came back exhausted and scarlet-eyed, as if he'd been engaged in a low-wattage war someplace. If you asked how work was he might say: "Work's work." Unless your dad was an astronaut or a cowboy—and nobody's dad in Cataract City had a gig like that—whatever he did for those hours held slim appeal.

Dunk's father worked at the Bisk, too. Chips Ahoy line. Our dads carried the smell of their lines back home with them. It became a forever quality of their clothes. It crept under their skin and perfumed the sweat coming from their pores. I used to keep score at the Bisk's company softball games; after a while I knew the batting order by smell alone: first up was Triscuits, second was Fig Newtons, third was Cheese Nips. The mighty Nutter Butter batted cleanup.

My father wasn't ambitious by nature—a more *aww, shucks* man you would not meet—but he was willing to work his ass off, had a supportive wife and a working-class chip on his shoulder. That chip was a familiar accessory on a lot of Cataract City men, but unlike other guys my dad didn't nurse his grudge impotently over beers at the Double Diamond. He looked at the men above him—*literally*: at the Bisk, management offices were glassed-in boxes overlooking the factory floor—and said to himself: *Why not me?*

He studied nights and by the time I was eleven he'd earned a business degree. He rolled this into a job as line supervisor, which led to a promotion to day-shift super.

Years later I asked him why he worked so hard to get that degree. He said: "I didn't want to smell like a Nilla Wafer in my coffin."

I wasn't a popular kid. I wasn't popular at any age, but in elementary school I'm not sure it mattered. The schoolyard hierarchy hadn't quite solidified. If anything, I was human wallpaper during those years. Whenever I grafted onto the edge of some group I'd get looks that said: *Oh, Dutchie—how long have you been standing there?* I was such a non-entity that I wasn't even teased.

On my report cards teachers wrote: *Dutchie seems quite thoughtful.* They didn't mean I was selfless—more that I often appeared to be absorbed in thought. Which wasn't really true. I had very little to say was all.

I first met Duncan Diggs when I was ten. We both lived on Rickard Street and went to the same school but had never spoken before. Dunk shared my loner spirit; he usually haunted the edge of the schoolyard by the tetherball poles in a jean jacket covered with iron-on rocker patches.

The day we met I'd been walking across the soccer field at recess when Clyde Hillicker tackled me from behind. Hillicker was a big dumb kid who'd grow up into a big dumb man, but at the time he was just puppy-clumsy and outweighed me by forty pounds. His fingertips were always stained Freezie-orange.

I crashed down with Clyde on top. My face hit the ground and my teeth gritted on a plug of dirt dug up by the aerator machine.

"Just lay there, Dutchie, okay?" Clyde said, all chummy. "I want to show Adam something."

He was with his friend Adam Lowery, an anorexic-looking boy with a ginger bowl-cut. Clyde sat on my back and grabbed at my helplessly kicking legs.

"Don't move," he whined, as if I was ruining his good time.

"Get *off*!"

"Hammer him," Adam said. "Hammer his face off!"

Clyde refused. "Bruiser Mahoney never punches. Bruiser Mahoney doesn't *need* to punch."

He grabbed my feet and tucked my ankles under his armpits. I lay face down with my body bent like a fish hook. A textbook Boston crab. Naturally, I screamed.

"Give up?" Clyde said.

"*Yes!*"

"He's still fighting!" Adam hollered.

"Are you still fighting?" Clyde asked.

"*No!*"

"Get off him!"

This was Duncan. He shoulder-checked Clyde hard enough that Clyde landed on his hands and knees, scraping up his palms. I gasped and curled up like a potato bug.

Clyde held his bloodied palms out to Dunk as if he was displaying stigmata. "We were just playing," he said. Dunk shrugged and kept his body in front of mine.

"We were just *plaaayin'*," Adam said in a singsong voice. "Come on, Clyde. These babies don't know how to have fun."

After they left Dunk didn't help me up, just hovered over me the way a lion does over a dead antelope. I dragged myself up and inspected the grass stains on my knees.

"Jeez. Mom's going to kill me." I didn't say thanks. Was this something you thanked a person for? "You like Twisted Sister?" I said, pointing to a patch on his jean jacket.

"It's my brother's old jacket. A hand-me-down."

"Cool."

I couldn't tell if he was amused or figured I was a shithead for thinking his twice-used clothes, which he probably hated, were cool. His T-shirt was old and there were holes along the hem as if mice had nibbled it.

Even though we were too young to have sorted out the true tough guys in the pack, Dunk struck me as someone you didn't want to tangle with. He wasn't big or strong. If anything, he was a bit skinny. But something in his eyes said whatever you started, he'd finish. Even if it took all day and left him a mess, he'd keep coming at you.

He was handsome, or at least he would grow to be, and his mom let him wear his hair long. It swept off the side of his skull in dark wings.

"Did it hurt?" he said.

"Yeah," I said. "Clyde's real fat."

Dunk laughed. "You're lucky. If Clyde put that Boston crab on the way Bruiser Mahoney does, you'd be dog meat."

"Who's Bruiser Mahoney?"

"Bruiser *Mahoney*," he said, like I must not have heard.

I just stared.

"Oh my *god*," he said solemnly, his tone that of a doctor who'd diagnosed my rare affliction: terminal idiocy. "Come to my house after school."

That afternoon I followed him home. He took me to the room he shared with his brother and showed me the faded poster on his wall.

That was all it took for me to become enraptured with Bruiser Mahoney. It was also all it took for me and Dunk to become friends.

Inseparable. That was me and Dunk. We'd both been looking for a person whose company we preferred to our own and once we finally found that person we practically lived in each other's pockets.

We'd have sleepovers, even on weeknights. Our parents, who'd likely been worried we'd go our whole childhoods friendless, indulged us.

I often ate breakfast at Dunk's house, even though his mom bought powdered milk that tasted like wallpaper paste. At our house we drank whole milk and ate real Corn Flakes. At Dunk's house we'd eat cereal that came in a bright yellow box with "Corn Toasties" stamped on the label.

We'd stay up late in my basement reading comics. On Friday nights we watched the Baby Blue Movie on Citytv. These were usually in a foreign language where the men rolled their *r*'s and the women smoked stubby black cigarettes. On the upside, the women were often naked while they smoked. Or if not smoking, they were running around medieval castles with their apple-shaped asses hanging out. The point of any Baby Blue Movie, so far as I could tell, was to leave preteens all over Cataract City confused and slightly sweaty.

One kid who watched the Baby Blue Movie religiously was Sam Bovine. His last name was Italian, pronounced *Boh-vee-neh*, but everyone called him Bovine like the cow. A skinny boy with thin wrists and a too-big head for his body, for a while Bovine was best known as the Hair Lice Kid. Twice a year we'd all line up at the front of class while a Rubenesque nurse picked through our hair with a pair of sterilized chopsticks—and she'd always find them wriggling in Bovine's hair.

"They're practically building cities," she'd say disgustedly.

Bovine enjoyed the attention but his folks were mortified. They bought special shampoo from the veterinarian that made his scalp smell like a freshly tarred road.

While no paragon of personal hygiene, Bovine *was* miles ahead of us in his knowledge of forbidden lore. He knew that if you spat on a hot light bulb it would explode in a shower of white glass and sparkling powder—which, Bovine claimed, would kill you if you inhaled it. He also knew that feeding a frog an Alka-Seltzer tablet would, in his words, "Make it blow up like a gooey green grenade." Most carnal was his knowledge of women, their anatomies, and how to satisfy them.

"Did you see last week's movie?" he'd ask Dunk and me at recess. "That girl who came out of the pond with her top off? Whoa! Some real humungoes."

Neither of us knew what to make of Bovine. Being around him gave you that feeling you got after eating too much candy on Halloween: hyper and a little sick.

"You know what women with big bazooms like? If you squeeze them like kneading pizza dough. It drives them wild. They'll rip all their clothes off if you squeeze their big knockers long enough."

Our neighbourhood was small, but like most neighbourhoods possessed its fair share of mystery. One night we were watching the Baby Blue Movie when it started to snow. Dunk and I crammed onto a chair, balanced on our tiptoes, and peered out the basement window that overlooked my front yard. Big fat flakes fell through the street lights, eddying in the updrafts skating down our narrow street.

"Holy lick," Dunk said. "*Look.*"

A woman was walking down the street. Slowly, with her arms upraised the way Pentecostals do in church. Not a stitch of clothing on her body. The naked woman walked upright as if the howling wind had no effect on her. For an instant I thought she was a ghost. She was as pale as chalk. She wasn't shivering, either. My skin froze just looking at her.

Pressed together tightly on the same chair, I could see Dunk's heartbeat through his wrist, hooked over the window ledge.

"That's Mrs. Lovegrove," he said. "She lives across the road, two down from me."

Elsa Lovegrove's body was similar to the bodies of other Cataract City women I'd unclothe years later. Her chest bones stood out like fingers under small breasts tipped with the dark rosettes of her nipples. She looked nothing like the women in the

Baby Blue Movie—those women's lush bodies were built for cavorting. Mrs. Lovegrove's body appeared to be composed of pure bone.

The wind whipped her long hair up to frame her face: it looked as if she'd lain down in a still pool of water. She may have been laughing or crying, I couldn't tell. Her husband rushed down the road and draped a blanket over Elsa's shoulders. Later we'd find out that her son had been killed that night in a late-season funny-car accident at the Merrittville Speedway.

On the weekends we would stay up to watch the *WWF Saturday Night's Main Event*, with "Mean Gene" Okerlund and Gorilla Monsoon broadcasting the action from exotic ports of call like the Pontiac Silverdome or the pearl of the Pacific, Honolulu's Aloha Stadium.

Dunk liked the high-fliers: Jimmy "Superfly" Snuka and Ricky "the Dragon" Steamboat. I liked the guys with a flexible moral code like Jake "the Snake" Roberts. He was flat-footed, wore a greasy T-shirt and carried a seven-foot python in a sack. He wasn't friends with anybody, but he wasn't a backstabber either. And when he cinched up his DDT move, your ass was grass and he, as Bovine would say, was the lawn mower.

Saturday afternoon wrestling was different. On those shows, you'd see marquee wrestlers matched up against jobbers—ham 'n' eggers, as Bobby "the Brain" Heenan called them. Poor saps like "Leaping" Lanny Poffo, "Iron" Mike Sharpe and the Brooklyn Brawler would get squashed by main eventers. But Saturday *nights*, the Main Event? No jobbers allowed.

On Saturday nights we'd get Randy "Macho Man" Savage and Miss Elizabeth. André the Giant squaring off against King Kong Bundy—the irresistible force meeting the immovable object. Meddling managers like Jimmy "the Mouth of the South" Hart.

Scheming villains like "Rowdy" Roddy Piper. Otherworldly crea-
tures like George "the Animal" Steele. Gorilla Monsoon saying:
"This place has gone bananas!" or "Ladies and gentlemen, Madison
Square Garden just literally exploded!"

The only wrestler we hated was Hulk Hogan. Mister "Train,
say your prayers, eat your vitamins, be true to yourself and your
country—be a real *American!*" How cheeseball could you get?

To Dunk and me, wrestling made sense in an elemental way.
Everything was defined and sensible within that squared circle.
There were your heels and your babyfaces. Cheaters would cheat,
schemers would scheme, but ultimately you paid what you owed.
We understood the crest and ebb of a match, its rising and falling
action. Even at ten years old we could appreciate the perfect finality to it all. When the Macho Man launched his flying elbow off
the top rope, it was over. When Hulk Hogan dropped the big leg.
When the Brain Busters hit their spike piledriver.

One Saturday night my dad came downstairs in his house-
coat. It was around the time he'd been promoted to supervisor.
Our house had been egged the week before; there was a suspicion that some guys at work had done it, though I found it
impossible to believe forty-year-olds would do such a thing.
Dad sat with a sigh that seemed to come less from his lungs than
his bones.

"Wrestling, huh?" he said. "Those fellas can sure fill out a pair
of tights."

Hulk Hogan was fighting "Mr. Wonderful" Paul Orndorff in
a steel cage match. Hulk Hogan bodyslammed Mr. Wonderful,
then cupped his ear to drink in the roar of the crowd. We cheered
our guts out for Mr. Wonderful, even though he was the heel.

"The Hulkster looks unstoppable," Dad said with a sly smile.
"Something tells me he's going to win."

"Bruiser Mahoney would beat the crud out of Hulk Hogan," Dunk said. "Bruiser would *eliminate* him."

"This Bruiser Mahoney sure sounds like something," Dad said.

"Mr. Stuckey, Bruiser Mahoney is the greatest wrestler who has ever lived," Dunk said with a bone-deep earnestness that my father surely found funny. "He's fighting in two weeks at the arena."

"Can we go?" I asked Dad.

"Is your father taking you, Duncan?"

"Yes, sir. We'll be sitting in the front row."

Dad nodded. "Let's go watch some wrasslin'."

And so the first Saturday of every month became father-son wrestling night. When the lights dimmed and Bruiser Mahoney's voice boomed over the loudspeakers—"You're cruisin' for a *bruuuuuisin'!*"—the place went electric.

Bruiser would storm down the Zamboni chute, sprinting to the ring so fast that his robe unfurled behind him like crimson wings. Vaulting over the ropes, he'd start to swing pure dynamite. He was untamed and breathtaking. His opponent didn't know what the hell hit him. Neither did I.

"That Bruiser Mahoney really is something," my father said that first night.

After that, Dunk's father began to drop by on Fridays for a beer with my dad. Mr. Diggs would bring Dunk with him, or Dunk would already be over. One beer turned into five, plus a shot or two of Famous Grouse, which ran seven-fifty a bottle over the river. Our fathers would talk while we horsed around in the backyard with Sam Bovine, who had a tendency to latch onto us like a burr for days at a time. The boom of the Falls carried over the treetops to merge with the hiss of beer can pull-tabs and our fathers' heavy, smoke-roughened laughter.

Physically they were different, my father and Mr. Diggs. Dad was taller but stoop-shouldered. As the years wore on, that stoop became more pronounced: his back bent until his body looked a little like a slender tree branch with a ripe apple hanging from it. Mr. Diggs was shorter, with the same dark hair that his son inherited; his body gave off this constant vibration, and I imagined the air closest to his arms and shoulders blurring the way it did around a hummingbird.

Other differences were harder for me to pinpoint, at least back then. One spring my father bought a new Chrysler Fifth Avenue with power locks and leather upholstery. When Mr. Diggs—who drove a second-hand Dodge Aspen—saw it, he rubbed one finger along his forehead.

"Jeez, isn't she a beaut."

My dad looked pained. "It's nothing special, Jerry. The bank owns most of it."

That same spring Dunk and I got our kits for the Kub Kar Rally. Our parents had forced us to join Cub Scouts the year previous; we both agreed it sucked rocks. Apart from one-match fires and knife ownership, Cubs was for shit. We'd sit around the school gym singing along to our leader's acoustic guitar. That, or were forced to hear what berries we couldn't eat if we got lost in the woods. Our sashes were almost naked. I got one measly badge for housecraft. Dunk earned one for . . . knots?

For the Kub Kar Rally we were each given a block of wood, four plastic wheels and axle pins. Our dads were allowed to help, but as my mother said: "I love your father, Dutchie, but as a handyman he's about as useful as tits on a bull."

Most men on our street had a tool room: a tight space in their basements where you'd find red vises, coffee cans full of nails and bolts, and corkboards with the outlines of tools marked in black

Sharpie. Our basement had dusty boxes of exercise equipment my father had become frustrated trying to put together. "Some Assembly Required" was, so far as my father was concerned, the most deceitful phrase to ever be printed on a box-flap.

Still, he tried. He took a few experimental hacks at the wood block with a saw. Next he set his hands on his hips and frowned at me.

"Well, what's *your* idea for this puppy?"

The next week we showed up at the rally with a lime-green thing that deviated only slightly from the block my Scout leader had given me. Dad wore a bandage between the webbing of his thumb and finger.

Thirty other boys were there with their fathers. Their cars had been lathed and routered and polished to a high shine.

"They should rename it the Daddy's Car Rally," my father said.

Bovine's car was a piece of crap, too. His dad was a mortuary attendant and apparently just as clueless as mine. At least he'd been allowed to write *Babe Magnet* on his block of wood.

"I can't wait to get my licence," he whispered. "If my car's a-rockin', don't you come a-knockin'."

When I asked what he meant, Bovine shook his head as if I was too dumb for words.

I spotted Clyde Hillicker and Adam Lowery. Their dads worked at the Bisk, too. Mr. Hillicker resembled a Saint Bernard with a beer gut. Mr. Lowery looked like a weasel that had learned how to dress itself.

"You help him build it, boss?" Mr. Lowery asked my father. He said "boss" the way other people say "asshole." "I guess some things you can't learn in books, huh?"

"I let him figure it out for himself," my father said. "We're not going to be around their whole lives, are we?"

Dunk's car had a flat black finish and flames licking off the front. He didn't seem that proud of it.

"That's a hell of a thing," Dad said appreciatively. "A real fire-baller."

"Thanks," Dunk said. Mr. Diggs smiled sheepishly.

My car came in dead last in its first heat. A wheel spun off in the next heat, disqualifying me.

"Good to see you're earning that big salary," Mr. Lowery said to my father, as if one thing had anything to do with the other.

Dunk's car came first in its preliminary heat and second in the next. Mr. Diggs sprayed WD-40 on the axle pins. It rallied past Clyde Hillicker's car in the semi-finals.

The final came down to Dunk and Adam Lowery. Their cars raced down the incline, plastic wheels clattering on the polished ramp. When Dunk won, Mr. Lowery downed his glass of McDonald's Orange Drink like it was a shot of Jack Daniel's, crushed the wax-paper cup and sidled over to our Scout leader.

Our leader—an ashen-faced man with a prominent Adam's apple—came over to Dunk and his father. Mr. Lowery and Mr. Hillicker flanked him.

"Mr. Diggs, these men are . . ." Our leader adjusted the knot on his scarf. "Well, they suspect a lack of fair play on your part. They think . . ."

"That car's heavy," Mr. Hillicker said. "It's heavier'n wood, that's for sure."

As soon as Hillicker said it, I knew he was right. The truth was there in Mr. Diggs' eyes. "I don't . . . didn't think . . ." he stammered. "You're saying there's some rule against . . ."

I'd never seen a full-grown man struggle so badly with his words. He shrunk two full sizes right there in the dusty gym.

Adam Lowery snatched Dunk's car off the track and handed it

to his dad. Mr. Lowery flipped it over and scratched its black finish with a pocketknife.

"Mmm-hmm," he said. He sunk the knife's tip in and popped off a square of carpenter's putty. Out fell a cube of solid metal, landing with a metallic *clink*. In the ensuing silence you could have heard an ant trundle across the wooden floor.

"You *cheat*," Adam said to Dunk. He pointed at Mr. Diggs and said: "Cheaters, the both of you."

A collective gasp went round from one boy to another. You could rag another boy about his weight or the fact his mom made him wear suspenders or just about anything, really, but you never, *ever* ragged on a grown man—especially to accuse him of cheating. Even if it appeared that was exactly what he'd done.

Mr. Diggs spoke in a thick, choked voice. "My son didn't know a thing about it."

"You can only use what comes in the kit," our leader said softly. "Plus paint and varnish. Did you read the instructions?"

Mr. Diggs ran the flat of one hand over his flushed face. Dunk was gripping his other hand so hard that his fingertips had turned white.

"I guess I didn't. Not properly."

"Cheating at a Kub Kar Rally," Mr. Lowery said. "Jesus, Jerry. Of all the skunky—"

"Just a second now, Stan," my father said. "The wheels on your son's car are thin as pizza cutters. Been bevelled, haven't they? You shaved them down right fine—or your boy did."

Mr. Lowery's lips pressed into a thin white line. His fingers twitched below the worn hem of his deerskin jacket.

"Well?" my father said to our leader. "Is that legal?"

After a moment our leader said: "Strictly speaking, no."

"You can't mean . . ." Mr. Lowery said. "The wheels are right out in the open. You can *see* them."

"I wasn't going to say anything, but rules are rules," my dad said. "That's something I learned in a book, Stan."

The rally was won by Kevin Harley, who'd come in third. Kevin's father kissed the stupid trophy and held it above his head, beaming, as if he'd just won the Stanley Cup.

Afterwards I overheard some of the other fathers talking about Duncan. *The apple doesn't fall far from the tree . . .*

Two weeks after the rally, as spring shaded into an early summer, the Eastern Wrestling Alliance returned to town.

The Memorial Arena was filling by the time I showed up with my father. I pushed through the turnstile, pulling on Dad's hand like a dog straining against its leash. Dad was still in his work clothes, tie hanging from his neck like a wet noose.

"Come *on*, Dad."

"Hold your horses, Dutchie."

The ring was bathed in a halo of light thrown by a mesh-enclosed lamp burning above. Dunk waved at us from the fifth row, wearing his Bruiser Mahoney T-shirt.

"We had front row but we couldn't save enough seats," he told me.

"You could've stayed," I said.

"Nah," he said. "Better to sit together."

The curtain-jerker was between Disco Dirk and the Masked Assassin. Dirk swivelled his hips and preened for the ladies, which was wasted effort seeing as there weren't more than a handful of them there. The Assassin caught Dirk with a pumphandle slam and pinned him, much to everyone's relief.

A few more matches, then an intermission. We stood in line at the concession stand. Further back stood Mr. Lowery and Mr. Hillicker with their sons. Mr. Lowery jutted his chin at my father and said something to Mr. Hillicker; their dark laughter drifted up the queue.

Our fathers bought two draft beers apiece, clinking their plastic cups with unambiguous grimness. Dunk was hopping from foot to foot.

"Bruiser's up next."

His opponent was the Boogeyman, who stalked down the aisle with his lizard-green face, stepped through the ropes and stalked around the ring flicking his bright red tongue.

"Let's go up close," Dunk said, tugging my sleeve. "It'll be okay. Trust me."

We ran down the aisle as Bruiser Mahoney's music began: *John Henry was a Steel-Drivin' Man.*

"Somebody is cruisin' for a *bruuuuuisin'*!"

The crowd rose to a thunderous roar as Bruiser Mahoney burst through a rainbow of sizzling fireworks. He ran with a high-kneed and almost clumsy gait, robe billowing off his heels. His face was set in an expression of controlled wrath—of *joy*. You could imagine a Spartan warrior running into battle with that same teeth-gritted, cockeyed look.

"*Bruiser!*" Dunk cried, stretching one arm over the barrier.

Bruiser Mahoney slapped Dunk's palm on the way past. It sent Dunk reeling into me. He just sat there with a blissful expression, staring at his reddening hand.

Bruiser Mahoney booted the Boogeyman in the breadbasket, stunned him with a shot to the solar plexus, flung him into the ropes and tagged him with a dropkick, then hauled him up and delivered a mat-shaking German suplex. The crowd was mad for blood and Bruiser was happy to oblige.

Looking back now, I could see why the guys we watched those nights never hit the big time—even Mahoney, who'd wrestled for six months in the WWF as Jimmy Falcone, working as a trail horse: a guy whose sole job is to lose and make his opponent look good while doing so. After that stint the promotion sent him packing to the carnival-tent and county fair circuit.

It wasn't that guys like Mahoney were any less muscular than the men who made their livings in the big league; it was more that their bodies lacked the requisite speed and grace. Their limbs seemed slightly disconnected from their brains. They moved at a plodding pace, more like durable tractors than souped-up race cars. And sure, there would always be a place for tractors, but it was not under the bright lights of Maple Leaf Gardens. The Garden City Arena in St. Catharines with its two-thousand-seat capacity was a better fit.

But we were too young to understand how men might be held back by their physical limitations—we figured these guys were fighting each other because they *hated* each other. We were fortunate that this was the arena they'd chosen to settle their blood feuds.

It was a see-saw of a match. The Boogeyman sprayed poisonous green mist—in fact, lime Jell-O—into Mahoney's face, then smashed him with a powerbomb. Normally that would be enough to put away the stoutest challenger, but the crowd rallied Mahoney back. He blocked the Boogeyman's double axe-handle chop and slung him into the ropes, tagging him with a crippling lariat clothesline on the rebound. He climbed the top turnbuckle. The lights hit every contour of his superhuman physique. Mahoney paused in that silvery fall of light—a showman aware of the moment—before spreading his arms and leaping.

He was only ten feet off the ground but from my vantage he could have had wings. For a moment he remained motionless—the whole world did—then the gears clicked and everything accelerated and Bruiser Mahoney slammed the Boogeyman, spiking him to the canvas.

One. Two. Three.

Bruiser Mahoney grabbed the microphone. "Yeah?" A wild cheer went up. He grinned. "Ohhh *yeeeeah!*"

The cheer was louder this time. It rose up and up, the sound of three thousand lungs emptying towards the roof beams.

"And I'll be here, I'll . . . be . . . right . . . *here,*" Bruiser said, stomping his foot on the mat. Three thousand mouths repeated his words—we all knew his mantra by heart. "I'll be here for *you,* fighting for *you,* always with *you!*"

Bruiser Mahoney's head swivelled towards the ceiling as he unleashed a mad-dog howl.

"Thank you! Good night!"

Next we were filing down the aisles, feet crunching over stale popcorn and paper cups. Lifeless, inert, shuffling like zombies under a buzzing Orange Crush sign.

Our fathers bought another beer as the arena emptied. I saw Mr. Hillicker lingering beyond the arena doors. He glanced inside, spotted my father, then turned over his shoulder and spoke to someone I couldn't see.

"Hey," Mr. Diggs said to my father, nodding towards the dressing room door. "You figure Bruiser Mahoney's in there?"

Dad chuckled. "I'd guess so."

"How would you like to talk to the Bruiser?" Mr. Diggs asked the two of us. "He's just a *man.*" I caught an edge of irritation in his voice. "A man like any other man."

"Like *us,*" my father said.

Saying this, he turned and walked towards the dressing room, striding purposefully albeit with a noticeable wobble, pulling me behind him.

The wrestlers sat on folding chairs arrayed haphazardly around a wide tiled room. Here and there were open duffel bags, knee braces, piles of sodden towels and grimy balls of tape. The room was foggy from the steam billowing out from the shower stalls. It smelled of Tiger Balm and something to which I could give no name.

"Hey, can I borrow your deodorant?" Disco Dirk said to the Masked Assassin.

"I wouldn't give it to him," one of the Lucky Aces said. "He's got that rash on his dick he picked up in the Sioux."

"Ah, go fuck your hat," Disco Dirk said as the other men roared.

One by one they took notice of us. None made any effort to cover up. The Brain Smasher brushed the tangles out of his hair, naked in front of the mirror.

"Bruiser," he said. "I think somebody's here looking for you!"

"Is it Estelle?" came Bruiser's voice from the showers. "I told that one it was once and no more. I'm no tomcatter."

"It isn't," the Brain Smasher said.

"Well who in hell is it?" Bruiser said, stepping into the room with a towel wrapped round his waist.

Maybe it was his wet hair hanging down his shoulders in dark ropes instead of the wild mane I was accustomed to. Or maybe it was the water glistening in the concavity between his chest muscles that I'd never seen before. Or the plastic cup with an inch of piss-coloured liquid in it that he downed quickly before tossing the empty cup into the showers. Or was it simply the shock of seeing Bruiser Mahoney in a locker room surrounded by naked men, amidst piles of spangly boots and neon tights? Whatever it was, he looked shockingly human for the first time.

"Mr. Mahoney," my father said, finding his voice. "This is my son, Dutchie."

"And my son, Duncan," Mr. Diggs said, guiding his boy forward. "They're your biggest fans."

"Oh, are they now?" Bruiser Mahoney said. "I must say they ought to be, that you'd bring them into this snakepit with these vipers!"

He laughed and strode forward, offering a hand that swallowed my father's own. He shook Mr. Diggs' hand next, then knelt down before me and Dunk like a man preparing to accept a knighthood.

"Look at you. My wide-eyed little warriors."

Up close his eyes were blue, terrifically blue, the skin around them scored with little cracks like the fissures in alabaster. He smelled of carbolic soap. The cleft in his chin bristled with untrimmed stubble.

"Welcome to the bestiary." He smiled. The point was broken off one eye tooth. "Fancy joining the carnival, boys?"

It was overwhelming to be so close to him, to all these men. I still struggled with the notion that the Masked Assassin might lend Disco Dirk his deodorant. Was it possible that any of these men actually *wore* deodorant, or stood in line at the post office to mail a parcel or behaved in any way like normal people? How could a creature like the Boogeyman have a job, a mortgage, a wife? It was impossible to imagine him grilling steaks in his backyard, his lizard-green face grinning above a *Kiss the Cook* apron. I had figured these men vanished behind the curtain after a match and lived in some nether-realm, squabbling amongst themselves like petulant demi-gods until they stepped back through that curtain to settle their grievances the next month.

"You're my favourite wrestler." There was a quaver in Dunk's voice. "You're sort of . . . well, *perfect*."

Bruiser Mahoney laughed. His breath washed over me. I caught the same smell that I'd once caught coming off my father when he'd stepped into my room late one night, watching me silently from the foot of the bed.

"Perfect, he says. You hear that, fellas? It's like I keep telling you!"

"A perfect boondoggle," Outbacker Luke cracked.

Bruiser Mahoney took our fathers aside.

". . . come by your house, do the dog-and-pony," I heard him say. Our fathers sunk their hands into their pockets and smiled politely. ". . . reasonable rate . . . wouldn't gyp you fellas . . ."

My father rested his hand on Mahoney's shoulder, patting it the way you might pat a dog. Next he reached for his wallet. Mahoney's big hand went to my father's wrist, trapping his hand in his pocket.

"Later," he said softly. "Either of you have a stick of gum?"

When he came back his breath smelled of spearmint instead of whatever had been in the plastic cup. He grabbed a Polaroid camera from his duffel, handed it to Disco Dirk.

"Take a shot of me with these little Bruisers," he said, kneeling to grab us around the shoulders. His power was immense: it was like being hugged by a yeti.

To Duncan and Dutchie, Mahoney wrote on the still-developing photo. *Two warriors in the Bruiser Mahoney armada.*

He signed it with his initials—*Yours, BM*—and for an instant I was terrified I'd laugh. Sometimes my mom would warn me through the bathroom door: "If you're taking a big BM, Dutchie, make sure you flush twice or you'll plug the pipes."

When Bruiser handed the photo to Dunk, Dunk stared at him gratefully and said: "I want to grow up to be just like you."

For a moment Mahoney's expression slipped. Under it was the face of a creature who was old, haunted and lost.

"Ah, you'll grow up, boy," he said. "You'll learn."

When we got out to the parking lot Mr. Lowery and Mr. Hillicker were there with their sons and some other Bisk men. They sat on the tailgates of their pickup trucks drinking cans of Natural Light.

"Look who it is," Mr. Lowery said. "The cheat and the gasbag."

My father gripped my hand. "Just keep walking, Dutchie."

The men hopped off the tailgates. Mr. Hillicker came towards us, bobbing on the toes of his boots while Mr. Lowery skulked low. They formed a semicircle of bleached denim, cigarette smoke and booze fumes.

"What's the matter?" Mr. Hillicker said to my dad. "Too big to talk to us grunts?"

"That's nothing to do with it," my father said. "It's been a long night, Dean. I'm taking my son home."

"And we're stopping you?" said Mr. Lowery. His teeth shone like tiny white spears under the lot lights. "Take him home, Stuckey. *Mister* Stuckey."

"You lay off, Stan," Mr. Diggs said with ice in his eye. "I'm telling you to just lay off."

Mr. Lowery showed Mr. Diggs his palms like a magician performing some dizzying sleight of hand. "I'm laying easy as a blind bitch in her bed, chum."

Clyde Hillicker and Adam Lowery watched from the truck. Adam's eyes were every bit as narrow and flinty as his father's; it was a scary thing to see in a boy my own age.

An awful electricity zipped among the older men. Shoulders jostled. Hands balled. Next the air was full of swinging fists.

Mr. Diggs' right shoulder dipped and his hand came up, crunching into Mr. Hillicker's nose. Mr. Hillicker stutter-stepped back on his heels, toes pointed up like in a Three Stooges routine; it would have been comical if not for the new dent in his nose and the blood that lay stunned across his cheeks.

My father pushed me out of the way as Mr. Lowery surged at him, low and sidewinding. It seemed unreal: Dad in his penny loafers and corduroy slacks fighting Adam Lowery's father in his chambray work shirt. Mr. Lowery hit my father in the stomach. The air whoofed out of him—"Dad!" I cried—then my father, who

I'd never seen throw a punch, brought his fist around in a sweeping roundhouse that clipped Mr. Lowery on the chin.

A pair of cop cars had been idling at the Country Style Donuts across the street. Now they crossed silently, skipping the curb and rolling into the lot. Four uniformed officers stepped out. They stood with their hands on their hips, smirking, not quite ready to get involved.

A hand grabbed my jacket and jerked me backwards. My shoulder collided with Dunk's—we were both gripped at the end of two huge muscular arms.

"Stay out of the fray, boys," Bruiser Mahoney said. "You're liable to lose something."

He sat us on the pavement and rucked into the fray. "Stop this mess!" he cried, towering like a colossus. He grabbed one of Mr. Hillicker's buddies by the scruff of his neck and rag-dolled him across the asphalt. "Cease and desist!"

Another man fell out of the scrum clutching his arm. Blood squeezed between his clenched fingers. "He cut me!" he shrieked.

I could have seen a flash of silver in Mr. Diggs' hand—something that shone like a sliver of moonlight.

"Break this shit up!" the cops shouted, wading in with their batons swinging. "Give it up, you bastards!"

Bruiser Mahoney stepped away, panting just a bit. Beads of sweat dotted his brow.

"Come on, boys." His hands gripped our forearms. He half led, half lifted us: only my toes touched the ground.

"My dad . . ." Dunk said.

"Your dad's in a whack of trouble, son. Nothing to be done for it."

The brawl raged on. The cruiser's lights bathed the scene in blue and red flashes. In hindsight, it was shocking that neither our dads nor the police saw us being led away by a goliath wrestler in scuffed cowboy boots and a buckskin jacket. Equally shocking was the fact that neither Dunk nor I called out to our fathers.

Bruiser Mahoney's brown cargo van was parked around back of the arena near the Dumpsters. He popped the side door and said: "Hop in, boys."

We sat hip to hip on the ripped bench seat. The van smelled of sweat and turpentine. The left side of the windshield was milky with cracks. A plastic hula girl was stuck to the dash. In the back were a few army duffels, boxes of bodybuilding magazines, sleeping bags and about a million empty Coke cans.

"What's going to happen to our dads?" I asked Mahoney.

"They're spending a night in the nick," Bruiser said, contorting himself into the front seat. His wide shoulders made it look as if a Kenmore fridge were occupying the space behind the wheel. "Buckle your seat belts."

The van hacked to life. Mahoney drove with his headlights off. The plastic hula girl's hips swayed as we bounced over the curb.

"It's nothing serious," Mahoney said. "Just grown men fighting. They'll be out tomorrow no worse for wear." He craned his head round and winked at us. "Every man ought to spend a night in the stony lonesome once in his life!"

He snapped on the radio. "Karma Chameleon" by Culture Club was playing.

"This glitzy fairy can really carry a tune," he said, snapping his fingers.

We drove down Parkside and pulled up beside a 5.0 Mustang. A farmer-tanned arm hung casually out the open window. There was a tattoo of a wolf howling at the moon on that arm, except the skin drooped so that the moon looked more like a teardrop—which would be poetic, I guess, if it had been on purpose.

Mahoney pulled up closer. I caught a flash of the driver: in his mid-thirties, his face deeply seamed and his skin a queer off-yellow like a watery cat's eye. He looked sick but probably wasn't. It's just how men grew up around here. My dad said Cataract City was a pressure chamber: living was hard, so boys were forced to become men much faster. That pressure ingrained itself in bodies and faces. You'd see twenty-year-old men whose hands were stained permanently black with the granular grease from lubing the rollers at the Bisk. Men just past thirty walking with a stoop. Forty-year-olds with forehead wrinkles deep as the bark on a redwood. You didn't age gracefully around here. You just got old.

Mahoney pulled into the beer store, left the van running and said, "Be right back."

"Do you think they're okay?" I asked Dunk while Mahoney was inside the liquor store. "Our dads?"

"I guess so," Dunk said. "Bruiser said so, right?"

Mahoney returned with half a flat of Labatt 50. He set it between the front seats and tore the cardboard open. The stubby was swallowed by his hand: only its brown neck protruded between his thumb and pointer finger. He upended the bottle, drank it, belched, sleeved the empty, popped the cap off a fresh one with the church-key dangling from the gearshift and veered onto the road.

"Need something to take the edge off," he told us. "The Boogeyman took it out of me tonight, that rat bastard."

"Where are we going?" Dunk said.

"What? You don't like hanging out with the Bruiser? Your hero?"

He stopped at a red light, downed the second beer, wiped froth off his lips and cracked a third. "Don't worry, boys. We'll cruise around until the heat dies down, then I'll take you home."

The van barrelled down Clifton Hill where the multicoloured

marquees of tourist booths and shops burned against the oncoming dark. Mahoney turned right and slowed past the Falls, unrolling his window to breathe the wet spray.

He drove down the river and pulled into an unfamiliar suburb. He circled one block three times, drumming his fingers on the wheel, before pulling into the driveway that divided a small fenced-in yard.

"Wait here, little warriors."

He skipped up the steps to the house at the end of the drive, spinning balletically to shoot us with finger-pistols cocked at his hips. His knock was answered by a teenaged girl. After a moment's hesitancy she let him inside.

"Do you know where we are?" I asked Dunk.

He leaned between the front seats and looked out the window. Then slumped back into the seat and lip-farted. Bruiser Mahoney came out of the house with the girl, holding her hand and pulling her the way you pull a dog away from an interesting smell.

He lifted her onto the passenger seat. "Ooh!" she said, laughing the way my mother did when we rode the Tilt-A-Whirl at the Falls carnival. Her long dark hair fell straight down her back and shone like metal in the domelight.

Mahoney clambered into the driver's seat and gave her knee a chummy clap. "Look at you! You're a pip—a real *pip!*"

The girl tucked a strand of hair behind her ear and stared out the window. Mahoney shot a look at us and waggled his eyebrows as if to say: *We're cooking now!*

"Hello," Dunk said.

The girl nearly jumped out of her skin. "Jesus!" she said to Mahoney. "Who are these—more of yours?"

The flesh crinkled around Mahoney's eyes. "Mine? Do you think I have a brood in every town?"

"I don't know why you'd think that might surprise me," the girl said.

"Don't be spiteful. These boys came to the show. They got separated from their fathers. I'm taking them home."

The girl was a high-schooler—the pleated skirt gave it away. She smelled of Noxzema and cigarette smoke. "Separated from your father, huh? Join the club."

We drove along the river. Mahoney pulled into a lookout along the water's edge.

"Yeearrrgh!" He stepped out of the van and stretched his long frame. "That air! Takes years off a man."

We sat at a picnic table under a canopy of spring leaves. The night air was moist like inside a greenhouse. Mahoney opened a beer and held it out to the girl.

"So," she said to us, "you're fans of the mighty Bruiser, I imagine?" There was a small, perfect coin of gold in the centre of her left eye.

"We are," Dunk said solemnly.

"So serious!" She sipped her beer. Mahoney watched her with a crooked eye. "I suppose you'd like to hear stories of his greatest matches, wouldn't you?"

"We would," said Dunk.

"Well, Bruiser?" she said. "Care to indulge them?"

"Dearest heart," he said, "what tale would you have me regale them with?"

The girl stroked her chin, considering. "How about Giant Kichi?"

Mahoney slapped the table. The *crack* of his palm caused a flock of nesting starlings to take flight.

"Aha! Giant Kichi, is it?" He rounded on us. "Kichi was the meanest wrestler on the Japanese circuit, one of twins born in Hiroshima. Their father was a madman. He raised cows on a patch of soil where the first bomb touched down, you see, and suckled his sons on the milk. When they were old enough, he had those same cows slaughtered and made his sons eat the irradiated meat. The radiation did something to those boys—lengthened their bones, gave them incredible strength. A pair of giants, the two of them!"

Mahoney upended his beer, then set one huge meathook on my shoulder and stared sorrowfully into my eyes.

"On their twelfth birthday, much the same age you are now, that madman led his sons into the woods. *Whichever one of you comes out alive is my true son*, he said, and left them there. Two weeks later, Giant Kichi came out. Torn up and scabbed and practically naked. Something had happened in those woods. He'd changed. Become a madman like his father.

"His father trained Kichi to become a wrecking machine. He brought in masters of each martial arts discipline. Wing Chun. Praying Mantis. Kung fu fighting. Everyone was doing it." He winked at the girl. "Giant Kichi sucked it up like a sponge. Big and strong he was, but also nimble. He beat holy hell out of his masters, full of rage and bloodlust. Finally his father stepped up and said, *How'd you like a piece of your old man?* Giant Kichi said, *I'd like that quite a lot, thanks*, and snapped his father over his knee like a stick of wood!"

"He did, did he?" the girl said.

"He did indeed!" Mahoney grinned. "Giant Kichi popped up on my radar years ago. I'd been touring the Eastern Seaboard with Killer Kowalski and Spider Winchell, eking out a rough living in the squared circle and doing some pest elimination on the side. I heard that Tugboat Sims—one tough S.O.B. and the only man to have beaten the Plague—had taken the challenge of this crazy Jap wrestler. Giant Kichi beat him so bad that Tugboat pissed his trunks and begged for his mama. Well, wouldn't you know it but two weeks later I'm at home dusting my knick-knacks when comes a knock at the door. I open it to see this little Jap fella with a wrinkly face like a cat's clenched bunghole. It was RiJishi, Giant Kichi's manservant. He hands me this funny scroll. It's an invitation to fight Kichi in the Tokyo Dome!"

Mahoney paced round the picnic table, stabbing his fingers through his hair.

"I took a steamship and trained as it sailed. Long hours in the boiler room, flinging lumps of coal into the greedy engine, my skin stained as black as night with the dust. The ship hooked past Greenland. I ran round the deck until icicles formed in my hair and jangled like castanets. I got bigger, stronger, as I knew I must to stand even a snowball's chance. And I swear, boys, I swear I heard Kichi's voice on the salt wind, calling me, haunting me, tormenting me.

"*Maaahoney,*" Bruiser mimicked. "*Maaahoney, I kirr you, Maaahoney.* Well, I'd be lying if I said I wasn't a shredded bag of nerves by the time I reached the land of the rising sun. A rickshaw ferried me to the Tokyo Dome and next I'm being led into the ring. A hundred thousand faces screaming for blood—*my* blood!"

Mahoney's expression darkened. He hooked his thumbs into his belt loops and shook his head.

"Ah, anyway. Let's talk about something else."

"No!" Dunk and I said in unison.

"Don't be a tease," the girl said.

Mahoney cocked a Spockian eyebrow. "I'm not boring you?"

She sighed. "Go on, you ham."

"Visualize it, then, boys. Set the picture in your mind. Giant Kichi—he was a man only in the way Goliath was a man. His head swept the rafters. You think I'm big? Oh, I was a *guppy* compared to this guy. But I'd vowed to lock horns, a deal had been struck, and then as now I honour my commitments."

The girl blew a raspberry.

"Yes, he was big," Mahoney said, after a searching look at the girl. "And his eyes . . . the darkest, most light-eating things I'd ever seen. I could tell right off he was nutty as squirrel turds, a whole flock of bats in his belfry, but I stepped through the ropes and scuffed my feet in the rosin all the same. Now boys, the first time Kichi hit me"—he slammed his fist into his open palm: *RAP!*— "I thought he'd caved my chest in. The crowd roared. I peeled myself off the canvas before he could land the finishing blow. I figured a man that big was like a tree: once he went down, he wouldn't get back up. So I chopped at him like a tree. Quick leg kicks, then scooting away. *Chop! Chop! Chop! Chop!*

"Kichi growled like an animal and lunged, but I managed to squirt away. *Chop! Chop!* I felt him weaken. *Chop! Chop!* The sound of my foot striking his leg was like an axe hacking into wet wood. When he went down—and yes, Giant Kichi did go down— it was with a cry that sounded like a gigantic baby sucking its first breath. He crashed into the mat with a rattle, the whole stadium shaking. I looked at him curled on the mat, helpless . . . and I couldn't finish it. He was raised a beast and that's what he became. So I left him there, may the Lord bless and keep him. And that, boys, was Giant Kichi."

The girl clapped. "Bravo!"

"Did it really happen?" I said.

Mahoney said, "Ask her. She was there."

The girl said, "It's true. Every word." She turned her bottle upside down, beer sloshing onto the dirt.

"What a waste!" Mahoney said.

"I've got to get back home," she said.

"Ah, come on. Another story."

"Another time."

Mahoney stared an instant, then rubbed his nose harshly with his palm. "Yeah, okay. Another time."

We drove back. Bruiser reached into the case. The girl briefly set her hand on his. He let go of the bottle, goosed the accelerator and said: "Is it to be like this, then? Is it?"

"I don't know what other way you figured it to be."

"Did you get the money I sent?"

"I don't need the money. Neither does Mom."

"The letters, then. You read them?"

She said: "I read them, yes."

"Everything I wrote, I meant."

"Sure you did. But that dog's not going to hunt."

For a moment Mahoney rested his hand lightly on the girl's knee. "We had some high times, now, didn't we?"

"You're a hell of a good time. Nobody would deny it."

"Are you telling me we didn't have some high ol' times?"

The girl offered him a distressed smile. "Why would I tell you anything when you already know it all?"

Bruiser drove back down the river route. The sky had lowered over the river, which had turned the colour of lead. Reaching across the armrest, Bruiser took the girl's hand. It covered her own like a tarantula clutching a cat's eye marble. She patted his hand with her free one, the way you'd stroke a tame animal: a toothless old bear maybe, the ones that rode tricycles in Russian circuses.

Mahoney appeared aggravated with this treatment; the tenderness of it, I figured. Or maybe the fact she stroked his hand as a mother would stroke her child's? He tore his hand away and punched the roof.

The girl's laugh said she'd seen this song and dance before. She turned to us and said, "Big Bruiser *maaaad*! Bruiser make heap big thunder!"

"Don't encourage her, please," Bruiser told us as we laughed. He sucked on his skinned knuckles and said, "If you encourage her she'll never grow up."

The girl stuck out her tongue at him. "I grew up like a thief, didn't I? Always out of your sight."

He beheld her with reproachful eyes. "When did you get so cold, girl?"

She stared straight ahead at that. I got the sense it was some kind of act, in which she was playing the hard girl. It didn't suit her, but she played it well enough.

We arrived at the house with the small fenced-in yard. The girl kissed Mahoney on the cheek.

"He'll get you home safe," she assured us. "You're in good hands."

When the girl left, it was as if she took some part of Bruiser Mahoney with her. Dunk and I watched in silence as he popped the glovebox and recovered a bottle of pills. He shook a few out and dry-swallowed them and jammed the bottle into one of the many pockets of his coat. Then he drove on. The only sounds were the loose muffler rattling against the undercarriage and the muted *clink* of bottles.

"Ah, Jesus," Mahoney said hoarsely, mopping his brow as a man with a high fever might. "Ah, Jesus, Jesus."

Dunk leaned forward to touch Mahoney's slouched shoulder. Mahoney flinched.

"God damn it." He unrolled the window, cleared his throat and spat. "I'm not perfect. Never claimed to be. Made mistakes—who hasn't? Look at you two. Your fathers get in some silly brawl and let a monstrous stranger walk away with their kids. *That's* good parenting? Smelling like damn cookies, the pair of them. What in hell's *that* about?"

"They work at a cookie factory," I said.

Mahoney's head rocked back on the stump of his neck. Maybe he was picturing it as I once had: a tree full of lumpen cookie-making elves, like in the commercials.

"I bet your dads have never taken you camping, have they?"

Dunk said: "We went to a cottage once."

"Great galloping goose shit!" Mahoney said. He pawed through the case for a fresh beer, opened it and swigged deeply. It clearly rejuvenated him. "Never gone on a camp-out? A couple of fine nellies you'll turn into."

"What's a nelly?" Dunk said.

"A pansy. A goddamn bed-wetter! That tears it—I'm taking you boys to the woods. It'll put some bark on your trees!"

We pulled onto the highway. Mahoney fled down the two-lane stretch, hair whipping round his head like snakes from the wind through the window. His face crept closer to the windshield; he crouched over the wheel, and I imagined him squinting at the yellow broken lines blurring under the hood.

A police car fled past in the opposite lane, lights ablaze and sirens blaring. When it was gone Mahoney laughed, a creaky-hinge sound.

In some dimmed chamber of my heart I realized I ought to be terrified. Yet I wasn't. Dunk grinned into the wind that screamed through the van, tugging at his clothes and stirring the drifts of soda cans behind us.

"Ever pitched a tent, boys?" said Mahoney.

Dunk said: "Never!"

"Ever baited a trap?"

"We lit a one-match fire in Cubs."

Mahoney snorted. "Your fathers should be bloody ashamed of themselves." He wrenched the wheel. We were off the main road— off pavement entirely—bouncing down a rutted dirt path. Long grass glowed whitely in the headlamps. I may've seen lights burning in the distance, the lights of an isolated farmhouse maybe, but soon those vanished.

We drove over the crest of some empty land, very flat, the path running as straight as a yardstick, and then came a stand of apple trees hung with winter-withered fruit that shone like nickels at the bottom of a well. Next came pine trees that dropped and kept on dropping. I was sure the van would rattle to pieces. My teeth chattered in my mouth. Bushes whacked up under the frame.

Mahoney remained hunched over the wheel, his face lit up by the dashboard's greenish glow. "Now we're getting somewhere." His voice possessed the mad certainty that the leaders of doomed polar expeditions must have held.

The path kept eroding. Soon it was only the phantom of a road; the woods loomed. Stones pinged off the frame. Branches yawned over the trail, raking the windows like skeletal fingers.

The van hit a lip. Metal shrieked as we bottomed out. I was thrown forward, shoulder striking the passenger seat before I slumped to the floor, dazed. Dunk helped me back onto the seat.

"Buckle your seat belt, man."

But we weren't moving anymore. Mahoney mashed the gas pedal, snarling through skinned-back lips. The wheels spun until the sound of smoking rubber reached the pitch of a gut-shot animal. Steam boiled from under the hood. Mahoney climbed out, stumbled in front of the headlights to survey the damage.

"We're here," he said, as if this had been our destination all along. He popped the van's back doors and flung out an army surplus tent, a blackened cooking grill, sleeping bags.

"You boys find some firewood," he said merrily. "Beat the ground in front of you, though—snakes out at this hour."

We explored the clearing that fringed the woods.

"Wait!" Mahoney called us back, removing a collapsible Buck knife from his pocket. After considering us at length, he handed it to Dunk. "Just in case," he said.

"I already got one," Dunk said, showing Mahoney the Swiss Army knife he always carried.

Mahoney pressed his knife into my palm. Warm from his flesh, the brass fittings greased with sweat.

We picked our way through the trees searching for sticks. An owl nested on a low branch, eyes shining like lanterns. The darkness of Dunk's hair blended with the blackness under the trees; he seemed as much a part of this wilderness as the owl. I fit my thumbnail into the groove on the Buck knife and pulled it open. The blade clicked smoothly into place—I could smell the oil in the mechanism. Moonlight played off the tiny hairline abrasions along the blade where Mahoney must've sharpened it on a whetstone.

When we returned from our mission Bruiser Mahoney was sitting cross-legged, assembling a tent in the van's headlights. One of the tent poles was bent at a broken-backed angle in his huge hands. Growling, he flung it into the bushes.

"Goddamn Tinkertoys."

He managed to get one tent up before the van's battery conked out. We built a ring of rocks and heaped wood inside. Mahoney doused the sticks with turpentine and lit a match.

"Phwoar!" he cried as the flames roared up.

Sap hissed and knots popped in the burning wood. Mahoney reached for a beer but the case was empty. He stood up the way a baby does—hands braced in front of him, walking his heels up to meet them—and shuffled to the edge of the woods. He pissed for a minor eternity—his urine sounded *heavy*, as if threaded with molten lead; I imagined it flattening the weeds and snapping twigs.

His body swung around and he returned to the van, hunting through it. He sat back down with a bottle of white liquor and a big silver handgun.

"I won it in a bet," he said. "Or I lost a bet and had to take possession of it. I forget now. We might need it tonight."

"Why?" I asked.

"You think we're the only creatures out here?"

As the night wore on, Mahoney was coming to resemble an animal himself. I peered through the flames at this shaggy man-beast fumbling with a loaded pistol. He looked like a bear trying to play the piano. The cylinder popped open. Bullets fell into his lap. He pinched them between his fingers and thumbed them back into their holes, then took crooked aim at the trees.

"Bang," he whispered.

He handed me the bottle. When I hesitated he said: "Your father never gave you a belt of rum? It's pirate medicine, son."

Whatever was in the bottle blistered my throat. I coughed convulsively and would've puked but there was nothing in my stomach.

Dunk took the bottle. Not only did he keep it down, he took another sip.

"It does taste like medicine," Dunk said.

"When I was your age I believed totally in the power of medicine," said Mahoney. "One time my grandfather was coughing. I gave him a cough drop. My grandfather had lung cancer. By the end he was hacking up spongy pink bits."

"Teach me to wrestle," Dunk said.

"A fucking *cough drop* . . . What?"

"To wrestle," Dunk said. "Teach me."

"Why? You want to grow up to be like me?"

"I do."

Mahoney sucked at the bottle and then wiped the shine off his lips. His teeth were the colour of old bone in the firelight.

"Up, then!" he cried. "Stand and fight!"

He leapt across the flames and landed nimbly. Dunk was crab-walking away on his palms and heels. Mahoney hauled him up with no more effort or regard than a man lifting a sack of laundry.

"Lock up," he snarled, setting himself in a wrestling pose. "Damn you, you wanted to learn so lock up with me!"

Mahoney got down on his knees. He grabbed Dunk's hands and slapped one on the back of his neck and the other on his shoulder.

"Like that," he said, settling his hands on Dunk's own neck and shoulder. "You control the other man this way, see? Now control my head."

The muscles flexed down Dunk's arm. Mahoney's head sat on his neck like a tree stump, moving nowhere. Dunk linked his fingers around the back of Mahoney's neck, screwed his heels into the ground and pulled as hard as he could.

"Has a butterfly settled on me?" Mahoney asked acidly.

"Owe," Dunk said, his face contorted with effort, "*help.*"

I wrapped my arms around Mahoney's bull neck. He wore the same aftershave my father did, the one with the blue ship on the bottle. The hairs on the back of his neck were as soft as the white spores on a dandelion before they blow away in the wind.

Mahoney said: "You're *huuuurting meeee . . .*"

His hands shot up, grabbing a fistful of our shirts. He pushed us backwards and we landed hard on our asses and elbows.

"Oldest trick in the book," he said, whapping dirt off his knees. "Never trust the wounded dog, boys."

Dunk's elbow was torn open, blood trickling to his wrist. His hands flexed into fists at his sides. Mahoney was by the fire, bent over his bottle. When he stood up Dunk was right there.

"What?" Mahoney said.

Dunk showed Mahoney his elbow. Not for sympathy, just so the man could see what he'd done.

"Sorry about that," Bruiser said. "Let's patch it up."

Mahoney found a box of Band-Aids in the glovebox and stuck one on Dunk's elbow. He took the bottle of pills from his pocket, shook a quartet into his palm and chased them with rum.

"That's wrestling, boys. Want to see what it earns you?" He rolled his trouser up past his knee. "I always wear tights in the ring. Now you see why."

His kneecap was shattered. The two halves of it lay under his skin with one half twisted to one side, the other sunk beneath his knee joint. It looked like a lunar landing photo. The cratered surface of the moon.

"A steel chair. *Whappo.* Some kind of no-holds-barred contest. The promoter didn't bother explaining it too well. He was drunk. Anyway, so was I. The guy who chair-shotted me, the Sandman, he was drunk too. I heard the bone crack. Sounded like a starter's pistol—*pow!*" Mahoney shook his head. "That was Texas. Never wrestle in Texas, boyos."

He ran his hands through his hair, parting the dark locks. A scar ran across the top of his skull. Pink, ribbed and shockingly thick—it looked like a garter snake frozen under his scalp.

"Razorwire," he said. "Some kind of crazy thing in Japan. Opened me up to the bone. Blood pissing all over the mat. That's how they like it over there. *Messy.* I kept wrestling. The both of us greasy with blood. I passed out. Came to in the emergency room with a sweet slant-eyed nurse stitching my head up."

Everywhere Mahoney had gone left a mark on him. The most crucial testament of his perfection—the fact that he'd come from outside of Cataract City, the great unknown where perfection was still a possibility—was the very thing that had ruined him.

Dunk said: "Did your dad teach you to wrestle?"

"My dad was a great man," Mahoney said. "A *beast*! When I was a boy he'd pinch my shoulders and say, 'Look at those tiny trapezius muscles of yours—they're mousetraps! You should have bear traps like mine! And your neck's thin as a stack of dimes—what use is a man who can't even support the weight of his own skull?' I was a small boy. Sickly. Born premature. Not much bigger than a kaiser roll, my mother said. She hardly realized I'd come out.

"I got picked on as a boy. Yes! After school I'd make it home a few steps ahead of my tormentors and hide. Then my dad would come home. He was a butcher. His days spent quartering hogs. He'd drag me outside to face the other boys. But before that he'd wad up his apron, still wet with pig blood, and stuff it in my face. 'Smell it!' he'd say. 'It should make you *crazy*! A mad *dog*!' And so I went out with my face smeared with blood and I'd fight. It made me a better man, and I think every boy should . . . Did you . . . Did you . . .?"

Mahoney was peering into the trees. He closed one eye like he was peering through a magnifying glass, then reared back as if he'd sniffed something foul.

"Did you *see* that?"

Dunk looked. I looked. There was nothing.

"What is it?" said Dunk.

"I . . . I can't quite say. But do you know who's out there?" He screwed his palms into his eye sockets and blinked furiously. "Every manner of psycho and degenerate. Where do you go when polite society rejects you? *The woods*. Eating skunks, biding your time, waiting for your opportunity."

Mahoney worked his jaw. The interlocking bones clicked beneath his ear. He scrounged the gun out of his jacket pocket. A log cracked in the fire. He wheeled about in a crazy circle, strafing the trees with the barrel.

"Who is it? Rotten-ass bastard, show yourself! I'll plug one between your eyes!"

We cowered as the pistol swung on wild orbits. Mahoney drank and wiped his lips with the back of the hand gripping the gun.

"There's no need for this." His voice took on a pleading note. "Come sit by the fire. We can—"

A rustling arose beyond the trees and for an instant I swore a face materialized. White as milk apart from the lips, which were as red as blood from a freshly torn vein. Teeth filed to crude points. A ravenous ghoul stalking us from the darkness past the fire.

Mahoney howled—"*Reeeeaaaggh!*"—and fired. Flame spat from the gun to illuminate the fear-twisted contours of his face.

"Weasels," he snarled. "Cowardly punks." He raked his finger-nails down his cheeks. "Think they can dog me out like that? You let a man dog you even once and he'll dog you until your last breath! Come on, boys."

"Where?" said Dunk.

Mahoney pointed to the trees.

Years later I'd wonder if it could possibly have happened as I remembered it.

The woods were black and cold, but not as cold as they would become later. I recall a lack of friction between my body and the things surrounding it—the trees, the spongelike quality of the topsoil—as if I was floating. I remember thinking I was in a place where none of my daily habits carried any impact. I tried to picture my bedroom with the wallpaper my father had put up: a panorama of the earth, small and bright and blue-white as photographed from the moon.

I slipped my finger through Dunk's belt loop, anchoring him to me. The long muscle that ran up Dunk's shoulder and neck to his hairline quivered with a nervous, tentative strength. Prickberry bushes tore gashes in my arms. The pain and adrenaline came together in my legs and fingers and head: a cool tingling under my skin, a hot buzz in my skull.

Bruiser Mahoney stalked ahead of us, a huge rumpled shape barely distinguishable from the darkness. He followed the silver finger of the gun barrel, his breath filling the space under the leaves. When he coughed the sound was that of an old refrigerator shutting down, the ancient tubes and fittings rattling against one another.

A serrated leaf feathered my cheek. I brushed it aside, startled by the whiteness of my fingers in the night, then walked through a spider's web strung between two saplings. The gossamer snapped over my lips and eyelids and for an instant I felt the hollow weight of a spider against my throat, but by the time I'd gathered my breath to scream it was gone, rappelling down my shirt.

"Take heart, lads," Mahoney whispered. "Fortune favours the brave."

My eyes adjusted. The woods took shape. Trees rose out of the black loam of the forest floor, bark covered in frost that glittered like pulverized salt. Streamers of fog snaked along the ground; I tasted the mineral wetness of it in the back of my mouth. We made no noise at all—even Mahoney, whose grace had otherwise deserted him—our feet sliding silently over the moist leafless earth.

"Wolverines out here," said Mahoney. "A wolverine gets hungry enough, it'll creep into your tent and eat your face off. Wolves, too."

As soon as he said that, I saw them: hunched shapes moving between the trees, much bigger than dogs, white-tipped fur bristling along their spines. Their smell rode the breeze, the stink of meat rotting between their fangs. My fingers tightened in Dunk's belt loop, which I guess made me a pussy but I was too freaked to care.

A stealthy clawing kicked up behind us. Mahoney whirled and fired. I fell to my knees, ears covered against the thunder. There was blood on Mahoney's cheek where the gun's hammer had gouged his flesh.

"It flanked round behind us, the sneaky bugger."

Mahoney trudged off in the direction of his gunfire. We found him bent over a small broken shape. Blood shone in a pool round its spike-shaped head.

"A coon." Mahoney laughed without mirth. "We've been chasing a damn raccoon."

The animal reeked of blood and piss. Its gums were already hardening, black lips drawn back from yellowed teeth. It looked like it had died very confused. Mahoney bent to pick it up by a hind leg. Back at the fire, he laid the dead animal down with reverence.

"I'm sorry," he said.

Who was he apologizing to, us or the raccoon?

"Hand me my knife," he said.

Mahoney unfolded the blade and slid the point into the skin between its front legs and sawed down its belly. The raccoon opened up in the firelight.

"If you kill an animal and don't eat it, you're cursed forever. Earl Starblanket told me that. He was a pureblood Navajo who used to wrestle as Big Chief Jackdaw."

Mahoney hacked through the gleaming knots of the creature's insides. The smell was indescribable. I couldn't imagine putting it in my mouth.

Dunk said, "*We* didn't kill it."

Mahoney looked up sharply. His hands were black with blood. "We all did. We were a hunting party."

Dunk shook his head. "Owe and me were just there."

"That's right, you were. You witnessed it. Do you want to put your mortal soul in jeopardy?"

Mahoney cut off a strip of meat. He gathered up the raccoon, holding its split body together the way a prim woman holds a purse, humped over to the trees and flung it away. He settled the metal grate over the coals and laid the meat down.

"You don't eat much," he said. "Just a bite or two, to honour the animal."

The meat sizzled. Mahoney speared it with the tip of his knife and turned it over. His lips shone with drool. He crunched some more pills. When the meat was cooked he hacked it into steaming chunks.

"Eat it," he said darkly.

It was burnt, which was a blessing: I assumed the taste of char was better than the taste of raccoon. Mahoney ate in silence, backhanding the juice that dribbled down his chin.

We lay in the grass. I was exhausted but couldn't let myself fall asleep next to Bruiser Mahoney—cold snakes squirmed in my belly just thinking about it. The stars were bright in a way they never were in my suburb. The moon was perfectly halved, like a paper circle folded over. The sky so clear that I could see calligraphic threads on the moon's surface.

"Did you know," Mahoney said, "that the Russians sent dogs into space? My mother told me this when I was a boy. Nobody knew the effects of space on a body, you see, so they sent dogs first. They found two mongrels on the streets of Moscow. Pchelka, which means Little Bee, and Mushka, which means Little Fly. They went up in *Sputnik* 6. They were supposed to get into orbit and come right back. But the rockets misfired and shot them into space.

"Whenever I look at the night sky, I think about those dogs.

Wearing these hand-stitched spacesuits, bright orange, with their paws sticking out. Big fishbowl helmets. How . . . *crazy*. Floating out and out into space. How bewildered they must have been. Freezing, starving, dying from oxygen deprivation. For what? They would have happily spent their days rummaging through trashcans.

"For all anyone knows those dogs are still out there. Two dead mongrels in a satellite. Two dog skeletons in silly spacesuits. Gleaming dog skulls inside fishbowl helmets. They'll spin through the universe until they burn up in the atmosphere of an uncharted planet. Or get sucked into a black hole to be crushed into a ball of black matter no bigger than an ant turd."

Bruiser Mahoney laughed. The sound sent a shiver through my gums. His laughter rolled out and out into the wilderness; the sound didn't touch anything I could recognize or draw hope from.

"Who *are* you?" I asked—the most searching, most innocent question I've asked in my life.

Mahoney propped himself up on one elbow. His fingers were black with dried raccoon blood.

"What do you mean?" he asked, a child himself. When he caught the aim of my question his lips curled back from his teeth. "Am I not still your hero?" he said, deathly soft. "The mighty Bruiser Mahoney? *Ooh*, you're a smart boy. You've figured me out, haven't you? Unmasked me. Well then, I guess that makes this the hour of truth. Let's lay all the cards on the table, hmm? Card one: I'm not Bruiser Mahoney. My name is Dade Rathburn. I was born in Orillia, Ontario. Before becoming a wrestler I was a janitor at a box factory. I've spent time in jail—once for beating a man half to death outside a bar, and once again for passing phony cheques. *Mahoney?* I don't have a drop of Irish blood in me! I'm a fake, boys." Coldness crept into his voice. "And I'll slap down card number two: wrestling's fake, too."

Dunk made a helpless noise in his throat, like the tweet of a small bird.

"Oh, yessss," Mahoney hissed. "Fake as a three-dollar bill! Fake as Sammy Davis Junior's eye! The matches are bunko. I win because we draw it up that way. The punches and kicks don't hurt—hell, most times we don't even touch each other. It's a big scam, and you bought into it."

"You be quiet," Dunk said. "You just shut up."

Mahoney laughed in Dunk's face.

"My opponent tonight, the Boogeyman? His name is Barry Schenk. Used to be a math teacher. Good guy. We head to the bar after our matches and have a laugh. We're *friends*."

Dunk twisted into a wretched ball. Mahoney's expression softened abruptly. He reached out and put his fingers on Dunk's shoulder. Dunk withdrew from his touch.

"I'm sorry, son," Mahoney said. "You shouldn't pay me any mind. I'm a drunk and a clown. You ever see an old clown, boys? No. Old clowns don't die, though."

He stood. His eyes shone like glass.

"Be like your fathers," he said. "Work a solid job. Build a family. Smelling like a cookie's a small price to pay for ordinary happiness."

A hellish noise kicked up in the woods: a high gibbering shriek that tapered to an ongoing moan. Mahoney spun on his heel, pistol jerked high.

"God rot you! I'll have your guts for garters!"

For the next several hours, until the sky lightened in the east, Mahoney blundered around in the forest. Every so often came the splintering of wood or a low animal bellow. Dunk and I lay together by the dying fire, dew silked to our skin.

At some point Mahoney emerged. His clothes were torn and

mud-streaked, his face badly scratched and his hair stuck with burrs.

"Goddamn bastards . . . thought you had me but I outfoxed you . . . didn't I, Daddy? Stinking of pig blood but I won. I *won*."

He shambled over to the tent, which was much too small for him. His cowboy boots stuck out the flaps.

I rose with the sun scraping the treetops. I'd fallen asleep on my side and woke up tucked close to Dunk. He was sleeping still. His spine bowed with each breath, touching my stomach.

My arm was pins and needles. I flexed my fingers, which felt full of static. My mouth tasted of burnt meat. The clearing was washed in new sunlight. Nothing in the trees except a chipmunk nibbling on a nut. Dunk rolled onto his side, blinking at the sun.

"You okay?"

"I want to go home," I told him simply.

He stood and stretched, catlike. We scratched our itchy bits and rubbed the dirt out of our hair.

I said: "Should we wake him up?"

"My dad doesn't like to get up after he's been drinking."

"So what are we going to do?"

Dunk stared at the sky as if he could tell the time by where the sun sat. "Okay, let's wake him up," he said finally.

Bruiser Mahoney's cowboy boots still jutted out of the tent. The toes were covered with muddy grass as if he'd been kicking holes in the earth. Dunk tapped one of them with his sneaker.

"Hey, Bruiser. We got to go home."

Dunk kicked harder. Bruiser's foot barely moved. His boot could have been filled with concrete. Dunk pulled back the tent flap. His nose wrinkled. "He must've puked."

Bruiser lay on top of his sleeping bag. His hands were covered in raccoon blood; it had dried and split, making his skin look like lizard scales. Dunk crawled inside the tent. I tried to grab him but he was already halfway in.

The smell was the same as when my dad had found our neighbour's cat under our porch, eaten by beetles. "That would gag a maggot," he'd said. Sunlight streamed through the tent's metal eyelets, picking up the dust above Mahoney's chest. His skin pale through the rips in his clothing. Quite suddenly I realized how *still* things were. Nothing but our own timid movements and the floating dust.

"Bruiser," Dunk said softly. "Hey . . . you awake?"

My knee knocked into Bruiser's leg. It was hard, like a mannequin leg. I pulled away, spine pressed against the tent's canvas. Mahoney's fingers were curled back in defiance of their bones. They reminded me of the Wicked Witch's shoes in *The Wizard of Oz*. I thought Mahoney might be taking a long breath. I held mine until my heart thudded at my temples. When I let it out he still hadn't taken a breath of his own.

Dunk leaned over him.

"Bruiser?" Shouting it: "*Bruiser!*"

Mahoney's face was the colour of the moulding clay we used in art class. His eyes were wide open, his eyeballs milky, snaky with burst vessels. White stuff that looked like dried shaving cream was crusted at the sides of his mouth. There was something the matter with his face. His upper teeth were ejected past his lips, connected to a strip of dingy pink plastic.

"Dentures," Dunk said quietly. "My grandpa wears them too. When he goes to bed he puts them in a glass of buttermilk."

Dunk pressed his thumb to Mahoney's teeth and tried to push them into his mouth. They wouldn't go. He pulled on Mahoney's chin until his mouth opened a bit. The sound was like a rubber band snapping. His dentures fell back into his mouth with a terrible *slunk*, the sound of an un-oiled drawer sliding shut.

Dunk pushed Bruiser Mahoney's dentures back under his lips and tried to pinch them gently together. But his teeth were too big for his mouth. Either they had grown—which was impossible, right?—or his skin had shrunk.

"Is he . . .?"

"I think so, yeah," Dunk said.

My heart was a wounded bird flapping inside my chest. I wanted to scream but the sound was locked up somewhere under my lungs.

"Should we close his eyes, Owe?"

"Is that what you do?"

Dunk nodded. "So the soul can go to heaven."

You think that's where it's going? I almost asked.

Dunk put two fingertips on Mahoney's eyelids and pulled them down. When he let go they rolled back up like window shades. One of Mahoney's eyes pointed towards his nose as if the muscles behind it had given up, letting the eyeball roll towards the lowest point on his face. It made him look comical and stupid.

"Fuck," said Dunk.

Outside the tent I wept. I wept because a man I'd idolized without really knowing him—it dawned on me that maybe this was the only way you ever really *could* idolize anybody—was gone and I was miserable because he'd died overnight, alone, in an army surplus tent with his boots on. And I wept because Dunk and I were in the middle of a big nowhere now. I wept because the only person who could have got us out of this was dead, his eyeball lazing into the centre of his face, and he'd left two dumb scared kids a million miles from anywhere.

Dunk opened the van door and sat in the driver's seat. He gripped the wheel so tight his knuckles went white, then punched it. The horn made a low *blatt*.

"Should we bury him?" he said.

I wiped scalding tears off my cheeks. It was the most serious question I'd ever had to answer. "We don't have a shovel."

Dunk nodded; he'd already registered that fact.

After some thinking, I said: "Could we burn him? That's what Bovine's dad does at the funeral parlour. There's a big oven down in the basement, Bovine says. The coffins go in on a conveyor belt. His dad sweeps the ashes into a metal vase."

"A vase?"

"I guess, like you're supposed to put it in your living room. Over the fireplace?"

"Where you hang stockings at Christmas?" Dunk said.

It *was* weird. I didn't tell Dunk that Bovine also told me that sometimes his father pried the gold fillings out of a dead person's teeth before putting the body in the oven. He gave the gold to the next-of-kin, who usually melted it down, Bovine said, turning it into earrings or doo-dads on a charm bracelet. People were weird about death. Looking at Bruiser Mahoney's boots sticking out of the tent, I could see why.

"How would we burn him?" Dunk said.

"We could stuff sticks inside the tent and light it."

"What about the sparks? They could fly off and set the woods on fire."

"We could build a ring of rocks around the tent."

Dunk touched his lip to his nose, considering it. "Would it get hot enough to turn him into ashes? Last summer we had a cookout along the river and my brother dropped his hot dog in the fire. In the morning it was a shrivelled black stick, like charcoal."

I pictured Bruiser Mahoney the same way: the meat cooked black on his bones, his body laid out like a stick figure. What would we do then? Snap his limbs over our knees—I imagined each break sending up a puff of sparkling black dust—and stack Bruiser

Mahoney in our arms? We'd have to carry him out of the forest like firewood.

Dunk climbed out of the van and walked to the tent.

"What are you doing?"

"Getting some things," he said.

He rummaged inside the tent. The points of his elbows strained against the canvas. Was he rolling Mahoney over? Rooting through the dead man's pockets? A series of loud pops, like shots from a cap gun, fired quickly. I wondered if it was the trapped air popping between the knobs of Mahoney's spinal cord.

That sound opened a hidden trap door in my head and quite suddenly I was staring at my own body in a coffin, my face propped up by a shiny satin pillow. I lay in a parlour with stained-glass windows; "Nearer, My God, to Thee" was playing. My father and mother were there, plus a few of my teachers and some aunts and uncles I hardly ever saw. My face was yellow from that chemical they pump into your veins to replace your blood—the same stuff our science teacher used to preserve dissected frogs. Stitches circled my head; the undertaker had brushed my bangs down to cover them, but not totally. I wondered if they had taken my brain out and if so, why? Maybe evil aliens had stolen it, like the ones in that television show Dunk and I watched late one night: *Invasion of the Brain Snatchers*. If my brain was gone, what was inside my head now? Packing peanuts like the ones that Dad's hi-fi equipment had come in? Some balled-up pages out of the *Niagara Falls Pennysaver*?

Staring at my own dead face didn't fill me with horror or sadness or much of anything, probably because I couldn't really *imagine* being dead. The whole scene felt like a joke—and then my dad began to bawl hysterically, soaking a platter of cucumber sandwiches with his tears, and the daydream fell apart.

Dunk came out of the tent with Mahoney's gun and knife and laid them on the driver's seat.

"Want a piece of gum?"

"Where did you get it?" I asked.

"You want it or not?"

We chewed gum. Dunk pulled the van's key out of his pocket and slid it into the ignition. The motor went *whirr-whirr-whirr*. Dunk popped the hood—it shocked me that he knew how—and peered into the engine compartment.

"It's fried," he said, and spat in the dirt.

Tracks of crushed grass ran out behind the van's tires. I didn't know how long we'd driven off the road, but it hadn't seemed all that far last night.

"Can we follow them out?" I said.

"Or wait here for someone to find us."

"Do you think anyone's looking?" My eyes drifted to the tent. Mahoney was laid out on his frayed sleeping bag, eyes open, dentures poking past his ashy lips. I was terrified he'd sit up. "Let's go, Dunk."

We found an old backpack in the van. Also a few cans of Coke, half a bag of barbecue chips, a Three Musketeers bar, some rags and a bottle of vitamin caplets big enough to choke an elephant. Glossy magazines with pictures of muscled-up men; other magazines of naked ladies—Dunk put one of those in the pack. We left the pills and empty beer bottles.

Dunk found a box of bullets in the glovebox and fiddled with the pistol. I was afraid it'd go off accidentally, leaving a smoking ring in his forehead. The cylinder fell open. Dunk picked out the spent cartridges, slotted in fresh ones and thumbed the safety. He put it in the backpack and gave the Buck knife to me.

What about the tent? We could burn it, or leave it open for the animals to find Bruiser. He had dragged us out here, got drunk, gone mad and died. What did we owe him?

"We could . . . roll him up in the tent? Put some stones on to hold it down."

Dunk sawed his arm across his nose. "He's just worm food now, anyway."

The stones were still warm from the fire. We rolled the biggest ones to the tent. Dunk kicked the tent poles away. It collapsed with an outrush of foul air as the canvas sagged over Mahoney's body. I could make out his face where the material lay across the hawklike bridge of his nose.

We heaped stones on the tent's edges. Dunk lifted the biggest one, cradled it to his gut, and dropped it. Mahoney's body bent at the waist—heels raising up, nose straining against the canvas—then lay flat.

Dunk shrugged the pack onto his shoulders and we followed the tire tracks out of the clearing.

The woods were alive with movement. Here a spooked rush of limbs. There a flurry of wings. All of it was timid. Funny to think that, in daylight, a pair of kids could be lords of the forest.

The only creatures who didn't fear us were the insects. Mosquitoes helicoptered around my ears, giving off a maddening whine. One drew so close that I was sure it would fly straight into the canal and then into my brain to suck the blood out of the grey matter. When it landed on the hard little hump above my eardrum I pinched it between my fingers; the bastard crumpled with a satisfying feel, like softest metal. The satisfaction was short-lived, as the bugs had found us by then: they were everywhere, crawling and whining and buzzing, drinking our blood and sipping our sweat. Soon my arms were covered in angry whitened bites.

The day was cool beneath the leaves. Shafts of sunlight sparkled, dizzyingly bright, moving in squiggly patterns on the ground as the wind stirred the trees. Gnats meshed above puddles of water, coiling up in bug tornadoes. The heat evaporated the morning's dew and gave the air a sweet green smell.

Dunk moved confidently, head down, thumbs hooked under the backpack straps. The scabs on his elbows shone like obsidian. Our breath came lightly as our feet flashed over the earth. We seemed to be making decent time, though our finish line was unknown.

We came to a break in the trees. A falcon circled in the sky, the white tips of its wings standing out sharply against the edgeless blue.

"I've never seen anything like that," said Dunk. A squashed gnat was stuck to his front tooth. It looked like a poppy seed.

A stream trickled across the path. Minnows like tiny silver arrows darted and settled in the glassy water, which ran around the rocks in eddies.

Dunk scooped his hand along the stream's edge and came up with a mudpuppy, an eel-like creature with stunted appendages like mouse paws. It thrashed in Dunk's palm, whipping back and forth in spine-snapping spasms. Dunk returned it to the water; we watched it squirm under a flat, sandy rock, turn and peer up at us from its muddy bunker.

The slime-covered rocks above the water's surface reminded me of Chia Pets. Dirty collars of foam surrounded most of them, and the water smelled funky: a waft of sulphur from a struck match.

"Be careful," Dunk said. "I don't want to carry you if you twist an ankle."

"You think I want to carry *you*?"

Dunk hopscotched across the rocks easily. I followed him but slipped on the last rock and got a huge soaker. "Fuckballs!"

Dunk hooted. My socks squelched, mud squeezing out of the eyelets. I flicked water at him off the toe of my sneaker.

"Hey, watch it!" Dunk skipped aside, still laughing.

It pissed me off. Dunk *always* beat me. In our two-man contest I always took the booby prize.

An expanse of sun-baked clay unfurled past the stream. The van's tires had left no impression in it. We walked to a spot where the clay gave way to a drywash. There was nothing but polished stones and nappy scrub that would have sprung right up after the van had gone over it, leaving no clue.

Dunk wiped the sweat off his forehead with the hem of his T-shirt. His hip bones stood out above his belt, as pronounced as ears. My wet shoe baked in the sun, its rotten-algae smell infiltrating my nose. I stood on my tiptoes, straining for sounds of civilization, the silky *shrriiip* of car tires on the road. *Something.* But there was nothing except nature, dominated by the throaty gurgle of the stream. For the first time in my life I found this to be a scary sound.

Dunk said, "Which way?"

I slapped a mosquito. It left a spiky blot of blood on my wrist above the big blue vein. I pointed. "That way looks flatter."

Dunk said, "Okay . . . but what did our Scout leader say about following a stream?"

I rubbed my temples, massaging the skin the way Mom did for Dad when he came home after a frazzling day. *It stimulates the thinking muscle,* she'd say.

"He said a small stream leads to a bigger stream, which leads to a river which leads to a lake which leads to a road," I said.

The streambed carried on for a few hundred yards before hooking around a clump of green bushes. A rime of earth ran along the stream's edge, making the side sun-cracked but passable.

Duncan said: "Let's follow it." He took a rag out of the backpack and tied it to a tree branch. "If we need to come back and go the other way, we'll know this was where we were . . . or if we come past this again, we'll know we're not very good at orienteering."

The stream meandered through the woods, a path of least resistance, splitting around molehills to leave small grass-topped islands. Water boatmen paddled in still pools, their bloated bodies moving in clumsy circles. Water skimmers zipped here and there. I'd once asked my father why they didn't sink and he'd told me they were so light that they could dance along the water without falling into it. "There's a skin on the water, like the skin that forms on top of pudding," he'd told me. "A water skimmer's body is lighter than water, believe it or not, so they can walk on the water just like you or I walk on a floor."

The temperature rose. Trickles of sweat cut down my face; wet patches formed under my arms. A dark T appeared on the back of Dunk's T-shirt. The sun dipped behind a bank of grey clouds but it didn't get any cooler—if anything it was *hotter*, as if the sun, beating down on those rain-packed clouds, threw a blanket of broiling air over us.

Dunk held a steady pace, hitching his pack up on his back, hopping instinctively over spots where the shore threatened to crumble into foot-soaking pockets of mud—pockets that I would've stepped in had he not been guiding. The stream grew steadily narrower. We followed it down a long slope through a glade of low-hanging willows whose branches dipped right into the water; it was like walking through a series of doorways strung with beaded curtains.

The stream was now narrow enough that Dunk could straddle it, his feet on either side. And now the woods changed, too. Where before everything was bright green, shot through with the gold of sunlight through the leaves, by afternoon it changed to the denser, darker green of pine needles so thick the light could not penetrate:

the sunlight lay on top of the needles, making it feel as if we were insects picking our way across a saw blade.

We followed the stream, which by then—as we'd probably both admitted to ourselves but hadn't dared vocalize yet—was only a sad trickle as it cut through a stand of pines. Big grey spiders suspended themselves on webs between the conifers. Dunk touched his finger to the centre of one web. A spider picked its way down like an inverted tightrope walker, the gossamer bowing with its weight. It stopped before reaching Dunk's finger, thrown off by the heat maybe, then danced onto his fingertip. Dunk held it in his palm: a bead of swirling, concentrated smoke.

"It's not poisonous," he said, returning the spider to its web.

"How do you know?"

"Well, it didn't bite me."

After that we didn't worry about walking through the webs. It felt nasty stomping like Godzilla through Tokyo, but we wanted to get back to our homes. The pines thinned to a stretch of waist-high bushes hung with bright red berries—the kind our scoutmaster called bird berries, because only birds could eat them. I was *so* hungry. All I could remember eating last night was licorice at the arena and a chunk of raccoon. I stared longingly at the berries hanging in plump bunches—couldn't I try just a few? But I pictured my stomach swelling and splitting, my red-tinted guts spilling out like a frog's who'd been force-fed Alka-Seltzer.

The air was shimmery with mosquitoes. Could you die of mosquito bites? I pictured my body full of tiny pinpricks where mosquitoes had pierced me, an empty skin-coloured balloon blowing in the breeze. Would a hiker find me, fold me up like a love letter, slip me in an envelope and mail me back to my parents?

Dunk shrugged the pack off. The straps left creases in his shoulders. We sat on a lichen-covered rock. The stream—what was left of it—trickled around the rock and down a shallow slope, disappearing into a series of puddles dulled with pond scum and alive with bugs.

We split the barbecue chips, which had been crushed into shrapnel during the hike. Dunk gave me one of the Cokes, warm and salty-tasting. I drank it too fast and got a head-rush. I belched and put the can in the pack. Maybe we could fill it with water later.

Dunk took the nudie magazine out. Its pages were greasy, as if they'd been sprayed with vegetable oil. The women were different than in the Baby Blue Movies. They had bruises. Some had weird scars on their bellies and others had black bars over their eyes. The women without bars stared with dead expressions, spreading their pinkish parts open.

Dunk said, "That girl has a black eye." He threw the magazine on the ground.

The sun slid across the sky to hang above the blue hills to the west. I shut my eyes and saw my parents at the kitchen table. My father was wearing black-and-white-striped overalls, the kind prisoners wore in old movies. My mother's fingers steepled under her lips, as if she were suffering in some manner I couldn't name.

Dunk reached down for the nudie mag and stuffed it back inside the pack. "We can use it to start a fire."

There was no choice but to keep going in hopes the stream would pick up again. The ground was as soft as stale sponge cake and the bugs were now *everywhere*—midges, maddening brainless midges that rose in seething clouds and flew up my nose, into my mouth and ears. They weren't even worth slapping; it worked best just to wave at them, batting them away from my face.

My sneaker punched through a stable-looking scrim of dirt into a syrupy pit of stinky mud. I reefed my foot back but the greedy mud held on to my Chuck Taylor, pulling it halfway off my foot;

mud flowed over the lip and into the toe. I leaned on a sapling—it cracked when I put my weight on it, rotted roots bulging out of the ground—and pried my sneaker up. Mud spattered to the ground like black pancake batter. I wiped out my sneaker with a handful of yellowed grass and put it back on. "My mom's gonna kill me for mucking up my new shoes," I said.

We were standing in the middle of a lowland marsh, what my dad called a muskeg. All around were dead trees, many of them split in half by lightning or snapped crossways under their own weight. Their bark was stripped and their trunks Swiss-cheesed by termites or woodpeckers. It struck me that the swampy ground was no more than a thin crust covering a vast pool of decay: a mulch of rotted trees and vegetation and the carcasses of whatever idiotic creatures might willingly inhabit such a place. Rising from still pools of water were more Chia Pet hummocks tangled over with vivid purple, ivy-like weeds. The air sang with midges and the dragonflies who dined on them.

"What now?" Dunk asked.

I squinted against the iron-grey sky. Was that a hint of greenery beyond the dismal grey? Maybe the stream re-established itself?

I took a tentative step, putting weight on my forward foot. My toe sunk down like it would on a soccer field soaked with a week's worth of rain; dingy water filled the depression. Up rose that horrid gassy stink.

Dunk stepped past, hitching the straps on his backpack. "Come on," he said grimly.

By the time we were deep into the muskeg—and it didn't take long—we couldn't have turned back if we'd wanted to. We hopped from one hummock to the next, clambering over blowdowns carefully so we wouldn't stab ourselves on the sun-bleached sticks. Before long those maddening flashes of green were visible in *every* direction—we may have even turned ourselves around, looking back at land we'd already traversed.

Dunk's shoulders hunched with the determined gait of a mule plodding into a stiff wind. I wished he'd taken a second to think before offering us both up to this awful grey netherworld, but Dunk didn't operate that way.

He hopped from an oozy patch of ground onto a hummock that wasn't a hummock at all—more a toupée of grass covering a sinkhole. Watching him sink through was comical, as pratfalls can be: his hands flew up like a supplicant at church. *Hallelujah, Lawd!* He tilted, grabbing for a jutting branch and bellowing in frustration when it snapped in his hand. He fell into a patch of dead sedge bristling with insects and lay there for a second. Drawing his arms under him, he performed a clumsy pushup. His foot loosened from the muck with a sucking *plop.* His leg was dripping with black sludge all the way to his crotch, his sock hanging off his foot.

"Sweet fuckity *fuck.*"

He rolled his sleeve up, exhaled heavily and plunged his arm into the black hole. His eyes squeezed shut, lips skinned back from his teeth. Dribbles of muck speckled his chin. He rooted around in the blackness, his arm jerking spastically: either he was tearing through roots and sifting through brittle insect carapaces or else he'd felt something brush against his arm—something that *lived* down there, which I hardly wanted to envision.

When he withdrew his sneaker, it didn't look like a sneaker at all; more like a dead, black-encrusted rodent. A thick stream of goo ran out of the heel, resembling the old motor oil Dad drained from his car. Dunk ripped a spongy beard of moss off a nearby tree and swabbed off his sneaker, then stood and surveyed our position. Just hummocks and shattered trees and whatever lurked under the ground.

I pictured the muck beneath us becoming deeper and more treacherous. Would it get deep enough to suck us under? What lived in those festering black pools? The creatures who did were probably blind—no light down there, right? Blind but tenacious, as you'd need to be to live in sludge. Blind and tenacious and *hungry*.

The sun slanted through the dead trees, creating gasoline rainbows on the oily water. Bugs coiled from tufts of boggy grass and crawled out of shattered tree trunks. They were all colours, but mainly that strange grey that suited a muskeg—bugs so grey they were almost translucent, an indication that these bugs were barely living, possessing no organs or brains. Creatures of idiotic instinct that pinged ceaselessly off my arms and neck. After a while I didn't even flinch as they danced around my head in a maddening corona.

An hour passed, then two. My mood soured as the ground grew swampier. I got a drencher as my foot slipped off a hummock into a moat of brown water. I earned another on my next footstep, sneaker sinking into a pocket of puddinglike mud that moulded to my foot so perfectly you'd think it had been custom-fitted just for me.

"Ah, shit-sticks," I said, too tired to care. "Crap on a cracker."

We decided it was best to take our sneakers off, reasoning that before long we'd sacrifice one or both to the sinkholes. We sat on a bleached log and pulled them off, knotted the laces and wrapped them around our fists the way boxers do with hand-wraps, their wet tongues lapping our knuckles. Some debate was given to whether we should doff our socks, too, but the idea of walking barefoot through the syrupy pools was too disturbing.

We began hopping gingerly, jeans rolled past our kneecaps. Shards of dead grass poked through my socks, stinging like nettles. We went from one hummock to the next, hoping each would withstand our weight, steadying ourselves with branches and the sick trees that pushed out of the earth like whitened spears. When those

weren't close at hand we simply held our arms out for balance—
a pair of dirty, inelegant Flying Wallendas.

I ran my tongue over my chapped lips—I was deliriously thirsty—
and got a taste of the mud I was tromping through. Pure *putrid*, like
biting into a carrot that had sat in a vegetable crisper until it turned
droopy, wrinkled, brown.

At last we reached a spot with no hummocks within jumping
distance. Fatigue hived in the dark half-moons under Dunk's eyes.
We steeled ourselves and then stepped into the stagnant water,
stirring up a platoon of water skimmers and releasing a reek of
boggy rot. We sank until the white orbs of our kneecaps shone
above the water. My feet squished through cold, congealed gravy.
Bubbles quivered up through the water to burst with a sulphury
stink; black shrapnel that looked like cockroach exoskeletons
swirled and settled back under the water.

We trudged in lurching strides, looking like a couple of
Dr. Frankenstein's monsters. The water's surface was dotted with
green blooms like baby lily pads. They detached from their moors
along the edges of the hummocks, trailing thin filaments that
reminded me of bean sprouts; these eddied round our legs like
stingless jellyfish.

The ground under the water was solid—or at least it wasn't
getting any *less* solid. It felt as if I was walking on a carpet of cow
intestines, the kind they sold at the butcher shop as "honeycomb
tripe"—I knew because Dad had come home with a plastic bag
of them one afternoon, so fresh that blood had pooled in the bag;
he'd hoped Mom would fry them with onions, a dish he'd eaten as
a child, but Mom said she'd just as soon eat boiled toenails.

Half-rotted sticks jabbed the soft webbing between my toes.
There were phantom stirrings against my skin, like the tails of
inquisitive fish—then they were gone. Worst of all, I wasn't certain

we were making headway. Moving, yeah, but to what purpose? I could see nothing ahead but dull grey edged by that maddening, elusive band of green.

My foot brushed something hard and covered in slime—a log, maybe. Or a petrified Burmese python . . .

. . . probably a log. No, *definitely* a log.

The afternoon wore into evening. A rock of despair settled on my chest. I couldn't imagine being stuck in the muskeg as darkness fell, forlornly perched on a hummock like a frog on a toadstool. The insects would drive me insane. But a glint of hope emerged as the band of green thickened towards the horizon.

"There," Dunk said, as much to himself as to me. "See? See?"

Our pace quickened; we'd grown accustomed to the cold custard underfoot. My feet got ahead of my body—I tripped over a root and pitched out full-length, splashing and sputtering. Brackish water surged past my gritted teeth and I gagged helplessly, tasting barbecue chips at the back of my throat. I was scared I'd swallowed bog water teeming with mosquito eggs. Would they hatch in my stomach and drain me from the inside out? No, I decided, settling on it as a simple article of faith. *Absolutely* not possible.

Dunk helped me up. We plodded on, sneakers thumping hollowly at our hips. The water got shallower: it sank to our shins, then to our ankles. Quite abruptly the land was firm. Greenness assaulted our eyes after what felt like a month of permanent grey.

We found a boulder. Dunk set his hands on it and pushed, halfway convinced it too would topple into a sinkhole. We sat and consulted over the state of our socks, which had torn off our feet— one of Dunk's was now a sweatband around his ankle.

We dried ourselves with the rags in the backpack. Dunk wrapped one around his foot, a poor substitute for his ruined sock. We pulled our shoes on with aching slowness—they were cold and clammy, and they reminded me of pulling on still-wet swim trunks for early-morning swimming lessons—and continued into the darkening day.

Twilight transformed the landscape. Everything blended into every other thing, the ground and bushes and rocks layering over themselves. My neck tingled. I'd managed to burn myself in the bog. Usually my mom never let me go out without a slather of sunscreen, plus a stripe of zinc oxide on my nose.

The wind curled across the earth, licking at the sunburn and the wet cuffs of my jeans and chilling me to the core. I thought back to that Coke I'd drunk about a hundred years ago. My tongue ballooned in my mouth, a dry sponge covered in raspy white bumps.

A shrill *peep-peep-peep* came from the bottom of a tree with yellow bark. Each peep sounded like a whistle being blown, as if whatever was making those peeps was using its whole body to make them. Hunting in the grass, we found a baby bird. I almost stepped on it—head tucked, it looked like a pinky-grey rock. "Jeez!" I yanked my foot back, cringing at the thought of its nutlike body pulped under my sneaker.

"He must have fallen out of his nest," said Dunk.

It didn't even look like a bird, or something that might turn into one. It had no feathers. Its wings were the colour of my grandfather's fingernails, its legs tiny thumbs. Its beak was the bright yellow of a McDonald's straw, splitting its dark blue head in half. When it peeped, the edges of its beak fluttered like tissue paper. You could see through its skin like through a greasy fast-food bag: the dark pinbone of its spine, the weird movement of its guts. There was a milky ball of fat where its tail would pop out.

When Dunk reached to touch it I grabbed his wrist.

"You can't. If it gets human smell on it, its mom won't take it back. It'll smell like us, not like a bird. Its mom'll be scared. She won't feed it."

"That's stupid."

"It's, like, a scientific fact."

Dunk hunted through the backpack and found a dry rag. He slipped it over his hand and picked the bird up in the same way you'd pick up a dog turd. The creature peeped crazily before settling. Dunk rolled the rag into a little nest with the bird in the middle.

"Stupid mamma bird," he said.

Crickets chirped in the green gloom. Through the trees, the sky was bruising towards purple. It's scary the way night falls in the woods: more abrupt, unsoftened by headlamps or street lamps. The only light comes from stars that bloom in the velvet sky, sharpening as darkness closes around each shining pinprick. Night in the forest falls like a guillotine blade: quick and sharp, cutting you off from everything.

The woods changed. Where before there was only the sound of our footsteps and breathing, now there were sly rustlings from all angles. Yet if I were to turn and peer into those black pools linked by long shadows, I'd see nothing. Whatever stirred would pause, hold its breath, melt into the landscape until I turned away—at which point it would stalk us again. A sense of desolation settled within me: a cold, slimy stone lodged under my lungs. There was nothing *happy* about the woods, I thought, especially at night.

We unpacked our belongings under a sweep of elms. What had seemed like plenty that morning now looked pitiful. A chocolate bar, a dirty flannel blanket, a book of matches from a club called Pure Platinum, a nudie mag and a gun and two empty Coke cans.

We built a ring of rocks. Dunk tore pages out of the magazine. I stacked a teepee of sticks over the paper. Five matches in the matchbook. The match-heads were a dull crumbly red. The striking strip was shiny-smooth.

We huddled over the firepit to keep the wind at bay. Dunk ran a match down the strike-strip. The paper shaft bent. The match didn't catch. He pressed the match to the strip with his thumb. It burst into flame. A fragile flame cupped in Dunk's palm. I held my breath as he touched it to the paper.

The wind snuck between us. *Whuff.* Darkness. Something rustled in the tree above, followed by a deep-throated cackle that ascended through several octaves before tapering to a weird shattering sob.

"It's a bird," Dunk said. "A stupid little *bird.*"

He tore another match. "Get close," he said, scratching it on the striking strip. The shaft tore nearly in half. He struck it again. The match-head went up in a hot spark and instantly burned out.

I hated everyone who'd had anything to do with those matches. Whoever made them, sold them or thought they were good for much at all.

Dunk handed them to me. "You try."

I tore one out and folded the book closed. The match felt worthless: flimsy, already damp with my sweat. It was the first time I'd ever really needed something to *work.* Sometimes your whole life came down to some silly little thing you never thought could matter, not in a million years. A stupid match.

I hunched so far over the firepit that I nearly nosedived into it. If I lit the match as close to the paper as possible, the wind wouldn't get a chance to snuff it. I ran it down the strip, flicking my wrist like I'd seen men do at the Bisk on their smoke breaks.

It caught. Dunk cupped his hands around mine. Light broke between our fingers in golden spears so bright they seemed solid, as if they might snap like icicles. I touched it to the paper. Flame leapt from match to paper. Relief washed over me.

Wind curled into the pit and between my fingers, silky-cool. *Whuff.*

Darkness—or not quite. A half-moon burned at the paper's edge, a fine orange band no bigger than a fingernail clipping. Then it went out.

"Fucking *wind.*"

"Scouts taught us how to light a *one-match* fire, right? We've still got two left." Dunk was smiling. His teeth glowed like chips of phosphorus. It amazed me that he'd find anything funny about this.

I blew on my fingertips to dry them, then tore out the second-to-last match. It *had* to light. Not because the law of averages said so, or because if it didn't we'd be stuck in the dark with that cackling thing in the tree. No, the match had to light because we were two scared kids lost in the woods. The universe owed us that much, didn't it?

It flared on the first strike. I stretched towards the paper, fingers steady. Wind licked at the flame, blowing it sideways but not quite out. I held it to a ragged edge where the paper had been torn from the magazine, the threadlike fibres oh so flammable, please please *please,* and the match burned down to my fingertips as the heat intensified, becoming unbearable, please *please PLEASE,* and the flame took hold along that edge, timid at first but becoming greedy, devouring the paper and Dunk let out a giddy *whoop* as the fire burned up and up, releasing oily smoke, eating a hole through the crumpled face of a girl with a black bar over her eyes.

We built the fire into a blaze, heaping wood up and laughing until we were out of breath, dancing a crazy jig round the flames.

The burning wood fell inward with a soft, cindery sound that sent a great coil of sparks up to extinguish on the overhanging leaves. The coals brightened and dimmed in the wind. The baby bird peeped softly.

"Do you think it's hungry?" Dunk said.

"I'm hungry."

"Me, too."

I found the bottle of vitamins in the backpack. Each was three times the size of the Flintstones vitamins Mom used to make me take at breakfast. They smelled like a barnyard, of hay and horses. It seemed wise to take them, like medicine.

"Do you think we can survive on vitamins?" Dunk said.

"We probably need other things, like . . . steaks and eggs and potatoes. Vitamins are just one thing."

"Popeye lives on one thing. Spinach."

"No, Popeye eats spinach to get strong so he can save Olive Oyl. He probably eats lots of other stuff—just not on camera."

"Oh."

I unwrapped the Three Musketeers bar, broke it in half and held the pieces out to Dunk. "You pick." The chocolate was stale with a whitened waxy film but still, it was the best thing I'd ever eaten. Once the rush wore off I realized how hungry I still was, and thirsty, and scared.

We lay down and stared at the sky. Dunk held the bird on his chest, wrapped in the rag. A red light flashed across the sky.

Dunk said: "Plane or satellite?"

"I don't know. Which goes faster?"

"I've never been in a plane," Dunk said. "Or a satellite."

"We took a plane to Myrtle Beach on vacation," I said. "And to Disney World."

"I used to ride my bike to the Point, where the river bends out before the Falls, y'know? I watched the planes come in. Some you couldn't see until they were just about on top of you. They came out of the clouds real low, a big *whooosh* and there they were. Sort of like sharks, you know? A shark coming at you in the water—you can't see it until it's just about in front of you. The grey planes looked especially like sharks. Scary but kind of cool."

The baby bird went up and down on his chest with each heavy inhalation. "Hey, Owe?"

"Yeah?"

"You think it's true what Bruiser said?"

"About what?"

"Those dogs."

"In the satellite?"

His face was still held by the sky, but I could tell this was pretty important to him. Could be he'd been sitting on it all day.

"Maybe, Dunk. I don't know . . . but not for sure."

"No?"

"How far is another planet from here? Real far from where we're looking, but maybe not. And a satellite goes pretty fast. Maybe they just drifted through space and landed on another planet."

"You think they could have?"

"Why not? A planet we don't even know about. Maybe it's sunny all the time there. Maybe the water's red."

"Red?"

"Or purple or gold. Anything but blue. Maybe the sun is blue. Maybe meatballs grow on trees."

He laughed. "Meatball trees."

"Or maybe it's a lot like here, but a long time ago. Like back in caveman times. Or . . . or nobody and nothing. Just the two of them."

"I guess they'd be scared."

I bent my knees and wrapped my arms around them. "But they'd already travelled through space, right?" I said, resting my chin on my kneecaps. "They climbed out of that broken satellite and breathed that fresh air and I bet it was pretty great. Mahoney said they were mongrels, right? They never had someone to feed them. They could hunt and kill and drink water from streams."

"Gold water."

"Yeah, gold."

"What would they hunt?"

I turned to face Dunk, resting my cheek on my knees. "I guess the same things they would hunt here. Rabbits and rats. Squirrels."

"You think they'd have rabbits on that planet?"

"Maybe. Or maybe there the rabbits are big as cars. Maybe bears are small. Maybe you could hold a shark in your palm there."

"So they would run away from giant rabbits."

"And hunt tiny bears. Or maybe there are animals we've never seen."

"Things with tentacle faces. Things with lots of teeth."

"Harmless things, too. Things that look like baby chicks, only ten feet tall."

"A ten-foot-tall baby chick?"

"No, just a yellow fuzzy thing who happens to be ten feet tall."

"Can it talk?"

"I guess, but not in a language dogs would understand."

I tried to think about fuzzy ten-foot baby chicks, but I kept thinking about things with tentacle faces and lots of teeth.

"Owe?"

"Yeah?"

"You think things might hunt *them*?"

". . . I guess so. But they travelled far and they were still alive. That has to count for something, right? So yeah, things hunt them. So what? Things hunted them here, too. The dog catcher, right? They just kept on going."

"Kept going, mmm, yeah."

"And maybe they found someplace safe. Or I don't know, maybe the whole planet is run by dogs. They get to be, like, kings of Dog Planet."

"Why would they be kings? They just showed up."

"Well, whatever. Maybe one of them gives a very inspiring speech and they make him the president."

"Of the whole planet?"

I shrugged: *why not?*

"Hey, Owe?"

"Yeah?"

"Meatball trees would be awesome."

"Totally. Eat them like apples."

"Oh, man! Big greasy apples . . . We shouldn't talk about food."

I rolled onto my side. If I curled up and held my stomach, maybe it wouldn't growl so much. Sounds came out of the darkness. Some like nails clawing into rotten wood. Others like the *click-click* of naked bones.

A slow, steady breathing wrapped around my shoulders then went out again, hugging the trees and sliding along the ground like the never-ending exhale of some huge creature with lungs the size of football stadiums. The heart of the woods beat through me: a soothing *thack*, a giant underground muscle pumping green blood through every root and into every tree, everything connected to everything else under the dirt.

I dozed and woke with Dunk settled next to me. He'd draped the blanket over us. His breath feathery on the back of my neck.

I fell into a deeper sleep and awoke with Dunk's fingers clutching my chest.

"Something's out there."

The worry in his voice sent a spike of ice down my spine. The fire was dead. My feet were swollen and numb inside my sneakers, the blood pooled.

"Listen," Dunk said urgently. "Can you hear it?"

The pressure of my held breath pressed against my eardrums, making it hard to hear anything. I forced myself to let it out in a shuddery hiss.

There were the usual clickings and rustlings that I'd almost gotten used to. But another sound, too. A soft noise atop those familiar ones, and beneath them at the same time.

"What is it?" I whispered.

Dunk blew on the coals, stirring the embers. An orange shine lit his face and gave me some confidence. He reached into the backpack. The light of a solitary star winked off the pistol's silver barrel.

The sound approached then drifted away, switching places to come at us from a new angle.

It's Bruiser Mahoney.

The thought snagged in my mind, a sticky black ball covered in fish hooks. Bruiser Mahoney was out there, alive but not really. He'd stalked all day and night and finally caught up. Sniffing us like a bloodhound, lumbering on all fours with his spine cracked out and shining like a half-buried centipede through the dead grey skin of his back. His dentures shoved past his sun-blistered lips and his face swollen with blood, his eyeballs two rotted grapes staring out of the piggy folds of flesh to make him look like a giant prehistoric slug. His fingernails matted with shreds of the tent he'd clawed free of. He'd followed us without stopping, blundering at first but becoming more aware, strides lengthening as he pursued us through the undergrowth. And now he was here.

You ever see an old clown, boys? Clowns don't die. But sometimes they come back . . . oh, yessss . . .

"It's him," I said. "It's Bruiser."

"It's not. It's something, but not that."

Except it *was* Mahoney. His hair hung in tangled, mud-clotted ropes. His stomach ballooned up with gas and his joints twisted with rigor mortis. Bones sticking out of his skin where he'd broken them on rocks, not noticing that he'd done so or not caring. The sounds suddenly made sense. The first was the rubber-band sound of Mahoney's naked muscles: with the skin stripped off his arms and legs, his tendons had cured in the sun and now they creaked when he flexed them. The sucking sound was Mahoney's rotted lungs.

God rot me, boys . . .

His lungs were filling and emptying—not because he needed to breathe, but because his body was still mindlessly doing what it had always done.

God'll rot you, too, soon enough . . .

Would he eat us? Or just tear us apart? His rage seemed so unfair. We couldn't have taken him with us—he weighed a million pounds.

The sticks caught. Firelight pushed back the darkness. Dunk stood, baby bird in one hand, gun in the other. Did he even know how to shoot? You could only learn so much from watching *The Equalizer* and *Magnum, P.I.*

Firelight bled to the edge of the clearing, flickering against the thickets. My heart was pounding so hard, my body so keyed up, that I saw everything in hyper-intense detail. Every dew-tipped blade of grass. The knife-edge serration of every leaf. My eyes hunted for the gleam of Bruiser Mahoney's black eyes, my nose probing the breeze for his decaying stench. A gun would do nothing against him. It might chip off a little hide but you couldn't kill something that was already dead.

"Over there," Dunk said.

It skulked out of the bushes, sleek body pressed to the ground. Its fur shone like pewter. Its skull was a sloped wedge like a doorstop, eyes midnight-black, the yellow tips of its canine teeth showing.

"Just a coyote," said Dunk. "A stupid coydog."

I'd never seen one up close. It was about the size of a springer spaniel. But there was nothing doglike about it, at least not like the floppy-eared, slobbering, ball-chasing dogs in our neighbourhood. This creature was built for wild living, a coiled tension in its every movement. It didn't run circles around the kitchen yelping for kibble: what it caught, it ate, and if it didn't catch anything it starved. A ball of muscle was packed behind its jaw, built by cracking bones to lap up the marrow. It made no sound at all: its next meal could be anywhere, so it had learned to creep silently.

"Go on," Dunk said sharply.

It melted into the darkness.

I woke with razor blades slashing my guts.

Air hissed between my teeth in a tea-kettle shriek. The slashing gave way to a steady pulse and grind: a clock's worth of rusted gears meshing in my stomach.

I crawled to the bushes. Dots burst before my eyes in crazy gnat-swarms. My gut kicked and I puked so hard that everything went black. My nostrils filled with bile, thick strings of drool swaying from my lips. I'd hardly thrown up anything, just a sad yellow mess in the clover. It was awful, feeling sick and starving at the same time.

I sat cross-legged, knees hugged to my chest, listening to terrible wet retching sounds from the trees. Dunk walked out wiping his lips. The skin around his eyes was butter-yellow and his hands were shaking.

"Must have been something I ate," he said, and managed to laugh.

The sun tilted over the scrub and tinder-wood, glinting off shards of granite in the rocks but not giving any heat. I was so thirsty. I wiped sticky white paste off my lips and smeared it on my jeans. I ducked behind some bushes and unzipped my fly. The colour of my urine shocked me: dark yellow, like I was pissing tea. I didn't know if I was sick or if it was the extra vitamins my body was getting rid of, the ones it couldn't use.

Dunk breathed heavily, bending over and bracing his palms on his knees.

"We should get going, Owe."

"I'm so thirsty."

"Me, too. Maybe there's a stream soon, like the one we crossed yesterday."

I thought about that stream with its Chia Pet rocks and muddy bottom. I wouldn't have drunk from it then, but if that same stream were running in front of me now I'd guzzle it dry.

We packed everything up, though there wasn't much left. The baby bird lay on its side in the rag, peeping softly.

"Must be hungry," Dunk said. He picked it up.

"What does a baby bird eat?"

"No idea. Let's go."

He walked ahead, hopping over rocks and stomping through low bushes. I had to pump my legs to keep up. Even if Dunk was sick—and he was, at least as sick as me—it wouldn't slow him down. He had that same machinelike intensity I'd seen the day we'd met in the schoolyard. He'd keep pushing until his body broke to pieces. It didn't matter if his opponent was another kid or Mother Nature herself.

The sound of rushing water was so sly at first—an almost imperceptible gurgle that knit with the rustle of the leaves. Dunk pushed an armload of whiplike willow branches aside and there it was.

The stream was much narrower than the one we'd crossed the day before. It was clear with an undernote of heavy blue, which might have been the darkened reflection of the sky on its surface. It bent like a gooseneck around an outcrop of ragged-edged rocks and continued on through some willows.

It looked like heaven.

We stood by the bank, dumbfounded. Dunk turned and gave me a sideways smile.

"It's probably okay to drink," I said.

"Aren't we supposed to boil it?"

"That's only water that's not flowing, like a pond or a lake."

It was as if, since there were no adults around, we had to try to act like grown-ups and make the grown-up choice. Which was stupid because we were kids and we'd make a kid's choice: we would drink the water no matter what.

We dipped our Coke cans, our hands trembling with anticipation. It was all I could do not to plunge my head in the stream. I tilted the can to my lips and tasted the water behind my molars: clean and sweet with the residue of Coke at the bottom of the can.

Had water ever tasted this good? Had *anything*? It hit my stomach like iced lead. I threw some up, took two deep breaths and forced myself to keep drinking. The buzz inside my head subsided.

We drank until our bellies were swollen and let go of giant, watery belches. Dunk wet his fingertips and let a few droplets fall into the baby bird's mouth.

We hopped over the stream, water sloshing in our guts. I was still starving but I felt a thousand times better. I spotted a heron downstream, balanced on one leg like a ballerina. White tail feathers and a monstrous air sac pulsating from its blue breast. Seeing me, it made a hoarse stuttering cry full of pips and croaks like rust in a pivot. It muscled itself into the air, arrowing into the lightening blue, and a part of my heart went with it, wanting to see what it saw, to know if we were near a house or a road or if—as I feared—there was nothing but marsh and scrub and hungering bugs.

Late in the afternoon we entered a glade of enormous maples and oaks. It was dark and heavy in there; the forest greenness tinted the air. I ached all over and my ass stung and my thighs chafed with every step.

My foot had been bothering me the last hour. I sat on a tree sawed in half by lightning and unlaced my sneaker. A blister had spread across my heel, the dead white skin at its edges milky like fish gills while the flesh inside was tender-pink.

"That's a doozy," said Dunk.

I pulled the sock on gingerly. Socks, matches—items you generally possess in such abundance that you forget how valuable they are.

Isolated raindrops pattered the ground. Soon the sky opened and rain sheeted down. Water collected on the leaves, draining into the glade in ragged streamers. Rain hit the back of my hand and ran between my fingers. A wave of despair rocked me; I concentrated on the things tying me to the world. My favourite movie was *E.T.* The number one song on 97.7's Top Nine at Nine countdown was "Pour Some Sugar on Me." My bed at home had a Star Wars bedspread with a grape juice stain on C-3PO's face.

We came upon an anthill that looked like a miniature volcano. It rose to a tall spouted opening, from which ants poured in abundance. They chained down the hill in the chlorophyll-green light, moving in dark shining braids like soldiers on the march.

"You figure the bird eats ants?" Dunk asked.

How would I know if a baby bird ate ants? Besides which, grubbing around in an anthill while the sun went down was a waste of time, and I said so.

But Dunk insisted. We got down on our knees and tried to catch a few. The hill's caldera crumbled the instant my fingers touched it. Ants poured out in a mad frenzy, racing up our legs and down our sleeves. It was funny—their legs tickled as they picked along the soft hairs on our arms—until they started to bite.

I'd had no idea ants could bite—*sting*, to be exact. Fiery needles stabbed me. Dunk and I jumped up, shrieking and swatting ourselves. Ants were everywhere: my chest, my armpits. Each individual bite wasn't so bad—yellowjacket stings were much worse—but they peppered me all over.

"My back!" Dunk said. "Slap my back!"

I did, raising puffs of dust from his T-shirt. He did the same for me. After what felt like an endless battle the stings lessened. I peeled my shirt off. My sweat-stung skin was dotted with inflamed bumps that itched like the devil. My body was smeared with ant anatomies: their thoraxes and antennae and abdomens and legs squashed all over.

"Holy hell," Dunk said, breathing raggedly. "That was a *baaaaad* idea, Kemosabe."

"I *told you* it was a dumb idea."

"No you didn't," Dunk said with a bewildered smile. "You said you had no clue."

"It was stupid." I was spoiling for a fight by then, uninterested in logical arguments. "*Moronic*," I said, a word I'd heard my father use in conversation with a drywaller who'd gypped him.

"Well, *sor-ree*," Dunk said. He slanted his head at me quizzically— but the slant held an edge of menace.

"It's not funny, man. My dad always says, Measure twice, cut once—which means think before you act."

"Yeah? My dad says don't be a fuckin' pussy."

"Your dad doesn't know what he's talking about."

Dunk's chin jutted. "He knows as much as your dad does."

"Then why isn't he in an office at the Bisk instead of on the line? Why doesn't he smell of aftershave instead of Chips Ahoy?"

Dunk rounded his shoulders and stuffed his bird-free hand in his pocket, where it balled into a fist.

"I'm not my dad, Owe. And you're not your dad, either." He chewed the inside of his cheek. His arms quivered all the way down to his fingers; the hand that held the bird shook it in its sock nest. Looking back, I can tell Dunk had to summon every ounce of self-control—otherwise he'd've punched the living shit out of me right then.

When the rain let up we exited the glade, Dunk leading and me trudging behind. Mist rolled over our sneakers, perfuming the air with the scent of every green thing.

Late-afternoon sun baked down, prickling the burn on my neck and the raw bites on my arms. Dunk and I were beyond tired now. It seemed as if every topic of conversation—our favourite TV show (*The Beachcombers*), our favourite gum (Gold Rush, which came in a cloth sack, the gum shaped like gold nuggets)—funnelled towards a senseless argument.

When you and your best friend start arguing about bubble gum, you settle on silence as the best policy.

The cave lay halfway up an embankment studded with straggly pines. The incline was rinsed with grey stones each the size of a baby's fist. Dunk picked one up and tossed it into the cave. It plinked somewhere past the mouth, giving way to a series of soft tinkles.

"Sounds empty," he said.

The cave fell away in layers of flat grey rock. We stood under the overhang taking in the scent of our own stink, sweat and grime mixed with wood sap and smoke and dirt and dead bugs. I was aware of my body in ways that a twelve-year-old boy probably shouldn't be. My guts were full of hardening concrete. Moon-slices of blood rimmed my fingernails.

We spent the next half-hour gathering firewood. I wondered if we ought to build the fire outside the cave, in the open where someone could see it. A helicopter maybe, searching for two lost boys. Late that afternoon I thought I'd heard the *whuppa–whuppa* of helicopter blades; they sounded incredibly close, just overhead, and a part of me actually believed that I'd look up and see it: a helicopter just like the one rich tourists rented out to get a bird's-eye view of the Falls, the one that had its own landing pad on the roof of the Hilton Fallsview hotel.

But when I'd peered above me, the sky was empty. Maybe what I'd heard was the drone of mosquitoes. Afterwards the notion was one I continued to fixate on: hundreds of searchers looking for us. Perhaps hikers had stumbled across Mahoney's van after it had showed up on a police all-points-bulletin sheet. If so, the cops and a small citizen's brigade might be stomping through the woods right now. They'd have dogs with incredible noses hot on our scent; they'd be armed with walkie-talkies and bullhorns. If the wind died down and I strained my ears, I'd probably hear the distant barks of the search dogs.

But as shadows thickened and the colour drained out of the sky until only black was left, I heard no dogs. The mental image of a search faded. I trudged into the cave, where I made a teepee of sticks with the scrounged wood.

"We can't do it there," Dunk said. "Smoke will fill the cave and we'll get affix . . . affix . . . affixated."

"*Asphyxiated.*"

"Whatever. We'll be *dead.*"

"So why don't we light it here and move it out front? We only got one match."

"Whatever."

Dunk dug the matchbook out. The match looked so pitiful, half bent with red phosphorus flaking off the head. I almost didn't care if it lit. If it didn't we'd probably die tonight. If it did, we were simply granted another day. The sun would rise and our lot would be the same: starving, thirsty, alone and lonely. We'd be more lost, more bitten and scratched and burnt under the merciless sun, and tomorrow night we wouldn't bother building a fire. We'd sit in the dark and freeze to death. Or the things in the woods with us would sense our weakness and take their due. Either way, we died. The only difference was that we'd suffer a little longer. Now or tomorrow or the day after. It was going to happen, right?

Dunk lit the fire. One match. *Textbook.* Our Scout leader would have shit a brick. We moved flaming sticks to the mouth of the cave. The fire sent up an orange cone that obscured everything beyond it, locking us in with its warmth and light. For the first time all day, I felt safe.

Dunk rooted through the pack. We both knew there was nothing in it. He pulled out the candy bar wrapper—it seemed like we'd eaten that about a billion years ago—and inspected it for leftover crumbs of chocolate. Finding none, he flicked it into the fire. The heat caved it in like a flower blooming in reverse. He picked up a pebble and put it in his mouth.

"Dad says if you suck on a stone it gets the saliva flowing so you don't feel as thirsty."

I put a pebble in my mouth, relishing its coolness beneath my tongue.

"Banana cream pie," I said.

"What?"

"My mom says that if you, um, really concentrate and pretend you're *eating* your favourite foods, you feel as full as if you've actually eaten them."

"Yeah?"

"She says."

Dunk scratched the ant stings on his legs—the heat was irritating my stings, too—and said: "Shepherd's pie."

"Tootsie Rolls."

"Tollhouse cookies."

"Sour cream and onion chips."

"What brand?"

"Pringles."

"*Nice*," said Dunk. "Hungarian goulash."

"Hawaiian pizza."

"Kraft caramels."

"Ballpark franks."

Dunk dropped his head between his legs. "I don't think it's working."

"Are you *thinking* about them? I mean, *hard?* You really have to picture it."

"I'm *seeing* them . . . it just doesn't work for me, Owe. Sorry."

You have a wild imagination. That was what my parents said to me all the time. Having a wild imagination wasn't so hot sometimes. I spat my pebble out.

Dunk lay on the cave floor and shaped his body around the fire. The cave stones glittered around his head, firelight making them move like insects.

I said: "You shouldn't sleep with your ear on the ground. Bovine . . ."

I laboured over it—one simple word, two syllables: *Bovine. Bovine* the word was attached to Bovine the person, who was attached to many other things: schools and malls and phones and pizza parlours and my parents . . . and to policemen who helped kids who'd lost their way. And all those things were so, so far away.

"Bovine what?"

"Bovine says that earwigs crawl in your ears when you sleep. Said his dad had to bury a guy whose whole brain was eaten away by earwigs."

Instinctively, Dunk cupped a hand over his ear. "How?"

"An earwig just crawled into the guy's ear. Guy didn't even know. Our brains don't feel any pain, right? No nerves. If it was just one earwig, no big deal. But it was a female earwig, man—she laid *eggs*. They hatched inside the guy's head and they started eating. Like, a giant buffet.

"But guess what? We only use ten percent of our brains, so it took a long time. Like, he'd forget where his car keys were. He was blinking all the time and couldn't stop. Finally he couldn't even remember his dog's name. When he died Bovine says his dad took the body into the funeral parlour to prepare it for the casket. When he touched the guy's face it caved right in. A million earwigs ran out of the eye sockets and nostrils and mouth. His dad almost went crazy on the spot, but he smoked a cigar to calm down."

Dunk pulled his hand away from his ear and laid his head down again. "Bovine's full of shit."

He was right, of course. Bovine was so full of shit he squeaked. I don't know why I'd even told the story. Maybe I'd wanted to scare Dunk just a little.

I'd been worried more or less permanently since Bruiser Mahoney turned off the main road into the wilderness. The worry had sunk so deep inside that I could only feel it now when it surged up from my bones: fear bitter in my mouth, thrashing behind my rib cage like a bird in cupped hands—but it was a needful terror and perhaps the last truly childlike instance of terror I'd ever feel.

As you get older, the texture of your fear changes. You're no longer scared of a dead wrestler stalking you through the woods—even
if your mind *wants* to go there, it's lost the nimbleness to make
those fantastic leaps of imagination. Your fears become adult ones:
of crushing debts and extra responsibilities, sick parents and sick
kids and dying without love. Fears of not being the man you thought
you'd become back when you still believed wrestling was real and
that you'd die in convulsions if you inhaled the white gas from a
shattered light bulb.

"Hey, Owe?"

"Yeah?"

"Want to tell another story?"

"What kind of story?"

"Like last night. The dogs."

"That wasn't really a story," I said. "Just something silly."

"Anyway, if you wanted."

I thought about it. The gears in my head meshed with a *clicka-
clicka-click*, and soon the story was gushing out of me.

"There's a place behind Niagara Falls, okay? Behind the water.
Back there the rock is dark and dripping . . . it shines in the
water that's always falling. A man lives there. He's been there
since the Falls have. He's old as the dinosaurs—older maybe. He's
short as a kindergartener. You can see his elbows and his knees and
knuckles through his skin, which covers his bones like Vaseline.
His body glows like those fish in the deepest parts of the ocean, the
ones you can only see through submarine windows, right? He has
no hair and his head is big and bulgy. Veins twist over it, but they're
not blue like the veins on my grandma's arms because . . . there's no
blood. The man is filled with something else. He can't hear anymore. The crash of water, it broke his eardrums. His eyes are milky
marbles but he can see very well. The man doesn't have a name

because he comes from a time before anyone was around to give him one.

"There's a tree behind the Falls, too. It grows out of the rock. The bark is the colour of fingernails and the branches reach high into the rock above. The tree has no top or bottom. It grows at both ends. The man sleeps in the tree . . . Actually, he doesn't sleep. But he slips into a hole in the tree, which is hollow, and stands inside. This is the only place he can hear. He listens to the water rushing on the surface, the buzz of bugs and birds flapping their wings and fish flipping their tails.

"A shovel is leaned against the tree. The blade is old and chipped. Behind the tree is a patch of dirt . . . except not dirt. Black rock, like the charcoal that comes in those bags you buy at Canadian Tire . . . You know people go over the Falls, right? They used to do it in barrels. Other people got lost in the dark and fell or got drunk and . . . or they jumped. Most of them, you can't even find their bodies. People think they get torn apart or trapped between rocks with the water pounding down. But they're not lost. *He* finds them.

"The man has a net," I said, "made from the thinnest threads. Thinner than fishing line or even spider's web. He walks to the edge of the water and throws it. He pulls in the bodies of those who went over. It takes him a long time. His face crunches up and the veins swell on his skull. It is hard work, and very lonely.

"The bodies don't always look so good. They are broken in many places. Sometimes he's got to throw the net more than once. When he has all the pieces he digs a hole in that splintery rock and buries the body upside down, legs facing up and head pointing down. Only the feet poke out.

"It's a special garden. Whatever's planted grows the wrong way, down instead of up. The feet keep going down into it—first the ankles then the heels then the toes. It's a swallowing garden. Before long it's empty again."

Dunk said: "Where do they go?"

"Wherever's under the Falls. Nobody has ever come back . . . except one. That was a man who went over the night before he was supposed to get married. Everyone thought he'd died in the plunge. His parents had a funeral. They put sacks of flour in the coffin. But five years later . . . he was naked, the way Mrs. Lovegrove was that one time. Walking down the low road along the river. His body was perfect. Not a scratch. He looked younger than when he'd gone over. He was smiling at first, but soon he started to cry. The loudest and scariest, the most awful-sad cry you've ever heard. When a car stopped and the driver asked what was wrong, he said, 'I wandered away. Why did I do that? It was so, so . . . *per-fect.*' Next his heart blew up. It popped like a balloon in his chest and he died."

"What was so perfect?"

After a while I said, "Who knows?"

"That's cheating."

But even back then I knew cheating was a big part of telling a story.

"That's BS, Owe," Duncan persisted. "Sincerely."

"How can you ask someone to tell a story then call BS when it doesn't turn out the way you want?"

"Aw, *maaan.* What a gyp." Dunk stirred the coals with a stick and grinned crookedly across the flames. "Still, cool story. A swallowing garden. *Creepy.*"

I closed my eyes. Firelight wavered against my eyelids. I thought about how I could fall asleep right there on the rocks— but if I did and if things stayed perfectly quiet, if the fire died and I felt nothing, I might never wake up. Whatever it was that usually pulled me back into the waking world just wouldn't be there. I'd be too deep in dreams. And that didn't really seem so bad.

"Hey, Owe?"

"Yeah?"

"I knew about the lead in the car."

"What?"

"In the Kub Kar. I was there when my dad cut the hole. We melted the lead down in one of Mom's old pots. It splashed Dad's hand and left a red mark."

"Why?"

" . . . I wanted Dad to win. He wanted me to win. It seemed really important to both of us, but when I think about it now I can't remember why."

The resigned slump of his shoulders reminded me of Dunk's father when Mr. Lowery took his penknife to their car, flicking the metal cube onto the gym floor.

"People aren't ever gonna let it go," he said.

Which was true. Cataract City didn't surrender such things so easily. Dunk Diggs, the boy who'd cheated at the Kub Kar Rally. Son carrying the sins of his father—but what had Mr. Diggs done, really, that all the other fathers hadn't? You could've hacked apart any one of those cars and probably found it pumped full of lead. It was just Dunk's bad luck to get caught.

"Everyone's gonna forget, man."

"Nobody ever *really* forgets, Owe. They just pretend to."

Noise came from below: a steady scrape and grind, drawing closer. It wasn't an animal—although how could I be so sure? Was I so locked into the rhythms of the woods that I could now recognize their sounds? It wasn't Bruiser Mahoney, either—by then I lacked the energy to summon horrors that weren't real and immediate. I knew Bruiser Mahoney was where we'd left him, dead in a tent with a rock on his gut.

A shape solidified. A man was clambering up the steep grade, boots gritting on the stones.

"It's just little ol' me," he said.

His head just about brushed the top of the cave. His legs and arms seemed to have more joints than they ought to, as if extra kneecaps and elbows lurked under his faded, streaked clothes. His hands hung from frayed sleeves that stopped halfway up his wrists, below which his long fingers twitched like a puppeteer's working a marionette. His face seemed to rotate in many directions. There was a yellow catlike tinge to his eyeballs.

"A voice told me to step into the light, so here I am." He dropped his pack and sat, grabbing each ankle and drawing them under his thighs. He smelled of dust and of something I couldn't name, something sweetly foul like the glop at the bottom of a carnival trashcan. "What are you doing out here all alone?"

"We're not alone," Dunk told him. "Our fathers are coming soon."

"You mean your father the *cheater*? Cheater, cheater, pumpkin eater?" The man diddled his earlobe. "The woods have ears and so do I."

"What are you doing here?" said Dunk.

"Do you own this fuckin' cave, kid?" The man thrust his sick-looking face forward. Bands of brown gunk edged each of his teeth. "Is this your forest?"

"I'm just asking if you're lost," Dunk said.

The man laughed. A dark chattering sound full of razor blades, broken bones and crawly things.

"Me? I'm *never* lost. Wherever I go, there I am!"

At first I'd been glad to see this man. He was an adult. He could get us out of here. But now I couldn't stop thinking about our next-door neighbour's dog.

Finnegan was a beagle. Mr. Trowbridge, our neighbour, would let me take him for walks. Poor Finnegan got bit by a raccoon and got rabies. *Contracted* was the word my mother used, as if rabies was something you'd sign for on a dotted line. The disease raced into his brain and made him go mad. Not angry-mad: *mad*-mad, like the old man at the bus station who yelled at pigeons. Mr. Trowbridge had to lock Finnegan in the backyard. I watched him through a knothole in the fence. Finnegan's muzzle was caked with yellow foam and there were squiggly veins shot through his eyes. He walked in dopey circles, head swinging side to side. "Finnegan," I called. He tore across the grass, growling and slobbering, hurling himself at the fence so hard the slats splintered. He smelled of vomit and of the shit caked in his fur. The dog catcher slid a dart gun through the fence and shot Finnegan. The dog lay down and died with a little shudder. Mr. Trowbridge cried in the driveway.

This man reminded me of Finnegan. The eyes. The *stink*. But Finnegan was a dog driven mad by disease. This man may have been born that way.

He threw his arm over me. A cold python slipping across my shoulders. "Now *you*—you tell great stories. Will you tell me another?"

Dunk grabbed my leg, pulled on it. "Sit over here," he said.

The man let his arm slide off me the way a child will let go of a toy he knows he can get back any time he wishes.

"So you're lost, uh? Happens a lot out here. You walk around for days, seeing things, losing your bearings, crying out for God. But He can't hear you. You can scream and scream but nobody'll ever hear you."

The man threw his head back and howled. "Aaaah-*whoooo!*" Tendons cabled on his neck as his voice echoed out and out into the night. "That isn't going to touch one set of ears." A wink. "Human ones, anyway."

He reached into his pack and pulled out a can of beans. Saliva squirted into my mouth at the sight. He set it in the V of his split legs.

"You must be starved enough to eat a bear's asshole. Or maybe any old asshole, huh?"

He tapped the tin with one finger, ran his ragged fingernail around the rim. He rucked up his jeans and took a knife out of his boot. The blade was thick, sharpened on both sides. It looked about a foot long.

"Don't got no can opener." He slid the blade into the banked coals. "Want some?"

"Yes," I said, unable to help myself.

The man cocked his head, staring at me. His tongue flicked out of the wet cave of his mouth, snakelike, to caress his canine tooth. "Well okay, but I can't just *give* it to you. It's worth something—a *lot*, by the looks of you. So you do for me and I'll do for you."

"Do what?"

"Oh, I dunno . . . You a dancer? Stand up and give me a twirl." He adjusted his position, pressing on his crotch with the heel of his palm. "I bet you just *strut*, don't you? Take your shirt off and swing it over your head. Twitch them hips. *Tease* me."

Dunk said, "No."

Their gazes fought above the fire. The man threw up his rubber-band arms in mock defeat.

"Can't blame a guy for trying, right? Jeez, it's not like I can make you do anything you don't want to . . . *right?*"

"You sure do look lost," Dunk said.

The man's gaze narrowed. A vein pulsed along his jaw.

"Ever play hide-and-seek, kid? I'm *hiding* now. Sometimes you've got to hide for a while. That's okay. I'm good at it. You know what else I'm good at? *Seeking*." He covered his eyes with his hands. Opened them like cupboard doors. "Peek-a-boo. I *see* you."

His knife slid through the coals, its tip glowing like magma. I wondered how it'd feel sinking into my stomach: would I feel much at all or would I only watch, dumbfounded, as the moon-sheened quicksilver slid into me, my skin parting like curtains? This man might not think two ways about it; he could have been sticking the knife into a brick of butter. He chewed the air, snapping big bites out of the darkness. His teeth snicked shut, opened, snicked again.

"I'm the rogue wolf. Know what a rogue is, kiddies? A wolf that doesn't play by the rules of the pack. He does what he likes. What feels *gooood*. Now the pack, they don't like the rogue. They try to pull the rogue in line." His lips twisted into an exaggerated pout. "*Waaah.* So the rogue, he takes five. Hits the powder room. But that's just fine and dandy, because a rogue doesn't need much . . . But even a wolf's got *needs*, yeah? His little taste of *meat*."

A knot of terror seized my stomach. I was prepared to die at nature's unfeeling hands; Mother Nature was unforgiving but at least she carried no agenda. But this man . . . if he hurt us, it would be brutal, careless, and he'd show no regard for our bodies. I'd be okay dying of frostbite or by falling off some rocks and snapping my spine, but not at this man's hands.

Wind whipped into the cave, howling round our shoulders and exiting with an outrush that batted down the fire: only trembling fingerlings of flame licked from the charred logs. In that instant I saw the man change form. His face elongated, nose and mouth pushing out from the windburnt flatness of his face, nostrils arching upwards before spreading and blackening into a rubbery texture. His face made awful noises as it melted and lengthened—the splinter of ice cubes in a glass—his skin stretching like fairground taffy. His hands curled into solid masses bristling with coarse dark fur; black claws slit through, each as wicked as a crow's beak. His skull crumpled into his forehead, deflating like an inner tube packed with shattering light bulbs, the bone solidifying again, as sleek and aerodynamic as a bullet. His ears crept up the side of his head, tapering into arrowheads fuzzed in grey fur. His jaw unhinged with the *crack* of a starter's pistol, mouth widening down each side as the skin tore across his muzzle with a silken noise, the edges upturned to make room for the new teeth crowding his mouth. Fangs pierced through his gums, as sharp and pale as bleached bone. The man was a wolf in all ways but his eyes: his sockets were empty, withered like two cored-out tomatoes.

When the flames kicked up, the gun was in Dunk's hand.

The man saw it pointed at his chest. He blinked, as if that might make it go away. When it remained in Dunk's hand he seemed baffled, an emotion that darkened into annoyance, then shaded into restrained anger.

"Where did you get that?"

"I took it off a dead wrestler."

The man laughed but stopped when neither of us joined in.

"You did, did you? You even know how to shoot it?"

"Is there that much to it?" said Dunk with a tilt of his head.

"Give it here. Let me see if the safety's on."

"No thanks."

"Come on, kid. You're liable to blow your hand off."

Dunk kept the barrel squarely on him. His hands didn't shake. The safety *was* on. I reached over and flicked it off.

"Cock it," I said.

Dunk thumbed the hammer back. The man gave me a look to melt bones.

"Listen, you want me to get you out of here? Take you home? I can, okay? I know the way. All that before? I was just blowing off steam. You think I was going to leave you out here? What kind of guy would I be if I did that?"

Dunk said: "A fucking psycho hiding in the woods."

The man worked his jaw side to side, grinding his molars to dust.

"Right. Which I'm *not*. So just hand it over and we can get going . . ."

He reached across the fire, fingers closing in on the gun. Dunk raised the barrel until it pointed at the man's head. I figure it must've been like peering into a very deep, dark tunnel.

The man's eyes rolled up to the top of his skull, oriented on the spot on his forehead where the bullet would drive in. He fidgeted, and I was convinced he'd lunge. I was equally convinced Dunk would shoot him. The man realized that, too. He'd caught that unwavering *something* in Dunk's eyes.

"Here's the difference between a knife and a gun," the man said. "A gun has many working parts that can jam up or misfire. A knife is foolproof. In tight quarters you get one chance with a gun. A knife . . . well, a knife can go as long as you've got strength to stick it in, right? A gun's for cowards. A knife's up close. Blood running down your knuckles. And if you get shot with a gun, you die. It's quick. With a knife, the pain goes on and on and on. With a gun you die once. With a knife you die a thousand times."

Dunk said: "I really don't give a shit how many times you die, so long as you're dead."

The man shook his head. He put the beans back in his pack. Uncrossed his legs. I watched for his calves to tense, any sign he'd spring.

"You boys have lost a chance to make a lifelong friend and benefactor."

"We're kids," said Dunk. "We'll make more friends."

The man withdrew his knife from the fire and stood up. "You're never getting out of here. You know that, don't you? You little fucks are going to *die*. Die without your parents and friends. With shit in your pants and your tongues sticking out like clowns. *Alone*. By the time anyone finds you the birds will have pecked out your eyes. Maggots overflowing your bust-open bellies. And me? I'll be laughing like a bastard . . . Well, toodles."

He picked his way down the slope gingerly, knife tip weaving a faint orange trail through the darkness.

Dunk held the pistol for hours, pointed out into the night. His shoulders must have ached. His wrists surely must have seized up. But he never put it down. The barrel never even dipped.

It rained overnight. It began as a *sing-sing* pattering on the leaves and rocks, moon-whitened needles falling like shards of starlight. By the time a grey dawn washed over the hillsides it was sheeting down. Thunderheads crowded the steely sky; every now and then a giant flashbulb would go off inside one of them, turning them translucent like tadpoles and showing the swirling purple-silver nimbus within. We edged under the overhang and drank the water that collected in our cupped palms.

The forest spooled out in the misty-hazy morning, spruces and pines holding a blue tint. The downfall had doused the fire. We sat shivering.

My hunger had fled overnight. All that was left was a dull gnawing in the bowl of my belly. My stomach was eating itself, I figured, or the nearby organs. I pictured a toothy split opening in my stomach as it devoured my liver, pancreas, spleen. Maybe that was why starving people had swollen bellies: their stomachs had eaten every-thing else inside them. The thought made me laugh.

"What's so funny?" Dunk said.

"Nothing," I said, because in fact there was nothing funny about starving to death.

I must have closed my eyes—that, or my consciousness was stolen away for a few minutes—because when I snapped to, Dunk was staring at a spider's web in the corner of the cave. A grasshop-per was caught in it. Its body was the green of a twig snapped off a healthy tree. Each time it thrashed, another part of it got glued to the web. The sticky threads vibrated like guitar strings.

A spider exited a hole in the cave wall. Its legs came first, flick-ing tentatively before spreading out like the metal ribs of an umbrella opening. It was as black as an oil bead, with red bell-shaped shadings. It picked its way down the web, walking upside down on a single strand before reaching the heart of the web where it spread its legs further. The grasshopper flung itself around madly. The spider paused as if in wonderment at the bounty it had been given.

We watched silently, hunched close, Dunk's head cocked, chin balanced on his fist. It didn't enter our minds to save the grasshop-per. We would never have thought of kicking a dog or tossing fire-crackers at a tomcat, but we watched nature in all its fascinating forms—as boys *should* watch, I think now, unapologetically, a right and ritual of childhood.

The spider raised its front legs like a bucking horse, then clam-bered nimbly over the grasshopper's head and sank its fangs into one convex eye. Its thorax pulsed as it pumped in venom. The grass-hopper went still. Next the spider was log-rolling the grasshopper, spinning its body rapidly, cocooning it in gossamer.

"Sucks to be him," Dunk said softly.

My heart pounded behind my eyes, each beat a miniature earthquake. I phased in and out of consciousness, sometimes rocking forward and other times snapping out of a dream state where the world was not so much different than this one, just slightly warmer and safer.

Eventually, the sun fought through heavy clouds to speckle the valley with light that pricked my eyeballs. I nodded my head at the world outside our cave. "We should try," I said.

"Okay," Dunk said docilely.

He set the gun's safety and snugged it in his pocket. The baby bird was sitting on his lap. It was still alive, breathing shallowly inside the rag.

The smell of sweet potato seeped out of the earth, which was raw and cold and flushed green from the rain. A curtain of mist was strung across the horizon. I inhaled the heavy musk of a deer's scat, rich with whatever it had digested. Worst of all I smelled Dunk and myself: sweat, sickness and desperation.

We came to a forest of tall pines through which the light slanted in dusty beams like rays falling through the stained-glass windows of an old cathedral. The ground was carpeted in layers of brown needles; it felt like walking on a horsehair mattress. At one point Dunk turned to me, distressed. He held his empty palm out, the one not carrying the bird.

"My knife," he said. "It's gone. It was in my pocket and now it's not."

He walked in a circle, lead foot stabbing out as though he was going to set off in one direction, then stepping back in, his free hand hitching at the loose hem of his jeans without seeming to realize it, round and round in a circle.

"It's okay, Dunk. How long do you think since you lost it?"

"I don't know," he said, staring at me as though I was a stranger—but no, it wasn't that: he was just stunned, the way I was the time Sam Bovine accidentally kicked a soccer ball into my face. "I don't know I don't know I *don't know*."

"It's okay, okay? Want to go back and look for it?"

"My dad gave me that knife—not for Christmas, Owe, not for a birthday, just *gave* it to me. I don't get things *just 'cause*, man. He's going to kill me."

I couldn't remember ever seeing him so freaked, and over what? A pocketknife. I didn't like seeing Dunk like this, antsy and weird, running a hand nervously through his tangled hair so continuously that he'd surely strip it out at its roots.

"Listen, man, your dad's not going to kill you. He's going to put you on a leash so you can't ever get out of his sight again. My dad, too. All he's going to think is how happy he is to have you back, right? Your mom, too, and my mom, and everyone else we know . . . except maybe Clyde and Adam, but *screw* those shitballs."

Dunk's pacing slowed and after a while he stopped, bouncing gently on the balls of his feet. He let out a shuddery breath and then laughed.

"Yeah, okay. It's just a knife. We've still got the other one."

"Totally. We've still got a knife if we need it."

"And my dad . . ."

"Your dad won't even remember the knife."

"You think?"

"Yeah, I think."

We kept walking. We found a stream and followed it until it emptied into a bog that gave off a sweet mulch smell that reminded me of the garden centre on Tamarack Road. Our sneakers squelched, footprints filling with grey water, so we headed for higher ground.

My muscles couldn't prop me up anymore—they were nothing but frayed balls of twine under my skin. I was constantly stumbling on stones and slipping on wet grass. My jeans were soaked from the brush of leaves. I walked with my chin tucked into my chest, hands flung out in front of me. I tripped on an exposed root and tried to get up, leveraging myself on a fallen tree limb close at hand—it splintered in my hands, rotted through with damp. I squawked as I toppled towards the broken end, turning my head so it wouldn't pierce my throat. My nose slammed into another exposed root, forcing stinging tears out of my eyes. I lay on the ground, staring at the woodlice squirming from the rotted branch in revolted fascination and thinking: *If I don't move soon those things will fall right onto my face—my mouth.*

I curled onto my side without quite realizing I'd begun to cry. My chest unlocked and the sobs doubled me over like punches. I thought my ribs might splinter but I couldn't stop. Dunk walked a short distance away; I saw him watching me through the fractured, watery prisms that sat over my eyes, standing with his hands in his pockets.

After a while he said, "Come on, Owe. Get up. Please." He offered me his hand.

I wouldn't take it. He sat on a fallen log and exhaled, chest caving in below his slumped shoulders. My sobs became sniffles. I wiped my nose on my sleeve and said: "He was right."

"Who?"

"That guy. We're going to die out here."

"Maybe," said Dunk. The fact he'd finally acknowledged it made me want to cry all over again. "But I don't want to die yet. I want . . . I want to see brake lights again."

"Brake lights?"

He nodded. "Last year Dad took me to a Blue Jays game. On

the way home there was a line of cars down the highway. All these brake lights were lit, a bright red chain through the dark. Around it were the lights of skyscrapers and the CN Tower. I thought how each one of those lights equalled at least one person. I hoped they were doing something cool with someone they loved, like I was with my dad." He searched my face and when he didn't see what he was looking for, he said, "I guess that's pretty stupid . . . You okay?"

"Yeah."

"Want me to spit in your mouth?" He grinned. "You probably dried yourself out with all that bawling."

"Man, that's just gross."

Things seemed sinister even in daylight now. I wasn't afraid of being pursued by the ghoul of Bruiser Mahoney or even the wolf-faced man. My unease came from the land itself, which had stopped changing: a flat stretch of swale grass studded with windblown trees extending to every vanishing point. The unchanging vastness of the land—*that* was sinister. It seemed to be running on huge hidden spindles, like a treadmill; the earth went round the spindles, the trees and prickerbushes trundling beneath the earth only to come up again in front of us. We walked the same endless expanse, bitten by the same mosquitoes while trudging through our old footprints. I cocked my ear for the sound of the Falls—the same sound that had backgrounded my entire life, reminding me (sometimes maddeningly) where I was from. I couldn't even hear that. The space above the treetops was still and noiseless.

We came upon a drywash and picked our way down the flinty shale. Dunk tripped, holding the bird up like the Statue of Liberty raising her torch. He slid on his knees, crying out. When I reached him his jeans were torn open, kneecaps already leaking red. We

were both a mess of blood: it dotted our shirts from the ticks and
blackflies and ants, which were joined by longer slashes from nettles
or twigs.

We were a pair of wind-up toys close to winding down. I thought
that eventually we'd come upon some impassable junction, a high
rock wall or cliff. But the land was sievelike. We had to step around
stagnant pools or small rock piles, but were met by no conclusive
barriers. We kept walking into the blue day, one foot here, the
other there.

Black specks peppered my sightlines. I couldn't tell if they were
insects or just spots of delirium chewing into my vision. The urine
in my bladder turned hot and painful so I let it go, which felt
incredibly good. I cried off and on but the tears were largely involuntary by now, constant as my own breathing. They didn't slow me
down at all.

Dusk rolled over the plain; bat-wings of shadow arched off Dunk's
shoulders. Full dark would come in an hour, maybe less. I didn't know
what we'd do then. It didn't bear thinking about.

A half-hour later, cold, moving gingerly through a field of thorns,
fully aware of my entire body, my hands, my mouth, my eyes stuffed
with looming darkness, my ears buzzing with insects or simply my
own disconnected thoughts, Dunk stopped and pointed.

"See that?"

Squinting, I saw a point. A triangle of black construction paper
taped to the horizon. It stood out because it didn't belong to nature.
Its angles were either too perfect or not quite perfect enough.

We walked towards this trembling apparition, this *point*, half
expecting it to vanish. We went down a small rise and the trees
closed in, making it harder to find that point in a maze of treetops.
But we found something even better: a path. At first it didn't seem
much of anything at all—a trail through the grass that could have

been tamped down by deer—but soon it became more pronounced, right down to the dirt, and Dunk laughed wildly.

Light bloomed ahead, a glimmer in the dense woods. It was gone then back again, like a blinking eye. My heart expanded with joy and fear at once: joy that it was there, fear that it could vanish at any moment. We approached cautiously, barely breathing for fear we might blow it out like a match. I don't know how long we followed that light, but it grew and took shape: a square.

The trees broke into a clearing. A house. The light was coming from its window. Electric light, so much different than firelight. It looked impossibly inviting, as if you could connect with all of civilization simply by placing your hands on the glass.

We crouched in the cover of the woods. Something held us back. Maybe we were half animal by then—part of the forest. Feral creatures of liquid eye, fur and claw and antler, skittish and curious at once.

Wind rustled the leaves as the night came alive with its little motions and stirrings. We broke from cover and crossed the yard—the grass had been cut and seemed too orderly to me, every blade perfect. We went round the front. A blue Chevrolet parked on the gravel drive. A garden gnome with a chipped porcelain face. So ridiculously *normal*. Such happiness ripped through my chest that I thought it would stall my heart.

Dunk knocked on the door with one grimed, blood-flecked hand. A middle-aged woman stood in the frame, light from the kitchen falling over her shoulders.

"It's you," she said. "The boys . . . those *boys*."

She rocked forward. I thought she might faint. She opened the door. The warmth of the house hit me, almost melted me.

"They've been looking for you everywhere," she said. "The police. Search teams. How did you . . .?"

"I'll sit out here, ma'am," Dunk said.

The woman nodded. "You do whatever you'd like. I'm going to . . . make a call. I've got blankets and—oh! *Colin!*" she shouted. "It's those boys!"

"Who?" came a man's voice from inside.

"The boys on TV. The lost boys!"

"Jesus!"

I sat on the steps with Dunk. The porch light snapped on, so much harsher than the gilded light of the moon. Dunk shook his head slowly, smiling as you would at a joke that's only half funny. His hands trembled and so did mine. I heard footsteps and craned my head to see a big man with one huge carpenter's hand clapped over his mouth, watching us in awe.

Dunk cupped the baby bird, his features set in mute confusion. Its body looked as hard as soap. Dunk touched it gently with one finger. It rolled over weightlessly, like a thing carved from balsa wood.

Dunk's head dipped to touch his knees. His body shook. Huge gulping sobs tore out of him, ripped out of his throat as if about to rupture his vocal cords, the most wretched noises I'd ever heard. I put my arm around his shoulders and felt the tension: it was like grasping a railroad track in advance of the onrushing locomotive. I didn't tell him everything was okay, because I knew even then that it probably wasn't. Not really, not ever again. I just let him cry.

"What the hell's the matter?" the big man said. "You're safe, boys." A mystified, barking laugh. "Don't you get it? You're *safe*."

There's a photograph of me and Dunk taken shortly after we wandered out of those woods to find the house—which was owned by Irene and Colin Harrington, a third-grade teacher and a construction foreman with a taste for isolation. It was shot by a reporter with the *Niagara Falls Review* who arrived with the emergency crews, no doubt alerted by the police-band scanner in his newspaper's bullpen. It's a tight shot, just our shoulders and heads, and the composition is off balance—by then there was a crush of firemen and ambulance attendants, so the reporter had to fire off a hurried snapshot in the scrum.

We are captured in close-up, in black-and-white, which amplified the stark slashes of blood on our shirts and the scrapes on our faces. My eyes shine like headlamps in the black pits of my sockets. We look like we've been released from a concentration camp, wearing expressions of grim futility. That sort of hopelessness grits into your face and posture, becomes a visible part of you.

In the photo my hand is up, covering Dunk's eyes. He was still crying. His head is tucked into the space where my shoulder meets my neck. The framing echoes something you'd see on the courthouse steps: a lawyer shielding his client from the hungering shutterbugs.

If you were to hypothesize about the events of those three lost days from that photo alone, you'd think it was me who dragged Dunk out of the woods. That I was the protector and he the protected. Which is why you should never trust photos to tell the entire story.

Our parents had arrived in police cruisers. They looked as haunted and haggard as we did. My mom gathered me in a bear hug that just about crushed the life out of me. Years later she got drunk at a cousin's wedding and told me she'd have left my dad if we hadn't been found. "I love your father, but I wouldn't ever have forgiven him. Getting into some stupid fight while his son's abducted. Celia Diggs would have done the same."

"Found?" I remember saying, a little drunk myself. "Mom, nobody *found* us."

Dad never spoke about that night outside the Memorial Arena when he'd punched Adam Lowery's father, but his regret expressed itself in other ways. To this day he will grab my hand in busy parking lots, even though I'm old enough to have kids of my own. He will stare at our clasped fingers and shrug sheepishly, but he won't let go. Which is okay by me.

We were taken to the hospital, where our guts were discovered to be full of worms. The doctor figured it was the raccoon meat. We were severely dehydrated and covered with more bites and stings than anyone could count. I was put on an IV drip and didn't take a dump for a week. Nothing inside me.

Dunk and I were put in separate hospital rooms. At night I'd roll over in a dreamy fugue thinking I'd feel him next to me. I'd find nothing but the over-bleached hospital sheets like spun glass against my cheek.

I still see Mr. Hillicker and Mr. Lowery around. They haven't aged well; eyelids drooping around their eyes like two sick hounds. I'd assumed they wouldn't feel much guilt for what happened, and I was right. To this day I think they ought to be thankful it wasn't Clyde and Adam who Mahoney decided to light out with. Not to brag, but odds are those two bastards would have ended up as clean-picked skeletons in a wolf den.

The police retraced our route from our hazy descriptions and the physical markers of our trek: a few blackened firepits. We'd covered over thirty-five kilometres, a twisting, doubling-back route that would shame any outdoorsman. Despite this, our scoutmaster claimed that we embodied the very pinnacle of wilderness survival.

We'd taken a wrong turn almost immediately. Had we gone east we'd have made it back to Stevensville Road by mid-afternoon. Instead we went northwest, into the forested territory fringing Old Highway 98 east of Bethel. But if we were unlucky early, we got lucky late. The Harrington house sat three kilometres from its nearest neighbour. Had Dunk not seen its roof we would have continued into the empty land south of Brookfield junction.

Nothing there but scrub pine and desolation, fifty miles to the nearest anything.

The wilderness took its toll on Bruiser Mahoney, too. The police found him where we'd left him, in a clearing some thirty miles north of Lake Erie. Through Sam Bovine I heard that his legs had been chewed off. Coyotes were the likeliest culprit.

"My dad used old mannequin legs from the women's wear department at Sears to fill out the casket," Bovine told me.

The rock on Mahoney's stomach may've been all that stopped the coyotes from making off with the rest of him. Or it could be that his taste didn't suit them.

The toxicologist said he'd died from an overdose of Clozaril, a knock-off of clozapine, an antipsychotic drug. The pills belonged to El Phantoma—birth name: Miguel Lopez—a Mexican wrestler with a history of bipolar disorder whom Mahoney had driven to a match in Gravenhurst the week before. Lopez had forgotten the pills in the glovebox and Mahoney had mistaken them for his pain medication. The Clozaril reacted badly with the alcohol to cause, in the toxicologist's opinion, "free-floating delusions, uncontrollable anxiety and a possible psychotic break with reality."

All of which seems about right to me.

Dunk and I went to Dade Rathburn's funeral. People figured it was some kind of Stockholm syndrome, or else we wanted to spit on the corpse. The big church was mostly empty. The girl was there, the one with the black hair and gold-coin eyes. It turned out she was Rathburn's daughter—one of many. He'd salted his seed liberally over his territory. She was crying. She hugged us both and apologized. "I said you'd be safe with him. I thought you would be. He wasn't a bad . . ."

"Anyway, it's not your fault," Dunk told her.

Dade Rathburn looked weird in his coffin. A deflated pool toy packed up for winter storage. His dentures were snug, at least, and his eyes were closed. Bovine said his dad had to cut the muscles under his eyelids so they'd roll down, then crazy-glue them shut.

I remember everyone watching us. I had no urge to spit on Rathburn. Whatever I felt was far too complicated to ever express.

After the funeral my father told me he'd prefer it if I didn't hang out with Dunk anymore. Dunk's dad was of the same mind. It seemed unfair, as if we were the victims of our fathers' guilty consciences. Had I been seventeen I would have told Dad to suck an egg. But I was twelve, and soon enough Dunk and I just drifted apart. I couldn't say how it happened. That strong childhood magnetism that draws one boy to another—sometimes that magnetism abruptly switches polarities, flinging those same boys away from each other, setting them on new trajectories.

My family moved to Cardinal Gardens, a suburb in the city north. Our new house had an in-ground pool and a two-car garage. The day the moving truck came, Dunk stood on the sidewalk dribbling a balding basketball.

"So you're moving, huh?"

"Is it that obvious?"

I'd meant it as a joke. He blew the hair out of his eyes—it was even longer than when I'd met him, the ends almost touching his nose—and smiled into the sunlight.

"You can always come visit," I said.

"And you can always visit back here."

That was the last I saw of Duncan Diggs for many years.

The next week I was in our new home flicking through TV channels and came upon an episode of *Superstars of Wrestling*. It shocked me how fake it looked. Punches and kicks missing by a mile. I watched a few minutes, then flipped to another channel.

DAWN EASED OVER THE ESCARPMENT, sunlight glimmering like a sine wave across the curve of the earth. I stretched my legs inside the car, wincing as the familiar pain cupped my kneecap. Fogerty's "Who'll Stop the Rain" had segued into Henley's "Boys of Summer," which had segued into a late-night call-in show about paranormal phenomena.

I had zoned out, lost myself down the memory hole, and now the dashboard clock was reading 5:26 and the gas tank was near empty. I stepped out of the car and began to walk.

The cut-off was fringed by long grass bent by a forceful night wind. Sun lightened the eastern fields. The world was cool, wind bearing the smell of burning grapevines. I had nothing on but a thin jacket, yet I didn't feel cold. Sunlight sparkled the tips of pine trees struggling through soil determined to spit them out.

I walked until the path began to collapse at its edges. It dipped and I followed . . . until at last a million tiny cogs seized in every part of my body and I stopped. The woods were closing in on me. Still, I didn't feel terrorized like I had as a boy. I took in the silky rustle of leaves, that cut-potato smell of the soil. Felt an odd jangle in my nerve endings. I couldn't quite leave behind the sight of a thin curvature of sunlight on the Lincoln's hood, so metallic and man-made and *human*. Couldn't abandon myself entirely to those woods.

Maybe if Dunk were here . . . or maybe there are some paths you can never go down again. I headed back to the car, laughing at my cowardice.

I dropped the Lincoln into gear and reversed down the cut-off. Back to the world as it existed. But it was good to remember that, long ago, it had been just Dunk and me, the two of us. Two boys in the woods. How far had we fallen from that?

I drove to the nearest gas station, filled the tank and paid the sleepy-eyed attendant slumped inside his bulletproof Lexan cube. It was rare for me to be up so early—under normal circumstances I'd be inert while my liver filtered whatever I'd drunk the night before—but I relished it. Soon enough the sun would climb to its familiar position, illuminating the sadly familiar sights of the city and ruining the sense of possibility. But until then, there was the lovely silence, the fresh, indescribable smell of a new day—if pure *possibility* had a smell, this was it—fledgling sunlight washing the grape fields and the rippling surface of the river.

Staring at that swift, dark-running water, a fresh memory hit me with the force of a ballpeen hammer.

I must have been seven years old—or eight? Anyway, I was in that human-wallpaper stage of my existence. My father had taken me to the river. We'd go every so often to skip rocks and hunt for crayfish. One afternoon while Dad was taking a whiz I'd spotted a Hefty trash sack bobbing at the river's edge. It had been sucked into a pool where the current swirled endlessly between the rocks; the pool was edged with the froth that built up at certain spots, crusty and opaque like the scum atop a pot of boiled pork.

The bag was of the heavy-gauge plastic you'd find wrapping scrap lumber in construction-site Dumpsters; the top was crudely knotted. I remember wondering what was inside, and tearing it open, driven by sudden wild curiosity—there was something about the placement of the bag, I guess; the *sullenness* of it bobbing in the shallows. At first I'd just stared, head cocked, profoundly puzzled. The contents looked like soggy balls of yarn, the kind Mom used to make macramé potholders and tiered flower holders. Except there was nothing vibrant about the colours: mixed muddy browns and washed-out whites. Then I caught a glimpse of a little arrow shape tufting from one of those balls and it was like when you stare at one of those 3D portraits just right—your eyes adjust and you see the sailboat or the train or whatever. When I saw the whole picture I reared back, horrified at a bone-deep, subcellular level.

Kittens. I could tell by that one tiny ear. How many? Four, five. I didn't look long enough to know. Kittens stuffed in a trash sack and hurled in the river. Even at that age, it struck me that they almost certainly hadn't drowned: the sack was so thick and the kittens almost weightless, so it'd probably just bobbed on the surface, too light to sink; perhaps the person who'd done it had watched the sack drift down the Niagara and said, "Huh." With awful clarity I imagined the kittens tearing at the sack with their little claws. But the plastic was too durable. They would have suffocated.

I stepped away, the horror so thick in my gorge that I thought I'd throw up. The bag shifted and I saw something else: the greenish plastic head of a glow-in-the-dark Jesus. A snatch of song came to me: *Well, I don't care if it rains or freezes / Long as I have my plastic Jesus / Riding on the dashboard of my car.* Whoever had done this must've been queerly religious, or else had a warped sense of humour. Jesus's head was shattered at the top, just above his crown of thorns. One of the kittens must've bitten it off.

I slumped back in the car seat, assaulted by the memory. But that's my city in a nutshell—or a trash sack. People around here think if they stuff their problems in a bag, huck it in the water, well, end of problem. And that theory has borne out, for the most part. In my line of work I see proof, over and over.

I drove home in the warm light, my mood curdling further when three police cruisers shrieked past in the opposite lane. I unlocked my apartment, stared for a moment at the empty dog bed in the kitchen, un-holstered my pistol and popped two pills to quiet the pain singing in my kneecap. I fell into a troubled, profoundly exhausted sleep.

PART TWO

DOLLY EXPRESS

DUNCAN DIGGS

T he city feels strange to me now. Changed in a million tiny ways that, taken together, seem massive. It's like not seeing your own face for eight years, then having someone hand you a mirror. *Who is that guy?* And then you realize: it's you. It's still you.

The day after they let me out of prison I awoke in the bedroom where I'd grown up. There wasn't a clock at the bedside, but I knew the time: 7:33. That was when the prison's halogens would snap on every morning, my eyelids snapping open with them. Would I wake up at that exact minute for the rest of my life?

I could've stayed in bed, which was warm, the mattress permanently sunken from the impression of my body—my teenage body, because I'd been that age the last time I slept in it—but I rose out of habit.

It was so strange to place my feet on carpet instead of cold lacquered concrete. And so wonderful to stand in the bars of honey-coloured sunlight that fell through the venetian blinds. Inside the pen, the sun had never felt the same as it did outside: it was as if the architecture of the place, or the compounds used to build it—the brick and steel and glass—leeched some part of the sunshine away. Not the heat—I could feel that—but its vitamins or the really nourishing part of it. When it had touched my skin in prison, it had felt as cold as the light from a bare bulb in a broom closet.

I stood in that bedroom sunlight for a long time. Drinking it in, the same way a plant does.

Could I open the bedroom door? I twisted the knob and, yeah, it swung open. It was stupid, but I'd been sure it was locked—even though the lock was on *my side*.

I took a long shower. It was the first time I'd showered alone in forever. Still, I glanced over my shoulder a couple times. The soap was Irish Spring, the soap my mother always bought. Cheap and reliable. It made a thick lather that perfumed the stall with the smell of . . . what was that smell? It made me think back to days I'd come home as a boy, filthy from the woods, with pine sap smeared on my hands; Mom would punt me into the shower, telling me not to come out until my hair squeaked.

When I went downstairs, Mom was sitting at the kitchen table in her uniform whites, her hands—her thin, birdlike hands—cupped around a ceramic mug. Her hair was salt-and-pepper: strands of jet-black threaded with coarser veins of iron-grey, pinned back behind her ears with silver clips.

"Coffee, Duncan?"

I nodded. "I'll get it."

I poured coffee into a ceramic mug. For eight years I'd drunk out of either six-ounce plastic cups or thick-bottomed plastic mugs with a handle big enough to fit a single finger—the kind of cheap, unbreakable dishware they used at summer camps. When those dishes broke, they left no sharp angles.

I added a tablespoonful of sugar, and after a moment, another.

I could have as much as I wanted. In prison everything was rationed: a packet of sugar, a thimble of cream. Now I could add sugar until my teeth ached. Hah!

I sat across from Mom. Sipped. Jesus, that was too sweet.

"You look good, Mom."

"Yeah?"

She touched her hair lightly with one hand. She'd visited me every month, just about—she and Dad both. The three of us would sit at a table bolted to the floor in the visiting room. Dad would drink a vending-machine Sprite. It was Coke for me, Diet Coke for Mom. A muted TV in a wire-mesh cage broadcasted old sitcoms.

We spoke during those visits, but it was surface talk. Sports, the weather—not that the weather made any difference to me. They never asked me what had happened. They *knew* what happened— everyone did—so only one possible question remained: was it necessary to take a man's life?

"So," Mom said with typical bluntness, "what now?"

"I haven't really thought that far ahead."

Her chin dipped. "Liar."

For two weeks straight, I walked the city, re-familiarizing myself with it—and with the scale of the outside world. Everything seemed bigger, crazily so.

One night I stopped at a 7-Eleven and stared at the Big Gulp cups so long that the clerk asked me if something was the matter.

"Nah, nothing." I shook my head. "People drink all of that?"

The clerk, adenoidal and bug-eyed, said, "All that and more. Free refills in the summer, right?"

Why was my confusion so surprising? Yes, it had been eight years, not a lifetime. Yes, I'd watched TV inside, read the newspaper.

I'd noted the shifts the world had taken. But that didn't prevent the system shock.

Things tasted better. Milk tasted richer, a Snickers bar sweeter. I had no explanation for that, just as there was no evidence to support my sense that penitentiary sunlight was a watery facsimile of the real deal. It was as though I'd gone into a protective cocoon that had mummified my sight and smell and taste, and now, back on the outside, my senses were hyper-attuned.

One day I zoned out on the sidewalk under a maple tree, tracking the progress of a caterpillar across a branch. I picked a leaf, then rubbed its waxy surface until I wore it down to the veiny substructure, chlorophyll staining my fingertips dull green.

"You okay, bud?"

A man stood beside me, his arm raised in a gesture of cautious aid. I guess I'd been rubbing that leaf and staring off into space for too long.

"I'm cool." I smiled, wondering if that was still what people said. "Just took a personal time-out there."

I was gripped by a desperate urge to hand the man my leaf. *Get a load of this leaf, man. It's dynamite!*

I walked a lot at night. I'd wake in my childhood bedroom, the shapes and smells all wrong. Sometimes I'd catch the wet, weeping smell of the cinderblock walls in the Kingston Pen. Or I'd reach for Edwina and never find her. That was the worst of it; I saw her ghost everywhere. I was back on familiar streets, and her shape was familiar to those streets. I'd catch the slope of her shoulders entering a doorway, or her legs folding into a stranger's car. But Ed had achieved escape velocity. This city would never see her shape again—a fact I both knew and somehow didn't, or couldn't, believe. Not quite.

I gradually backtracked to spots I was familiar with. Some grisly compulsion carried me past the Bisk just as the shift whistle blew. Workers trooped in and out, their hair frosted white with flour. I spotted Clyde Hillicker, who looked a lot like his old man except for the deep dent in his right cheekbone. Hillicker had spent a few years in the stony lonesome, too—we finally had something in common.

I returned to places where I'd hung out with Owe and Edwina, mooning around like a lonely mutt. I'd stand on the ground we'd occupied together years ago, closing my eyes; weirdly, I could hear the whisper of their voices in my ear—but when I opened my eyes it was just me, alone in the dark.

One afternoon I walked down the Niagara Parkway, skirting Oak Hall golf course where early-morning duffers were shanking balls into the rough. I kept well off the fairways; the course marshal might've spotted me and called the fuzz. I tromped through stands of dense pines—and you know what? They whispered in the wind, just like in those old country and western songs.

I cut south at Upper Rapids Boulevard until I reached the river. A fine layer of mist clung to its surface, evaporating as the temperature inched upwards. A raccoon trundled through the bushes to my left, unafraid of me. I hunted for flat stones along the shoreline, skipping them. Me and Owe used to have skipping contests. *Owe.* I thought about him a lot. Almost as much as Ed. He'd visited me in prison only once, to clear up some lingering business. I can see why he kept his distance. He had every right. But I'd need his help soon—for the plan taking shape, growing stronger with every step I took through my city.

Would he help? He didn't owe me anything. What we had together, those old loyalties—that was a long time ago.

"What're you doin'?"

The girl had snuck up on me. She was tall and reedy, wearing orange shorts and a blue hooded sweatshirt with the sleeves hacked off. Her spindly legs rose out of a pair of vulcanized rubber boots. They looked like flower stems poking out of a pot.

"Just skipping rocks," I told her.

She cocked her head. Her red hair coiled into ringlets that framed the wide angles of her face. Her eyes were green—made greener by the sunlight streaming through the canopy of trees—and they were wide and alert, but with an alertness different from the wary kind I was used to in the eyes of inmates. Her eyes were simply interested.

"I've never done that," she said.

"It's not that hard. You can watch me, if you want."

She sat on a rock, eyeing me. My shoulders tightened slightly under her gaze. My first rock only skipped twice.

"I could do *that*," she said.

She heeled her rainboots off. Her bare feet had the clammy look feet get when they're wet and compressed: like turnips gone wrinkly in the bottom of the fridge. She dipped her toes in the water.

My next rock skipped seven or eight times, with a few dribblers at the end I didn't count. The girl didn't look too impressed.

"Your hands," she said. "They're pretty trashed."

I stared down at them. "Trashed?"

"I mean, like, *fucked up*."

I felt my brows beetling, the skin drawing inwards at my temples. I stuffed my hands in my pockets. "How old are you?"

She said, "Thirteen."

"Oh. I thought you were younger." She was about the age that Edwina's kid would be—the one who'd left that scar on her stomach. The one she'd given up for adoption. "Anyway, that kind of language . . ."

She blew a ringlet off her forehead. "You can't tell me how to talk."

I lifted my shoulders. "I'm not telling you nothing. It's just, I thought we were being friendly is all."

She smiled. "Sure we are."

I shifted my feet. The tips of my sneakers were wet from the river. "Anyway, you do as you like. I'm not your dad or anything."

Her smile persisted. "You could be, for all I know."

We walked together down the Parkway until we reached Burning Spring Hill Road. The Dufferin Islands rolled off to the north in a haze of overgrown sedge and water-rotted sycamores. The Derby Lane dog track was still there, but it had seen better days—although, now that I thought about it, had the place ever seen *good* days?

"This place is creepy," the girl said as we walked past the grounds.

I could see why she'd think that. The swaybacked spectators' gallery seemed to be collapsing into itself like a jack-o'-lantern left sitting on a porch until mid-November. Every single bulb in its marquee was busted, likely the work of punks with an obsessive streak.

"It used to be nicer," I said. "A little, anyway. I had a dog. My friend and me, we both did. Greyhounds. We raced them here."

"Bullshit," the girl said cheerily.

"Not bullshit." I walked across the lot, glass gritting under my soles. "Dolly Express. That was my dog's name."

"That's weird."

I acknowledged her complaint with a nod. "Racing dogs have silly names. We just called her Dolly."

She touched her chin, eyes gazing skyward. "That's an okay dog name. You okay?"

"Yeah," I said. "Just thinking."

We'd walked only a little further when the girl said, "This is me."

A low-rent apartment block sat in the shadow of the escarpment. I watched while she climbed up the front stairs. She went ten steps, turned, and waved.

"See you."

I waved back. "See you around, maybe."

Her shrug said: *anything's possible.* I watched until she was safely inside the building. She waved me off as if I was being stupid, she could handle herself.

I walked back to Derby Lane. Wind whipped off the river and howled around the marquee, singing off every point of busted glass. A burning ripcurl surged up from my stomach. This was a vital part of my life, right here. And it was gone now. I felt sick with nostalgia. Memory like a sickness, memory like a drug. I stood in the lengthening shadow of the lane, swallowed up by the black hole of my past.

———

BACK WHEN I WAS A YOUNG WORKING STIFF, I often sat on a bench in the locker room after my night shifts, soaking my hands in a bucket of warm water. A weird smell had started leaking out of my pores after my first few shifts at the Bisk, sweet and spicy like a Chinese bakery. I'd noticed that food tasted different, too: drinking a Diet Coke was like sucking on a battery. But I needed the money. Always, the money.

The regular night-shift mechanic had busted his leg falling off a stepladder in the deep-chill; now, whenever the rollers on the industrial conveyors went wonky, I had to tighten them with a three-foot pipe wrench. I wore heavy-duty work gloves but they didn't stop the calluses: four dime-sized patches on each hand. Thick and hard, they put pressure on the nerves.

One night, same as most others, I'd scraped off the dead skin with a butter knife. It flaked away in curls, collecting in my palm. The new skin was pearly-white like cooked haddock; it turned pink with the rush of blood.

I dabbed on ointment, emptied the bucket and made my way past the factory lines to the exit. Machines stretched down the floor. I had to remind myself that we made cookies, the kind that kids liked.

Back then I used to dream about those machines growing into me—I mean, into my *body*.

The dream started with me tightening a lugnut on the conveyor belt, something I would do fifteen, twenty times a shift. Both hands on the wrench, torqueing my shoulder to feel the quiver of the machine across my stomach. Next the silver head of a screw pierces my skin. The tip's winking in the middle of my hand. I'm like, *huh?* But no pain. I'm shocked, but because dreams are driven by their own weird logic, I'm not terrified.

The screw has driven through the wrench and through my hand, anchoring me to the machine. Pressure builds up my spine; I lean sideways, putting weight on my right foot. Which is when steel bolts punch through my Caterpillar workboot. *Tink! Tink! Tink!* When the concrete dust clears I see the bolts have twisted into a snarl that pins my foot to the floor. I laugh. It's so *strange*, it's funny.

I sink to one knee. *Aaaaahh.* Feels great to take a load off. The moment I do so, small hooks—like fishing hooks but with a crueller curve, the hooks surgeons use to tug catgut through an open wound—pierce my trousers and sink into my skin. Each hook is attached to a leader like the ones my father used to catch steelhead: braided wire, so the fish can't rip through with their hacksaw teeth. My dream-skin tears easily. My flesh is chalky and full of holes, like

Wonder bread. Still, nothing hurts too much and there is never any blood, a fact that seems more sinister when I'm awake.

I begin to notice the other men around me—the generic Cataract City guys you see around. Their heads sprout like cabbages along the line. They're talking over each other, babbling away.

". . . saw him down at the Hillcrest Tavern and knocked his dick in the dirt . . ."

". . . knocked her up and now she's figuring to have the damn kid . . ."

. . . gonna put a supercharger in it. It'll blow your doors off, sonnyboy . . ."

I try to remember just how I got there but the lines don't meet up, the teeth don't groove. How did this happen? The way everything does, I guess. One thing follows another, naturally.

After my shift that night I met Edwina in the parking lot. She was heading inside dressed in flour-caked overalls and a hairnet but she was beautiful for all that—or more beautiful because of it. The lot lights burned against the night, making golden rings around her irises. I wanted to paw at her like a lusty dog but I knew she wouldn't stand for that. She was older—as she often reminded me—and more experienced, as she also reminded me.

"Your hands?" she asked, taking them into her own.

"They're going to have to come off, Ed," I told her, fake-sad. "I'm cutting them off at the wrist."

"I'll kiss them all better."

There were places in Cataract City where you could buy a cold beer at seven in the morning. Two blocks north on Lindy a sleepy-eyed Mexican was still serving icy Sols out of an orange picnic cooler; he could be handing me one in five minutes and I knew just what he'd say: *Wrap your leeps around a cold one, partner.*

I was a working man, unlike a lot of guys my age—Owe, for one, who was off at college earning his police services diploma. So I drank, sure. Not at campus bars where girls wore perfume that smelled like a Mounds bar. At the Double Aces and Blue Lagoon, where women sat with their elbows polishing the bar alongside the guys and everyone ordered "a shot and a Hed": a shot of rail rye and a glass of Hedley Springs, cheapest beer on tap.

A shot and a Hed, a shot and a Hed, a shot and a Hed, and you wake up feeling like you've been shot in the head!

Instead I drove to the house Ed and I rented on Culp Street. I caught a whiff of vanilla—I'd spilled concentrate on my hand the other week on the Nilla Wafers line and the smell had crept under my skin. I smelled like a cookie, same as every other long-time stiff at the Bisk.

Dolly met me at the door, her tail tucked between her legs. Dolly's a greyhound. I found her in a Dumpster. I was fifteen, maybe. Sixteen?

I'd been riding my bike to the Bisk; my dad had forgotten his lunchpail. The sun was just up, the city asleep. I was coasting past the Food Terminal when a cube van went screech-assing past, laying rubber. A couple of townies who had been ridding their guts of last night's piss-up behind the supermarket, was my guess. I dropped Dad's lunch off and rode back, slaloming lazily between the shopping carts in the Food Terminal lot. At first I thought the yips were just gravel popping under my tires. I braked, ears straining. Were they coming from the Dumpster?

I cracked the lid and found two puppies on a flattened Del Monico tomato box. They mewled when the sunlight touched their skin. Another few hours and they would have broiled to death. They were so damn small; I remember feeling their heartbeats through their skin—or was that my own heartbeat pulsing in my hands?

I can't tell you why, exactly, I took them to Owen's house.

I showed up on his doorstep breathing hard from the ride. Sweat dripped off me in pints, which freaked me out because I was in Cardinal Gardens. The houses all looked pretty much the same, and they were real swish: the lawns a checkerboard green you could only get with a riding lawn mower, the bushes trimmed into leafy bells. I figured the Neighbourhood Watch was going to come along and say: *Son, don't you think you ought to bust your ass back to where you belong?*

I knew where Owe lived, even though we hadn't talked for years, since the Mahoney thing. Our dads had made that choice. But by the time I showed up at Owen's house I had my learner's permit in my pocket and I even knew a guy, Slick, who'd buy me a six-pack of Black Label from the beer store (at double the retailer's suggested price). All I'm saying is, I had some freedom—I didn't always do what Dad said anymore.

I popped the kickstand and shrugged off my backpack. The puppies were nestled on a bed of torn-up *Pennysavers*, the pack's zipper halfway open so they could breathe.

Mr. Stuckey answered the door. He wore a striped shirt with Pearlite buttons, and a slice of buttered toast was clamped between his teeth.

"Good morning, Master Diggs," he said around the toast, in an English-butler voice. "How ya been?"

"Okay, Mr. Stuckey. Owe around?"

For a sec I figured Mr. Stuckey was going to slam the door. I knew nobody would nominate me for sainthood but still, I'd never had the "bad influence" tag slapped on me. That was for guys like Sam Bovine, who'd been caught selling single pages of his father's old fuck-book—*The Well-Spanked Farm Girl*—for a quarter a page. Adam Lowery had ratted Bovine out; Adam bought two pages and was pissed that all he got was four paragraphs about some chick milking cows and the autumn twilight settling across the prairies—but was it Bovine's fault that a spank-book writer had literary dreams?

"Come on in," Mr. Stuckey said after forever.

I waited in the hall, soaking up the air conditioning. The window unit at my house had gone balls-up that summer; we had a half-dozen fans stirring the humid air around. The backpack squirmed against my sweaty skin.

Owe came downstairs rubbing sleep from his eyes. Last I'd seen him was about a year before. My dad had been driving me home from baseball practice and we saw him with some buddies. One guy had a crewneck sweater knotted around his neck.

"Your old friend is palling around with yuppie twerps," Dad said, frowning.

Owe went to Ridley Academy, a private school. The school—sorry, the *Acchaaaadhemy*; in my head I always heard it spoken in a windbaggy British accent—had a fleet of rowing boats, called "sculls," which the "oarsmen" raced at the Henley Regatta. I'd pictured Owe in one of those old-time rower's getups: striped bathing suit like the ones women wore in the 1920s, a goofy straw hat perched on his head. Which I admit was a shitty thing to think. Could Owe help it if his folks could afford better?

"What's up?" he said.

"Hey, man. Can we talk somewhere quiet?"

Owe glanced over his shoulder, where his parents sat at the kitchen table pretending to read the newspaper. "Okay . . . downstairs."

The basement was unfinished. Dusty exercise equipment was heaped in a corner. Owe looked freaked. Did he think I was going to slug him, or confess I'd been having kinky dreams about him?

I shrugged the backpack off and unzipped it.

"Holy shit," Owe said. "Where did you—?"

"In the Dumpster behind the Food Terminal. Someone . . . they threw them out like trash, man."

The puppies were so small you couldn't tell what breed they were: just wrinkly things with closed eyes. Their flopped-over ears were the size of fingernails and their paws were bright pink, like a human baby's hands.

"What should I do with them?"

Owe said: "Keep them?"

How could my parents say no? It wasn't like I was begging for a dog from the pet store. This was more like a humanitarian intervention.

"There's two," I said. "I was thinking maybe . . ."

"I don't know," Owe said. "My folks . . ."

"It's okay," said Owe's mom, who'd crept down the stairs. "It's the right thing to do."

After heeling off my workboots, I walked into our unlit kitchen. Dolly padded softly behind me. I set my lunchpail on the counter— it was my dad's old pail, covered in Chiquita Banana stickers— opened the fridge, shook the milk carton. Only a few mouthfuls left; I gulped straight from the carton, bachelor-style. Then I tore rags of dark meat off a rotisserie chicken. Dolly ate them in that weird, gluttonous way dogs do: snapping her head back and flinging the meat down her throat.

"You hog," I said softly. She watched me, eyes shining in the fridge-light.

I showered, towelled off, lay in bed. The clean light of morning pulsed behind the curtains. Dolly hopped up, settled her head on my hip. Her heart beat hard, driving the blood through her veins.

Next week she'd race her first A-Class event. She was unbeaten in her career.

And there was a part of me that really hoped she'd lose.

You know when you're driving on a hot day and there's heat-shimmer on the road? As a kid you figure you'll catch up to it if your folks drive fast enough. Eventually you realize it's nothing that can be caught because it doesn't stay put.

A greyhound . . . now a greyhound will chase that shimmer until its heart explodes, and right up to that very moment it will believe, with every atom of its being, that it'll *catch* the thing.

They're all muscle, greyhounds, all *go fast* muscle. Their legs are triple-jointed, and in full flight all twelve joints are at work: a smooth piston-like *pump, pump, pump.* Sometimes I figure it's nothing but wind shear that keeps them on the ground, y'know? There is no other animal on earth whose skull looks more like it ought to be coming down the barrel of a gun.

Racing greyhounds have got a heart the size of a fist, double the size of a Labrador retriever's. But they've also got heart in the fighter's sense: a greyhound's got the deepest bucket of any dog. They'll run themselves to death if you let them, because that's what they want to do—what they've been *made* for. But to be a real runner means you must be faster than anything else . . . which means you've got to be forever alone at the head of the pack.

When pure racers spring from the starting traps and hit the straightaway, some of them *whine.* They're going so fast that you might mistake the sound of their bodies slicing through space for that of a low-flying jet.

A lot of people want a dog who is always happy to see them. Who'll sit in their laps. But that's not a fair hope with a greyhound. You've got an animal who is a Ferrari with a brick permanently weighting its gas pedal. The lives of greyhounds are all open stretches and endless horizons.

Of course, neither Owe nor me knew a thing about greyhounds when we found them. And it was a steep learning curve. I mean, Jesus, how would we have known about milking a puppy? That's what the veterinarian called it: *milking*.

"They'll have to accept milk that doesn't come from their mother," he told us as our puppies squirmed on his examination table. "They're still whelps. You've got to feed them as their mother would."

He sent us home with Esbilac, a formula especially for pups. Dolly needed constant feeding. I'd be up at four in the morning when she whined in the shoebox beside my bed. I'd pluck her from her cotton-batten nest, feed her until she burped, and fall asleep until she whined again.

"No eating my newspaper, no tearing up my carpet, no shitting on my floor" were the ground rules my dad laid out for the animal he called the Amazing Dumpster Dog.

I named her Dolly. My great-grandmother's name. She'd come up from the South, Mom said, to marry a man she'd fallen in love with at a revival gathering. When that love faded she'd met my great-grandfather, ditched the other guy, remarried, and *that* love stuck fast.

"People didn't get divorced back then," Mom had told me. "Oh, god, it was the very mark of shame. But Dolly didn't care. To hell with all that, she figured. It took guts."

My Dolly had guts, too. She'd been ripped away from her own mom and chucked in a Dumpster. For a few terrifying days she couldn't keep the Esbilac down and became so weak she couldn't stand. One morning I came downstairs to see a pale blue box on the kitchen table; it had once held a Hummel figurine my father had bought for Mom on a whim.

"If the poor nipper goes," Dad said, "we'll bury her in that. Out in the backyard."

Mom came downstairs, spotted the box and my wounded eyes.

"Jesus, Jerry. Do you have a brain rolling around in that thick head of yours?"

"What did I do?" my dad said, genuinely shocked. "It's the nicest box we own."

Fact is, Dad cared about that dog. He'd hunker over her shoebox cooing softly, same as he'd probably done with me in my cradle. Later on, when Dolly was ripping up his sneakers and his flower-bed, Dad was much less kind. "That goddamn mutt won't see her first birthday!"

When she was only weeks old I got permission to bring Dolly to school. She lay in her shoebox beside my desk as I slogged through trig and chem. In shop class I sat her atop the tool caddy while rinsing crusty gunk out of ancient carburetors.

Nobody ragged me about bringing a puppy to school. I already had a rep as a rough ticket. I didn't really enjoy fighting, but I wasn't afraid of getting hit and dealt a hard lick. If anybody was making jokes about Duncan Diggs, Dog Boy of Westlane High, it was strictly behind my back.

Meanwhile, girls who had no clue I'd even existed were suddenly stopping by my desk to ogle Dolly. Even Francisca Bevins, head cheerleader and a shoo-in for the Total Bitch All-Stars, was charmed enough by the Amazing Dumpster Dog to pass the time of day with me.

The dogs brought Owen and me back together. I'm not saying that was my aim. But when I found those creatures in the Dumpster the first thought through my mind was: *Owe.*

Owe's greyhound was a boy. He named it Fragrant Meat.

"It's what they call dogs in Mongolia," he told me. "The ones they eat. At the supermarket, that's what they label it."

"Why would you name him that?"

"A dog doesn't know any different. Fragrant Meat. Shithead. Ass-licker. As long as you say it with *kindness*."

It bothered me that Owe chose that name. Sure, the dog wouldn't know, but wasn't it disrespectful all the same? Owe eventually shortened it to Frag; he probably got sick of explaining it to people.

Frag developed a life-threatening kidney problem. One morning he stumbled into Owe's bedroom disoriented, bumping into the walls. When Owe picked him up, Frag burped up warm, white foam.

"Frothy, same as a milk shake," I remember him telling me.

For a few days it was touch and go. Puffy red rings were permanently fixed around Owe's eyes. But Frag pulled through. The vet put him on a special diet; Frag had to guzzle a gallon of water a day to flush his kidneys.

We used to take our dogs on walks along the river or down in the valley of the escarpment—always keeping the road firmly in sight. We talked about tons of stuff. Girls, of course, but also our friends and whatever might be waiting for us out in the great wide world—the casual bullshit that makes up the bulk of all conversations.

The dogs brought us together when a lot of things could've pushed us apart. We went to different schools. In the summers I worked on the horticulture crew at Land of Oceans. Those same summers Owe was at basketball camps in the Carolinas, scrimmaging against future ACC and Big Ten recruits.

That's an important part of this story, too: how Owen "Dutchie" Stuckey became known in Cataract City simply as Dutch. For a while people knew him by that one name, the way divas are known. Cher. Whitney. Dutch.

He earned the moniker for one simple reason: the boy was straight-up *murder* on a basketball court.

Before his talent blipped on the city's radar screen, Owen was Dutchie. Little Dutchie Stuckey with his cowlicked hair, the joints of his limbs like knots in a rope. Then Dutchie shot up a full foot and began to drain twenty-seven-foot jumpers with a defender's hand in his face. After that he was Dutch.

His skills were an unsolvable riddle to me. I'd grown up with spazzy, knock-kneed, tangle-foot Owe. Whiff-at-kickball Owe. But put him on a basketball court and that clumsiness went away.

Dad and I went to the last game of his junior year, at the height of Dutch mania. He'd posted some crazy averages that season: thirty points, twelve assists, four steals, five rebounds, one and a half blocks. We sat on risers in the Ridley Multiplex, crammed shoulder to shoulder with spectators. The crowd was ritzy: lots of elbow-patched blazers and Hush Puppies. The gym was so packed that sweat and breath caused hazy halos to form around the sodium vapour lights.

On the first play after opening tip, Owe caught the ball on the wing. He dribbled once, got his defender to bite, crossed left, got his defender going back that way and crossed *back* right—an ankle-snapper, they call that move. His defender went down on his ass as Owe pulled up for a silky-smooth jumper. The nylon gave that sweet stinging *snap* it makes when the ball barely grazes the iron.

The crowd raised a foghorn cry: "*Duuuuuuuuuuuutch.*"

I'd never seen a human being move the way Owe did back then. Tall but still gawky—the body of a muscular stick insect. He didn't bull through defenders: he flowed around them like mercury, squirting through the tiniest seams until he was at the rim for an underhand scoop, or whipping the ball to a teammate parked at the three-point arc for a wide-open look.

This will sound crazy, but even his eyes were a different colour on the court. They'd always been blue, but on the court they seemed brighter and colder—I don't mean unfeeling, just the purest cold imaginable: like ice in the polar icecaps.

He went off for fifty-three points that night. After showering and giving a quote to the local hack for the morning edition, he hopped in the truck with me and Dad.

"Hell of a game," Dad said.

"We ran up the score," Owe said. "I asked Coach to bench me to start the fourth. Game was in the bag, right? But the college scouts were up from the States—it was my showcase game. So he kept me in, kept running plays to goose my total."

I remembered the frown that had darkened Owe's face after he'd canned each late-game shot. As if he wanted to miss, but couldn't.

"It's the zone," he said. "When you're in it, the hoop gets as big as a barrel. Any old junk you toss up goes in. It's like . . . white light. Sounds stupid, I know, but it's the only way to explain it. This very bright light at the edges of your vision, crowding everything out until it's only the ball and the hoop. No sound, no distractions. It's so easy in the zone." He smiled helplessly. "To be honest, I'm happy when I come out of it. I really don't think humans are meant to live too long in the zone."

"Dutch Stuckey," my father said dreamily after we'd dropped him off. "That boy's going to put this city on the *map*."

There was awe in Dad's voice—probably at the fact that anyone from Cataract City could be so good at anything.

Looking back, it's easier to spot the signs. I remember one afternoon when we were at Valour Park, shooting on the hoops. We'd taken Dolly and Frag for a meandering walk and they were leashed to the bench next to the court, lying contentedly in the shadow of an oak tree.

I'd always been athletic and even became a half-decent slotback for our football team, but I was no great shakes at basketball. I could set screens and rebound—I'd happily do the grunt work. Owe was good but he hadn't yet made the leap. His shot was there already, though: this smooth arc that hung forever at its peak, unbothered by gravity, before falling crisply through the net.

He'd dusted me at H-O-R-S-E when Adam Lowery and Clyde Hillicker showed up. They went to my school but I never took notice of them anymore; they were just two guys I vaguely disliked floating through the halls with the jocks and stoners, the skids and skells.

"Hey, shitheads," went Adam.

My shot hit back iron and bounced over to Clyde. He tucked it under his arm.

"Finders keepers."

"Throw the goddamn ball back," I said, in no mood.

Adam took it from Clyde and lofted a shot. The ball dropped nicely through the rim and rolled back to him. Bouncing it on the tips of his fingers, he said: "We'll play you for it."

Adam considered himself a JV basketball badass. The coach, Mr. Weaver—everyone called him Mr. Weave because he wore a noticeable hairpiece with frosted tips—must've blown some top-end smoke up Adam's butt.

Owe said, "Sure. Play you for *my* ball."

We agreed that the first to seven points wins, all baskets counting as one point. I matched up with Clyde, who was six inches taller and fifty pounds heavier than me. Thankfully he was built like a pile of Goodwill parkas, meaning I could muscle him around.

Owe and Adam guarded each other. As soon as Owe checked the ball, Adam shot. *Swish.* Owe checked the ball again, and again Adam shot. *Swish.* Owe checked the ball but this time he closed out, forcing Adam to pass. Clyde caught the ball and brought his elbows around, clipping the bridge of my nose. Red lights popped in front of my face and my brain hit *Tilt.* Clyde spun clumsily and clanged the ball in off the backboard.

"First one's free, Clyde," I said, rubbing my nose. "The next one'll cost you."

They were up 3–0. Adam dribbled left, nearly had it stolen, and hoisted up a clumsy jumper that barely grazed the iron. I collected the rebound and fired it out to Owe, who immediately fed it back to me. I pump-faked Clyde, who bit, then blew past him only to bank the ball too hard off the backboard.

Adam took the ball at the top of the key, passed inside, got it back, stutter-stepped right and hoisted a rickety jumper that toilet-bowled around the rim and in. 4–0. A clumsy fadeaway by Clyde— he tossed it just over my outstretched fingertips—made it 5–0. We were getting skunked.

On the next possession Owe checked the ball, timed Adam's jumper and blocked it cleanly.

"Foul," Adam said.

"Bullshit!" I shouted.

"Honour the call," Owe said.

Clyde missed a desperation hook shot. I collected the rebound and passed it out. Owe passed it back in. I whipped it out and growled, "*You* take it."

It was as if he'd been waiting for permission. He jab-stepped Adam, got some space and lofted a shot that dropped through. 5–1.

"Lucky shot," said Adam.

Owe took the ball at the top. That coldness I would come to

know well was in his eyes. He crossed Adam over, sending him sprawling. He drove and kicked the ball to me under the rim. I banked the open shot in off the backboard. 5–2.

Adam's road-rashed knees wept blood. He got right up in Owe's face, barking, "Take that shot, punk. Go on and shoot that weak-ass shit."

Owe dribbled back until he was thirty feet from the hoop. Adam put his hands on his hips. "You really going to take that?"

Owe did. The ball barely grazed the back iron as it fell through. 5–3.

Next, Owe dropped a pair of long bombs and a fadeaway that banked in softly. His second shot led to a dispute: it dropped through the netless rim so cleanly that Adam argued it was an airball. Owe just shrugged and canned his next shot from the exact same spot.

"Was that an airball, too?" he asked Adam.

"Fuck off, Stuckey."

After a nifty up-and-under move where he faked both Adam and Clyde out of their shorts, he shovelled the ball to me for a final easy bucket.

Final score: 7–5.

Adam snatched the ball after the game-winner. "We're keeping it, anyway. You fuckers cheat."

"You can leave with the ball," I said evenly, "or you can leave with your teeth."

Our dogs were barking at the commotion.

"Shut up, you fucking *mutts*," Adam hissed.

I punched him in the gut and he fell back like he'd been pole-axed, dropping the ball. Clyde stepped in uncertainly and when I cocked my fist he flinched like the big marshmallow he was.

Owe collected the ball. Adam grabbed at his chicken-chest like an old woman clutching her pearls. A venomous look came into his eyes. He scrounged a nickel out of his pocket and flipped it onto the concrete.

"Take that home to your daddy," he wheezed. "You two melt it down, win yourselves another Kub Kar Rally."

The incident with the Kub Kars was years past—but because this was Cataract City, it may as well have happened yesterday. The city's got a wet-sidewalk memory: press something into it and the impression remains forever.

Things were gearing towards a scuffle when Owe noticed Dolly had slipped her collar. It lay empty on the grass beside the bench. The park bordered the heavily trafficked Harvard Avenue. I knew greyhounds had zero road sense—most of them figured they could outrun a car.

I sprinted over the grass, shouting her name. "Dolly! *Do-lly!*"

I ran down the sidewalk, dodging people, imagining every horrible outcome: she'd been hit by a car; she'd been attacked by another dog, a raccoon, a skunk; she'd been stolen by a dog-thieving prick in a white cube van.

I rounded the corner where Harvard met Brian Crescent and there Dolly was, cradled in the arms of Edwina Murphy.

"Lost something, Diggs?" she said, laughing as Dolly licked her chin. "She's a quick little bitch. You ought to race her down at Derby Lane."

Our mothers had a nickname for Edwina Murphy: the Jezebel.

Owe and I first got to know Edwina—everyone called her Ed— when she was fifteen, three years older than we were at the time. Owe's folks hired her to babysit.

Ed lived down the street, in a house of boys. The Murphy brothers were known hellions; more than a few nights I'd wake to the light of police cherries washing my bedroom windows as one or more of the Murphy boys was dropped off or picked up.

Ed had some hellion in her, too, a wildness that reminded me of comic book vixens: Red Sonja, the Black Widow. Her long dark hair fell straight down and when the sun hit it right, it shone like a curved mirror. She swore like a dock worker and punched you on the shoulder to punctuate her sentences. Still, we thought of her as being different from her thuggish clan. She could be charming when it suited her.

Ed was almost criminally easygoing as a babysitter. Her rules were: No fighting, no drinking, no pills, no lighting fires. Other than that, open season. If Owe wanted Marshmallow Fluff for supper, Ed's shoulders would lift and she'd say: "Going to rot your teeth out, hombre, but they're your choppers."

Sometimes when Owe's folks were working late Ed would pick us up at school. We'd find her lounging against the flagpole sipping a bottle of Coca-Cola. The male teachers drank in greedy eyefuls of her, and her attitude suggested she didn't blame them—looking was free, after all.

"Fine afternoon, isn't it, Pete?" she'd say brightly as our grammar teacher hustled to his car. "It's a hot, hot, *slut-hot* ol' day."

We'd walk home in the cooling afternoon, puppy-dogging Ed's heels. She often stopped by Scholten's Convenience on Abilene, rapping sharply on the back door with her knuckles. Mr. Scholten would slip her a carton of cigarettes, which she sold as singles to her classmates. Every city has hidden doors that require secret knocks. Ed knew a lot of doors. How had she learned the knocks? I knew better than to ask a magician how she did her tricks.

Ed smoked her own product, and her brand was the absolute *worst*: Export A, in the green deck. The Green Death.

"It's my last one, boys. Promise," she'd say.

"But you have another pack in your pocket," Owe would insist. Ed would just smile.

I'd sleep over at Owe's when Ed babysat. There was no such thing as a curfew. We could stay up until we heard the garage door rumble on its tracks, at which point we had to hotfoot it to bed and start sawing logs.

We'd watch the *MuchMusic Top 20 Countdown*, hip-checking each other along to Twisted Sister and the Beastie Boys. We introduced Ed to the Baby Blue Movie. She declared it wimpy and flicked channels way up to the 100s, where the scrambled pornos played in a never-ending loop.

We watched the grainy broken images and listened to the goofy dialogue—Female: *Are you the plumber?* Male: *That's right, and I've got a biiig pipe to install*—set to cheesy *ohm-chaka* guitar riffs. Every so often the picture came clear in reverse polarity: we'd see a silicone-pumped tit looking like the huge eye of a squid or a man's face frozen under a blue-white glare, teeth shining like halogen track lights. I found it a lot less sexy than the Baby Blue Movie: the images spoke of adult lust, the desperate kind that took place in murky peep theatres. Ed seemed to sense this and switched back to the Baby Blue.

"That's too harsh for you boys," she said, levelling a finger at us. "Don't watch it again. I'll kick your asses if you do."

It was hard to take her threats seriously. Ed literally wouldn't hurt a fly: she used to catch bluebottles buzzing against the windows and let them free outside. Once she found a brown bat in the toilet—it must have flown in through the open window. She fished it out with her bare hands: its body the size of a peach stone, wings thin as crepe paper. She rested it on the picnic table in Owe's backyard, under a shoebox propped up with a stick. The bat dragged itself to the table's edge and flew off.

"I was sure it was a goner," she said, then asked herself, "Could I have handled that?"

Then, one night, Ed demanded we go to sleep at our regular bedtime. "You best hit the sack, buckaroos," she said, hooking her thumb upstairs.

Soon after, I heard the front door. Ed walked up the stairwell with Tim Railsback, her boyfriend. They went into the bathroom. The bathtub ran. We got out of bed, curious. The bathroom door was open a crack. To this day I wonder if Ed left it that way on purpose.

Ed and Tim were stripping naked. Steam rose from the tub the way mist rises off lawns on a summer morning. Their bodies were silked with sweat. Railsback was very tall; the top of Ed's head rose to where his collarbones came together. Her body had none of the hardness I'd see in Elsa Lovegrove.

They sat in the water, Ed between Tim's parted legs. A dull surge of jealousy washed through me. The knobs of Tim's knees rose above the tub like whitened stadium domes. His hands moved over Ed's body without settling anywhere. His expression held many things: sadness and queasy expectancy, regret, hopefulness.

"What is it?" Ed said.

"It's just . . . it's happening real fast."

Ed laughed. "It's okay, boy. We don't need to do anything."

Ed was the kind of girl who'd call grown men *boys*. Me and Owe stood trembling, our eyes shining in the doorway. Ed turned her head until her face met Tim's. Something in her eyes said *Don't make me ask for it. Just tell me.*

Tim said, "I love you."

And he must have. Almost everyone who spent any time with Ed came to love her. It made her careless, the way people can be when such a hard-won thing is given over so effortlessly. But I think she loved him, too, at least in that moment. Ed needed a lot of love—but she'd give it, too.

None of us heard the garage door. Owe and I *barely* heard the back door shut, and the warning gave us just enough time to dash back to his room and dive under the sheets.

Ed and Tim weren't so lucky. Owe's folks caught them bare-ass. *In my house! Under MY roof!* Owe's mom shooed them out, cursing as they fled into the night. Tim wore only his underwear; he left his Letterman jacket on a bathroom hook.

Of course Owe's mom called my mom and related the sordid tale. Which is how Ed became the Jezebel.

That night at Owe's was the last time I'd see Edwina until the afternoon years later, on the corner of Harvard and Brian, when she stood in front of me cradling Dolly in her arms.

"You got to keep an eye on this one." She tsked, handing the dog over as Owe rounded the corner with Frag.

"Tweedle Dumb and Tweedle Dumber," Ed said. "You two still attached at the hip? And you've bought matching dogs, too. How cute."

Owe said, "Dunk found them in a Dumpster."

This set Ed back for a beat. Then she said, "Who says you can't find treasure in the trash? You ought to take them to Derby Lane, see if they can run." She rubbed her thumb and fingers together, giving us the international sign for moolah. "You could be sitting on a mint. I know a guy there, Harry Riggins. Runs the kennels. He can tell you if they're any good and if not, *hey!* Still one hell of a pet."

The Derby Lane racetrack was a lot like Tinglers, the porno shop on Leeming Street—I mean, everyone knew it was there but only a certain type of guy actually *went*.

Derby Lane had been around since the seventies. As my dad said: "Used to be an okay fallback if you were looking to wager a few bucks on animals running in circles and didn't have the energy to make it down to Fort Erie to catch the ponies."

But with the casino going up on the Boulevard with its *tinkle-tinkle* of one-armed bandits and $5.99 buffet, the dog track was dead as disco. It only attracted the saddest of the sad, lonely old men in shiny-elbowed blazers and Florsheim shoes that had been stylish forty years ago. It was the sort of place that mocked the very idea of luck; even if you won, it was by Derby Lane standards, which meant parlaying a 100-to-1 shot into a measly payoff.

Me and Owe showed up on a Sunday morning. Sam Bovine dropped us off in his dad's old hearse—he was an apprentice mortician by then, a calling that I thought didn't suit him but that Bovine embraced with gusto.

"I'd stay," he said, "but I've got to get back to the stiffs or else they may wander away, *Living Dead*–style."

Owe said, "Three's a crowd, anyway."

Bovine bristled. "Ah, screw you two. And screw your dogs, too. Get them out of the casket croft—they're stinking up the upholstery."

We waved as Bovine swept the hearse around in a wide arc, flipping us the bird as he tooled off. We walked the dogs across the lot, which was empty except for one ancient pickup truck. The sun glinted off metal flarings outlining the park's dingy marquee. As we passed the pickup truck I noticed the bed was carpeted with dried-up dog turds. They looked like stubbed cigars.

We walked through the Winning Ticket Lounge, crossing a threadbare paisley carpet that gave off the stink of fry oil and wet dog. We passed down a line of ancient Silver Chief penny-slots, most of them unplugged, cords wrapped around the levers.

"Our family came here for Chipped Beef Friday," I said. "Before, y'know, the kitchen got shut down. Roaches? Mice? I think roaches."

Huge windows smudged with oily fingerprints overlooked the track. Ashtrays were set into the armrests of the gallery seats. The track itself was an oval surrounded by billboards for the Flying Saucer restaurant, Murphy's Pegleg Tavern and other local haunts.

We made our way to the track. Litter drifted around the empty risers. Dolly strained at her leash as we crossed to the far left of the track, passing a row of metal boxes with a swinging grate attached overtop. The starting boxes?

The kennels were in a boxcar-shaped building with tin siding. I remember thinking that it must get deadly hot come summertime. Owe knocked. When nobody answered he toed the door open.

The howls began at once—like a dozen busted foghorns going off. The kennel was bright white, clean and well lit. Industrial fans rotated above the dog pens. To the left was a deep basin sink and a big steel hook hung with leather leashes. Beside it was a hamper of dog muzzles and another of neatly folded racing jerseys.

A man entered through a side door, yelling, "Shush it! *Shush!*" He was in his late seventies, short and pot-bellied, wearing carpenter's overalls and orange galoshes.

Edwina followed him, waving sunnily. "Here's the Bobbsey Twins!"

The old man ambled over and stuck out his hand. "Harry Riggins at your service, boys." He edged his glasses up his nose. His eyes were watery behind thick, scratched lenses. "I take care of the dogs. Feed 'em, exercise 'em. I also work the mechanical hare on race nights. You know much about greyhounds?"

"They run pretty fast," Owe said.

"They can run, that they can." Harry knelt, opened Frag's mouth and ran one squared-off finger along his gums. His other fingers roamed up Frag's face and opened his eyelids. "*Eeesh.* Too much pressure behind this one's eyes. Makes them bulge out. Quirk of the breed. You happen to know their bloodlines?"

I said, "I found them in a Dumpster."

"Oh," Harry said. "That does happen. Some trainers . . . goddamn slugs."

Ed said briskly, "Well, let's see if these mutts got any pep in their step."

The dog runs were hundred-yard-long fenced enclosures laid out behind the kennels. Greyhounds dashed down the nearest run, skidding to a stop at the fence before barrelling back the other way.

Harry said, "Let's put your two in with this wild bunch, see if they can ruck in."

Frag and Dolly tried to join the racing pack. Almost immediately they got tangled up and hit the fence; the chain-link made a strained musical note as it was stretched back against the posts—*phimmmm!*—like an overtuned banjo string. They tumbled across the dirt, scrambled to their feet and raced to rejoin the dogs.

"Yikes," said Ed.

"They're young yet," Harry said. "The bitch seems game."

I didn't like Harry calling Dolly a bitch. He didn't mean anything by it—I knew that, technically, it described what she was—but the term put a burr under my ass.

I'd never seen Dolly running with a greyhound other than Frag. Now I observed how muscle was packed in fat balls where her chest met her front legs. She ran with abandon: legs outflung, mouth wide open in the closest thing to a smile that a dog can manage.

"They ain't much as pets," Harry told us. "Lap dogs, I mean. You probably figured that out already. Looking to sell them? Probably get a couple hundred for the bitch. The male's more of a giveaway."

"They don't want to sell, Harry," said Ed. "They want to race."

Harry cocked his head at Ed. Stubble glittered along his jaws like flaked mica.

"Come on now, Edwina." He turned to us. "You just finished telling me you aren't any kind of dogmen, right?"

"We've never raced dogs," I admitted.

Harry said, "Then I'd urge you to sell. Still some decent dogmen at this track. They'll treat the nippers well enough, maybe even turn the bitch into a decent B-leveller . . . Could you really want to keep them as *pets?*"

Ed said, "Harry, why not let's just see what these dogs have got?"

He looked leery but said, "For you, darlin'? Anything."

Minutes later Harry met us at the track. Leashed at his side was a young greyhound with a coffee-cake coat.

"Steadfast Attila," he told us. "I didn't name him. He'll race in D-Class soon. That's the lowest level at the Lane. Attila's a stayer— he'll race right to the line."

Harry left Steadfast Attila with Ed and approached the mechanical hare. It wasn't a hare at all—just a ratty teddy bear lashed to a five-foot buggywhip pole. Harry pulled a squeeze bottle out of his overall pocket and sprayed down the bear.

"Rabbit piss," he said. "Don't ask how I get it."

We led the dogs over to the hare and let them take a sniff. Steadfast Attila started pogo-sticking on his hind legs. Fragrant Meat sat on his haunches and gnawed on his own ass.

"That's not an encouraging sign, son," Harry told Owe.

Dolly just cocked her head at the hare, and I figured she knew exactly what it was: a piss-soaked teddy bear on a pole.

Fragrant Meat raced Steadfast Attila first. Owe and I lined up the dogs at the start line. Steadfast Attila barked madly, screwing his haunches into the dirt. Fragrant Meat flattened himself out with his tail straight as a ramrod.

Harry hauled himself into the operator's seat. "When it gets thirty yards out, let 'em go."

The mechanical hare zizzed down the rail, spitting blue sparks. The dogs tore off, kicking clods of dirt back into our faces. Fragrant Meat's rear legs had a noticeable sideways kick. Steadfast Attila worked the outside edge, his brindle coat a beautiful brownish blur against the rust-coloured dirt.

Fragrant Meat held the lead when they hit the turn, but Steadfast Attila pulled into a dead heat around the hundred-yard mark and outdistanced Frag down the stretch. Frag kicked hard to the finish, though; there wasn't an ounce of quit in that dog.

"I don't like to dismiss dogs on their first offering, but he's got the sidewinder legs," Harry said to Owe, a doctor delivering sad news.

"Sidewinder legs?"

"It's like hip dysplasia," Harry told him. "There may not be a lot on your dog, but greyhounds are like precision instruments—even a little is too much when you're talking about races won by a fraction of a second." He clapped Owe's shoulder companionably. "The boy's got sass. But it's like running with a clubfoot."

"He *does* have sass," Owe said. "He ran his guts out."

"A good dog only loses because his body can't compete," said Harry. "That's the difference between greyhounds and men—a man's mind'll fold, even if he's got all the tools to win. Some say a dog won't quit just because dogs are dumb animals. I don't subscribe to that theory."

Harry lashed a fresh teddy to the whip. He had a burlap sack full of them: teddy bears and rabbits, pigs and penguins. "I get them from a carnival supply company," he said. "Used to go to the Goodwill but they'd give me weird looks."

He led Steadfast Attila to the kennels and returned with a fawn-coloured greyhound who walked with the high, hopping gait of a show horse.

"Trix Matrix," he said. "Didn't come up with that name, either. I call her Trixy. She's earmarked for great things, I'm told. She'll earn foreign interest—some of our best dogs are bought by Irish breeders to run at the top tracks overseas."

Harry led Trixy over to Dolly. The dogs stood nose to nose. Dolly nuzzled her snout into Trixy's throat. Trixy snapped at Dolly, who whipped her head aside to avoid Trixy's canines, dancing back, paws stuttering as if the ground was hot as glowing coals.

"She's got moxie," Harry said, a smile touching the edges of his mouth. "But plenty of scrubbers do."

Dolly toed the line beside Trixy. She stood stock-still, rear legs flared, front paws spaced with one slightly in front of the other. Her pulse raced under my fingertips. She looked back at me with a quizzical expression. *You don't have to hold me so tight*, the look seemed to say.

When the hare raced down the rail, Trixy bolted—god, that dog could boogie. You didn't have to know much about greyhounds to see she was a true racer: the fibre of her being spoke through her running form.

And Dolly? Well, Dolly just stood there.

"Girl?" I whispered.

Then I felt the run building inside her body: all the little parts gathering momentum, energy coursing through her skin. It was like a giant muscle contracting before it flexed into action. Her entire body recoiled—legs pistoning backwards, haunches dipping low—and there was this awesome tension, every fast-twitch muscle committed to the goal of forward motion. Then she was gone.

At first Dolly's strides were clipped and violent, paws churning up chunks of dirt until she hit the seventy-yard mark. There she lengthened out into a powerful running motion, her streamlined skull bobbing with each stride.

Trixy ran high, head up, spine bowed. Dolly ran low: head on the same plane as her shoulders, spine prone, slicing through the air like a ballistic missile. She managed to get the same leg-spread as Trixy, though, with her lower gait: her legs scissored under her, tucked paws brushing her belly before they jackknifed out again, barely grazing the dirt.

Trixy held the inside position when they hit the turn; she angled her shoulder towards the rail, steering like a stock car around a high-banked oval. Dolly's paws skidded for purchase as she muscled herself back into position, her shoulder colliding with Trixy's; their heads came together, teeth flashing, fighting with each other even as they fought desperately for position.

They raced round the bend. Me, Ed and Owe ran to the rail. The dogs were so close that I couldn't separate one from the other: there was just an elongated shape, two dogs fused together. They disappeared behind the tote board.

They shrieked around the turn and hit the final stretch. Dolly had flared out to the right, far from the rail, meaning she'd have to cover more ground. Trixy pounded down the track, head upflung, mouth open and tendons flexed down her throat and across her brisket: she looked like she was screaming. Dolly's legs pumped so hard it was like watching a machine reaching the point of failure, spindles trembling as it threatened to fling itself to pieces. A red berry was splotched on her coat—Trixy must have bitten her hard enough to draw blood.

They tore down the homestretch. Dolly angled across the track, closing in at the rail. Her form was slipping: her front legs speared wide as her head jerked up and down. Still, she drew even with about forty yards to go. Trixy kept pace for another ten yards before Dolly blazed past with a vicious finishing kick, accelerating over the line.

Harry ambled down from the operator's box. He scratched his belly through his overalls and smiled in the way old men do when they see something fresh and exciting—with an element of bewilderment.

"She's a real dandy, son. And what a low drinker."

"Low drinker?"

"Old dogman's saying," Harry told me, "for a dog that goes down real deep in their running stance, so low their belly's almost dragging the dirt. They look like they're crouched by the river lapping up water."

Ed slapped my back. "Looks like you won the lottery."

When I went to pick up Dolly she was hopping around, favouring one of her paws.

"What is it, girl?"

She whined thinly, babying her paw in that confused way animals do, as if they can't quite believe their bodies might break down or fail. She'd run so hard that sand was compacted between her paw-pads. Must've hurt like hell.

"It happens when they start racing," Harry told me. "Buy a bottle of Tuf-Foot—it'll harden them right up." And he suggested I take her to the vet.

When the vet instructed me to help Dolly onto the examining table, she buried her snout into the soft spot between my clavicle and neck. Her breath had the ironlike tang of raw liver, which I took to be the smell of pure animal fear. She shook when the vet flushed her paw with peroxide, but she didn't nip—just beheld him with tragic, injured eyes.

The Tuf-Foot worked. Dolly never had that problem again. But I was worried, and that worry never did go away.

Every time Dolly raced she'd enter the zone, the same as Owe did on a basketball court. And like he said, human beings aren't meant to exist there for too long. Why should dogs be any different?

But it was Dolly's element, you know? Blazing down the track so fast her skin must've screamed. She was happiest there.

Owe and I became fixtures around the kennels. We'd help Harry sweep out the cages and dole out kibble. There was a fair amount of turd collection, too—it required a wheelbarrow and a shovel. In return, Dolly and Frag got to run with the others. They're group animals, greyhounds; they do best in a pack.

Sometimes Harry let them rip around the oval. Frag was a scrubber—damn those sidewinder legs. Still, that dog loved to run. Dolly was something else. She had the gift, Harry said. But after seeing her almost self-destruct in that first test against Trixy, I worried a little about racing her seriously—and anyhow, I couldn't legally register as her owner until I was nineteen, since Derby Lane was a wagering circuit.

This was how Ed fell back into our lives, too—fell into Owe's life, specifically. Something kindled between them. I don't know how it began, but by the time I found out, it was blazing hot.

One night I came off the track into the Winning Ticket Lounge. It was empty, but I heard soft noises from the coatroom. I walked over expecting to find the janitor. Instead, Owe and Ed were pawing each other in the gloom. Owe was taller by then; his shoulders jingle-jangled on the empty hangers, a strangely musical sound. His hands cupped Ed's breasts forcefully, pressing her up against the plywood wall. Ed's eyes were closed and her hands were clenched in Owe's hair and her tongue was in his mouth.

A gutshot feeling rocked me as I turned away soundlessly. I'd thought that, if anything, Ed was more suitable for me. Our families still lived on the same block. Our ambitions seemed more in keeping . . . But what the hell did I know of Ed's ambitions? I felt like a creep, catching them. It reminded me of the night we'd spied on Ed in the bath with Tim Railsback.

But I couldn't help thinking: Hadn't Owe already had enough goddamn good luck in his life?

"You're a good kisser," I heard Ed say in a husky voice.

Owe laughed, breathless. "Beginner's luck?"

When they came back outside I saw different things. In Ed I saw something more than simple lust. I got the sense that she had scared herself—as if she wanted to reach for Owe's hand but didn't quite dare.

Owe looked bemused. As if he was thinking: *Hey, that was pretty cool. Wouldn't mind doing that again if I had a chance.*

One day, when Ed left us at the track to go to her job, we followed.

This was almost a year after I'd seen her and Owe in the coatroom. Owe was in the midst of his breakout basketball season. The two of them weren't dating, exactly—I don't know who was keeping who at arm's length, but I suspected it was Ed keeping Owe at bay. Or maybe I just wanted to believe that.

She was working part-time at the Bisk. Ritz line. But she also worked at a bar. She wouldn't tell us which one. So one night Owe and I followed her.

"Why bother?" I'd asked him earlier.

"She thinks we're kids, Dunk. Screw that! I say we go cadge drinks off her."

We followed her in Owe's father's car, a late-model Olds. Ed's Mercury Topaz went down Rickard to Ellesmere, turning left up

Stanley to Lundy's Lane. The night was cool with the smell of creosote and the hum of crickets.

She pulled in at the Sundowner. She wore jeans ripped at the knee and an oversized *Flashdance* sweatshirt. She went in through a black door set into a dingy brick wall.

"Huh" was all Owe said.

The bouncer was a huge black man with a greying goatee. Seeing Owe, he mimed shooting a jump-shot. "You're that boy with the sweet shot, am I right?" He ushered us inside without ID'ing us.

The Sundowner existed in a purplish, glittering perma-twilight. Winking lights ran along the floor like the ones marking the edges of airport runways. The place was packed: well-heeled guys, construction workers, prowling sex tourists, college students nursing pitchers of twenty-dollar draft. An elevated stage swelled into a bulb, where a brass pole shone up to the ceiling. Half-naked women drifted around us like shimmery butterflies. I figured half the world's supply of body glitter was concentrated right there.

We lucked into a stageside table just as two other guys were leaving. There was a pit in the middle of the table where a girl would dance if you paid. A DJ's voice piped up: "Gentlemen, put your hands together for Shah-Shah-Shah-*Shasta!*"

The Scorpions' "Rock You Like a Hurricane" blasted. A woman stepped through the tinsel curtain. She was gorgeous but clearly also drunk or stoned or both. She waggled her ass and stepped out of her bikini bottoms the way kids do: by yanking them down to her ankles and stomping until they came off. She strutted down the catwalk, skidded in her high heels, almost fell, didn't fall, then tossed her hair around like a boat propeller. Her face was blank as a test pattern.

"Yeeeeeah!" someone went.

My mind spun: Ed might be the bartender, right? Or a waitress— and *they* didn't take their clothes off, did they?

A girl sat between us. Cute and thin with boobs that didn't belong on a frame her size, drinking a Corona through a bendy straw. "Wanna dance, sweetheart? Champagne room. Fifty bucks each."

All I had in my wallet was seven dollars. I said, "You're very pretty, but—"

"Stow it," she said. "It was a yes or no question."

She pulled a cigarette out of her purse. It was five inches long and looked like it would take a year to smoke.

"Fucking *hot* in this sonofabitch," she said, lighting it with a platinum Zippo. "I'm from the Sioux. Cooler up there."

"I've heard it's nice."

"It's a shithole. My ex is from the Sioux. He beat a man half to death with a skillet." She batted her eyes, pixie-like. "A *skillet*, dude."

The DJ said: "Gentlemen, put your hands together and welcome to the stage Dah-Dah-Dah-*Disneeeeeeee!*"

Edwina stepped through the tinsel. She knelt and placed her cigarettes and pack of Dentyne on the edge of the stage—would they have been stolen backstage, I wondered through my shock—and strutted down the stage with scissoring steps. The black lights shone on her legs, sleek as cobalt. She didn't even see us. I'd heard what girls do at these places is pick a spot on the wall and focus on that. Who'd want to focus on all that desperate *need* howling up at them?

Owe laughed—a brittle, brutal sound. It stole above the sound of Springsteen's "Hungry Hearts."

Ed's gaze snapped towards us. Her hands flew briefly to her mouth—then she hopped down nimbly, gave our ears vicious twists and marched us out.

"Fucking hell, Ed!" Owe said. "That hurts!"

The crowd catcalled as Ed bulled us through the club and out the front door. "You *bastards!*" she screamed, shoving us into the parking lot.

I saw tears in Owe's eyes but it was hard to tell if they were from his laughter or from Ed's fingers: she'd pinched my ear so hard that a line of blood trickled down my jaw.

"What the fuck, Lou?" she said to the bouncer. "You check ID or just stand there looking pretty?"

Lou held his hands up. "Boss wants numbers, baby. Butts in seats."

She stood in the parking lot in a spangly G-string, a dental-floss bikini and teetery stripper heels. Tourists ambling down the strip stared pop-eyed.

"You little *pricks*. This your idea of fun?" She got right up in Owe's face, chest thrust forward. "This what you came to see?"

Owe gripped Ed's shoulders gently. It struck me as strange how high he loomed over her.

"Listen, I'm sorry. I just . . . you said you were a bartender."

"I told you I worked at a *bar*," she said fiercely. "I didn't lie."

"I'm not saying you . . . I'm not angry, just surprised. You do whatever you want, Ed."

I saw terror leech into Edwina's eyes—she could tell Owe *meant* it. He really didn't care.

"It's a temporary thing." The cups of her eyelids were brimming. I'd never known Ed to cry.

Owe lifted his hands off her shoulders, holding them up like he was being threatened at gunpoint.

"Ed, listen, I don't know why you're getting so upset. I'm sorry we came. That was wrong. I won't do it again."

"I just don't want you to think . . ." She brushed a palm across her eyes, smearing her mascara. "The Bisk . . . layoffs, okay? I was low-est on the totem pole. A girlfriend of mine used to dance here. She said . . . What the fuck?" She hammered a fist into Owe's chest. "Why do I have to explain it? I didn't want you to know because . . ." She threw her hands down her body, a *taa-daa* motion. Her lips were pressed tight, her chin dimpled like a golf ball. "You know? It's nothing. Doesn't mean that I don't . . ."

She looked at me with pleading hopefulness, as if I might know what to say. And I'd have done anything for her if I'd only known what she could possibly need.

"Ed, it's cool," Owe said. "It's *aaall* cool, yeah? Me and Dunk are gonna go now. I'll call you tomorrow."

Her jaw went hard, like she was struggling not to say the word. But she did. "Promise?"

Afterwards Owe drove to Queenston, to a footbridge that arced out over the river. Clouds of midges gathered under the bridge lamps.

"It's not such a big deal," I said.

"Not really," he agreed. "Did it surprise you all that much?"

"Sure it did."

In time he said: "Okay, me too. But . . . did you see that scar on her stomach?"

I'd seen it. A twisting milky thread rising above the hem of her G-string like a cobra from a fakir's basket.

"She had a kid a few years ago," Owe said. "C-section."

"She did? With who?"

"Not my business."

I wondered if Ed had tried to make it his business, share that secret part with him. Maybe he'd told her not to bother. He'd have put it in gentle terms, but still he would've said it.

"She gave it up for adoption. Hasn't seen the baby since."

I said, "Does it matter?"

Owe's blue eyes glittered like the moonlit water along the quay. "Does what matter?"

"That she had a kid. That she gave it up."

"That's her thing. Y'know, I just want what makes her happy. I'm out of here soon," he said. "Scholarship offers pouring in. Once I sit down with Coach and make that choice, I'm gone. A vapour trail. *Hasta la vista*, Cataract City. Ed's smarter than you and me put together, Dunk."

It was true. But even back then I knew that intelligence and hope run on different rails. Ed was a relic of Owe's old life: back when he was Dutchie, not Dutch. He was becoming something else. His body moved with new smoothness, joints lubricated by the magical oil of self-confidence. He was coming into his own while Ed remained what she was: a tough girl from a rough brood whose body moved like pure sex under the black lights.

I reached into my pocket and pulled out a piece of newsprint. I'd unfolded and refolded it so often that the paper was splitting at the edges. I showed Owe the For Sale ad circled in red ink. "Honda CB550 motorcycle," I said. "Hundred K on the odometer, but Hondas run forever. Five hundred bucks."

A smile creased the deeply tanned skin around Owe's eyes. "Where would you go, Dunk?"

"Don't know." *Away* wasn't a place so much as a goal, was it? "It would be nice to *motorvate*, you know? Yesterday is history, tomorrow's a mystery."

I wanted Owe to know there were a million ways out. That I could do it, too. But then I had a sudden vision of myself as I knew I'd be in a few years—a vision of such unflinching truth that my mind settled around it with shocking ease: I was sitting at some local wet-spot, the Four Hearts or The Gate. My legs were kicked out, toes pointing up, and I slumped in my seat, mimicking the way men sat around here—each of us carving his little plot. I wore overalls dusted with flour from the Bisk. My hair was clipped short and was white at the roots. I was drinking a Hed and a shot, smoking counterfeit cigarettes. My wife worked at the Bisk, too. For a holiday we'd rent a room at the Mist-Eye Motel on the other side of the river;

we'd swim in the unnaturally blue pool wearing the irregular bathing suits from the factory outlet centres on Military Road. When the sky was clear we'd be able to see back across the river and catch a glimpse of our own fucking house.

I said: "I'm glad you're going, Owe. Not *glad*-glad, but . . ."

You can't hate your best friend for taking the opportunities he'd been given. That would be the worst sort of hate, wouldn't it? Because it would mean you hate yourself, too.

After that night, I saw less of Owe for a while. It was a familiar drift—we'd done that slow fade out of each other's lives before. The first time, our fathers had instigated it; this time it felt more natural. It's weird how two guys can grow up on the same street and share the same everyday sights, sit in the same classrooms with the same teachers, roam the same woods, like the same girls . . . then one zigs, the other zags, and soon enough they're strangers to each other.

But you have to understand this: Cataract City is possessive. The city has a steel-trap memory, and it holds a grudge.

Nothing that grows here is ever allowed to leave.

On the night that changed Owe's future, Edwina found me in the lunchroom at the Bisk. I was a trainee by then, working on the line with my old man. The two of us were sitting next to the Coke machine, eating the PB-and-banana sandwiches Mom had packed.

"Mr. Diggs," Ed greeted my father.

Dad knew about the Jezebel business but had never held it against Ed. We could tell by her face that something real bad must've happened.

"Dunk, it's Owe. He's in the hospital."

A bite of sandwich stuck in my throat, dry as wormy wood. "What?"

She squeezed her eyes shut. "I don't know . . . my friend's the intake nurse at Niagara Gen. She called to say he's been admitted."

I set a land-speed record driving my dad's pickup to the hospital. Owe was laid out on a bed with his right leg elevated in a contraption whose many braces, straps, pulleys and lacings drove a spike of dread into me. His mom sat beside the bed in her nurse's whites.

"He called out for you," she said to Ed, her eyes dull with shock. "I dropped the dosage. He surfaced for a minute. He called for me, for his dad . . . and for you."

Two bags of fluid hung on a metal pole and drip-drip-dripped down a tube into a needle poked into his arm. Owe's right knee was black and swollen to twice its size: it had a rotten shine to it, like the skin of a fruit that's about to split apart and leak its insides. The kneecap was swivelled so that it now sat under his leg like a giant tumour.

He'll never play basketball on that knee again was my first thought. My second was: *Never walk properly, either.*

Ed cupped Owe's face. His eyelids fluttered.

"Whoa, Nelly," he said with a loopy smile. "I got a doozy of a lump, huh?"

"What happened?" I said.

His endless smile terrified me. "I was coming out of the A.N. Myer gym—playing some pickup, right? Walking down O'Neil to the bus stop, dribbling my ball . . . This car or truck or I don't know what . . ."

He swallowed. His throat made a dry *click*. Edwina gave him water to sip through a straw.

". . . this car skipped the curb and *whap!*" Owe clapped his hands with sudden violence. The sound ricocheted off the eggshell walls. "Then *whoosh*. Guess they drove off. I heard . . . laughing? *Laughing*, man."

He licked his lips and stared at the wreckage of his leg. His worry seemed mild at best; whatever was dripping into his veins spared him the full extent of the horror.

Ed took his hand. "It'll be—"

Owe snatched his hand back with casual brutality. "Gonna need a cane, man!" he said in a druggy singsong. "Gonna need a solid gold *caaaane* to get me down the street!"

By the time he passed out again I was already moving out the door.

I'd kill them.

A curtain of blood had dropped over my vision. It was all I could see, all I could smell.

I drove. Edwina sat in the passenger seat. At first I'd told her not to come but she refused to listen. Fair enough. She deserved blood as much as I did.

She said, "You know who did it?"

"I have an idea."

"You know *why?*"

"No good reason."

"Drive faster."

"You gonna pay the fucking ticket, Ed?"

I knew where they drank: the Gunnery, a dive on Dorchester. I knew because everyone knew where everyone else did their drinking in this city. You pick your watering hole and cling to it the rest of your life like a drowning rat to a bit of Styrofoam bobbing in the sewer.

I doused the headlights as I turned into the lot and parked next to Adam Lowery's shitbox Tercel. The thing shone like fresh blood in the moonlight, drops of water drying on its hood. He'd probably gone to the Coin-Op carwash on Philbrook and given it a good scrub. The front bumper was crushed on the passenger's side. I pictured Lowery flipping on the high beams at the last instant, pinning Owe in the glare.

The Gunnery hosted some rough customers. The Murphy boys bent their elbows there. The chimes above the door tinkled as I stepped through, Ed right behind me. Her brothers gave her confused smiles from their corner table. Beer-warped floorboards creaked under my feet. The Rock-Ola jukebox was playing a Smiths tune.

Clyde Hillicker turned on his stool, squaring his shoulders. The curtain of blood darkened until I could see only his outline like a charcoal etching on the sidewalk.

I cut fast across the distance between us. Clyde threw a punch that caught me on the neck with a flat *smack* like a double-cut pork chop slapped on a marble slab. I stepped through it and lowered my head, bringing my right hand up from below my belt.

I won't claim it was a thing of charm or grace. It was a mean punch, a pure *ugly* one, and I summoned it from the blackest depths of my soul.

It clocked Clyde on the chin. He fell and his skull hit the rail with a sweaty *thud* as my momentum carried me over his sagging body into the bar. Nobody offered to pick him up.

Ed slit her eyes at her brothers and mouthed, *Where?*

Her eldest brother hooked his thumb at the toilets, smiling out the side of his mouth. Ed grabbed a pool cue from the rack and crept to the men's door.

"Any of you see Adam Lowery," I said loud enough so he'd hear, "tell him we have issues to discuss."

I booted the bar door open but stayed inside the bar. The chimes tinkled as the door closed.

Adam Lowery cracked the bathroom door a titch and poked his head out. Ed swung the cue into his face. It landed flush, shattering his nose. Adam squawked; his hands flew up as he fell back through the door. The Murphy brothers laughed.

Ed followed Adam into the bathroom, hitting him with the cue as the door swung back and forth on its bat-wing hinges. Adam was on the floor with his hands up to ward off the blows, but then his hands fell and the cue broke and she went to work with her feet. The door stopped swinging. Ed didn't step out for a while. Adam was lucky Ed was wearing flip-flops.

She came out breathing heavily. Her brothers offered a round of applause as if she'd finally fulfilled her familial obligations.

We drove away fast. I still couldn't cope with the idea that Owe's dreams were toast. And over what? A stupid blood-grievance nurtured since childhood—the sort that festered all over this city—acted upon in a moment of opportunity. We were *snakes*. A knot of venomous rattlesnakes balled up under a rock. If one of us made a break for daylight the ball constricted, every one of us tightening, pulling that rogue snake back in.

"He could rehab it," Ed said.

"Sure he could," I said. "Sure."

The knuckles of my right hand were split: the skin had opened in crude Xs like the tips of dumdum bullets. The fight hadn't solved a goddamn thing. It hadn't even felt good. Clyde would suck his dinner through a straw for a week or two. Adam might need a transfusion but then he'd be fine.

Those facts didn't un-fuck Owe's ruined prospects one bit.

Clyde Hillicker earned a five-year hitch at the Kingston Pen for the hit-and-run, the maximum punishment under the law. Apparently he'd been behind the wheel—although it wouldn't surprise me to hear Adam convinced him to take the rap. Adam was dumb but cunning. Clyde was just dumb.

Adam spent nearly a month laid up. His nose is still so flat that his nostrils run horizontal to his face. They look like coin slots.

Owe never played basketball again. Not at the level he had, anyway. His knee healed as best it could but after six or seven surgeries, the steel pins and bone-screws, his joint had to be fused. The docs outfitted him with a bulky brace.

After a too-short rehab Owe tried to make a comeback. But in basketball, you really need to be that half-step ahead. Owe still had the IQ and that sweet jumper, but he'd lost the speed to make defenders fear him. They stuck tight to his jersey, suffocating him. He got victimized on the defensive end by speedier guards.

The college offers were revoked. He ended up signing a ten-day look-see contract with Lotto Delmonte, a Mexican team run by the banana kingpins. They thought he might have something left in the tank. He didn't. They cut him loose. He spent a few months drifting and drinking around Marina del Ray. Word spread that Dutch Stuckey, Basketball Boy Wonder, was a bust. Beneath the sadness and resignation, lurking like a foul pocket of mud in a riverbed, was relief. Owe's failure re-established the status quo in Cataract City.

When he returned from his wandering, Owe threw a prolonged party at Sherkston Shores, a trailer park bordering Lake Erie. He rented the largest trailer on his folks' dime and invited everyone to stay.

His body was deeply tanned, his eyes a washed-out Windex blue. He reminded me of a scarecrow that had hung too long in a desolate field. The only creature who didn't seem to notice the change was Fragrant Meat; he was also the only creature capable of bringing a real smile to Owe's face.

During the day, Owe drank vodka and soda, a habit he'd picked up down south. He sat on the beach, staring out over the slate-grey water and sky welded together without a joint, piling warm sand over his knee. "It's Ayurvedic medicine," he'd say cryptically. "The Swami Vishnu gave me the *secret*."

At night he'd switch the soda for Jolt Cola and become beet-faced and weird. We'd stoke big bonfires, driftwood piled in a rickety heap. Owe doused it in kerosene and lit it, shrieking giddily as the fire ate the bleached sticks.

"Remember?" he said to me one night over the flames, his grin a grim rictus. "In the woods? What we'd have done for a fire like this, huh? *Hah!*"

He acted as if the last few months of his life, everything post-injury, had never happened. He'd brought a bunch of stuff to the trailer with the intent of giving it away: old jerseys, a laminated four-leaf clover, photos he'd snapped during a camping trip in Banff. "I brought this just for you," he'd say, pressing something into someone's hands as if the item had specific meaning to its recipient. But I'd watched him try to give the same things to different people.

His buddies from Ridley showed up, guys with names like Thad and Chad and Bradley-not-Brad, girls with names like Pris and Elle whose tennis skirts danced around their thighs. They drove ragtop Beemers, drank Bartles & Jaymes wine coolers and smoked skunky dope. They came, stayed awhile, filled themselves with the unshakable sense that something was deeply the matter with Owe and left. Owe waved from the beach as they drove off, his hand floating above his head, loose as a balloon on a string.

I kept visiting, though, and Ed was there the whole time. She'd been rehired at the Bisk; she used up all her vacation days to be with him.

But Owe wasn't *there* in the truest sense. During the day, his eyes would dart along the sand as if he were tracking a sand crab or a shred of litter. But there was no crab, no litter. At night, he'd flinch as if sparks from the fire were popping in front of his face. I'd stay up in the trailer, listening for his voice. Sometimes I'd hear him: a low acid chuckle rising from the beachhead, lapping over and over with the waves.

Ed tried to rouse him. But it was like trying to transport sand with a sieve. When he was happy it was with a manic-sick happiness; his smile sat on his face like a Halloween mask, twitchy-dark things beneath. When he was sad, the melancholy seemed bottomless and incurable. He was never just Owe, the Owe we knew.

At night Ed stumbled into the trailer and fell asleep alone in the woodsmoke-smelling darkness. I wanted to go to her, comfort her in whatever way I could. But I didn't. *Couldn't.*

One night we sat together on the beach. Owe had been drinking all day and was zonked in the trailer.

"He'll get back to himself," Ed said, as if she had the power to make it happen.

I said, "He won't stay this way forever."

"You're solid, Dunk." She peered at me in the glowing remains of the bonfire. "You know? You're not too high, not too low. You're solid . . . safe."

"I don't know how safe I am."

"Oh, very safe. Trust me."

"Well, I don't plan on being here my whole life."

Her eyebrows took on a troubled slant. "What's so wrong with right here?"

I couldn't frame an answer. There was the moon casting its glow on the water, breeze curling off the shore. There were Edwina's legs stretched out, toes smoothing the warm sand at the fire's edge.

"Nothing, I guess," I conceded. "It's pretty . . . perfect."

She laughed. I loved the sound rolling alongside the lake, easing softly into the other night sounds. I thought how I could listen to it for the rest of my life. Dolly trotted over and stretched out between us.

I was just nineteen, but nineteen wasn't young in Cataract City. I knew that a moment comes when you've got to make your best hand and stand pat. I'd always felt Ed and me were the right fit— but did that doom her in some weird way?

I also knew that she might never love me the way she loved Owe. And Owe was my very best friend. He was sick and he needed me.

But I loved Ed, and sometimes love makes you helpless.

I held my hand out. If Edwina hadn't put her hand in mine I wouldn't have blamed her one bit. I wouldn't have chased it any further.

But she did, y'know? She put her hand in mine.

We told Owe in Lions Club Park. He was wearing a pair of grey sweats with a Dijon stain on the left knee. His cheeks were furred with stubble. He watched us approach from the bleachers with his head cocked, as if he'd read our intentions on the breeze.

"Hail, hail, the gang's all here."

A T-ball game was in progress, and our walk towards Owe was punctuated by the metallic *tink* of an aluminum bat striking a stationary ball. The stands were packed with parents who seemed a little *too* keen, as if they expected their five-year-old to launch a moonshot over the outfield fence. The day was warm and sunny, and kids were buying Ghost-cicles and Rocket Pops from a Dickie Dee man.

When Ed told him the news, Owe's face set in a leering grin.

"You figured you'd tell me out in public so I wouldn't make a scene?" he seethed. "I don't give a *fuck* what any of these assholes hear!"

Ed and I stood there; in Owe's eyes we must've been Hester Prynne and Benedict Arnold. He jerked himself up, ignoring the hissing scolds of the parents—the game had come to a standstill, kids staring gape-jawed at the sloppily dressed guy who'd been the city's saviour scant months ago—as he gimped down the stairs, giving it the full Quasimodo treatment so we'd feel like even bigger heels.

"You're a bum, Dutch!" an enormous woman catcalled, her butt spreading across the risers like dough. "You got no heart. You never did!"

Others in the crowd voiced their approval. These were the same people who'd cheered Owe wildly not long ago. They'd loved him and now they hated him—and they *loved* hating him.

Ed went after Owe. He shrugged her off viciously, knocking her down. She sat on the clipped grass watching him hump away.

"Jesus," she said. "*Not* how I pictured it happening."

That was all we heard of Owen until a letter arrived.

Dear skunks:

Enjoy each other. Trash attracts trash, right? I leave you to your trailer-park lives. I hope you pop out a brood of revolting, zero-IQ blobs, as nature surely intended. You have my blessings!

Yours most sincerely,

Owen Jeremy Stuckey

Now that pissed *me* off. When I hammered on the door of Owe's house late the next afternoon, Mr. Stuckey answered, same as he'd done years ago when I showed up with two baby greys in my backpack.

"Come in, Dunk."

I went inside with Dolly. A half-hour later Owe dragged his ass out of the basement. Eyes bloodshot, jowls furred with a scraggly beard, but skin so milky I figured he hadn't seen daylight for a week. Frag padded obediently at his side.

"What do you want, man?" He sounded exhausted.

"Let's go walk the mutts."

He stared blankly. "Okay."

It took him nearly an hour to get dressed, and even then the attempt was half-assed. One white sock, one black. It'd do.

Thanks, Duncan, Mr. Stuckey mouthed as we left.

Owe walked with a cane. He'd chosen it himself—a giant gnarled stick like a wizard's staff with a grey rubber stopper on the end. It accentuated his disability, which I'm sure was his aim.

Dolly and Frag nipped playfully at each other; they hadn't roughhoused together in a long time. Owe shuffled along, cane going *phunk* on the sidewalk. He stank. I told him so.

"Ran out of deodorant, man."

"You can never technically run out of deodorant so long as you're committed to the idea of, y'know, buying more of it."

Owe gave me a wry smile. "That was a very scholarly bit of ball-busting."

"Not bad for a zero-IQ blob, huh?"

The knee brace made him look like a cybernetic monstrosity cobbled together in a secret government lab.

"You really need that thing, Owe?"

"Eh. It's a pain to take off."

"You were never *that* fast on the court, anyway."

"Is this some kind of radical therapy, you prick?" He shook his head, smiling. "But yeah, no, I never was that fast. I was never even"—he lowered his voice mock-conspiratorially—"that *good*. Good for Cataract City. Good even for some Div One programs. But *good*-good? NBA good? Nah. Not even Euroleague good. Too slow, too short, no hops."

"Ah, come on. I wasn't trying to say—"

He held a hand up to shush me. "You asked, didn't you? There was one skills camp down in Indiana. I was matched against this redheaded point guard. Skinny enough that he might slip down the drain in the shower. The first few plays I victimized him. Easy layups and long threes. But then this guy started timing me, figuring out my moves and getting a hand in my face. I wasn't air-balling shots but I was missing consistently. Meanwhile he's playing steady dee, hitting his open j's and dishing to his slashing power forward. A slow, steady demolition. Out-hustling me, outsmarting me—and that's what *I* did, Dunk, to all the athletic guards with their pogo-stick legs. That guy got a scholarship at Wake Forest. Div One, yeah, but not Duke, not Kentucky. If he's lucky he'll play a few years in Europe. And he *killed me.*"

We watched Frag and Dolly, not speaking. The day had darkened into evening. Stars salted the sky.

"You know what I miss?" he said. "I never thought I'd say it, but I miss the zone. I used to hate it, you know? I couldn't breathe . . . or I could breathe *too much.* But that feeling of the outside world and everything in it collapsing into a perfect point, everything within that point coming so fucking *easy* . . . I miss that."

After a stretch of silence he said, "I didn't mean what I said to Edwina."

"Owe, listen . . . I love her. Have for a while."

He nodded. "I could tell. And before, I would've been happy to let you have her. You're the better fit, you two. Plus I figured I'd be dating sorority chicks. But all this happened and I . . . I freaked. Everything narrowed. I grabbed at what was there."

"So what now? I love the hermit look you've got going on, real corpselike and greasy, but that can't go on forever."

He smiled distantly. "I heard what you did to Lowery and Hillicker."

"I don't know what you're talking about."

"Of course not. You do them both?"

"Whoever did *that* probably had help."

His smile widened. "You don't want to fuck around with Miss Edwina Murphy."

"No, you do *not*."

"Hey," he said after we'd walked half a block in companionable silence, "there's a police services course at Sir Sandford Fleming College."

I laughed. "You? Johnny Law?"

"It'd be a big change. But after what happened . . . righting wrongs isn't the worst job on earth, is it?"

My life remained in Cataract City. It was a small, contained existence—the kind I preferred. Edwina and Dolly and me: a closed circle I was wholly content to stay within. But this city being what it is, me being who I am, things were bound to go sideways.

It started with Dolly. I had raced her four times since I'd turned nineteen, the age that I legally qualified to be her trainer. That was also the year I'd started to date Ed seriously, and the year Owe went off to college. You take the good with the bad.

For years I'd brought Dolly to the track just to hang out. She enjoyed running with the pack, and Owe and I liked spending time with Harry Riggins. But as she got older and came into her body, Dolly began to consistently outrun the pack on the practice loop— even the pure-bloodline dogs.

"You should race her," Harry said one afternoon. "You're old enough, Dolly's old enough."

"Ah, I don't know. She's just a house dog, really."

"She doesn't run like a house dog, son. What's the harm?"

She first ran in the D-Level sweeps, the lowest on offer at Derby Lane racetrack. The Winning Ticket Lounge showcased its usual sad collection of rum-soaked schemers that day—women with bleached high hair, and nickel-betters with their trousers pulled past their bellybuttons.

"I've probably contracted lung cancer just looking at them," Edwina remarked, nodding at the divot-cheeked smokers under a pall of bluish smoke.

We'd met Harry earlier, in the corral. He'd filled out Dolly's Bertillon card: her length from haunch to brisket, weight and bloodlines (Ed wrote: *unknown*). And we'd given her a proper racing name: Dolly Express. It was Harry's idea: a takeoff on the Daily Express, the VIA Rail line that once connected Niagara Falls to Hamilton.

Harry had snugged a racing jersey around Dolly's legs. "Needs to be tight," he'd said, "otherwise she might get a leg trapped under the straps in full flight—at that speed a dog will snap a leg just as easy as you'd snap a stick of spaghetti."

The racers were led onto the grassy infield by the Niagara Falls chapter of the Young Jaycees, giving bettors the chance to eye the dog flesh. The tote board flashed betting lines—Dolly had gone off at 12–1; she looked stringy and bandy legged compared to her competition.

We herded Dolly into her trap. She'd been slotted in number 3. Along with traps 2 and 4, they're known as coffin boxes: the dogs in these traps are hemmed in by the rail-runners and wide-runners, meaning they can't open up down the stretch.

The traps flew open as the mechanical hare zipped down the rail. Four greyhounds went pounding down the track like the hammers of hell.

Dolly remained in her trap. One second ticked by. Another. The other dogs were already twenty yards gone and accelerating fast.

Come on, girl, I thought. *One foot in front of the other . . .*

An explosion of fur and flesh blasted out of the trap. Dolly launched herself wide, banking round the high side of the track. I remember a whistling inhale—the sound of breath caught in a hundred throats—as hardened railbirds and casual dog fanciers alike leaned forward in their seats.

Dolly went wide on the first bend. There was something gyroscopic in the way she ran the track: banking high around the turn only to arrow in on the straightaway. She covered more ground than she needed to, but she'd also ramp up to a faster max speed. Maybe that's why she'd waited in the traps: she wanted to avoid the jostling of the pack so she could blow by on the homestretch.

She caught up with ninety yards to go and slingshotted past the pack, winning by four lengths. Her breakneck running style, late dash from the traps and wonky manoeuvring had the crowd buzzing.

Hell, *I* was buzzing. I turned to Ed in the Winning Ticket Lounge and said, "Will you move in with me?"

I lived on my own by then, in a teensy apartment overlooking the Fairview Cemetery. It was barely big enough for me and Dolly, but I had a steady job at the Bisk—the Fig Newtons line—and nursed a hope for something bigger.

Ed threw her head back and laughed—a tinkling sound like glass wind chimes in a high breeze. "Dunk, you live in a shoebox with a view of the boneyard. If we're going to do this, you're moving in with *me*."

I told my landlord the very next day; he was happy to see the back end of the high-strung dog that left scratch-marks on the linoleum. I loaded my few possessions into Bovine's hearse and drove to the house Edwina rented on Culp Street—which happened to overlook a boarded-up middle school. It wasn't much better than overlooking a graveyard, but I kept this opinion to myself.

Dolly was elevated to B-Class for her second race soon after that—and the tote board listed her at 2–1 odds. She won. Then she won two more races in that class. And that's when she was deemed ready for A-Class.

A few days later, Ed and I watched as Dolly smoked her A-Class debut over Silent Cruise, who had been tabbed as a world-beater. Afterwards an old gaffer sauntered up to me and in a deep Irish brogue asked, "Is that great galloping bitch for sale?"

He had associations back in Tipperary, he claimed, and was an informal scout for punters at the famous Thules dog track. "She may not always win," he said of Dolly, "but Lo', she puts on a rollicking show. The yobbos back home would love 'er."

He hadn't been surprised to hear Dolly wasn't for sale.

"You're smart to hold on to a bitch like thaa. A gold mine on four legs!"

How much longer would I let her race? The way she ran made it a huge risk every time the traps sprung. I couldn't live with myself if she got hurt. I'd have stopped if not for the fact that Dolly seemed happiest in full flight.

By the time we got home that evening, the heat had set in. There were rolling blackouts across the city and our A/C was on the fritz. Edwina was edgy. We lay on the sofa reading by the light of tea candles. Her legs thrummed across my thighs. She screwed a knuckle into my ribs and play-slapped me.

"What's up with you tonight?"

"Just feeling silly."

The sticky warmth lay thick inside the walls. We had been sweating just to breathe. She stood up, pulling me into the bedroom. It may simply have been a way to break the heat inside of her, the same way a good thunderstorm will break a heat wave.

She undressed in the moonlight falling through the window. Her body seemed carved out of that moonlight—a part of it, and distant in the same way. Before Ed, I'd had no experience with women. Sure, I'd kissed Becky Longpre on the Lions Club baseball bleachers, got my hand up her shirt before she protested about being a good Baptist girl, but that was it. My breath always quickened with Ed. My heart beat so fast I felt it over every inch of my body.

It was always a struggle to control myself, but Ed sensed that. She'd brace her hands on my shoulders and ease the shakes out of me, eyes telling me to take it slow. I only had to listen to her and obey.

I wondered what she was thinking in those moments. Part of her, maybe the deepest part, was locked off—even then, when we were that close. I figured a woman can't be understood the way a man can. Women have purposes men can't even imagine.

And then I felt that sweetness coming up from the balls of my feet. It wasn't just the physical part; it was the body-closeness I would come to crave. But it's never enough, is it? Two people can't share the same heart, can they?

Afterwards she let out a jittery breath. "That was nice. You always try real hard, Dunk. A girl appreciates that."

A girl appreciates that. It was as if she was giving me advice for down the line, when I'd find myself in bed with someone else.

Early the next morning I'd awoken for no reason I could name. Dolly's head was perched on the edge of the bed, inches from my face. The weight of her skull spread her dewlap across the mattress. Had I been talking in my sleep? Had I called out to Dolly?

She snuffled softly and licked my cheek. Her tongue smelled of shaved iron. It wasn't her style; Dolly was a standoffish creature.

Maybe something about the stillness of night had rewired the circuits in her brain, drawing her to me? I lay motionless, not wanting to break the spell.

Three weeks after Dolly's A-Class win, a murmur passed through the Winning Ticket as Ed and I entered. The punters had pegged me as the owner of the mutt with the million-dollar legs. Ed slapped me on the shoulder and whispered in my ear: "You're basking in the reflected glory of a dog. Drink it up, big shot."

A weedy fellow in boater shoes and a brushed velvet coat wormed out of the crowd.

"The number four bitch in tonight's final heat—yours, yeah? Is she well?" he asked. "Not got the shits, I hope? Should I put a ten-spot on her to be first on the bunny, first over the line?"

Other dogmen pressed in, twisting their racing forms in white-knuckled fists, waiting for my reply.

"She's not shitting any differently than usual, if that helps."

They peeled away like buzzards from a clean-picked carcass, grumbling as they drifted over to the betting wickets.

Harry waited for us in the kennels with Dolly. "This is the big time," he said. "Open Class welcomes dogs from all over. The purse is decent enough that you'll get dogmen coming up from New York and as far east as Maine. Your girl better not make her customary late dash—these dogs'll be too quick for that."

"Do you know any of the other dogs?" Edwina asked.

"Not so much the dogs as owners. Teddy Simms from Cheektowaga's got one in trap two, a bitch named Hurricane Jessie. Simms works with some *fast* bloodlines. Lemuel Drinkwater's here, too. He breeds over at the Tuscarora Nation outside Buffalo. A real bottom-liner, is Lemmy—loves a winner, no use for a loser. A couple years back he got DQ'd for the season. The vet was giving one of his winners the usual post-race once-over and wouldn't you know it if a jalapeño pepper didn't slide out of the poor dog's ass."

Harry took in our shocked expressions.

"Old dogman's dirty trick. Slit a hot pepper with a razor blade, get those juices leaking out, stick it up your dog's fanny. You better believe it'll get him hopping."

"Why is he still allowed to race?" I said.

"You take a look around this place? Not exactly a hive of morality, son."

We sat in the stands for the prelims. The spotlights beat down on the red dirt of the track. Midges and no-see-ums rose from under the risers, dancing in the gathering dark. The tote board chittered as the odds rose and fell.

Railbirds clustered along the finishing stretch with tickets clutched in their sweaty fists, pounding the spectators' rail as the dogs thundered down the final leg of each race. Afterwards the winners crowed—"I knew that boy was a mucker!" or "What a stayer, just like I told you!"—as the losers tossed their stubs on the blacktop alongside cigarette butts and crumpled beer cans.

Before Dolly's heat I went down to the lockout kennel where the dogs were housed before each race. Harry stood with a tall man in his early thirties. The man wore pegged blue jeans and a jean jacket, his red-brown face shadowed by the brim of an Australian outbacker hat; fake crocodile teeth were strung around the brim like bullets in a bandolier. He reminded me of Billy Jack, the star of those seventies action flicks, except he didn't have that actor's face.

"Duncan," Harry said, "meet Lemuel Drinkwater."

We shook. Drinkwater's hand was dry and chilly; it was like gripping cold muscle. He smiled but there was no kindness in it, no heat or nastiness either: he had a perfectly blank expression, reflecting nothing.

"We were jawing about your dog." Drinkwater pronounced it *darg*. "How'd you train her to run that way, wide all the time?"

"I didn't do anything. Just how she runs."

He nodded the way a man does when he doesn't believe you. But some men figure everyone's lying to them all the time.

"She's a quick dog," Harry said. "Whoever chucked her in the garbage as a pup must be kicking themselves."

Drinkwater shrugged. "Garbage is the best place for some of them."

Harry pursed his lips like he wanted to say something but wouldn't.

"Guess I got lucky, then," I said.

"You know what they say," Drinkwater said breezily. "Even the blind squirrel finds a nut." He swaggered off, cowboy boots pink-a-pinking on the cement floor.

"What a dick."

"He's got his qualities," Harry said diplomatically.

Harry handed Dolly over to the lead-outs and we headed to the traps.

"That's Hurricane Jessie, Teddy Simms' girl." Harry pointed to a muscular greyhound with Dalmatian markings on her coat. "And that's Drinkwater's entry, War Hammer."

War Hammer was jet black with a frost of white hair fringing her muzzle. Her ears were pinned flat to her skull and she had the mincing gait of a boxer during his ring walk. She moved like a creature that wanted to outrun its own skin.

Dolly drew trap number 4. Hurricane Jessie was in number 5, the outermost. War Hammer would run the rail from the 1 spot, with Primco Posy and Tilda's Vinton filling out the other traps.

The mechanical hare zipped down the electrified rail. The traps sprung open, unleashing a fury of muscle and bone. At first it was difficult to separate one dog from an other: they were nothing but a mad blur of limbs like smears of paint on a canvas.

The crowd rose to a quick roar as the hounds hit the front stretch. War Hammer led with Primco Posy running outside her heels, boxed in on the outside by Tilda's Vinton. Hurricane Jessie had established her spot on the far right. Dolly was in last place, a yard or so behind Tilda's Vinton.

She was running higher than usual; she couldn't find room to open up. Hurricane Jessie had the long body to make a wide break difficult, plus Dolly would sacrifice too much distance against War Hammer on an outside pass attempt.

She rolled her shoulders and ducked in at Tilda's Vinton, trying to squeeze past. The dog met her charge nimbly: Dolly's head snapped off Tilda's haunch, killing her pass attempt.

The dogs hit the turn. War Hammer rode the rail so close you'd think she was zippered to it; her positioning ensured she kept her lead over Primco Posy, who ate a faceful of dirt. Hurricane Jessie eased into her turn, running smartly but dropping her speed. Suddenly an opening presented itself.

Dolly shot the gap between Hurricane Jessie and Tilda's Vinton. She gunned up the high side of the track, finding open space. She angled her shoulder to the bend, banking like a fighter plane on a make-or-break manoeuvre and battling every inch of the way.

I hopped on the rail hoping for a better view but all I could make out was the dogs' cresting shoulders. I stared into the stands at Ed, trying to gauge the race from her face. Her fists were clenched, her mouth open in a frantic O.

The bunny rocketed down the homestretch. The lead dog was War Hammer. Next came Dolly, wide on the outside, fully into her stride.

Then a funny thing happened: War Hammer went low. Not as

low as Dolly, but her body flattened and became streamlined like a street racer tapping the nitrous oxide for the final kick. But Dolly was just naturally faster, plus she'd done her work early in the race—she was running flat out.

Dolly and War Hammer hurtled down the last fifty yards. Their strides were so long that they covered seven, eight yards at a go. Dolly's head was down, eyes fixed on the finish line. She was the most beautiful thing I'd ever seen.

They crossed the line at a dead heat. The results went out over the loudspeakers: Dolly had won by a quarter of a second—razor-close, even by dog-racing standards. A small cheer went up from the stands.

Harry shook my hand like I'd had something to do with it. "A magical dog," he said. "Merlin on four legs!"

Drinkwater collected War Hammer. He smacked her ass hard enough to rattle the poor thing's bones, and shot me a challenging look—*What, you're going to do something about it?* He said, "Talk about your bullshit luck."

I should have resisted, but I couldn't. "Winners win and losers go home."

"This one's won plenty," Drinkwater told me, stroking War Hammer's skull so hard that the skin peeled back from her bulging eyes. "Why else would I keep her around? She's beaten far better than your jumped-up sidewinding bitch."

"I guess we'll never know."

"Guess we could," Drinkwater said. "I'll put her up against your slippery little greaser any time. Do it right here, after hours. Harry can set it up, can't you, Hare?"

"I'm not getting involved," Harry said.

"You already are," said Drinkwater. "Let's put some money on it, why not?"

My gaze drifted into the stands, where Ed watched Dolly take her victory lap. In a two-dog race Dolly could go wide and blow the doors off Drinkwater's mutt.

It was a foolish bet. But there was a need in me that ran deep. I couldn't finger the root of that need, but it ripped at the dearest parts of me with phantom teeth. It had something to do with the rumble of the Falls inside my Cataract City bones; something to do with the fingernail of rust on the wheel well of my pickup and how the sight of it chewing into the paint brought an invisible weight crashing down on me.

Drinkwater named a bet. Twenty thousand. My heart rate spiked.

"Sounds fine," I said, calm on the outside.

"I don't take food stamps."

"And I don't take loose cigarettes."

Drinkwater said, "Shake on it?"

I offered my hand. Drinkwater reached into his mouth, took out the wad of gum he'd been chewing and stuck it in my open palm.

I almost punched him. But I'd seen the bone-handled knife sticking out of his boot and Drinkwater struck me as a guy who'd know how to use it.

The days leading up to the race passed strangely. Not in a dream, exactly, although I did feel disconnected from the fabric of the world. The only constant was the zing of electricity in my blood.

I worked nights at the Bisk. Heat filled my arms on the line, and an odd feeling echoed through my jawbone on those nights—not panic, because there was no immediate danger; more like a taste of faraway lightning under the tongue. After work I'd drive through the early-morning fog, listening to the Falls, that sound in the background of my entire life. I tried to imagine myself someplace absent of that sound and could not: it followed me like a lost dog.

Edwina knew about the race but not the size of the wager. Twenty thousand dollars; where would I find that?

"I'm in," Owe said when I floated the idea. We met on a weekend when he'd come down from college. He looked good: healthy, with muscle back on his bones. He walked with a cane but at least it *was* a cane; the wizard staff was gone.

I said, "Just like that?"

He shrugged. "Sure, why not? Dolly's a killer, right?"

"It's not a sure thing."

"You trying to talk me out of this?" He laughed. "You've made your sale. I'll bet the last of what that Mexican banana impresario gave me for, y'know, stripping me of my athletic dignity and so forth."

A part of me had hoped he'd say: *Dunk, it's a stupid idea, put it out of your mind.* Still, it was great to see the old Owe back. Maybe the wounds between us had healed for good.

Meanwhile, I spent a lot of time at Derby Lane with Harry, who kept Dolly loose on the practice loop.

"Things can happen," he said. "A dog can pull up lame, cramp up or spring a hole in their bucket when the traps open."

We watched Dolly sprint down the rail in pursuit of the bunny, which zipped to the end of the circuit and stopped. She raced past, breaking into a run that carried her around the bend.

"Scientists say that in fifty years or so, Olympic records will quit being broken," Harry said. "Humans will have hit our limits. Only so fast a man can run, right? That's what these eggheads figure. But when I see a greyhound run, I think one day a greyhound's going to fly. One day a greyhound's going to find a nice flat stretch and break into a full-out *scream*. It'll be like a plane taking off. Higher and higher till it's just a speck in the sky."

Harry grinned, enjoying the possibility. "It could happen, gravity notwithstanding. Why? Because a racing dog doesn't know it's *not supposed* to fly. And if I own the dog that finally does it I'll holler, *Go on, you crazy bastard! Send me a postcard from China!*"

Dolly blazed around the near bend, gobbling up great bites of the track. Harry said, "You've got to be mindful, though, seeing as any creature who fails to accept its limits can be a danger to itself."

We led Dolly to the wash station. Harry hosed dirt off her paws, massaging her pads to release the grit. Dolly rested her chin on his skull, looking like a boxer receiving a rubdown from his trainer.

"Guess it's too late to tell you that Drinkwater's a nasty piece of work," Harry said. "Rumour is he once fed a fistful of Mars Bars to a greyhound his own dog was set to race. It got real sick, chocolate being the worst thing for a dog, and ended up dying on the track. Other awfulness, too."

"Like what?"

"He runs that shop on the Tuscarora Nation, Smokin' Joes. Cheap cigs, booze, that sort of thing. Makes a small mint. But he loves his dogs, or loves what they earn him. Not just racing dogs, either. He breeds fighters. Pit bulls. Fights them in the warehouses out behind his shop, though I'd never watch such a thing. And it's not only dogs who do the fighting. Word is, men fight there. But you've got to be one desperate soul to tussle for Lemmy Drinkwater."

"So you figure he'll welsh?" My half of the wager was mostly drawn from the college fund my folks had set up. They'd put away a little nut out of every paycheque for years. They'd let me know that if I said to hell with it and went to work at the Bisk, that was okay, but they wanted me to have the chance.

Harry shook his head. "Lemmy'll square your bet if he loses, but I wouldn't put it past him to stack things in his favour. All I'd say is, don't risk anything you're not willing to part with."

———

The day before the race we almost lost Dolly.

Edwina and I took her for a late-evening walk on a path running parallel to the canal. Dolly's retractable leash snarled around a rusted metal pole, raking a sharp spur. The leash sliced in half clean as a thread drawn across a razor blade.

The severed end of the leash whipped back into its holster. Dolly looked at us, head cocked at a quizzical angle. When Ed called her name—"*Do-lleee*"—it sounded like a moan. Dolly bolted. Her rear leg kicked over a hummock in a crazy flailing motion of pure joy.

We sprinted after her. There was nothing but brush and long grass for two miles until you hit the canal. My feet flashed over sedge and crabgrass as the clouds thickened and night came down. To the north the skyway bridge bent against the sky, pale sunlight winking off its spine. I splashed through puddles shimmering with gasoline rainbows—the land had once been a dumpsite and old poisons were still bubbling up.

I became aware of all the little noises around and inside of me: blood rushing in my ears like a buried river, the hot thrum of crickets in the grass, the ongoing *cree-cree-cree* of starlings and somewhere, far away, a barking dog—but not Dolly.

Edwina and I split up. She went in the direction of the bridge, I went south towards the subdivisions edging Queen Street. My limbs had loosened and I ran in an easy rhythm, making small adjustments, relaxing my shoulders and swinging my head side to side to scan for encouraging signs.

I was ninety-nine percent positive I'd find her; then ninety-eight percent. Soon a persistent doubt burrowed under my skin like a chigger. I knew there are holes buried in the fabric of every ordinary day that can swallow you up. My feet flashed over the darkening earth as I hunted, finding nothing but coils of rusted metal and the shattered bottoms of old soda bottles that shone from the ground like huge glass eyes. Blisters burst on my heels, shooting waves of coin-bright pain up the backs of my calves. I was nearly hyperventilating, but this had nothing to do with exhaustion. Part of my concern was generalized: Dolly was a dumb dog and she was lost and probably didn't know it yet. And part of my fear was particular: Dolly was more than just a dog. Dolly had become *our* dog, a special dog.

Water ran darkly down a narrow streambed. The light of a fresh moon winked where it rippled around the rocks. I strained my ears, hoping a telling sound might separate itself from the mad-dening noises of nature. When none did I picked a clumsy path across the stream. My shoes slipped on a wet rock and I plunged into the knee-deep water. The chill crawled up my legs and thighs past my balls to my gut, where it collided with the fear, shattering into silvery minnows that zipped around my belly.

She's gone, said a voice inside my head—a terrible, nasty voice that I hadn't heard since I'd been lost in the woods with Owe.

It happens. Things you love fall off the face of the earth. Nobody ever knows what became of them. And that would be worse, I thought, than if Dolly were to die. At least then we'd know she was gone. Lost is an infinitely more terrible idea. Lost was the most unsolvable puzzle: a mess of possible outcomes like a movie miss-ing its final reel.

"Dolly! *DOLLY!*"

I crashed through the underbrush, branches gouging my rib cage and nettles raking my face, eyes burning in my sockets like heated ball bearings. The fear shot through me now, bright green and juicy-bitter as the chlorophyll in an April leaf. My dog was gone. Ed and me had been talking, in a not-so-serious but sort-of-serious way, about having a kid. How could we, when we couldn't even keep a dog safe?

The trees opened onto a strip of concrete along the canal. Wilderness gave way to civilization, that abrupt mash-up that sometimes happens in cities. My eyes scanned frantically but twigged on nothing more than the sidewinder movement of a snake sweeping upriver against the current. Squares of light burned along the escarpment. The moon shot veins of white across the water. I smelled summer in the air, wood resin and horsehair and the greasy smell of barbecue briquettes bursting into flame.

I moved west or maybe north, disoriented for the first time since that night with Bruiser Mahoney. As I walked along the salt-whitened quay my mind drifted for an instant—one of those instants big enough to hold your entire life. I saw how a city could sink into you, trapping its pulsing heart inside your own heart—except it never feels like a trap. A trap snags you out of nowhere, violently and without warning. But I knew every inch of my trap, didn't I? I knew the dirt path that led down under the Whirlpool Bridge to a fishing hole stocked with hungry bass. How to jump off the old train trestle in Chippewa and hit the rip of slack water so I could paddle safely to shore. Cataract City was like those fur-covered handcuffs you could get at Tinglers—Ed had come home with a pair of them after a stagette party, embroidered with the phrase *Prisoner of Love*. The city of your birth was the softest trap imaginable. So soft you didn't even feel how badly you were snared—how could it be a trap when you knew its every spring and tooth?

I heard it then: a thin whine drifting across the water. At first I mistook it for the sound of my own wheezy breaths rolling across the water only to hit some unseen barrier and rebound back. My feet stuttered to a halt and I held my breath. *There*—the sound was hidden somewhere within a stand of pines canted at a crooked angle where the quay crumbled into the canal.

I picked down the incline, pine sap smeared on my palms and the rustlings of the timber above, stiff-arming through snarled branches to the polished rocks gleaming at the shore.

Oh, Dolly. She stood at the water's edge stamping her feet. She dipped one paw and withdrew it, growling restlessly.

It dawned on me: she was upset that it stopped her from going forward.

I crept to her quietly, certain that she'd bolt. Ten feet . . . seven . . . five . . . She turned, but I'd already hemmed her in: rocks to each side, water behind her.

"It's okay, baby. It's just me."

Her haunches dipped and she began to shake. I grabbed her collar in one hand and wrapped the other around her neck. When I felt her in my arms I reared back and swatted her backside.

"Bad dog. *Bad.*"

It was the first and only time I'd ever hit her. And I knew it was wrong of me. She'd only taken advantage of an opportunity that any dog would. I hadn't struck her out of anger, but just to burn off that pent-up fear.

Dolly shivered against me. Her flesh pressed to mine, but I realized with a small shock that there was no real closeness—a wall had been set between us, thin as crepe paper but solid as brick.

Later, as a weary and relieved Ed and I watched Dolly run laps in her sleep, I wondered, What do greyhounds dream about? Endless open fields, I supposed. Escape velocities. I thought of those Russian dogs in the satellite. I knew that if Dolly had been in that satellite, she wouldn't have felt a shred of fear. She'd have experienced speed at its purest, a gravitational pull slingshotting that satellite around the curve of the earth fast enough to make it glow hot. I pictured

Dolly in the cockpit as she hurtled into deep space. Loving it. And that scared me.

Dolly's spirits were high the night of the race. So much so that she got into Ed's purse and chewed up a tube of her mascara.

"Holy shit!" I said when I spotted the ragged black ring around her lips, teeth black as stalactites.

"She's full of beans," Edwina said, wiping Dolly's mouth with a paper towel.

"What's in that stuff? Could it make her sick . . . could it make her *slow*?"

"Take a pill, Dunk. The tube was nearly empty."

We arrived after eight o'clock. Owe was waiting in the parking lot with an envelope full of cash. The two of us had gone to the bank earlier that day to make our withdrawals. The teller had wetted her fingertips with a sponge in a dish and counted the bills with sleepy eyes, as though she worked with that kind of money all the time.

A silver pickup pulled up beside us. Drinkwater got out with a large man wearing engineer's overalls. He shot Dolly a look. "She looks like shit—been eating it?"

The mascara had left a dirty ring around Dolly's mouth. Ed smiled cheerily and said, "Go fuck yourself."

Drinkwater smiled back. "Ooh, a smart-mouthed bitch from Cataract City. Never seen one of you before."

Owe and Ed and I took Dolly inside. The Winning Ticket was shuttered, the stands empty. Spotlights shone down on the groomed dirt. Harry waved at us from the kennels.

"I dragged the smoother around twice," he said. "The track's pristine. Where's Drinkwater?"

"Out in the parking lot."

Harry's brow creased. "Go on, take Dolly in back. I'll be with you directly."

We took Dolly to the prep room, where Ed babied her onto the scale. I considered writing her weight on her Bertillon card, but why bother? This evening's event was like a pro boxer fighting a bare-knuckle match in a parking garage.

When Harry showed up, he paced the length of the prep room and said, "Did you keep an eye on Drinkwater in the parking lot? You got to mind that man, didn't I tell you? Didn't I?"

"What's the matter?" I said.

"The man's got no care for his dogs. They're just motors to be gunned until they conk out. I already told you about the hot peppers, but there's other tricks. One is using that boner pill, what's it called?"

Owe said, "Viagra?"

Harry snapped his fingers. "The very thing. Stuff one of those down a dog's throat and it'll get the heart racing, open up the blood vessels and give it extra pace down to the wire."

"Drinkwater's in the parking lot feeding his dog *Viagra*?" said Owe.

Harry said, "I took a peek in the lot and the two of them, him and his buddy, they weren't feeding that dog anything. I do believe they were *injecting* it."

"Jesus," Owe said softly. "So what—bet's off?"

Harry offered his palms. "You got no grounds to welsh. No drug tests before or after. All you got are the suspicions of a half-blind old man."

We met on the track. Drinkwater's associate looked exactly like the sort of man who'd inject Viagra into a dog. War Hammer stood at the man's side, body flexed tight as a railroad tie, unblinking, nostrils dilated, breath coming in whimpering gasps.

We loaded the dogs into the traps. War Hammer in trap 1, Dolly in 5. Drinkwater gave me a queer look: the outside trap meant

Dolly needed to cover more ground. War Hammer went into her trap robotically—she looked as if she might explode like a firecracker inside a tin can.

We retreated to the spectators' rail while Harry climbed up the operator's box. The mechanical hare warmed up, sparks popping off the electrified rail. I tasted it in the back of my mouth, sharp as ozone.

The hare sped off. At the thirty-yard mark it tripped an electrical circuit that sprung the traps.

The dogs shot out in a fury. Dolly stumbled out of the gate and I turned to Drinkwater thinking he'd rigged it somehow, greasing the dirt, but it was just a slip, a simple slip that could happen to any dog and might set them back half a step—nothing but a bit of bad luck.

War Hammer was ten yards ahead and accelerating. A terrifying mania ran through her limbs; she was totally out of control and fear-stricken: she ran as if pursued by wolves. The dogs stormed down the dirt, the thunder of their paws matching the thunder in my blood. Dolly dropped a level, spine flattening like a dancer going under a limbo stick.

That's it baby, drink looooow.

They blazed past us and it was as if the passage of their bodies sucked every sound from my ears: they now ran in a wrap of silence like dream animals, untouched by friction or gravity. When they hit the bend War Hammer was still in the lead. Their spines humped over the far rail for the first hundred yards before they both went low enough to vanish. Sound washed over me again as Owe and Ed hollered a single ongoing encouragement:

"*Gooooooo!*"

The dogs rounded back into view. Dolly was outside, banking high, screaming around the turn. Her stride was strangely even,

almost conservative—which is when I realized that she'd finally figured it all out. Her speed was there—hell, she was *faster* than ever—
but she was under control. Somewhere on the far side of the track
she'd dialled it in. And she was perfect. Perfect the way Owe had
been on a basketball court, the way Dade Rathburn had seemed to
be in the squared circle. War Hammer was a few yards ahead, but
Dolly had saved a little something for the finishing kick. Her eyes
bulged from their sockets in a way that might have seemed comical
if not for the frothy ropes whipping from her open mouth. It was no
longer a matter of who was faster—it was a matter of whether Dolly
could catch War Hammer before she ran out of track.

With 125 yards to go, Dolly's spine arched and her shoulders
rose. She looked as if she was preparing to climb an invisible ramp.
Her front legs—*was I really seeing this?*—appeared to push off from
thin air.

I pictured Harry watching from the operator's booth, whispering, "I *told* you it could happen."

Another step, maybe two, and she'd have lifted off. I truly believed
that would've happened.

And then—

One time at the Bisk someone dropped a screw into the gears
of an industrial mixer. It pinged around the machine housing
before sticking between the teeth of two huge tumblers. Nine
times out of ten it wouldn't have stuck: the gears would have spat
it out or snapped it in two. But it got stuck fast and the gears
seized—and the pent-up torsion tore the entire machine to
pieces. Gears stripped off spindles and rotors burned out. Busted
gears punched through the housing. The machine was a smoking ruins.

That was what I thought of watching Dolly break apart.

The simplest explanation is that Dolly's rear right paw snagged in her jersey. A thin nylon strap ran across her belly; Harry had snugged it tight but it must have loosened. Dolly's paw got under the strap, where it was trapped between it and her stomach.

It could've happened a million other times and nothing would've come of it. Maybe it was the way she brought her leg down. Maybe it was the angle of her spine. When Dolly flexed into her next stride her foot remained snagged on the strap. Her leg kept going. The strap had no give—they aren't designed that way. Dolly ran on the unshakable belief that her leg was going to come down again; she put all her weight into that belief, and in doing so she busted her own leg.

It went just like Harry said: a stick of spaghetti.

Her body flung forward, her leg flapping behind like a ribbon in the wind. She hit the track and unravelled.

My hips were already clearing the rail as War Hammer crossed the finish line. I sprinted to where Dolly lay in an awful tangle, snorting like she had pollen in her nostrils. She rolled onto her side and got up. Maybe I'd seen it all wrong—maybe she'd just twisted her limb? She put her right leg down to see if it might work. It hung like a limp thing with the paw twisted off at a horrible angle.

She lifted it up again—lifted her haunches which lifted her dangling leg—then tried to put it back down, lifting and putting it down with puzzled helplessness.

"You're going to be all right, girl," I said, because in my heart I still hoped.

I pulled Dolly into a hug, stroking her head like a father trying to soothe the fever of a sick child. Her body softened into mine and I knew some part of her acknowledged the situation or gave up. Or maybe she was just sick of running.

The following hours passed in a haze. I remember Ed taking Dolly's muzzle in her hands and how Dolly licked her face crazily—startled by Ed's tears, maybe. And I remember Harry's crestfallen expression, tears hanging in the cups of his eyelids as he said: "I should have tightened those straps. Should have known she'd run that jersey right off her back."

I said there was no faulting anything he'd done, but I could tell Harry didn't accept it. Some men can't.

I remember barging into the vet's office as they were closing. The vet injected Dolly with something that made her eyelids roll down like shutters before testing the leg with his fingers, feeling all the places where it had been ruined. He made a long incision down Dolly's leg and as soon as it was opened shards of bone from her shattered leg simply fell out; they looked like crushed glass.

He told us the best he could do was amputate—that, or euthanize her. I almost strangled the man.

Ed and I smoked too many cigarettes while the vet operated. Ed cried on and off. When it was over Dolly hobbled out on three legs with a plastic cone around her head, woozy from the anaesthesia.

On the drive home she snoozed on Ed's lap, her chest rising and falling in the moonlight that fell through the windshield. An immeasurable weight lifted from my own chest.

There are things I didn't see, but I do know they happened. I know that War Hammer died shortly after the race from whatever toxic brew Drinkwater had shovelled into her. Owe told me that she'd staggered into the finishing pen, turned a few wonky circles and collapsed. He also told me he'd handed Drinkwater what we owed him—a bet was a bet—and that Drinkwater stuffed the envelopes into his pocket and walked to the parking lot.

Harry and Owe buried War Hammer in the soft loam along the river, five hundred yards behind Derby Lane. "You got to bury them deep," Harry said. "Otherwise the shore freezes in the winter and they get spat up out of the earth in the spring thaw." When Owe asked how he knew that, Harry said simply, "I've buried a lot of dogs, son. Only a few of them my own."

Dolly never quite found her old footing: she could walk just fine, a funny little hop-step, and developed strong shoulders from putting more weight on them. Ed called her Tripod. She even became a little fat, like an athlete gone to seed. When Ed and I were still together, we'd take her for walks in the park. Ed would toss a tennis ball. Sometimes Dolly would tear after it and I'd see her body drop into that old stance, her belly nearly brushing the clipped blades of grass. But then she seemed to sense it, too, that natural runner rearing up inside her. She shut it down to a trot, no longer wishing to access that old aspect of herself.

I'd never say I was happy for what happened that night at Derby Lane. The sight of Dolly flipping end over end . . . sometimes it'll pop into my mind and I'll shudder. But here's something I've never told anyone: the accident made Dolly more touchable. Afterwards, I could hold her—just for a few minutes, but that was something. She allowed me to show her love and accepted it as much as her nature allowed. Her breath would fall into a calm rhythm as I stroked her coat. That nub of bone poking my thigh . . . it always wrecked me. But then I would feel her big heart beating at almost the same tempo as my own and think: *Maybe it was for the best.*

———

"WHAT ARE YOU STILL DOING HERE?"

I craned my head over my shoulder and saw the red-haired girl in the rubber boots. The girl who'd been so unimpressed with my rock-skipping skills.

"I've been watching from my window," she said, hooking her thumb at her apartment block. "You're standing here like a zombie."

The wind gusted, blowing ancient litter around the Derby Lane lot. The door of the Winning Ticket Lounge blew open and banged shut on its rusted hinges, issuing a thin squeal. How long had I been standing there? Too long for the girl's taste, clearly.

"I was thinking."

"About what?"

"Personal stuff."

The girl unhinged her jaw, letting her eyes roll back. "*Laaaame.*"

I bristled, aware that she was a child but unable to help myself. "You're not very nice, you know. Not as long as I've known you."

"We just met," she said evenly.

I kicked a rock, sent it skittering across the tarmac. "Well, anyway. I'd better get going now."

"You're too sensitive." The girl set her hands on her hips in a schoolmarmish gesture. "This city is going to eat you alive."

I waved goodbye to her and walked down the Parkway, heading towards Clifton Hill. Edwina and I used to walk Dolly down here sometimes, but I hadn't seen either of them in nearly eight years. I wouldn't be seeing them any time soon, either.

As I walked, I thought back to that night at Derby Lane—those fleeting moments on the homestretch when Dolly almost flew. I used to see her in a dream, which replaced the one with the hooks and screws. In that dream she was perfect, yet never more so than she was that night. She lived so well in that dream simply because she really could have stepped right out of it, blitzing down the backstretch like coiled thunder.

In that old dream Dolly scorched the earth with such fierceness that I swear sparks snapped off her paws. No earthly creature was meant to go that fast, but she *did*. Strange wonder she didn't burst into flames. In the last few seconds of her racing career Dolly broke free of physics. She broke free of my understanding of them anyway, and in that way she entered the dream.

I can only imagine it was a scary place to have gone. It asked everything of you and could break you to pieces so easily. I guess Dolly figured the juice wasn't worth the squeeze.

Maybe it's the same with Owe. In all the years since his knee was shattered, I don't think he's picked up a basketball more than a few times. He didn't even teach kids at the summer skills camps, despite the frequent invitations.

I only remember seeing him on the court again once, a few months after he'd returned from Mexico. I was driving home after a late shift at the Bisk. It was just past midnight, and as I skirted Lions Club Park I saw a solitary figure shooting hoops. His gait was a bit wonky—there was a hitch in his giddy-up, as they say around here—but that form was unmistakable. The ball travelled through the sparkling midnight mist trapped under a lone spotlight, effortlessly beautiful.

Swish.

I idled in darkness under the trees, watching. Sweat gleamed on Owe's brow. His shot dropped through that net as if guided by pure mathematics or pure grace: the ball mapping God's own perfect angle.

In that light, in that moment, Owe looked like a kid again. And I wished we could *be* kids again, just for a while. Revoke for just one day our breaking bodies, our tortured minds. I would have given anything to spend one more day as we once had, even if it was one of those piss-away afternoons reading comic books in Owe's basement while the rain clicked in the downspout like marbles.

Owe had tucked the ball under his arm. Regret was carved into every crease of his face. I figure if I'd looked in the rear-view mirror I'd have seen it in mine, too.

He left the court. I let him go.

PART THREE

FIVE MILLION
CIGARETTES

DUNCAN DIGGS

———

I t was night again when I left my childhood bedroom. I slipped silently down the hall, avoiding the spots where the floor creaked, knowing my mother was probably awake anyway, her ears pricked to the sound of my socks whispering on the scuffed linoleum.

I pulled on boots and a dark hoodie, let the door click softly shut behind me. The air was cool, clean, laden with the alkaline taste of the river. I walked under the street lamps, many of them popping and fritzing—there was something permanently wrong with the city's power grid. Brownouts, blackouts, phantom outages or surges. People would come home after a weekend away and find their fridge motors burnt out, their eggs gone rotten. My father kept the old Kenmore—nickname: the Green Meanie—going on compressors salvaged from the city dump. Nobody bothered petitioning the city hall about it: to live in Cataract City was to accept many disappointments.

I trekked down the hill to a quiet stretch of blocks off Bender Street. There was a pay phone near the Sleepy Eyes Motor Inn. I let the Plexiglas door swing shut, hunted the name out of the book and plugged quarters in the box.

Five rings later, a sleep-syrupy voice answered. "Yuh?"

"Hey, man. It's Dunk."

The phone line scratched with static as Owe moved around. He was sitting up in bed, maybe. A glassy knock was followed by deep swallowing sounds.

"I wake you?"

Owe yawned. "You figure?"

"Sorry. How are you?"

"I'm okay. Yeah, not bad. You?"

"Keeping on. Listen, I want to talk to you. I . . . It's nothing I'm expecting of you."

Another swallow, then Owe said, "How are you liking it so far, man? Some guys have a harder time adjusting, is why I'm asking."

"It's nice, yeah. The openness."

"I figured," Owe said. "Easier to breathe?"

I nodded, even though I knew he couldn't see me. "Like I was saying . . ."

"You looking across the river right now, Dunk? Somewhere in the direction of the Tuscarora Nation, maybe? Are you thinking about who I *think* you're thinking about?"

After a while I said, "I'm not putting you on the hook. I just—"

"I know what you *just*, man. You got blood in your eye?"

I thought about the past eight years, the nights without sleep and the constant edgeless terror; I thought about Edwina because my mind was never far from Edwina; I thought about the fact that cosmic fairness is a mysterious commodity, not something you can buy or sell, but sometimes that great wheel really ought to come around—and if it didn't, you had to wrench it around yourself. I was a son of Cataract City, and around here we understand payback. You pay what you owe, or you're *made* to pay.

"I've got a spot of blood in there, Owe," I said quietly. "Yeah, I do. And it's been screwing with the way I see for a while now."

The next afternoon I sat in a booth at the Double Diamond with Sam Bovine, a good-ol' shitkicker jingle playing on the Rock-Ola. It felt so *roomy* with no bull-necked guard looming on my blindside.

Bovine looked not bad, considering. His nose was threaded with busted veins and he had a sun-starved look about him, but that was sort of how I'd always pictured him at this age. I laid out my idea. Bovine set to poking holes in it.

"*Three* guys?"

"Or four," I said. "*If* I get the first couple down fast and don't take too much on the chin doing it. Three's probably the max. He's got to have at least three scratch fighters he can call, right?"

Bovine reached across the table to push up the fringe of hair over my forehead. I flicked his hand away.

"What are you doing?"

"Looking for the lobotomy scars, Dunk! Jesus, *Lemmy Drinkwater?* And why three? Why not, y'know, *one?*"

"That's small beer, Sam. This'll be a trifecta—triple the risk, triple the reward."

"But it's not triple the risk, is it? Triple the risk is fighting three guys over three nights, months apart, with time to heal. You're talking about fighting three guys in a row, *bang-bang-bang*, the same night."

I sipped beer and savoured it. Held the glass up to the light to watch the cascading bubbles.

"I guess you're right," I said. "Math isn't my strong suit."

"You seem remarkably put together for a man who could end up crunching on his own teeth like breath mints."

Bovine had been with me for every fight at Lem Drinkwater's place before I went to prison; I used to cross the river for a match every few months. Bovine had been a mortuary attendant by then, same as his pops, so he'd been comfortable around busted flesh.

The door banged open, throwing a shaft of late-afternoon sunlight across the floor. Owe slid into the booth. Bovine's hands curled into fists.

"Relax," I said. "I asked him to come."

Owe put up with Bovine's stink-eye; given our shared history, maybe he figured Bovine was allowed to be just a little bit pissed.

"What was it you wanted to talk about?" he said to me.

I told him the plan.

"The fights still go down over there," Owe confirmed. "Every month or so."

I said, "You still keeping an eye on him?"

"Me personally? No. Drinkwater's a smuggler, and that cottage industry is down with the dollar's hovering at about par. The whispers are he's gone soft, lost his touch. I don't believe it—Drinkwater could find the angle in a circle. Why are you even mixing yourself up in this? It's none of my business—"

"That's right," Bovine said. "It's not."

Ignoring Bovine, Owe turned to me. "I got the impression you were going straight."

"The road, she is a-bendy."

"Only if you insist on bending it."

Something swam up in my chest, a swirl of angry colours.

"Are you standing against me, then?"

Owe said, "Have I ever?"

NINE OR SO YEARS AGO, my phone rang. It was Bovine, clapped up in the drunk tank at the Niagara Detention Centre. This had put a real bug up my ass. I was fighting in a few hours and not only had Bovine agreed to drive, he was supposed to be my goddamn cutman.

"You got to spring me, Dunk."

I could smell the Old Grouse drifting out of the mouthpiece. "Jesus, Bovine. I mean, seriously. Here I am dozing, trying to get my mind right—"

"Sorry, Dunk—didn't I just say sorry? I'm not drunk, even," he said sulkily. "Not *that* drunk."

I sat on the edge of the bed, curtains pulled against the evening sun. The sheets smelled of the vanilla body butter Edwina wore.

"I can't be released on my own whatever . . ."

"Recog—"

"Yeah, recognizance. But you spring me and I'll pay you right back."

I could have left him there. Bovine was no stranger to the drunk tank. He probably had his own cot, with monogrammed sheets. But what was I gonna do? I'd known the guy forever.

"Be there in a bit."

I brushed my teeth. Some fighters don't brush before a fight, a little fuck-you to their opponent. Other fighters, their breath stinks but it's just the adrenaline souring in their mouths. Me, I bear my opponents no grudge. I'll even slap on deodorant.

I filled my palms with water and ran it over my skull. My hair was cut short—just like everyone's at the Bisk. The industrial flour got past the hairnets and stuck to your head; at shift's end you'd take a shower and it was like lathering with plaster of Paris. So we shaved our skulls to the wood. The staff softball photos looked like recruit-ment posters.

Despite my fighting, I'd been lucky with my face. I had hairline scars under both eyes and one on the edge of my forehead that looked like a Y. But my nose had never been broke, and my cheeks neither.

My hands were another matter. We're talking a pair of ugly bust-up mitts. The knuckles were all crushed, except for one: if I laid my hands side by side, that lonely knuckle looked like the final spike on the EKG machine before a heartbeat flatlines. In the places where I fight, you can go into the ring with open-fingered gloves, with wraps, with nothing. I bare-fist it. You tab a man flush on the but-ton with a bare fist and it's good night, Gracie. The problem is, my fingers tend to split over the joints.

Bovine was training to be a mortuary attendant by then, and when he was sober he was a decent cutman. He had this stuff called Negatan, a kind of formaldehyde gel that cauterizes the insides of a stiff's nostrils and gums. The first time he used it on me it turned the skin on my hands to pig leather. It'd been scary to watch the skin go dry and hard as buckskin. But it killed the blood, so what did it matter? I wasn't a hand model. I'd caught the other guy with an overhand right ten seconds into the next round and laid him down soft as a baby into bed.

I threw clean clothes into a duffel and went downstairs. Dolly's head rose from her dog bed in the kitchen. She padded over, tail sweeping the lino, and tugged at my tearaway pants, popping a few snaps.

"Stop, you pest," I told her, and fed her a meatball from last night's supper as I rummaged for juice in the fridge. Ed hated it when I fed Dolly from the fridge.

I didn't leave a note. Edwina would never tell me not to go—even if that was what she really wanted. Ed would never say anything because she was harder than me. Most of us in Cataract City were hard because the place built you that way. It asked you to follow a particular line and if you didn't, well, you went and lived someplace else. But if you stayed, you lived hard, and when you died you went into the ground that way: *hard*.

I guess I was hard enough, but Edwina had always been harder. And so I found that you could love a person even more fiercely for their hardness.

Dolly nosed around the back door as I slipped on my sneakers. She was hoping I'd take her along.

"Sorry, girl. Not tonight."

Best to keep your dog far away from Lemmy Drinkwater. Best to keep anything you loved far, far away.

The detention centre's night-shift guard tipped his hat as I stepped inside. I nodded sheepishly, as if it was me who'd done wrong. One-hundred and fifty-three bucks later, Bovine sauntered out of the drunk tank. He made a point of shaking the guard's hand.

"This is the last time you'll see me."

"You said that last time," said the guard.

"This time I'm being sincere."

The first thing Bovine did was hug me. It's the first thing he always did. He stunk of rye and sweat and there were pinpricks of blood on his untucked shirt.

He did a soft-shoe number down the cracked stairs of the D.C., tripping over his feet and pitching onto the sidewalk. I didn't bother asking what had landed him in detention this time. Seeing as he didn't look super-drunk, I figured he'd been pinched for the "disorderly" half of "drunk and disorderly." Why did I hang out with this fool? For one thing, Owe had toddled off to join the boys in blue. My circle of friends, never big to begin with, had shrunk.

Bovine reached into his pocket, produced a thick fold of bills and peeled off a mitt full. I took what he owed and gave the rest back.

"Aw, come on, Dunk. For pain and suffering."

He knew I needed money. I was still trying to recover what I'd lost on Dolly's race a few years back. Then last year Dolly had come down with a case of gastroplexy that nearly killed her; five thousand bucks and one stomach resectioning later, she was a healthy pooch.

We drove down Clifton Hill, past the teenybop meat markets, and crossed the Rainbow Bridge. The falls were lit with red spotlights; it looked like a spray of blood was frothing from the basin.

We cleared customs and headed up Niagara Street, past the OxyChem plant's smokestacks pumping grey vapour. We turned right onto Packard, skirting the Love Canal. Bovine tossed a bottle out the window; it smashed on the pavement and the sound sent Velcro spiders scurrying up my spine—the fight was crawling into me.

We hit Saunders Settlement Road and crossed onto the Tuscarora First Nations land. I eased on the brakes and pulled into Smokin' Joes Trading Post. I drove round back to the warehouses and parked beside a pickup truck with a giant novelty ball-sac hanging from the trailer hitch—it was that kind of crowd.

Bovine grabbed his cutman kit. Taking his face in my hands, I stared into his eyes. His pupils seemed about right.

"I don't need a drunk working on my face."

"Come on, Dunk. You know I'd never if I was shitfaced."

The warehouse door was propped open with a cigar store Indian, a cigarette duct-taped in its mouth. A couple of guys were passing a flask outside the entrance.

"How you feeling tonight?" one asked.

"Buy the ticket, take the ride."

Their rasping laughter followed me into the warehouse. Boxes and crates stacked high; the smells of patent leather and tobacco.

We walked down aisles towards the light and buzz of a milling crowd.

A half-dozen sawhorses formed a ring on the shellacked concrete floor. A hundred-odd spectators stood or sat on stacked pallets. It was your standard fight crowd: fat and magpie-eyed, drinking Hamm's tallboys. A few cheered at the sight of me: I guess they'd cashed in on my ass before.

Lem Drinkwater was dressed in his usual pegged blue jeans, a chambray shirt with pearl-snap buttons, his Crocodile Dundee hat with a ring of alligator teeth round the band.

"You feeling it?" he asked, eyeing me down his nose.

"All I want to feel right now is the bills in my hand."

Drinkwater's laugh wasn't really a laugh, just bared teeth with air hissing through them: *hsh-hsh-hsh!* "You'll get paid after."

"That's not how it worked before."

"S'the way it works now. Roll with them punches, Diggs."

I scratched behind my ear. "You got me over a bit of a barrel, Lemmy."

"That's not my aim," he said—and maybe it wasn't, but I also knew he didn't give two sweet fucks whether anything he did happened to put me over a barrel.

"And if I walk out right now?"

He shrugged. "Plenty of warm bodies willing to step in, I'd say."

"I'd say. Same purse?"

"Same as same as."

I waded through the railbirds into a small cement-walled room to warm up. A single bulb burned on the end of a cord. I did some jumping jacks and ran in place, high-legging my knees to touch my chest. Sweat beaded my upper lip and my breath fell into an easy rhythm. I rolled my shoulders and snapped out a lazy left jab—my teaser punch, my bait: look at it out there, pesky, a bothersome gnat . . . you won't see the right steaming behind it to steal your lights away.

Fighting didn't tickle my nuts, just happened to be something I've always been half-decent at. I swung my right hand and things went down. There were a million better ways to turn a buck with your hands but I wasn't good at any of those.

I chased the money. And I preferred to fight men drawn to the money—money's clean, money doesn't have agendas or psychoses. Sometimes I fought men who'd fallen way down the ladder. It's rough work, tussling with a guy who's trying to claw back up to that bottom rung. Other men wanted to figure something out about themselves, so okay, I'd oblige.

And some men were just batshit crazy. Those guys were the worst. Those guys you just about had to *kill*.

I'd taken a few bad beats myself. The worst was to a fellow from right there, the Tuscarora Nation. Wasn't a big guy, but he was fast and wiry and once he'd gone slick with sweat I couldn't lay hands on him. He didn't rough me up so much as whittle me down, peppering me with stinging jabs and hooks like a man with a small, sharp knife taking thin peels off a big log. After a while my chest was greasy with blood and I'd swallowed so much of the red stuff that I needed to puke. It was all I could do to grab and hold him close, waltzing with an unwilling partner. At one point I sent up a little prayer: *Let him knock me cold, God. Take me out behind the shed and put one in the back of my skull.*

But he just kept at it, quick and relentless. By the end the punches came in the dark—my eyes were two pissholes in the snow—and I felt like I was being beaten with a black sack over my head. That guy, he shaved me down until I was thin as a toothpick and then I just . . . *snapped.*

Everything comes back to that question of hardness. I came from a hard place, yeah—a place where shopkeeps sell loose cigarettes because by the time that third Thursday of the month rolls around, most of their customers can't afford a whole deck. But that guy, he probably grew up in a tarpaper shack, sleeping on the floor with eight or ten brothers and sisters, and had a dog in the yard chained to a radial tire. That's another level of hardness, and I couldn't find the place in my heart to match it.

The door to the dressing room opened. My opponent tonight was about my size, maybe a bit taller. He didn't look much older than nineteen, twenty. A kid, really. His eyes pinned me. I gave him a look that said: *You don't have to show me your dick's bigger, okay? All that'll sort itself out soon enough.*

He wiped his nose and rolled his eyes to the ceiling as if to say he'd been expecting worse than he'd drawn. "You fight before?"

"Few times, yuh," I told him. "You?"

"First time."

"I'll go easy."

I leaned against the wall and watched him warm up. He was quick but gangly and it didn't look like he could throw a straight right to save his skin—I started feeling sorry for him, then wiped those thoughts away.

"Know something?" he said. "You smell like Fig Newtons."

His skin was drawn tight over his cheekbones. I reminded myself to aim for those spots.

Drinkwater opened the door. The bare bulb winked off the teeth on his hat.

"Let's go, you pigs."

The first punch tabbed me flush on the jawbone and that's when I knew he didn't have the ol' *boom-boom* to put me away. Him and me were only dancing a little dance that would end with me landing a starcher that left him snuffling concrete.

The punch landed solid, and it lit my head up like a slot machine: *Cherry—Pineapple—Star*. Yeah, I'd have a fat lip, and yeah, I tasted blood in the chinks of my teeth, but he didn't quite have the juice.

I spat warm blood and stared into the crowd: a couple of dudes with the stringy-haired, strung-out look of fairground carnies sat beside a young girl, frighteningly skinny, in a Megadeth shirt: *Peace Sells . . . But Nobody's Buying*. Her eyes were riveted on my opponent.

Were they together? God, I sort of hoped not.

I circled left and let my right hand hang at my hip, like maybe he'd really stung me and I was trying to haul the scrambled shards of my brain back to where the neurons would start jumping the gaps again. He circled with me—*come on, friend, just a little closer now, let me get one good clean look*—and the muscles flexed up his side, tightening over the ladder of his ribs as he stepped into a clumsy uppercut.

I shifted so his fist could pass harmlessly between the outer edge of my shoulder and my neck and for a heartbeat it was there: the knockout button of his outthrust chin. I planted my leg and dropped my head. My right came up in a swift arc; my shoulder joint swivelled in its socket, well-oiled with adrenaline, and my fist passed my ear on its downward flight, falling fast, a bomb splitting the clouds. Hell, it may have whistled like a bomb.

It met his chin flush. Something broke deep down in my hand. The impact jangled up my arm and hummed like restless honeybees in the hollow of my shoulder socket. He sagged into me, our chests touching. I felt the shuddering beats of his heart through my skin.

Bah-dum . . . bah-DUM . . . bah—

The kid's face had gone pale. Beads of milky sweat leaked from the skin under his eyes, which were rolled so far back in his skull that I saw the twitching, vein-threaded whites.

—DUM . . . bah-bah-DUM . . . bah-dum—

His heart beat out of true. An arrhythmia, could be. A year ago Jeff King, batch mixer on the Oreo line, just lay down in the lunch-room, shut his eyes and died. A heart murmur, I heard. King was 225 pounds with a pulse like a jackrabbit. It was nothing he could guard against; a defect in his nature, was all.

I felt it in this guy, too: a structural weakness knitted tight to his body. He wasn't built for this kind of rough work. I was terrified that if we kept at it, he'd die in my arms.

I held him until the fog left his eyes and he was able to collect his feet under him. When he stood, staggering back, I raised my arms.

"I'm done," I said. "You win."

The guy, still stumblebum, swung at me and missed. He tucked his fists tight under his chin, swaying unsteadily as I backed off.

I found Drinkwater in the crowd and said, "There's something the matter with him. His heart or something."

"You're hilarious," he said. "Get your ass back in there."

The railbirds hissed and catcalled. A plastic cup struck my shoul-der, spilling Orange Crush down my shirt.

"Can't do it, Lem," I said. "If it goes sideways, we both got to carry that."

"I'm not gonna carry a damn thing—and you, you're just chickenshit."

"Sure, Lem. That's what it is."

I looked at Bovine, jerking my chin towards the warm-up room. The kid stood in the centre of the ring, fists still tucked, as we walked away.

Lemmy Drinkwater shouldered open the presswood door and let it fall shut, muffling the din of the crowd. "You sure as fuck aren't a people-pleaser, are you?"

I pulled my hoodie on, stuffed my feet into workboots. "You shouldn't let that kid fight again, Lem. Something's off with his ticker. I felt it."

"Who are you, Trapper John?"

It was easy to hate Drinkwater, and I did. He was a killer—of dogs, at the very least—and a sadist. It tore me up to find myself in his service. Yet he seemed to me the sort of man who could do with his life exactly what he wanted, and I held some whipped-dog respect for that.

"I'm not paying you a red cent for that shitshow you just put on," he said.

"I didn't expect you would."

He scrutinized me through a fringe of dark hair. "You just fight?"

"Just fight what?"

"I mean," he clarified, "to make rent. Just fight?"

"I work at the Bisk . . . part-time now."

"Tough times, I hear. Cutbacks."

"Times are tough all over."

Drinkwater nodded to say he understood this to be the way of my life, yet to indicate it wasn't the way of his own. His eyes were coldly, darkly serious—I felt I was being measured for some future possibility, and in that instant I desperately wanted to show Drinkwater whatever it was he hoped to find. It sickened me, my *need*.

"Something's coming up," he said. "I need somebody on the other side."

"Of?"

"Of the river. Off the rez. You can't trust Nationers—they don't know how to act with that kind of money."

"What kind of money?"

Drinkwater knocked the air in front of him with his foreknuckle.

"No kind. I was just asking a question. If you were interested."

"In *what?*"

Drinkwater looked as if I'd answered already. "Maybe we'll talk," he said.

As I walked away between walls of stacked boxes I heard the sound of dogs fighting, which wasn't much of a sound at all: low, almost sexual yelps. It struck me that my own fight had been a curtain-jerker for a couple of mutts.

A knot of men stood beside the cigar store Indian in the parking lot. As we passed, one of them shouted, "Cracker candyass!" A bottle sailed over my shoulder and shattered against the warehouse wall, shards rebounding at me. A thick blade of glass whickered past my face, drawing a line of ice across my brow; I ducked instinctively, hands pawing the wound, feeling the quick rush of blood curving down my jawbone.

I turned and saw the men who'd done it. There were five of them—not one real specimen among them, but they stared back challengingly and I knew the beds of their pickups would hold bats and axe handles.

"Come on," Bovine said.

We continued across the lot. My opponent was helping the girl in the Megadeth shirt into his car. The girl seemed sick, but beyond her thinness I couldn't tell how. He was so gentle with her, taking her legs and folding them carefully inside the car, leaning in to kiss her cheek. I pictured the two of them driving to a small house on Chemical Row, near the OxyChem plant, where he'd fold her out of the car with the same tenderness. I didn't know why he'd fought, whether for money or pride or sickness, but I could see he loved her and wanted to believe their life together was a happy one.

I got in my car, and Bovine checked out the cut over my eye. He decided I didn't need stitches and slapped a butterfly bandage over it.

"Another memory to add to the Dunk scrapbook," he said.

"There's a million stories in there."

"Nope, only one," Bovine said. "Man takes on world, world wins. But you get to write it over the course of a lifetime—so you've got that going for you."

"Oh, fuck off."

Bovine howled.

Edwina was waiting in the dark.

She was lying on the couch in the room off the front hall—a room that had seemed so big when we'd moved in from her old house on Culp Street. It had seemed as if we'd never gather enough stuff to fill it.

She drew on her cigarette and the room seemed to quiver, the red ember floating.

"Ed . . ."

"You win?"

I shook my head, but wondered if she could see my face.

"You get hurt?"

"Not bad. My hand."

"Let's take a look at you."

She got up, snapped on the bathroom light and sat me on the toilet. She wore a shimmery black robe—irregular in some way I couldn't see—that she'd bought at a clearance warehouse over the river. Perched on the tub's edge, she drew on her cigarette, squinted into the smoke and traced her pointer finger over my butterflied brow; she brought her fingertip down slowly to touch the split in my lip.

She plucked the cigarette from her mouth and with that same strong, quiet hand reached over my shoulder—the ember singing the fine hairs on my earlobe—to snatch a Kleenex from the box on the toilet tank. She set the cigarette between her lips, twisted one corner of the Kleenex into a rope and pressed it to the split.

Ed had a smooth, open, brown-eyed face with a spray of freckles over her cheeks. She was still as beautiful as when I'd first met her, but a harder breed of it: the dagger-sharp points of her cheekbones, the way the light threw itself off the straight edges of her teeth.

As she leaned forward over my swollen hand, my eyes fell upon her clavicle bone. I wanted to run my tongue along it—post-fight randiness—but I couldn't just lean across and do it: you need permission for such things, if unspoken, even from those you love.

Ed gathered the front of her robe in one small, casual gesture. Then she put her head far back—very far back, almost like a contortionist—and shook her dark hair loose so that it hung free down her neck.

"Can I have a drag?"

"You don't smoke," she said.

"One drag."

I pulled the cigarette from her lips and drew thinly. The paper tasted of cherry lip gloss. There was no stamp on the filter; everyone at the Bisk bought their smokes off-brand from a guy who sold them out of his trunk in the parking lot.

I turned my head to cough and spotted a lottery ticket on the sink ledge. Ed played them all: 6/49, Lotto Max, Dreamhome Sweepstakes, always ponying up for the Bonus, the Encore. She played with some girls at the Bisk, too. A year or so back they'd picked six out of seven and split a few grand. "If I'd been born on the fifty-sixth of January instead of the thirteenth, we'd have all quit on the spot," she'd told me, laughing but not really.

She never used to play the lotto. For a long time our life together hadn't been about waiting on a lucky ship to come in—it had been about building that ship ourselves, with the toil of our own hands, and sailing wherever the hell we wanted.

She pinched the cigarette from between my lips, put it back between her own, then stood in front of the mirror. My gaze rode up her feet, which were strong-toed and callused from hours on the Nutter Butter line, up her calves roped with muscle, past the dimples in the back of her knees to her thighs, which were just starting to go. I stood behind her and my arms went to her hips . . . and when she didn't protest, around her waist. The bathroom light reflected off the mirror, doubling itself, and for an instant I felt trapped: a man stunned in the motion-sensor halogens snapping alight along a prison's barbwire fence.

Some questions you can look at two ways: *What might I have been without you?* One coin, yeah, but two sides. Ed must've looked at both sides of that coin, too.

When Wally Cutts called me up to his glassed-in office above the Bisk's factory line, I knew what was coming.

I'd showed up early that morning to shower. The showerhead at home was calcified—the chemicals that were dumped into the city's water supply crystallized, meaning many of us in Cataract City had to replace our showerheads every year. I'd stood under the nozzle as the water melted the remains of the fight from my skin and nerves, working my swollen hand under the hot water.

Then I'd dressed in my whites with the other men, each of us smelling of our lines, put on my hairnet and latex gloves and passed through the disinfectant chamber onto the factory floor. We stood in a loose semicircle while the safety inspector ran his tests. There was no sound but the ticking down of the giant grey units stretching deep into the factory. A haze of flour hung in the air—our lips were already whitened with it.

While we waited we limbered up using the exercises the productivity expert taught us: deep knee bends and hip swivels. We looked like an old-timers football team prepping to take the field. Knuckles and knees cracking, elbow joints popping—I could tell whose elbow or knee without even looking: each man's body had its own sounds.

The red lights flicked green and the line leapt to life: worn canvas cloth chattering over steel pins, *chukka-chikka-chukka*. We inclined our heads over the line and tried to hold that pose for eight hours.

At the end of the shift I climbed the stairs to Cutts' office and knocked.

"Come in, Duncan. Sit down."

Wally Cutts was the line super—it was the same job Owe's dad had once held. His degree hung on the wall, same as Mr. Stuckey's had. At last summer's corporate picnic the shop steward, a ratlike creature named Stan Lowery—Adam's older brother—hung a piñata from the crotch of a tree: a leering burglar with a black mask over his eyes. Lowery had painted the burglar's feet to look like workboots, just like those Cutts wore while walking the shop floor. Lowery stood with his gang of line-pigs, good ol' boys with swollen wine-cask bellies, all of them laughing as their kids beat holy hell out of that piñata. Cutts stood there with his wife and young boy, chewing potato salad and ruffling his son's hair as if this was a big lark and he was in on it.

"Hurt your hand?" Cutts said now.

I nodded.

"But you're okay?"

My shrug indicated it was nothing he should bother himself about.

"Duncan . . . you know how it's going, yes?"

I squinted at him dumbly, as if I didn't, or couldn't.

"First of all, production's way down. Not because we can't make the stuff, but because people aren't eating it. It's a healthier world, Duncan—and that's fine and dandy, unless you're baking cookies."

Cutts was chubby-edging-into-fat with a beery face that broke into laughter at a great many things that weren't funny. He'd walk the line filling a paper sack with warm Chips Ahoy, plucking them off the moving belt.

"How old are you, Duncan?"

"Twenty-five."

"Twenty five," he said, as if it was impossible for him to recall ever having been so young. How the hell old was he—thirty? I could've happily murdered him in that moment. "We're letting you go."

"Just like that?"

He saw I was smiling and said uneasily, "It's a seniority thing, pure and simple. You had a lot built up, you'll recall, but then you took that year off to go to college—that put you back down near the bottom."

Cutts showed me his palms like I was a dog who figured he was hiding a doggy treat. "We're offering a month in lieu. Most guys are taking that."

"The pension plan I've paid into?"

"Duncan, retirement age is sixty-five. You've got forty years left to get a good pension under you. Edwina's job is safe, I promise."

We shook. His hand felt like boiled suet stuffed into a surgical glove. When I got back downstairs Stan Lowery was waiting.

"We're going to grieve it!" he told me, sounding like a teacup chihuahua yapping at the mailman. "We're grieving this fucker all the way up, Diggs, you set your watch to it."

He'd made the same promise to the guys turfed before me—and most of them now spent their nights patrolling hotel parking lots with a flashlight. I nodded to a few guys on the way out. It dawned on me how little I knew them. I'd worked at the Bisk for six years, yet I couldn't recall most of their wives' names.

"Well," Bovine said, "I'm sure she was nice on the inside."

The woman was old—how old I couldn't really say. She lay on a steel table in a white-tiled room in the basement of the Harry Bohnsack Mortuary, a white sheet draping her from neck to toes. She may have been pretty once.

"Let's get that pesky blood out of you, dear heart," Bovine said sweetly.

I'd spent the afternoon at the Blue Lagoon, pumping Jack and Cokes into myself. Ed was working, Dolly was sleeping, and any way, I liked watching Bovine work.

He wore painter's overalls and a black vulcanized apron. He shook out a length of surgical tubing and fitted one end to a long, thin needle. He fitted the other end to the toaster-oven-sized recovery unit—a funny euphemism for a machine that sucked blood out of dead folks.

Bovine worked briskly, whistling "The Old Gray Mare" while rolling a blue drum with *Nestlé Formalin* written on it. How strange that a company known for its chocolate syrup would be a leading producer of formaldehyde. One whiff and I was back in grade ten science class on frog-dissection day. Bovine threaded a surgical tube into the drum, clipped it with surgical shears and attached a stent, joining it with two more lengths of tube. One end of the tube went into the recovery unit; the other end was fastened to a second needle, which Bovine slid into the big vein in the woman's neck.

He flicked the machine on. Yellow formalin flowed up one tube. Black blood trickled down the other, collecting in a plastic jug. While the woman drained, Bovine used a pair of industrial clippers to cut her hair off, then her eyebrows.

"Don't worry, my dear," Bovine said, hunting through a bin of sterilized wigs. "Only your hairdresser will know for sure."

At first I'd found it creepy that Bovine talked to them. But then I figured we all had our coping mechanisms. He opened a tackle box, the kind you'd keep fishing lures in, and grabbed a pair of ocular suction cups.

"You going to look away, pussy?" he said.

"You want me to throw up on the poor girl, ruin all your hard work?"

Bovine took a swig from a beaker of gin and tonic on the steel slab and eased the woman's left eye open. The cornea had gone milky as if it had been bleached. What's worse, it had taken some sort of awful elevator to the basement of her skull.

"The brain shrinks from lack of moisture," Bovine said. "Eyeballs get sucked into the cranial vault."

He peeled the sticky-tab off a suction cup, attached it to her eyeball and pulled. That sound always got to me: it was like hearing a rubber boot pulled out of thick mud. The eyeball popped into the socket. Bovine ran a bead of glue down the eyelids and pressed them together.

"Just once I'd like to leave the eyes wide open," he said. "See the guy peering up out of the casket like: *The fuck you looking at?*"

The buzzer rang.

"That must be Dr. Jekyll," said Bovine, in a lispy Vincent Price voice. "He's bringing more carcasses . . ."

While he answered the door I stood over the body. Blood still dripped from the tube into the collection jug, dark as tar. A dead person's blood smelled a little like silver polish. The formaldehyde had put some life back into her: she could've just put her head down for a nap.

Bovine said, "Check out what the cat dragged in."

I looked up and there was Owe. He was about twenty pounds heavier than last I'd seen him, but the eyes and chin were the same.

"I saw this guy propping up a bar stool the other night," Bovine said, "and thought, Jesus, that bastard looks a lot like another bastard I used to know. And it was that very bastard!"

"How are you, man?" Owe smiled, displaying a big chip in his front incisor.

"I'm hanging on." I hadn't seen him in what, four years? The last I'd heard he was living out west. Calgary? Edmonton? "What brings you back?"

"Change of scenery? The mountains were getting stale."

"How long you been back?"

"Not long."

"You're still on the force?"

A quick nod. "Caught on with Niagara Regional. I just want to do something *valuable* with my life, Dunk."

The sarcasm escaped him like a poisonous mist. He scanned my damaged hand and the new scab bristling along my eyebrow. His eyes had a peculiar movement: snapping back and forth, taking things in while his face remained impassive. That was the first real difference I noticed: those insurance adjuster's eyes.

"*Stuckey's back in toooown*," Bovine sang to the tune of "Mack the Knife." "He's taken an oath to protect we noble savages of Cataract City."

Owe nodded towards the body and said: "You dressing her up for a date, Bovine?"

Owe and I smiled at each other in the old familiar way and I felt myself relax, the old rhythms taking hold.

"I guess you want to know why I've called this meeting," Bovine announced grandly. "I've come up with an extracurricular project for you wastes of skin."

He led us into a storage room stacked with heavy-duty card-board sheets. A few of them had been folded into coffin shapes.

"You've got to be kidding me," Owe said.

"What?" said Bovine. "Our budget burials."

"People get buried in *cardboard*?"

Bovine said: "Once you're in the ground, who cares?"

"You don't put them out for display in one of these things—right?"

"We've got rental caskets, all the nice ones. Evermore Rest, Celestial Sleeper, The Camelot, The Eternal Homestead. We display bodies in a rental, then bury them in cardboard."

"That's just so weird," said Owe.

"Who buys a tux you're only going to wear one night?" Bovine said equitably.

"Okay, Bovine, but who wants their mother buried in a shoebox like a hamster?"

"Dutch, tell me. On garbage day, do you see people putting ornate wooden boxes with little brass handles out on their curbs?"

"What do you do for a headstone—tape two Popsicle sticks together?"

Bovine said, "When I die, stuff me in a Hefty sack, drag me through the parlour while the organist plays 'Dust in the Wind,' on out the back door into an open grave. Bingo, bango, bongo."

The storage-room door opened into a garage that housed a pair of Cadillac hearses. Bovine pointed to the old model. "That's mine now, free and clear."

"Congratulations," I said. "You'll have no problem picking up at goth bars."

Bovine mimed whacking off. "You're hilarious. I'm thinking we smash it up. Merrittville Speedway, y'know? Demolition Derby night." He slapped the hearse's wide back end. "Just keep backing this baby up into the other cars. Reduce 'em to rubble."

I said, "Where would we fix it up?"

"The auto shop at the high school," said Bovine. "I talked to Finnerty and he said sure, so long as we do it at night."

The first day of what would become an informal but binding "situation" between Lemmy Drinkwater and myself ended with me holding the bloodied body of a pit bull named Folchik—Mohawk for "Little Hunter"—in my arms.

The dog was shivering uncontrollably, shiny with blood under the sodium vapour lamps overhanging the fighting box. Her foam-flecked tongue lolled out the side of her mouth, warm as cooked liver on my forearm.

Little Hunter had fought like a monster but her opponent, a blue-nose pit bull up from the Carolinas named Seeker, had been just that little bit slicker. Seeker sat with her owner: a fat dog breeder wearing a train engineer's cap and hacked-down combat boots. The dog's two-tone eyes—one blue, one yellow—were riveted on Little Hunter. Seeker's sides expanded like a bellows as the blood from her own wounds leaked down her legs to the rosined floor.

It shocked me, how fast it had happened. Only minutes ago Folchik had been a whole creature, full of blood and life. Next? Nothing but a connection of exhausted muscle and torn flesh, opened up in ways no creature ever should be. I felt her heart shuddering under my fingertips at an insane gallop and smelled her adrenaline—the same smell in dogs as it was in men.

The day had begun with me waking next to Edwina.

I had lain still while the bedroom fell into place around me, listening to Ed breathe: long, slow inhales, smooth exhales. She faced away from me but I figured she was awake, as she usually was at this hour: eyes open to watch the sun spread across the bottom of the windowsill, immersed in her own unknowable thoughts.

I curled into her, slipping an arm down her rib cage. When we were dating she'd once said I didn't know how to cuddle right. *Your body doesn't fit itself properly to mine* is how she'd put it. At that age I was worried about being a decent lover—the fact that I might've been a piss-poor cuddler never entered my mind.

It's true that we'd started living together young, but that was how people did things here, as if we were ticking off boxes in an exam called *Life*. But I knew I'd found the real thing with Ed: the spark, that unquestioned connection. So I'd held tight. I regretted nothing and could only hope Ed didn't, either.

Ed sat on the edge of the bed and stretched. The tendons in her back flexed and she worked her fingers loose as she did every morning—after years of picking busted Arrowroots off the conveyor, it looked as if tiny balloons had been inflated inside her finger joints.

I lay still while she showered. She whistled "The Log Driver's Waltz": *It's birling down a-down white water / A log driver's waltz pleases girls completely.* She dressed in the thin yellow light and clipped her photo ID to her overalls.

"So," she said. "What's your schedule today?"

I smiled wolfishly. "Today I find my ass a new job."

She nodded as if this was firmly within my abilities.

The Port Weller dry dock was a cathedral of rust.

There wasn't one exposed strip of scaffolding not pocked or slashed with it. The hulls of ships in the shelf docks were so eaten through that the metal would crumble in your hands like schist. Skycranes tilted against the black-shouldered cliffs of the escarpment, ferrying girders caked in marine paint. Even the air had teeth:

a million tiny fangs gnawed at the exposed skin above my collar.

I walked through the main gates along a strip of canal that shone silver in the new day. Sunfish snatched at zebra mussels clinging to snarls of rebar jutting from the seawall. Gulls circled; they must have followed these hulks in from sea and now, their meal ticket gone, the air was alive with their confused screeches.

The foreman waited at the punch clock: a solid guy with an oily, pancake-flat face.

"You Diggs?"

"Thanks for meeting with me."

"Part of my job." His head jerked to indicate I should follow.

We passed over hatboards to a walkway alongside the flank of a ship rooted in deep dock. I trailed my fingers over the metal, which trembled under an assault of air-hammers and riveting guns. An arc-welding torch snapped alight above; a soft blue glow streaked the hull, following the roll-lines of the steel. A spray of golden sparks cascaded off the tin overhang, touching the arm of my denim jacket and leaving scorch marks almost too small to see.

We stepped through a porthole door into a small, dark, rust-smelling chamber. A smelter was working beneath us: sweat instantly popped along my brow. Around us were chains and pulleys rimed with dark, granular grease. The points of naked hooks swung in front of my eyes, their chains clanking like wind chimes.

The chamber broke onto a narrow footpath spanning the ship's hull. Men worked thirty feet below: all I could see were the yellow plugs of their hardhats. The sun broke through the ship's unfinished angles, glinting off the aluminum gangplanks.

The foreman led me into a makeshift office. "Go ahead and go sit down."

I took blueprints off the chair facing his and set them carefully on the floor. He pulled my crumpled resumé from his pocket.

"The Bisk, huh?"

"Cutbacks. A couple guys I used to work with said I should try here."

"Yuh, they been through already." His snort seemed to say we'd been fools to throw our lots in with a multinational conglomerate while he'd had the good sense to stick with ships. "English Literature certificate?"

"I took some classes up at Niagara College."

"Why?"

When I didn't reply the foreman massaged his forehead with the stump of his pointer finger—I wondered if he was doing this to call attention to the missing digit.

"Can you weld?"

"I've spot-welded."

"Spot we don't need. Mig? Tig? Acetylene?"

I shook my head.

"Can you run a Wheelabrator?"

I shook my head.

"Plasma cutter?"

I shook my head.

"Oxy-fuel cutter?"

I shook my head.

"Profile burner?"

"No."

"Metal lathe?"

"No."

"Boring mill?"

"I can learn."

"Just about any walking stiff can. Only takes a year's apprentice-ship up at the college. Same one that taught you those English classes." He pronounced it *clarsis*.

"Listen, I need the work and I've got a strong back—"

"What do you think we do, haul sacks a cement? This is a skilled labour site. What'd you do at Nabisco?"

"Batch mixer, mainly. A bit of line maintenance."

"That's not a skill we're in need of. Sorry."

He didn't look one damn bit sorry. Maybe he was one of those men who enjoyed pressing his heel into the back of his fellow man's neck. I squinted at his ID badge, which was melted and heat-scorched. *Sonny Hillicker.* One of that clan, then.

"You related to Clyde?"

"My kid brother."

"I know Clyde."

"Yeah. Clyde knows you, too."

Jesus—wasn't that just Cataract City? The old snake-ball. Fighting just to fight, even when the battle's long been lost.

"You smell like a cookie," Sonny Hillicker said, and he laughed. "Alla you Biskers do."

Hot coals burned at my temples. But beneath the fire was the insistent scrape of desperation: the dull edge of a knife down the back of my neck.

An hour later I was in the Coffee Time off Drummond eating a cruller that tasted of cigarette smoke and flipping through the job ads. The cell phone buzzed in my pocket.

"Yeah?"

"Diggs."

"Yeah."

"Where are you?"

"Who's this?"

"Drinkwater. Sounds like you're someplace busy."

"Coffee shop."

I picked up a weird abrasion on the line—Drinkwater's stubble grating on the mouthpiece? Dogs barked in the background.

"You healed up?"

"I'd be okay to go. Anything happening?"

"Why don't you come over."

"My cutman's at work."

"Don't need him. Just you."

"This a job?"

"This isn't anything if I'm on the phone with you another five seconds."

"What do you know about fighting dogs, Diggs?"

"I know I wouldn't want to fight one myself."

"Smart, paleface."

Drinkwater had showed up at Smokin' Joes in a chromed-up Silverado Crew Cab. Joes was the size of a small-town supermarket and sold everything from motorcycle jackets to authentic Tuscaroran birdhouses, but I'd yet to see anyone come out with anything except suds or cigs.

Drinkwater, as always, was all sharp angles and unforgiving bone. I took in the raised pink scar that fish-hooked from his hairline around one ear. He wore the same stovepipe jeans I'd seen him in since the first day I met him, the kind you had to work in like a catcher's mitt. He retrieved a pit bull from the truck bed, wrapping the leash around his fist.

"Get your ass in gear, Diggs."

We passed through a gate into an acre-wide impound housing six U-barns: corrugated tin scabbed with rust, the sort of things built to shelter twin-prop airplanes. The far north warehouse was the fight house. The other five? I had no clue what they held.

Drinkwater met with four men inside the gates. They had the same look: the old-style blue jeans, jackets with knotted fringes of fur, the wide-brimmed black bowler hats with partridge feathers stuck in the band. They spoke with their backs to me.

Thunder kicked up over the flatlands. A sleek black helicopter rose over the earth's hub, hovering over the compound. The air swam with rotor wash, the shimmer of gas fumes. The smell of industrial bearing lubricant hit my nose: it was the same cherry-scented lube we used at the Bisk to grease gears. The chopper rode too high for me to make out its occupants—all I saw were sunglasses whose tinted lenses shone like lynx eyes in the reddening sun.

Drinkwater and the other men held their bodies stiff against the blade-wind as it rose to a fierce howl, ripping fans of dust off the ground. The helicopter banked southward over the band centre and the squat architecture of the rez.

Drinkwater didn't say anything about the helicopter as we walked the ruddy scrub behind Smokin' Joes, down a row of fenced-in pens. At the sound of Drinkwater's voice, dogs tore out of their cheap plastic doghouses to leap and claw at the chain-link.

They were pit bulls—some black, some brindle-coated, some the glossy grey of a luxury sedan. And they all had the same physique: a dark heart-shaped nose, black eyes canopied by a jutting forehead, docked ears and a jaw that looked to have been worked into shape by chewing an India rubber ball. Their musculature flared like a cobra's hood down their ribs, which were prominent when the dogs held certain positions; those bones looked like giant skeletal fingers flexed under the flesh. The males' penises were sheathed in folds of skin that lay nearly flat against their stomachs like the hood scoops on muscle cars. None of the dogs looked more than sixty-five pounds but they seemed monstrous. It was as if they were made out of well-matched chunks of stone wrapped in jeweller's velvet.

"There is no breed to match the pit bull," Drinkwater said. "Americans love two tons of Detroit rolling iron and supersizing *everything*, so of course breeders used to figure the biggest dogs were the toughest. German shepherds, Dobermans, Rottweilers, Great Danes, Tosa Inus—all hat, no cattle."

Dogfighting was big on the rez. Dogmen came up from the Carolinas and as far south as Florida to fight Drinkwater's studs. He'd set up a closed-circuit TV link; the fights were broadcast in Vegas and drew heavy wagering.

Drinkwater bashed a stick against a pen. The dog inside leapt and yowled. Its neighbours did the same, biting at the fence and leaving runners of saliva dangling from the metal.

"This is my million-dollar gal," he said. "Folchik. My Little Hunter."

I remembered War Hammer, another one of Drinkwater's million-dollar gals. When he opened the pen door, Folchik bounded out. She looked not much different than the others. I told Drinkwater as much.

"It's not the look," he said. "It's the *game*. Game is the dog that won't quit fighting—the dog that'll fight with two broken legs! Game is the dog that will toe the scratch knowing it's already dead. Game is crazy, but game dogs taste more of life because they have no fear of death. And Folchik is *dead game*."

Drinkwater stick-whipped the dog's ass. The blow sent seismic ripples down the dog's flanks, but Folchik didn't register it at all.

"Another breed, that would be abuse," Drinkwater said.

I ran a hand down Folchik's hide. Muscle throbbed under her skin, strands lapping each other like tight-woven wicker. Her coat held the reflective sheen of the tinted windows of a downtown high-rise, like nothing possible in nature.

"They're good with people," said Drinkwater, "but murder on other dogs."

"We had a bull mastiff for a while growing up, before I got Dolly." Drinkwater shook his head as if this was the saddest news he'd heard all day. "Some guy brought a mastiff round for a roll. Neapolitan variety—I guess they're supposed to be bad-asses. Hundred-fifty pounds and jowly, folds of skin hanging off its muzzle. Disgusting thing! I refused to roll my stock—wasn't that dog's fault it had a moron for an owner. Another guy had a beat-up old pit bull cur that was practically a bait dog—one you chuck in with the gamers just to keep them lively—but still, a pittie. That little scrap of shit tore the mastiff's throat right out. The mastiff's owner bawled his guts out."

Drinkwater leashed Folchik and together we walked to one of the tin-sided sheds. Inside was a treadmill with a two-foot-tall metal cage over the track. Drinkwater swatted Folchik inside the cage and knotted her leash to the treadmill panel. He ramped the elevation to max and cranked it. Folchik fell into a quick run as the treadmill's belt ripped round the rollers.

"I want to show you something," Drinkwater said.

"We're leaving her here?"

"She can run for days."

We walked to a warehouse dominated by a giant machine, green like a '70s-vintage fridge. It was working at a furious pace, well-worn parts ticking with the sound of silenced bullets shot from an automatic rifle.

Drinkwater walked me down the line. Bricks of tobacco went into a shredder on one side, cigarettes spat out the other. The cigarette filters chittered down one funnel, where they were attached to the paper, rolled with the tobacco and fastened with a golden band. The machine was manned by chain-smoking Natives; they picked fresh cigs out of the hoppers and lit them off the stumps of their last. One guy smoked like a Frenchman, holding his cig between his third and fourth fingers.

Drinkwater eyed me down his nose. "You wouldn't squeal on your old pal Lem, wouldya?"

When I didn't reply he led me outside, back to the shed where Folchik was still running strong—if anything, stronger. Her tongue hung out of her mouth, thick and pink.

"She's rolling tonight. Got to taper my baby down."

He took her out and scratched her ears and under her chin with all the tenderness of a man clawing at a tick bite. The clipped nub of Folchik's tail wagged gratefully—and Drinkwater cuffed her head so hard that her snout bounced off the dirt. Folchik's lips rippled along her gums to expose her teeth but she didn't bite.

"Good girl," Drinkwater said softly. "You build the aggression by antagonizing them, see? Turn them into a stick of TNT with a very short fuse, yeah? Come with me."

A bearlike specimen waited by Drinkwater's truck: he was fifty pounds heavier than me, with a dewlapped face. His nose was mobbed with broken veins. He stood spread-legged against the bumper dressed in the same deep-blue dungarees Drinkwater wore and a wifebeater. "Diggs," Drinkwater said. "This is Igor."

"Igor? You're joking."

Neither man spoke so I said, "Hey, Igor."

"Hiya," Igor said, deadpan.

Folchik rode in back. I rode bitch. Drinkwater pushed the big truck up to eighty down unpaved roads, throwing up a rooster tail of dust. We gunned past houses that weren't much more than huts held fast by L-clamps and the grace of God. Soon even those were gone: only the uncluttered scrub of the rez where, as they say, a man could watch his dog run away for days.

Drinkwater said, drily, "What bounty you've given us, paleface.

What beauty to behold. I guess you'd like it if we were gone—yeah? Sure. We give you heap big headaches. But the ol' typhoid-infested blanket trick didn't work, did it? The firewater, though. *That* was a smart move."

He hurled the truck round a blind corner, wheels flirting with the ditch. The momentum threw me against Igor's unyielding bulk.

"But you let us hang around, you white devils with your white devil guilt, and now we're dug in deep."

The dirt road gave way to tarmac. The tires bit down and we screamed off the rez into the world of concrete light stanchions, dotted yellow lines and Piggly Wigglys. Drinkwater took us down a switchback hill that emptied into the Niagara river basin. He stopped in front of a puntboat tied along the shore.

"Let's see what you can do with this tub," he said.

The river was greenest at the shore, greying as it went out and black where it ran deepest. It was five hundred yards wide where we stood, and hooked sharply a half-mile down, around an outcrop of Jack pines. The sun carved over the trees on the far shore, glimmering off a million leaves so that it seemed as if the distant banks were on fire.

We picked across jags of rock slick with algae at the waterline. An insane glittering of gnats danced above the greenness. We each scooped up a handful of cold river water and ran our fingers over our teeth until we heard the squeak. It was something all men did around here.

My uncle used to take me fishing for steelhead in a puntboat before the bank took it away. Drinkwater's boat was a long, flat-bottomed pug with rings of rust around every rivet. He and Igor stood at the bow while I shucked the tie-downs and slid us off.

Once we'd floated free of the rocks I pull-started the old Evinrude and guided us into the deepest seam of the channel. The current held a complex urgency: breaking around rocks and into sucking crevices, forming again, fighting against itself like a thing made of many strings being pulled different ways at once.

Drinkwater watched me without watching me. Igor's face remained stony as an Easter Island idol as the dying sun lit it from behind: he looked sandblasted, with divots of shadow on the places he must've had acne as a teenager.

Drinkwater shifted his hips and I saw the curved bone handle of his knife sheathed where his belt ran round his spine. I thought that you didn't need to be strong or skilled to slide a knife into someone— you only had to core that worm of mercy out of your heart. That was the hardest line, one I couldn't cross; it put me at a disadvantage with guys like Drinkwater.

"Cut the motor," he said.

We drifted. Igor whispered into Drinkwater's ear; Lem laughed without mirth.

"What I need of you . . ." he said to me, still laughing.

"How many?" I said.

He wasn't laughing now. "How many what?"

"How many cigarettes and what's my cut?"

Drinkwater squinted. "Five million cigarettes. More maybe, next time. No cut. Flat rate. Ten K."

In Cataract City, as in any border town, smuggling was common. Most of it penny-ante, done for a cheap thrill. When I was a kid, Bovine's dad had installed an extra-large windshield-washer-fluid reservoir in his Impala. He'd drive over to Pine Street Liquor and fill it with Comrade Popov's potato vodka—five gallons of the swill. *Anything to declare?* the border guard would ask. *Just that you've got yourselves a real swell country over here*, Bovine's dad would answer with a shit-eating grin.

"Fine, I'll do it."

Drinkwater picked his fingers along the teeth in his hatband. "Just like that?"

"Just like that. I want half now."

"I'll give you two now."

"Fine."

"Igor will be going with you."

"When?"

"When you do it."

"Igor's okay with that?"

"Igor's okay with anything I tell him to be okay with."

"When do we do it?"

"I'll let you know when it becomes critical."

"Let's head back. You give me the two now and call when you need me."

"What, you don't enjoy my company?"

"Not really, Lem."

Drinkwater's lips skinned back from his teeth and he doubled over, laughter sobbing out of him in a high, breathless wheeze. Straightening up, he flicked away tears from under his eyes with one finger.

"Hell, ain't that a shame. I like you well enough."

We returned to the Tuscarora without speaking. Once we'd slipped past the razorwire fence, Drinkwater said, "I'll pay you after the fight, which I need to get back for."

"I'm not watching two dogs maul each other."

"If that's all you see you aren't watching close enough. Anyway, cash doesn't leave my pocket until the roll's over."

Inside the warehouse, in the same spot where I usually fought, sat a plywood pen. It was waist-high, roughly seven foot by seven. The crowd was mostly Native men in dungarees and jean jackets; a pall of cigarette smoke floated over the fighting box. The men who'd thrown that bottle at me might've been there, but I couldn't remember their faces. The old man who smoked like a Frenchman was there, watching with eyes like peach pits sunk in the net of wrinkles on his face.

A trio of white men huddled on the far side of the pen, all three of them fat—southern deputy fat. They wore overalls, train engineer's caps and Caterpillar boots. They had handkerchiefs in their back pockets and they stood on pigeon toes in a rough circle around a dog crate.

"No dog beats a pittie," Drinkwater said to me. "The only fact left up for debate is which pit bull bloodline is best. Folchik's a red nose—best, I say. Those boys came up from Carolina with a blue nose bitch whelped by Grand Champ Negrino, the original slaughterhouse on four legs. So I guess we'll see."

I thought about how, right now, people were looking into problems of great importance. Curing cancers, puzzling out how to make a combustion engine run on orange peels and egg shells, stuff like that. Those kinds of people didn't live in Cataract City, though. Here were the things my people investigated: which type of dog was the best at killing all other types of dogs. The better I got to know Lemuel Drinkwater, the more I came to see he'd built a laboratory for himself. He was a scientist, you could say, and his field of study was suffering. And now I'd made myself a part of that, too. I was another one of his lab rats.

One of the fat dog-breeders came over with his cap in his hands, nervously rubbing the hatband's sheen with his hammerthumbs.

"I 'preciate the opportunity," he said, showing teeth that were shockingly white and straight.

Drinkwater said: "So who's this one you brought?"

"She's a game bitch," the man said. "Green, yuh, but plenny game. This yours?"

"She is," said Drinkwater. "Folchik."

"You rolled her ever?"

Drinkwater pointed to her flank and said, "Figure she got those scars shaving?"

The man set the toe of his boot between Folchik's front legs. "Lotta space between them legs. Blue noses is narrower across the brisket."

Drinkwater said, "They must tip over easy."

"I ain't never rolled no tippy dog, mister."

The fat breeder's pit bull, Seeker, was sleek and streamlined. She had terrifying aerodynamics: she didn't move so much as *flow* like grey water. Her skull was a wedge trimming towards her snout, and she had a small overbite—the points of her canines protruded below her top lip.

The dogs were lifted into the pen. Their noses touched. Seeker licked Folchik's chin.

"Razor them," Drinkwater said.

Both men made a cut in their dog's flanks—Drinkwater with the bone-handled knife, the fat breeder with a box-cutter clipped to his overalls. They wet their fingers with the blood and rubbed it onto their own dog's nose first, then the other dog's. Folchik snuffled blood up her nose and sneezed, spraying red on the shellacked concrete.

The dogs nosed up at the scratch-line. The blood had jacked the fight into them. They lunged, forelegs battling, teeth daggering in the smoky air. And still they made no sound: only the soft hiss of breath escaped their lungs.

"God damn," the breeder said with real admiration. "That's a gamer."

The dogs were drawn back to their corners, held tight by their scruffs. Seeker yowled and snapped at the air. Folchik sat still as stone.

"Release," said Drinkwater.

The dogs flew at each other like stones from a catapult. Folchik closed the distance and leapt; Seeker dropped levels, flattening as Folchik sailed overtop. For a split second their teeth flashed: Seeker's head twisting sideways and darting upwards to snap at Folchik's belly, Folchik's head straining down to rip at her opponent's flanks as she passed overhead.

Folchik's paws hit the cement and skidded, leaving milky scars in the rosin. As she wrenched her body awkwardly around, claws seeking purchase on the slick floor, her haunches slammed into the plywood with a thump that shook the pen and her rear paws kicked off the barricade to slingshot back at Seeker, who was spinning to meet her.

Folchik bulled forward, angling for the killshot, skull snaking side to side—but she found nothing except air as Seeker back-pedalled smartly, feinting, dodging, her throat half an inch from Folchik's gnashing teeth. Folchik backed Seeker up to the pen's edge, trying to bully her into a corner but failing. Seeker slipped to one side, batting Folchik's head with her paw, then tilted her head slightly and arrowed in at the spot just behind Folchik's jaw.

It took an instant. Less. When Seeker's head came away there was a shiny pink disc on Folchik's throat. It rapidly filled with red that dripped down the dog's leg.

The fight found its truth in that moment. Seeker's manoeuvre was that of a picador baiting a bull, making it believe in its own invulnerability before sinking his little dagger, the *pica*, into the bull's neck.

The dogs met in the centre of the pen. Both rose on their hind legs, forelegs locked over each other's shoulders like waltzers in a death-dance. Folchik's mouth was a blur of enamel; ropes of saliva hung from her jaws, stretching and snapping with the crazed movement of her head. Seeker held her own head aslant, parrying Folchik's crazed thrusts, crow-hopping lightly on her hind legs. Her head stabbed forward when she found an opening, clinical cobra-strikes that opened the skin around Folchik's jaw and shredded what was left of one docked ear.

The noise that came out of Folchik caused my guts to contract: it was a confused whine like that of a child confronted with a puzzle she cannot solve.

Folchik torqued her body and jerked her head to strike at Seeker's belly. Her jaws fastened onto Seeker's brisket, but as Folchik was rucking in for a better grip Seeker leapt off her hind legs, tucked her head smartly and flipped over Folchik's back. Her haunches hit Folchik's spine and she spun to the side with eerie grace; her head ended up even with Folchik's back legs. Now Seeker's teeth flashed like razors—she didn't need an instant to orient herself; she knew exactly where she was—two quick strikes into Folchik's right rear leg. By the time Folchik spun round to fend off the attack, Seeker had ducked clear. What looked like a nest of wet red wires hung from a deep wound in Folchik's thigh.

"Break!" cried Drinkwater. "Time!"

Drinkwater and the fat breeder climbed inside the pen to fetch their dogs. Seeker licked Folchik's bloodied flank lightly, the way she might have licked one of her newborn pups.

In the corner Drinkwater petted Folchik with great tenderness, whispering, "My beautiful, my beautiful." He had a bag much like Bovine's and from it he removed a packet of Monsel's solution, which he painted onto the dog's wounds with a wet Q-tip; Folchik stood silent as her flesh hardened into brown jerky.

In the other corner the fat breeder filled a bowl with Gatorade for Seeker. He saturated a cottonball with Adrenalin 1:100 and eased it up Seeker's rectum with one squashed-flat thumb.

My gaze drifted into the crowd. The old Native guy was working his jaws around another cigarette—his lower lip came up too far for him to have teeth. I hated having anything to do with these ugly men whose stomachs were falling through the shiny denim of their jackets and whose skin hung like wet laundry off the warped dowels of their bones. But I knew we shared one thing: we were fascinated by these creatures, who were perfect in some exquisite, unknowable way—and we would probably watch one of them die.

Folchik limped to the scratch-line. Her eyes were marble-hard and tacky as peeled grapes; she wasn't blinking anymore. Seeker ebbed out of her corner like liquid.

"Release!"

Folchik tore in at Seeker, who backpedalled madly, seemingly unsure of herself for the first time; the Little Hunter's rush had the grey dog's paws scrabbling under her belly, losing traction, at which point Folchik faked a strike at Seeker's leg. Seeker ripped at Folchik's head except her head wasn't there anymore. Folchik had reversed to strike at Seeker's opposite leg, picking it up and wrenching it sideways, flipping the fat man's dog onto her side, and for a harried second Seeker's throat was exposed: the *killshot*. Folchik was straining madly for it and I was sure she'd end it right there—*wanted* her to, because a part of me hated the silky perfection of the other dog—and the crowd rose to a quick roar, sensing the hometown favourite was making her move as the dogs' fangs buzz-sawed the air. But then Folchik reared back and it was clear something had gone wrong: her muzzle was shredded like cheesecloth to expose the pink rack of her gums and the blood-flecked pegs of her teeth. Seeker sported a long rip down one side of her face but her throat was unhurt.

"Pick her up," the fat breeder told Drinkwater. "She's close to dead."

He refused.

"What's the *matter* with you?" I said.

Suddenly, it was as if Folchik had lost her heft: the iron had been ripped from her spine. Seeker bullied and harassed her, striking at her retreating forelegs, tearing pink gouges into her coat and rag-dolling her across the pen.

Next I was stepping over the boards into the fighting box. It was an involuntary reaction, like breathing or blinking my eyes. When I elbowed Seeker clear, she lunged, her teeth ripping into my fore-arm with enough force to pierce the flesh, but only once—whether this was a matter of training or because she had no interest in hurt-ing me, I couldn't tell. She backed off and sat on her haunches, eyeing her breeders.

I bent beneath those staggered faces under the vapour lamps, wrapping my arms around Folchik, who was shivering uncontrolla-bly. I picked her up, cradling her head in the crook of my bloodied elbow. She buried her face in my armpit. Her bladder let go in a warm trickle that went down my side and soaked the band of my jeans.

I stared at the men ranged round the box. Not disapprovingly, not for sympathy, but to see what they'd make of it. I didn't see anything other than dark-eyed stoniness. Men with their hands in their pockets stared back at me with no knowable emotion; I could have done what I'd done or not, it mattered very little to them. The only man who seemed to care was Seeker's primary keeper—he inclined his head at me, the smallest of nods.

Drinkwater stepped into the box with his knife out. He held it low, tip pointing at my belly.

"Put my dog down. We're not finished."

"I think so, Lem. I really think this is finished."

He brought the knife up, the edge pressed to my neck. He raked it against the grain of my stubble, the vibration radiating along my collarbones.

"Lot of witnesses, Lemmy."

"I own every eye looking at you."

"People know where I am. It's a whole lot easier to make a dog disappear than a man. White man, especially."

Drinkwater squeezed one eye shut. He put the knife back in its sheath.

"Bad dog," he said softly. "Bad, bad dog."

Edwina was asleep, or pretending to be. I slid past the bed and stashed the two thousand dollars in the toe of an old workboot.

When I turned, Ed had shifted up on one elbow, face glossed by the moonlight falling through the window. The sight made a small sweet hole in me.

"You find anything?" she said.

"They weren't looking at the dry docks. Something'll come up."

"Why are you dressed like that?"

I wore my overalls, the only clothes I'd had in my truck. The ones I'd been wearing were covered in blood. After the fight I'd wrapped Folchik in my shirt and left the warehouse. Nobody bothered trying to stop me. I'd driven around town with the dog in the passenger seat; the street lamps shone through the windshield, picking up the sheen of blood on her coat. She'd pawed at the seat with what little energy she had—it dawned on me that she was trying to climb down into the footwell, where it was darker, which was I guess where a dog would prefer to die.

"Hold on, girl," I'd whispered. "Just a little while longer, okay?"

I'd stopped at a pay phone on an unlit block. The receiver was ripped off but the book was intact. After hunting up the address, I'd driven down Lockport Road, skirting the airport—shark-coloured planes were lifting into the twilight, reminding me of when I'd ride my bike to the Point as a boy and watch them ghost out of the clouds—and pulled into the SPCA.

It was closed, but a sign read EMERGENCY SERVICE and an arrow pointed round back. I left the truck idling and gathered Folchik in my arms, worried that she'd bite—she must have been terrified, delirious, confused—but she only whimpered as I lifted her. She weighed nothing at all.

I stepped from the truck with Folchik in my arms. I smelled raw adrenaline dumping out of the dog's pores and below that, the smell of warm pavement. I banged on the door hard enough to strip the skin off my knuckles. The woman who answered was in her late sixties—a volunteer, I figured. She wore glasses on a beaded string and when she saw me standing there, they slid down her nose to rattle on her chest.

"I found her on the side of the road," I said. "You have to take her."

"Oh *Gaad*," she said with a strong upstate accent. "What happened?"

"I don't know . . . someone might've hit her with their car."

"*Savages*. Why wouldn't they have stopped?"

"Jesus, listen—I don't *know*." I held Folchik out to her. "She's real bad off. Do you have a vet on staff?"

She nodded. "Always one on call. I'll have to—"

"Call whoever it is. Hurry up, you have to—"

The woman stepped aside, waving me in. Beyond the door lay a small, clean, white-tiled room dominated by a steel examining table.

"Lay the dog down," she said. "I'll call the police, too. We have to file a report. You'll have to talk to them."

A quick scan of the room told me there was no phone. I said, "Go make the calls."

"Okay, yes. Oh *Gaad*," she said, hurrying out.

Blood had soaked through my shirt. Folchik had been breathing shallowly, but her inhales seemed steadier now.

I left before the woman returned. I drove to an all-night car-wash on Pine Street and cleaned my truck out, scrubbing the upholstery until my hands turned a chapped red. I changed into my overalls and drove to the Tops Market, where I bought bandages and peroxide in the pharmacy and grabbed a case of Hamm's from the cooler. In the parking lot, by the glow of the truck's domelight, I debrided and bandaged my arm where Seeker had bit me. The punctures were ragged, throbbing with a dull, bone-deep heat. I hoped they wouldn't get infected.

I'd driven back to the border, where I declared and paid full duty on the beer. Then I wound through the quiet streets of my city, drank four beers real quick at the end of my block and finally rolled up the driveway with the headlights off.

"You been drinking?" Edwina said.

I stared at the beer at the end of my arm. "Bovine bought a couple cases over the river. I bought one off him."

I was shocked at how easily the lie came to me. Dolly padded over and nosed around my legs, snaffling the exposed skin at my ankles. Her tail stiffened.

"Have you been seeing other dogs?" Ed asked.

"A stray wandering around the shipworks." Another effortless lie.

"Hmm. Dolly's jealous. Come here," Edwina said.

We lay in the moonlight. The breeze played on the wind chimes hanging in the window: it was hammered bronze and shaped like tumbling water. A friend of Ed's had bought it for us at a tourist trap on Clifton Hill. Might as well buy wooden shoes for a Dutchman.

"There's something on your neck," Ed said. "Is that blood?"

"Oil, probably. From the docks."

She rubbed my thigh . . . then rubbed higher. I liked her this way, all coy and mothering. I needed her to carry me away from the sight of Folchik broken open on a warehouse floor. Maybe she needed it too, really *needed* it, like me, instead of just wanting it to satisfy the urge.

Lately when we made love, I'd been seeing Ed as someone else. She'd angle her head as she lay on the pillow and the outline of her bone structure would seem more purely arousing to me. But then I'd realize it was still Edwina—just a younger version. Her hair not yet leeched by the bleached flour that constantly hung in the air at the Bisk. Her forearms not yet twisted with thick blue veins. And I'd look at my own hands and they were no longer ruined things, either. It was as if our young selves reappeared . . . the strangest thing.

But those younger, *other* selves are never really gone, are they? All their possibilities. Why would they be? They're only waiting for you to chase them down and reclaim them, right?

Who'd have figured wrecking a hearse could be so much fun?

Owe, Bovine and I drove it to Westlane High School, where, as promised, the auto shop teacher let us use the tool bay. We jacked the meat-wagon on a pneumatic hoist and tore it apart.

It was just the three of us drinking Lakers and busting the hell out of the hearse. We took a sledgehammer to it. We stomped the windshield until the Saf-T-Glas webbed, caved and folded into the front seat. We loosed war whoops while crowbarring out the side windows, which broke with such a sweet tinkling. I crawled into the back and ripped down the velvet curtains—*pik-pik-pik!*—off the brass hooks.

Bovine popped the hood. We stood around it.

"Well," Owen said. "I'm pretty sure that's an engine."

At least Bovine had half a clue what to do. He purged the gas tank and rerouted the flow to a hose fed through the glovebox and then into a jerry can duct-taped to the back seat.

"Can't be any gas in the tank during a demo derby," he said. "Unless you want a field of flaming fireballs."

One night I cracked the door leading into the hallway and when the alarm didn't blare we walked into the darkened school. Our boots squeaked on the tiles, that haunting sound echoing down the hallways.

"Darla Dinkins," Bovine said, tapping his beer bottle on a locker. "Ol' Double D. I asked her out dancing at the Blue Lagoon—I had fake ID. Ah, god, did she shoot me *doooown*."

"She works at the Shoppers Drug Mart on Portage," I said. "Married to Doug Kirkwood, who sells Chevys at Mullane Motors. Two kids . . . one's named Ekko, I think."

We passed the trophy case, our bodies reflected amidst the golden armatures. The three of us looked younger in the half-light, relieved of the years sunken into our flesh—the effect was so compelling I found myself reaching out to touch our faces where they lay trapped in the glass.

Back in the tool bay we spray-painted *THE DEVIL'S DUE* down each side of the hearse. Bovine hacked down the muffler with an acetylene torch—miraculously without melting his fingers off. The big hulk howled like the hounds of hell.

On the night of the derby we flicked on the hearse's hazard lights and crept down the back roads to the Merrittville Speedway.

Bovine had spent the afternoon stuck down a bottle, so I drove. Bovine hummed softly in the back seat as wind rushed through the empty windows to carve the hair back from his widow's peak. The narrow road shone like a runway in the moonlight. Stars salted the sky above the escarpment. I fiddled with the radio and pulled in "Take Me Home Tonight" by Eddie Money.

"*Beee mah little bay-bee,*" Bovine crooned in a drunken falsetto.

The Speedway shone under a ring of spotlights. I pulled into the grassy staging area teeming with chopped-down derby rides. The inspector did a circuit around the hearse, casually snapped the antenna off and said, "Got a helmet?"

"No," Owe said.

"You can rent one over there. Ten bucks."

"That's highway robbery!" Bovine cackled from the back seat.

"That guy better not be driving," the inspector said.

Owe begged off, seeing as his knee was held together with Silly Putty and carpenter's glue. Bovine slapped me on both cheeks and gave me a woozy hug. "Steady on, Highlander!"

While Bovine and Owe made their way to the bleachers, I scoped the competition: a rusty delivery van with a giant plastic chicken on its roof; a slab of Detroit rolling iron, cotton-candy pink, with *THE SHOCKER* on the hood; a purple Buick with an armless, legless mannequin lashed to the grille. Two guys sat on the Buick's hood passing a flask; their laughter floated up towards the stars.

Drivers hopped into our cars. The air was soon hammering with pistons, thick with exhaust fumes. The inspector waved a red flag. I pulled out behind a Nissan Micra that must've been some masochist's idea of a swell ride. We drove a lap past the stands. The lights shone down with the intensity of tiny suns. Owe and Bovine stood, beers in hand, cheering their guts out. I blew them kisses.

The cars idled on the sloped oval, grilles aimed into the centre. When the air horn *blatted*, I threw the tranny into reverse and tromped the accelerator; the tires stuttered, spitting loose stones against the undercarriage until finally they bit, rocketing the hearse up the slope and away from the fray.

The delivery van collided with a Dodge Aspen; the plastic chicken sailed off the roof to explode like a snow globe on the Dodge's hood. Wrenching the wheel, I swung the hearse into a sloppy arc as the little Micra caromed off my bumper and pinballed like a BB.

I threw my arm over the passenger seat and cranked my neck over my shoulder. The purple Buick fell directly in my crosshairs: it sat in the centre of the bowl, fishtailing on two flats. I punched the gas and shot downhill—the pink behemoth charged past my front bumper in pursuit of a lime-green Gremlin—lining up the hearse's trunk with the Buick's mannequin hood ornament, which swelled in the rear window until—*CRANCH!*

The impact threw me forward. My face bounced off the wheel; flaming spiders scuttled before my eyes. The mannequin's head bounded off the hood and burst under the passing tires of the delivery van. I jerked the transmission into D and goosed the gas; my bumper was snarled with the Buick's fender and the unlocking of all that twisted metal was accompanied by a metallic shriek that set my teeth on edge. The air above the oval was blue with exhaust; my head swam with the fumes but my adrenaline was redlined. Absolute clarity settled over me, a sensation I'd felt only once or twice in my life.

The hearse accelerated up the oval; I spun the wheel casually, using just two fingers, blood on the back of my hand in perfect red droplets. I must have bloodied my nose when it hit the wheel but never mind, this was a hell of a time. The big car swung around at the top of the oval as if on autopilot, back wheels flirting with the fence; the thunder of the hearse's muffler trip-hammered against my eardrums while I paused at the height of the incline to survey the madness below. I selected the delivery van that was meshed with the Aspen; their back tires smoked as they tried to separate. My foot mashed the gas and the view expanded, blown up big as all outdoors, before shrinking to a pinprick as I shot the gap and *SHRRAASH!* barrelled into the van, hitting it broadside and rocking it up on its side.

For an instant I thought I'd tipped the van over but soon gravity took hold and it smashed back down, axles snapping, hood jackrabbiting up and a torn fan belt hurtling skyward like a bird. I took in the green piss of antifreeze and the stink of cooked wiring and screamed in triumph, tasting blood between my teeth.

That was when the hearse rattled and died. I gripped the wheel, white-knuckled, laughing as I twisted the key. Nothing. Laughing harder now, these hysterical giggles, I jammed the transmission collar into P and reefed the key. The hearse coughed to life and I let loose a war whoop as the Micra blazed down the decline and ran straight into me.

The collision jolted me—each knob of my spine was robed in cold flames—as a glowing-hot lugnut pinged off the roof and hit the passenger seat, melting through the upholstery and sending up tiny curls of smoke. I peered groggily over the hearse's hood at the Micra, which was folded up like an accordion, the driver laughing like a hyena with the flesh split above his brow. I was laughing, too— "You're a wildman!" I shouted, and he must've heard because he grinned as if to say, *Buddy, you don't even wanna know!* He threw the Micra into reverse, backed clear and went after the pink behemoth.

When I dropped the tranny into D, the hearse whined like a sick animal. The stink of broiled creosote seeped through the vents. I navigated a wasteland of shorn metal and cracked engine blocks hissing steam to the low side of the oval. A busted car horn emitted an endless high-pitched honk—the *whooonk* of a terrified goose. I gunned the hearse up the track incline, gears grinding, unsteady on tires shredding from their rims, then swung around and scanned the field. The Micra was rammed into the ass-end of the Aspen. The pink thing's trunk was torn off and there was a huge dent in its left side, but it still moved. It angled round until we faced each other, three hundred yards apart. My heart swelled up to fill my chest.

I stood on the gas pedal. The big block V8 shrieked as the hearse leapt like a scalded cat. The pink car was boogying, too: vaporous

streamers of smoke peeled back from its crunched hood. The spotlights shone off the still-bright chrome of the dash, which glowed
with its strange circular geometries, and I inhaled the mustard leatherette of the seat and thought about the bodies that had occupied the
berth behind me, laid out in coffins with their formaldehyde-stiff skin
white as candle wax, wounds sewn tight with black thread, and then
I braced my hands on the wheel as the pink car blasted into me.

A crash of earthbound thunder. Our hoods were welded with the
weirdest metallic symmetry. Steel buckled, the alloy became liquid: it
tumbled off the front of the hood in silver waves like steel-tinted winter water over the Falls, throwing me against the wheel so hard that I'd
wake the next morning with the bright welt of its shape on my chest.

The impact shocked the air from my lungs. My next inhale was
tortured, the sound you make after being under water so long it has
almost killed you. I sucked in the steam roiling off the hearse's engine
block—the taste of a blowtorch's blue flame. As the motor rattled
down I smelled gas—on me?—and watched as small flames licked
from under the pink car's hood.

"Hey! You okay, buddy?"

The derby inspector hung his big fat melon through the window.
I blinked my eyes and tried to focus.

"Derby's over, man. You got yourself a bloody nose."

"I'll be okay. Say, did I win?"

The inspector shook his head. "The Micra took it."

When I burst out laughing, the inspector insisted I check in with the
on-site medic: unprovoked laughter was a symptom of a concussion.

After the race we took a cab to the Blue Lagoon. A pair of gay divorcees danced together on the postage stamp of a dance floor. Their
pancake makeup shone under the black lights, making them look
like lost mimes.

I drank a pint of Laker and soon the plugs of Kleenex stuffed up my nostrils were wet with beer foam. Bovine had kept himself well lubed on two-dollar drafts at the derby and showed no signs of flagging. Pinpricks of sweat glittered in the hollows of his eyes, and his hair looked like a half-deflated soufflé.

"Take it easy," I told him. "You don't have to drink your body weight."

Bovine said, "Who are you—my mother?"

He staggered onto the dance floor, grinding up on the divorcees. Arms above his head, a highball glass in one hand and a pint in the other. When the women abandoned the floor, Bovine danced by himself in the strobes, thrusting his crotch.

Owe winced, fished in his back pocket and tossed a deck of cigarettes on the table.

"You smoke?"

Owe shook his head. "Sitting on them funny, is all. Screwing with my spine. They're evidence, actually." He exhaled casually. "Know much about cigarette smuggling?"

"Nothing. Why, should I?"

Owe tore the cellophane off the package, tapped one out. "These're counterfeits, but they look and taste almost like the real deal." He rotated the cigarette with his fingertips. "The band's a little different—the only way to tell. Dull yellow instead of glossy gold. It's big money."

"That so?"

"Half a billion a year—can you believe that? Mainly on the reserves down in Cornwall. The Akwesasne Mohawks in the U.S., the Kahnawake tribe on our side. When the Saint Lawrence freezes they hoof 'em over the ice. In the summer it's speedboats."

I said, "And nobody arrests them?"

"You can't walk onto a rez and start slapping on cuffs. The Six Nations never ceded to the Crown. They're a sovereign people who walk the path as brothers and equals under the law—but our laws don't apply. They can cross the border freely. No guards. No duty. They got their own police force, but . . ."

"It's complicated?"

"Ever been down to the Akwesasne? Right out of *Mad Max*, man. Where does the money go? Not into infrastructure. Tough tickets, the Mohawks." Owe smiled as if to say, *Crazy, huh?* His insurance adjuster's eyes slid over the slope of my shoulder to my nose, the plugs of bloodied TP, his gaze resting comfortably on mine. "Our old pal Drinkwater's neck-deep in it."

"That so?"

"It is a fact," said Owe. "Makes him a whole lotta wampum. That's racist. Sorry. He smuggles across the river into Canada. A risky game, but his rake is huge. Plenty of money on both sides of the river— in Drinkwater's pocket on that side, in the distributor's pockets over here. But the river itself . . . that's where the smugglers operate. They're low-level mules, totally expendable. Here in Cataract City, you can't walk five feet without tripping over one of those poor fools."

My bladder tightened. I got up and went to the toilets, and stared at my reflection in the fly-spotted mirror. Did Owen know? Had he seen or heard or somehow read the thoughts bouncing inside my head? Owe was smart—smarter than me. I couldn't outfox him. He'd give me a heads-up, wouldn't he? Let me know which way the wind was blowing?

A quickie vacation—that's how I floated it to Edwina. Don't ask where the money came from. Don't ask me to justify it. Just say you'll come.

We'd planned a similar trip years ago, to New Orleans. We'd made it to Kentucky before my old pickup's engine blew, which was just as well—something burned deep inside my bones the further I'd gone from the city.

But I remembered even the smallest details from that trip: Ed's feet on the dashboard, the chipped candy-apple of her nail polish. How we'd sat in a café in West Virginia eating eggs whose yolks were the size of quarters—pigeon eggs, Ed had called them—with sunlight falling through the yellowed windows. How Ed had grabbed my hand impulsively and bit the knuckles. I still had knuckles back then.

She had sat on the bed in one of those no-tell motels along the interstate, cupping her breasts, laughing and telling me casually, "I really like my tits." Later that night, dehydrated and ravenous, we'd ransacked our pockets for quarters and wrapped our naked bodies in the motel duvet and crept out to stock up on cold Cokes and Ho Hos, giggling like kids in the glow of the vending machines.

During that trip I'd realized you can't have it all in a relationship. Constancy and the ability to thrill—these rarely dwelled within the same person. So you took the best of what you could reasonably expect, made your choice and held to it.

This time we drove north into Pennsylvania Dutch Country. The grey sky held a perpetual hesitancy, as if it could open up at any moment. The exit signs fascinated me. Turn off at any one and the possibility existed that you could be somebody else entirely. The miles dropped under the hood and tension eased out of my chest. In Cataract City everything was a struggle. It knit itself deep inside you. What was the most awful thing about living as an adult on the same streets where you grew up? It's so easy to remember how perfect it was supposed to be. Reminders were always smacking you in the face. Good things happened—sure, I knew that. They just happened in other places.

"Am I a gift?" Ed asked me one night in an interstate motel. "Because you're a gift, Duncan Diggs. And I treasure that gift. Really, I do."

"So do I, Ed. I treasure you, too. Why wouldn't I?" But the refrain in my head said, *Just tell me not to do it, Ed. Whatever it is, whatever you think, just tell me not to go through with it—and I won't. I swear to you, I won't.*

But she wouldn't say anything about how I'd managed to find the money for the trip or what I might be planning. It wasn't Ed's way. Looking back, I believe she was making plans even then. The trip had that end-game undercurrent.

We drove back through unending rain. My cell rang outside Buffalo.

Drinkwater said, "How's it going, paleface? Get your sea legs ready."

The night before the job, Owe called.

"Got a minute?"

"Sure, always."

He was drinking—a slurred tempo to his words. I pictured him in his well-ordered cop apartment drinking whatever cops drank.

"You never asked me about Fragrant Meat, man. You never asked how my dog was doing."

I sat by the window overlooking the street. Dolly's head rested on my lap. I scratched her ear flaps and said, "How is he?"

"Dead."

The fact hung between us—*dead*—like a squashed bug on the sidewalk. Owe laughed, the same mirthless, thousand-yard laugh he'd started using after his knee surgeries.

"I'm sorry, man. I knew you really cared about—"

"No, no. Just *listen*, okay? Listen." When I didn't say anything he carried on. "So a stupid fuckhead gets off his stupid fuckhead job on Friday afternoon. The stupid fuckhead has a few too many drinks with the other stupid fuckheads he works with and then hops in his truck and goes screaming down a neighbourhood street at ninety K. That neighbourhood was my neighbourhood. Southern edge of Calgary—I couldn't see the Rockies from my house, the angle wasn't right, but the area *felt* safe, Dunk, and that mattered because I never really felt safe on the job, right?"

The clatter of glass, the sloppy *gloh-gloh-gloh* of liquid sloshing out of a bottle. A heavy exhale, then two convulsive swallows—I heard the click of his Adam's apple. He'd reached that state of drunkenness where cold clarity settled in. He spoke fluidly.

"I was walking Fragrant Meat. But I didn't call him that any-more. Wasn't any sort of name for a creature you loved, right? He slept on my bed, which was fine seeing as the ladies weren't exactly lining up to share it with me. I heard the truck before seeing it. The *grrrrr* of its engine. It rounded the bend, skipped the grassy strip dividing the street, hopped the curb and . . . there was no time to do anything. I tell myself that now, Dunk, and . . . really, that's the truth I think. But it *felt* like I had all the time in the world. But that's only because time slows down in a crisis—that's what every-one tells me, anyway.

"The fuckhead hit Frag so hard his collar snapped—the impact knocked the blood through him in a wave, the vet told me, bulging his veins and snapping the collar. All I felt was a slight tug as the leash followed the movement of Frag's body—like a big fish biting the bait off your hook before the line goes slack."

I could hear Owe moving—had he stood up, was he stumbling around? I listened to the familiar squeak of the brace on his knee: an awkward contraption he never bothered to oil. Then came a crash, the squeak of shoe heels on linoleum and a tortured outrush of air.

"Jesus." He hissed through his teeth. "I've fallen and I can't get up."
"You okay?"

"I'll live. Unfamiliar surroundings." His breathing calmed, then he said, "I didn't see Frag go airborne. But when I close my eyes, Dunk, sometimes I do—Frag tumbling over and over in the air as if he's rolling up an invisible hill before gravity inevitably takes hold. His legs tucked stiff to his body like he's already dead, rigor mortis setting in. And y'know, I *hope* he was dead. I *hope* the impact knocked the life right out of him.

"The fuckhead's truck smoked on down the sidewalk. To this day I have no idea if he even *knew*. Frag was slumped halfway under an ornamental shrub on somebody's front lawn. His flesh was split right through his coat, man. Can you imagine the pressure?"

My eyes drifted to the house across the street. It'd been vacant a few months. The owners had defaulted on their mortgage— happened a lot, even in low-rent neighbourhoods—and the bank hadn't resold it. It sagged into itself the way neglected homes tend to, as if, vacant of life, the wood and brick surrender their strength and the whole works sinks slowly like a mammoth into a tar pit. The windows were dark but I could see something moving behind the glass.

"Engine coolant had bled down the street," Owe said. "I followed it. The truck was parked in an alleyway covered in a blue tarp, the kind you drape over cordwood to keep out the damp. The front headlight hung from its mount. Frag's collar was meshed with the grille. That's when I felt it, man. The *snap*. I'd heard that term around the precinct. The snap is that moment, that *sight*, that breaks a cop. One guy snapped when he found a baby stuffed into a vacuum cleaner bag by its drugged-out father. He unzipped the bag and saw an ash-grey little face clung with lint and cat hair and . . . For me, it was a dog collar stuck in the grille of a Dodge pickup.

"So fuckhead's sitting on a lawn chair in the backyard, smoking a Chesterfield with a freshly cracked beer. Bloodshot eyes, blood down his shirt: he'd busted his nose on the wheel. I showed him my badge. He goes: *I've got my rights, don't I?* After the evidence crew showed, I wrapped Frag up and carried him home. I laid him on the kitchen table. Where else . . . where do you put a dead dog? You'd think that'd be the end of it, right?"

He lapsed into silence. I didn't break it. He rustled around, stood up maybe. Next came the grating scrape of a lighter's flywheel being flicked.

A trembling flame lit the bay window of the house across the street, illuminating a figure standing in the darkness.

I listened to a ragged inhale, a prolonged hack.

"You smoking?"

"I don't, as a rule," Owe said. "Only on stakeouts."

My heart double-tapped—two solid mule kicks behind my rib cage.

"Big case, uh?"

"Not really, man. Penny-ante, to tell the truth. But guys get themselves shut away for nothing sometimes. But then it's not my job—"

"To talk people out of being stupid?"

Silence again.

"Fuckhead's lawyer got him house arrest. Ultimately he got two years for drunk driving. It was only a dead dog, right? He stood before the judge and was all, *I have a disease. Look into your heart.* Three priors—a pair of DUIs and another for driving with a suspended licence. Your garden-variety fuckhead driven by garden-variety demons. Anyway, here's the part you need to know. The fuckhead who killed my dog went for a smoke every night. Right before bed. He turned in late—two in the morning. How did I know he smoked, Dunk?"

I didn't say anything. The answer was obvious: because he'd watched him.

The line was so quiet I could hear the paper of his smoke crackle as it burned.

"Four nights I watched from my car in the alley. At one o'clock on the fifth night I got out with an iron pipe. Fuckhead smoked in the backyard, under the patio's bare bulb. I crept into his yard, unscrewed the bulb so the contact points weren't touching. Then . . . well. Next day Chief calls me into his office. Said nobody would be trying all that hard to find the guy who assaulted fuckhead, shattering his kneecap and crushing his orbital socket . . . but maybe police work wasn't my bag."

The ember brightened in the dark house across the road. Owe's breath feathered the mouthpiece, gently rasping.

"And I'll tell you, because why the hell not . . . there are moments you realize that when you carry through with a given plan of action, you're gonna come out a changed man. Won't be noticeable on the outside but you'll never be the same behind the eyes. Standing in the dark in fuckhead's yard, waiting, a small part of me kept yammering: *this isn't you*. But who are any of us, really? We inhabit different states of being. Some are fleeting and some become permanent. Sometimes what we are, or who, or . . . it's just a question of circumstance, y'know? How far would you go? How much does it mean to you? How much do you need it?"

Dolly whined thinly, then heaved herself up and padded into the kitchen. I listened to the dry click of nails on the linoleum, the dry crunch of kibble between her molars.

"Anyway, that's Frag. I cremated him and scattered his ashes on his favourite walking trail . . . favourite, *I think*, because who can tell a dog's mind? It's hokey as hell, but whatever. I loved him, uh?"

"I know you did."

"He was sorta stupid but I love stupid things. Like you, Dunk."

"Awww, aren't you a peach."

"Don't do it, man."

I said, "Do what?" but the line was dead.

I sat watching the figure across the road. The figure watched me back.

At some point Ed returned from work.

"What are you looking at?"

"Nothing, beautiful. The stars."

The next night I didn't say goodbye to Ed, just slipped into my boots and left her sleeping. I flagged down a cab at the top of the street and told the driver to hit the casino. It rolled down Clifton Hill, the neon-lit marquees watery behind a curtain of rain. I bought a ticket for the casino shuttle. A couple of old warhorses in Sansabelt slacks stumbled on the bus, moaning about the rigged slots.

At the Rainbow Bridge a bored-looking border guard checked my passport. The shuttle headed east along the river and turned right at the aquarium before heading up Pine Street.

The driver stopped at the Piggly Wiggly. I stepped out, jacket pulled tight around my shoulders. The night seemed colder on this side of the river.

The bell chimed as I stepped inside the store. The clerk was eighteen, zitty, tending to the hot-dog rotisserie. I headed to the dairy case, grabbed a quart of full-fat milk. Moo juice, as my mom called it. The bell chimed. I turned to the pastries, craving something sweet and body-wrecking. A Hostess Choco-Bliss, maybe.

"Dunk?"

Owe stood behind the swinging glass of the soda cooler. He let it fall shut and squared his shoulders. His expression betrayed nothing.

"Hey, Owe."

"Fancy seeing you here."

"Yeah, fancy that."

I picked up a cellophane-wrapped bearclaw and rubbed the serrated edge of the wrapper against my chin.

"What are you doing over here?" he said.

"Meeting somebody."

"Anyone I know?"

"Don't figure so. We met after you left town."

"Where you going?"

I said, "What are you doing here?"

Owe smiled sheepishly. "Pizza and wings at Sammy's."

"By yourself?"

"Why—want to come with? I don't like eating alone."

"Sorry, but like I said. Plans. Another time."

A car pulled into the lot. The horn honked.

"You can't go halfway down the rabbit hole, Diggs," Owe said before turning away.

I paid for my milk, walked across the lot and got into the grey Ford Taurus. Igor was squashed behind the wheel. He pulled out, driving with the squinty determination of the elderly.

A pit bull sat in the back seat. It was about the same size as Folchik, white with a black stripe across its eyes.

"That's Bandit," Igor said. "Don't pet him."

"Where's Drinkwater?"

"Not coming," Igor said. "Never does."

"Just you and me?"

"On this side. Others, other side."

"You got my money?"

Igor's head swivelled slowly, as if his neck was operated by a balky crank. When he didn't answer I glanced over my shoulder. Stuck hadn't followed. He couldn't possibly know where we were going—even I didn't know that.

Igor said, "What's your problem?"

We hit the I-190 and out across the night river where it split at Navy Island. The street lights vanished as we drove through Buckthorn Island, then came back as we hit the Red Carpet Inn off Grand Inland Boulevard. The wheel looked as thin as copper wire in Igor's meathooks. I felt the shape of the box-cutter in my pocket. I was ashamed to have brought it—a Dollar Store weapon, something a punk would carry.

We hit the West River Parkway and swung round the traffic ring into Beaver Island State Park. Light stanchions shone on an empty road glittering with frost. Igor tapped the brakes and eased onto an unlit corduroy road. Bushes whacked up under the car, rattling the coins in the cup holders. Igor pulled under some trees, cut the engine and unrolled the back window enough so Bandit could hop out.

"We walk from here."

The long, open rush of the river and the dampness of the woods crawled up the back of my neck. We trudged through leaf mould that collapsed beneath our feet, boots sinking into the twisted roots that clawed up through the earth.

Igor moved slowly, tripping once and whistling air between his teeth. Trees with bladelike leaves, willows maybe, grew thickly along the bank. I pushed them clear with hands numb from the cold. The river opened before us.

It was black, as all night water was—as if the night dissolved directly into it, filling it with the same nothingness that must exist between stars.

"Those are them," Igor said.

I peered at one puntboat, one swift-looking Zodiac. The puntboat was a wide-bottomed hulk topped with a tarpaulin. Under the tarp sat cardboard boxes stacked high, flaps fastened with packing tape.

"You in this one." Igor pointed to the punt. "I follow in the Zodiac."

The cry came from somewhere behind the willows. Owe. I knew it instinctively, because although years had passed and we were now double the age we were back then, and Owe's voice had changed and deepened, when we scream—any of us, when we are truly shocked and scared—we sound like boys. Owe screamed as he had when we were boys lost in the woods.

Instinctively I leapt from the puntboat and moved towards him—which was when Igor smashed a fist into the side of my head. The night swung out of balance, stars pinwheeling as I crashed on the rocks with Igor's bulk following to crush the air from my lungs.

"Knew you were dirty . . ."

His hands clamped round my throat. My legs thrashed uselessly as Igor hipped himself up on my chest, bearing down with all his weight, shoulders torqueing forward, hands constricting to crush my windpipe.

Darkness hemmed my vision, a deeper and more profound darkness than night. I brought a fist up and cracked Igor in the mouth but my strength was fleeing, my reflexes too, and I don't think he even registered it. I slid a hand between his thigh and my stomach, feeling for the box-cutter that lay trapped against the tight denim of my pocket. I clawed for it, my tongue thickening as the pressure of blood swelled behind my eyes.

My hand closed on the plastic shaft of the box-cutter and I thumbed the mechanism convulsively. I jerked my arm, the box-cutter slicing through my pocket as my hand came up under Igor's thigh—there was a sensation of things coming apart, a terrifying new looseness—and next my hand was free and in it lay three inches of glinting razor.

Igor's hands clenched my throat tighter. White balls burst in front of my eyes. Then warmth was spreading across my chest. Igor's grip loosened. He stared down with a look of befuddlement. His jeans were dark, as was my shirt and jacket.

"Wha—?" he said.

He stood with difficulty. A clean, straight slit ran through his jeans, two inches to the left of his zipper. Blood ran along each edge. His hands trembled at the wound. He pushed as if he might somehow push the blood back inside. He staggered towards the water, still ten or twelve feet from the shore.

Igor got down carefully on his knees; blood splashed the stones, or was it the splash of water? Part of me wanted him to die, but that same part knew I was doomed if he did. That part also knew it was beyond my power to control now.

Igor crawled to the river. He was moaning somebody's name, I believe, yet the sound came out as a hateful hiss. He fell face first into the water. I staggered to the waterline, rolled Igor over. His eyes were already glassy like a doll's.

Run, said a rabbity voice inside my head. *It's all you can do now. RUN.*

The Zodiac ignited with an easy rumble. I piloted it onto the river, skipping across lapping wavelets, swallowing compulsively because it was hard to breathe. Where was I going? I had no idea. My mind said, *Just go.*

The Zodiac's motor stripped out across the water. I angled towards the Falls, charting the bend of the river by the solitary lights hovering above the scrim of the shore. Red and blue lights flashed in the low-lying blackness on the Canadian side, disappearing as the cruisers dipped down a hill and reappearing as they crested it.

A trap door opened in my stomach. *Edwina. Owe.*

I cycled the motor to surge upriver. There were the lights of Clifton Hill. The Falls were lit with red and green spotlights, and a white bowl of mist foamed up from the basin. The sound was loudest here: a pressurized thrum against my eardrums. I thought fleetingly: *You forget how powerful some things are. You take their beauty for granted.*

A helicopter rose up from the Falls basin, blades whirring over the tumbling water. Its spotlight illuminated the river. I almost laughed. I spun around and cut back downriver. I screamed into the cold air that wicked off the water, let it fill my mouth with the taste of wet steel. The taste of home.

The searchlight crept across the river until it found me. A cone of light shone down like the finger of God himself. The chopper dropped low; water foamed over the Zodiac's gunwales. A bullhorn-amplified voice shouted something, but I had no idea what.

Then the puntboat slid out of the darkness in front of me, Owe at the wheel. His skull was clad in a helmet of blood. Jesus, was he okay? I cut the motor and floated forward. The noses of our boats touched, then bounced gently away.

I showed Owe my palms like a magician following some sleight of hand. Ta-*daa*. The helicopter's searchlight cored a circle of whiteness out of the night.

"I'm sorry I had to run you down," he might have said, but his words were carried away by the rotor wash of the helicopter.

"You never had to do anything," I may have said back.

"You made me."

"No, Owe. You made yourself."

We floated in that perfect halo of light. Cataract City men, fully made.

———

IT WAS NIGHT AGAIN WHEN I LEFT my parents' house, walking to a quiet stretch of blocks off Bender Street. I'd thought about taking the folks' car, but my licence had expired while I was in prison and I was done taking stupid risks. Almost done, anyway.

There was a pay phone on the street, near the Sleep Easy Motor Inn. I stepped inside, let the Plexiglas door swing shut, plugged quarters in the box and dialled.

I hadn't tried the number in years. Would she have kept it?

One ring. Two. Three. Four. Five.

I was getting ready to hang up when a voice said, "Hello?"

My breath hitched. I felt my heart as a discrete part of me, shuddering in my chest. I couldn't speak; my voice was lodged tight and hard as a fist somewhere below my lungs.

"Duncan?"

After an endless gulf during which I was certain she'd hang up, I squeaked, "Yes."

A pause, then a long exhale. "So," she said, "are you going to try to find me?"

"Depends," I answered. "Do you want to be found?"

She laughed—a husky, frayed-edge sound. The most beautiful sound in the whole world.

PART FOUR

DONNYBROOK
&
LIONS IN WINTER

DONNYBROOK: DUNCAN DIGGS

——

That first night in the Kingston Pen I lay in the dark above my new cellmate, a huge specimen from Sioux Lookout named Nathan Bainbridge. Bainbridge gave off a billygoat odour: trans-3-methyl-2-hexenoic acid, in fact, which Bainbridge, a borderline schizophrenic, leaked out in his sweat. The poor bastard was plagued by night terrors. His legs thrashed wildly, rattling the bedframe we shared. Sometimes he unleashed piglet squeals, horrified by whatever creatures stalked his dreams.

I breathed shallowly, trying not to wake Bainbridge. Searchlights strafed the yard outside the window. I listened to the living engine of the prison: mice squeaking, inmates hacking wetly, screams that died soon after they were born. I'll admit it freaked me out.

My own toughness wasn't something I'd had cause to question. It was an aspect of my makeup, same as my black hair and the cleft in my chin. Still, I understood that I was Cataract City tough, with a head-down, fists-cocked grittiness that'd only get me hurt in here, where all a man really needed was ratlike cunning and a willingness to sink in the blade. In prison, every blind corner held a threat. I got used to it in time, the way a guy living beneath a flight path gets used to his windows rattling every time a 747 cruises overhead.

Night washed slowly into day. When sunlight began to creep over the floor Bainbridge rolled out of bed, walked to the commode and flopped his dick out of his PJs. While his piss hit the steel with a ringing tinkle, Bainbridge stared at me blankly and crooned Phil Collins: "*It's just another day / For you and me / In paradise.*"

I'd killed a man. That much was known around the pen. That the man had been Iroquois earned me points in some quarters, hatred in others. I didn't bother clarifying the facts to anyone; that night on the Niagara River had taken on a dreamlike quality in my memory—a nightmare of moon-silvered steel and blood the colour of tar.

At the trial the prosecution had submitted grainy photos of a man laid out on a riverbank. His body looked deflated, a tire with a pinhole leak, limbs wrenched at odd angles on the rocks.

Seeing those photos, a bony-fingered hand squeezed my heart muscle. I hadn't wanted it—hadn't *meant* for this to happen.

I got nine years for involuntary manslaughter in the killing of Igor Bearfoot, plus three and a half years for attempting to introduce a controlled substance across international borders. Which meant I earned statutory release after eight.

In his sworn testimony, Owen Stuckey stated the killing of Bearfoot had been a matter of life and death. At the time of the pretrial hearing the bruises on my throat had mushroomed into a purplish-yellow collar, testament to his claim. When asked to identify the suspect from the witness box, Owe's eyes met mine unblinkingly. He'd fingered me with his right hand—his left was still heavily bandaged from his encounter with a pit bull, Bandit, owned by the deceased.

Bearfoot's body was returned to the Tuscarora Nation, to be

buried in keeping with Iroquois custom. No charges were levied against Lemuel Drinkwater.

Those first few years inside I punished myself.

The prison weight pen was available during out-of-cell hours—I got two daily—and I spent the first half of it curling ancient barbells and strapping heavy weight plates around my hips to grind out wide-grip chin-ups. I performed each move silently, my features wrenched into strained expressions; I could feel the thick veins radiating from my temples. I must've looked like one of those hooded monks in frescoes at the Sacred Heart church, stripped to the waist, lashed with iron-tipped whips—men dedicated to acts of extreme penance. Flagellants, my mom called those guys.

A boxing ring was set off the weight pen. In the second hour I'd smash my fists into the heavy bag so hard that the leather groaned against the hanging chain and the skin over my knuckles split open. Afterwards I wrapped my shredded mitts with prickly prison-issue toilet paper—even the TP was designed to remind us of our sins—and if I was lucky I'd fall into an exhausted sleep, riding those maddening night hours where time could draw itself out like a blade.

Often I'd jerk awake from dreams where I was adrift on the Niagara as Igor Bearfoot's head swam out of the black water, eye sockets picked clean by sunfish.

One day while I was hammering the bag a young inmate ambled over. He was of medium height and build, with reddish-brown skin and hands graced with long, clever fingers. He flipped me a pair of hand-wraps.

"They're my old ones," he said. "Keep you from busting your mitts up any worse than they already are."

Silas Garrow was a full-blooded Mohawk Indian from the Akwesasne rez. Other than me, he was the only inmate to make use of the boxing setup—Garrow had once been the Native American Boxing Council's top-ranked middleweight.

"Twenty-one wins, three losses." He gave his biceps a little pump. "A regular rambling rumbler—reservation-to-reservation, swinging TNT every place I went." He held his fists under his chin. "These babies had 'em trembling in their teepees, limping back to their longhouses."

But his boxing ambitions were cut short after he got pinched for smuggling.

"They caught me driving a rig of Bronco smokes across the Saint Lawrence in the middle of February," he told me. "The ice broke, right? Soon the rig was just a-sinkin'. I was only twenty-two, my first run, so I flung the doors open and started hucking boxes out. Well, next the emergency crew rolls in and I'm still stuck . . . a skidoo, a skidoo, my kingdom for a skidoo! Even a pair of fuckin' ice skates—throw a dog a bone!"

When I tried to explain my own situation, Silas held up one hand.

"I know all about the Tuscarora. Who was it? Dale Hawkwind? Lemmy Drinkwater?"

"Drinkwater, yeah."

"There's a verse we were taught in school," Silas said. "*Learn to be patient observers like the owl; learn courage from the jay, who will attack an owl ten times its size to drive it off its territory* . . . I think that's how it went. Anyway, Lem Drinkwater learned how to do business from Raven—the Trickster. You killed one of his men?"

"An accident . . ."

"Always is, man. What was his name?"

"Igor Bearfoot."

"*Igor*? Sounds like an apple."

"An apple?"

"Not a real Indian, man. Red on the outside, white on the inside."

We started training together. I'd never truly learned to box: I just bulled forward, swinging lefts and rights, a tactic that tended to work against the tomato cans Drinkwater had thrown at me. But Silas was rangy and oh so slippery. I'd hem him into a corner, shutting down angles in hopes of landing a crushing shot. Silas would pop a few jabs in my face—*yip! yip! yip!*—with enough sting to either back me off or make him throw a clumsy haymaker. Next he'd slip out of the corner slick as oil.

A greased eel's got nothing on this guy, I'd think—usually just before getting blitzed with another of Silas's crisp jabs.

"The Great Spirit has conveyed tremendous power into these vessels," Silas would say, kissing each of his fists. "He told me, *Go forth, Silas Garrow, and wreak great havoc on the white man and all their wicked ways.*"

"The white man? Silas, all your fights were against Indians."

"Yeah? Well, they had it coming. We all do."

I'd *tsk-tsk*. "You're such a racist."

"I'm a self-hating Indian, man. Learn to spot the difference."

We sparred four days a week, and the other three I nursed my various hurts. Black eyes and fat lips and a hematoma on my forehead big as a boiled egg, the blood wrapped tight as a fist under the skin. One day my guard stopped by my cell and whispered, "We can't help unless you tell us who does this to you."

I said, "I ran into a doorknob."

"Suit yourself, hard guy."

Sometimes, without quite admitting the instinct, I'd lean into one of Silas's shots—Silas was a pitty-patter fighter anyway, no real gas in his pistons—and let his fist fillet my face. Once or twice he got an inkling about what I was doing; he'd cut a hard look at me, yank off his gloves and say, "The point of boxing is to *not* get hit."

"Keep it coming, man. One more round."

"You think I like kicking a dog down the street?"

"Come on. Give it to me like you mean it."

One day Silas simply refused to go another round. "Listen, man . . . we're all in here for good reason. Everybody'll tell you it was a judge on the warpath or crooked cops, but facts sit square against that. The only sunlight I see is this one ray coming through my window in the morning—and man, I put my face to that ray, drink that shit up like Kool-Aid. We all owe and we're all paying. But you don't got to pay extra, okay? And if you're bent on it, fine, but don't go making me your fuckin' Shylock."

Silas won when we sparred because Silas was naturally gifted, but I picked up a few nifty new tricks. Every once in a while I'd catch him with a sweet hook to the short rib; the natural red would fall out of his face, to be replaced with puréed chalk.

Afterwards we'd sit on the apron, faces flushed and leather-burnt. Silas would tap me companionably on the back of the head with his glove. Sometimes his expression became solemn—or mock-solemn? I could never tell. "Can't believe I'm actually *friends* with a paleface. This is going to fuck my cred all to shit if they ever find out on the rez."

Edwina visited me only once, a month after I entered the pen.

She looked as beautiful as I'd ever seen her. Believe me when I say this had nothing to do with the fact that all I saw otherwise was the pitted faces of long cons. Hers was a raw beauty, and any changes I could spot were minor: she'd done a little something to her hair or her skin, imparting a fresh lustre.

We sat in the visiting room around circular steel tables that looked like playground carousels. Rays of sunlight carved through the barred windows—heatless in here, as always.

The other inmates snuggled with their wives and girlfriends like high-schoolers under the bleachers, copping feels just to touch flesh that had touched the outside world. Ed and I sat at opposite ends of the table. Ed's hands stayed on her lap.

"You shithead," she said flatly.

"I'm a shithead," I agreed.

She fed quarters into the vending machines and came back with a Coke, a Diet Coke and a honey bun wrapped in cellophane. She slid the Coke and bun across to me.

"Was there a reason you didn't tell me?"

"About what, Edwina?"

"About all of it."

"What would you have done if I had told you?"

Edwina had the same hard-boned face as a lot of women in Cataract City, but the difference was in everything going on under that calm surface, nuances expressed in the smallest movements and dilations. I smiled; it was so good just to *be this close* to her, to see the gold coins of light dancing in each of her eyes.

"Jesus, Duncan. You killed a man."

The finality with which she spoke those words—it was as if the act itself had attached itself to my name like a cocklebur. I *was* a killer. Not a murderer, but definitely a killer.

"Did you ever think?" She stared searchingly into my face. "I mean, in a million years . . .?"

"No, Ed. Never in a million years."

"How did it happen?"

But this was almost like asking somebody how they'd come down with cancer: you accumulated bad habits and bad luck, I figured, and the next thing you know, something takes root. You don't set out to get cancer. And I'd never set out to kill a man.

Ed exhaled heavily, blowing a bang slantwise across her forehead. I wanted to reach across the table and tuck that lock of hair behind her ear.

Later, I found a single strand of Ed's hair in my cell, laid across my pillow like dark thread. I don't know how it got there—I'd been stripped and scrubbed before entering the pen; everything I'd owned had been taken from me. And we hadn't touched once during her visit; not a hug, not a handshake. But it *was* her hair. I knew this simply by feel, the way a man knows the shape of his wife's body in the dark. A single strand of hair; all I had left of her. I held on to it for years, if you can believe it. I'd lie awake at night twining it around my finger, desperately afraid it'd snap. It never did—I was always gentle with it. If my orange jumpsuit had had pockets, I would've carried it close to me all day. But since pockets were banned, I slicked the hair with saliva and smoothed it to the metal frame of my cot in a spot where it wouldn't be disturbed when the sheets were changed. It lasted three years, that strand of hair. Then one day I reached for it and it was gone. I hunted madly, making Bainbridge get up so I could search the floor under his cot, but no luck. Maybe it simply dissolved from all my handling.

Next Ed said, "Do you actually think I'll wait?"

No, I knew she wouldn't wait for me—not because there wasn't any love between us, but because she'd freely given me the chance to save myself, and I hadn't taken it. I couldn't bear to consider her question, and so my mind fled back to the night when we'd first danced.

It happened months after we'd first held hands at Sherkston Shores. I'd asked her to dance on the postage stamp of a stage at the Wild Mushroom bar. The bond had been there in the curve of our bodies as we leaned into the music, heads cocked as we stared at each other. We'd danced to a Beatles song, "I Want to Hold Your Hand." Ed held her hand out to me, her eyebrows raised in a silent question. I'd taken and kissed it, earning a round of desultory wolf-whistles from the rubber-necking barflies. Ed laughed and rolled her eyes. We'd danced to the next song, by the Tragically Hip, "Everytime You Go," and I'd lip-synched the lines that ever since have been seared into my mind, meshed with the sight of Edwina's hips swaying to the beat: *My girl don't just walk, she unfurls . . .*

Afterwards we'd walked down Clifton Hill, which was nearly dark at that hour. Stars pinpricked the sky. We took sips from the can of Laker I'd cadged off the bartender at last call. We stood at the observation rail as water hit the cataract, sending up a mushroom cloud of spume. I'd slid my coat around her shoulders and told her about the things that had mattered to me back then: the motorcycle I'd planned to buy but never did, the cut on my hand I'd picked up on my first shift at the Bisk. She told me about the death of her father from esophageal cancer and the all-girl band she'd played in before getting into a fistfight with the lead singer.

I'd smiled, knowing I was hers now: all body, all soul. I'd been waiting to give myself to somebody that way ever since I could remember.

"I'm taking Dolly," she said to me in the pen's visiting room.

"Taking her where?"

"Just away, Dunk."

I kept my head steady, my gaze calm, but my insides were chewing themselves to pieces. "Okay, sure. She loves you best, anyway."

"Dogs love everyone the same."

She stood up. Her jaw worked like she was going to say something else. She looked at the visiting room guard, flustered for a moment, then back at me. "You want another Coke before I go?"

That's when I realized it was going to end this way: with the woman I loved awkwardly asking if I wanted another soda.

"It's okay, baby. But thanks."

She walked out and kept walking. She took Dolly and never looked back. Edwina did the one thing I'd never fully brought myself to do, despite all the dreaming and planning: she left Cataract City.

I grew my hair long, shaved my skull to bare scalp then let it grow again. My body fleshed out: I had thick striations across the chest and marbling on the delts, lats flaring in a noticeable cobra's hood. I hammered the bag until my body was clad in a fine oil of sweat and every joint rolled smooth in its socket. I sparred with Silas and sat with him at dinnertime in companionable silence. I watched my hair go grey at my temples in the steel mirror above the shitter—everything in the pen was steel, and no reflection was quite right—and wondered if it was something about the character of the light that had given me a permanent squint.

Prison subtly ruins you. The grey cafeteria chow cored a hole through my insides. The pressure of living with five hundred caged animals carved deep lines in my flesh. I saw a man stabbed in the ear with a sharpened toothbrush. Saw another man kicked half to death with bare feet in the showers, his attackers slipping on the tiles as their cocks slapped their thighs. The only solace was that these victims probably deserved it, more or less.

After a time, I was no longer a new fish, but not an old fish. A middle fish, if there was any such thing. Sometimes I'd feel a click in my throat when I swallowed: Igor Bearfoot's huge hands had partially crushed my Adam's apple.

As the long-timers said: I worked my time and tried to make it work for me. I enrolled in correspondence English classes, completing the diploma program I'd started years ago. My verbiage improved considerably—the iron bars became *ferrous shackles*; a pretty actress on TV became a *toothsome seductress* . . . you'd never speak that way in the pen, of course, unless you wanted an ass-stomping. But I liked my newfound words, my bons mots—they pushed the walls back just a little, gave me space to breathe. When the book trolley came around I'd say, "Surprise me." Police procedurals, horror pulps, outdoorsy narratives.

The Count of Monte Cristo—that one I asked for specifically.

Some days I figured I'd do my years quietly and earn my release and life would continue at a lower wattage. I'd stay with my folks and visit my probation officer, get a job—something I could do with my hands—go to the Cairncroft Lounge on Saturday nights for a wobbly pop with Sam Bovine, meet a woman who wasn't put off by histories and scars. Get a little house off Drummond Road, have a few kids.

It wasn't such a stretch, was it? Perhaps it wasn't the life I'd envisioned—but who ever ends up with the life they imagine as a child? Screw anyone who does. What's to say they hadn't dreamed too small in the first place?

Other nights I lay in bed with the pads of my feet clenched tight as if I was teetering over a balcony ledge thirty stories up, terrified I'd get cancer and die in this strange grey place. Or maybe a vein would pop in my skull and I'd twitch to death in my sleep with Bainbridge squealing beneath me. Mainly, though, my worries echoed those of most cons: when I got out, what would be left for me? The world would have progressed and I'd have lost my fragile place in it. I'd already lost Edwina—what else was left?

Each New Year I stood in the common room wearing a goofy party hat as Dick Clark announced the ball drop on TV. It was the only way I bothered marking the passage of time. I didn't count days anymore, or even weeks. They'd welded together, a polished steel rail that I could slide right over.

I awoke to each new day and let it carry me through a familiar routine. I sat at the same table for meals, met Silas at the appointed time for sparring, showered with the same faces, stuffed in earplugs and struggled to sleep. I even got used to Bainbridge's smell.

In my sixth year Silas Garrow was released. The guards let him throw a little bash in the laundry room: a few bottles of Jack Daniel's, a sandwich platter. Silas bequeathed me his collection of spank mags.

"Treat them with reverence, paleface."

I held one up. *Fifty and Nifty.* "Really, Silas?"

"Older ladies need love, too. See you on the outside?"

"Of course."

Were they true words? Silas would never leave the Akwesasne and I'd plant myself back in Cataract City. The only place we'd meet again was back inside these cold stone walls.

One night Bainbridge started shrieking and kicking up a mighty fuss. I said to hell with it, reached down and shook the huge man's shoulder.

"Nathan, god damn it, wake up! You're having a nightmare."

Bainbridge blinked his cowlike eyes and spoke in the voice of a child. "Geez, what a crazy dream. There was this ugly witch with a wart on her nose and she was cackling like a loon and—" He swallowed heavily. "She was pulling on my . . . *scrotum.* Tugging so dang hard I thought she'd rip the dang thing off."

"It's okay, man. See? No witch."

Bainbridge shuddered. "Thank you, Duncan. Sincerely."

The rail narrowed and then, one day, it ended. On that day a guard handed over the items I'd been arrested holding: a handful of change, half a roll of cherry Life Savers. I peeled the paper and popped two of them in my mouth—the candies were stuck together with age. They tasted just about as good as I'd remembered.

I dropped two tarnished quarters into the prison's pay phone. I called Owe.

And then I was out.

And now came payback.

———

THE DAY AFTER MEETING with Owe and Bovine at the Double Diamond and outlining my intentions, Owe and I drove across the river, through customs, and onto the Robert Moses Parkway. A bullet-pitted road sign said: ENTERING THE TUSCARORA NATION. Owe pulled into Smokin' Joes. The steel warehouses where Drinkwater's real business went down still stood behind a fence of electrified chain-link.

The shelves in Smokin' Joes looked as if they'd been rifled by survivalists. The leather jackets were so old they'd lost their smell, dust collecting on their shoulders. We wandered around aimlessly. I saw the cashier pick up the phone.

Five minutes later Drinkwater pulled into the lot. His silver pickup was dinged and rusty. He stepped inside his store with a hulking, sallow-faced sidekick in tow. The awful thought struck me that the sidekick looked a lot like Igor Bearfoot.

"You're out of jail, my pretty," Drinkwater said when he saw me. "And look! You've brought your little dog, too."

I said, "You look haggard, Lem."

Drinkwater's fingernail *scritched* the stubble on his chin like a wooden match pulled over a striking strip. "You look well, Diggs. Prison life must have agreed with you, uh? Three hots and a cot. Yeah, you'll never get those years back, but you put on a few solid pounds of jail beef."

I pulled a Coke from the cooler and drank half in one go.

Drinkwater said: "Plan on paying for that?"

"Think I'd welsh on you, Lem?"

"I don't know what you'd do—you're an ex-con, Diggs. Better get used to people having trust issues." He glanced at Owe, then back to me. "I would have thought you two might have trust issues of your own."

"I want to fight again, Lem."

Drinkwater drew back as if shocked. "Diggs! Need I remind you that you're in polite society? Your animalistic ways don't fly out here."

Owe said, "How's business, Lemmy? Lookin' a little sluggish. You ought to rotate your merchandise."

Drinkwater's tongue played on the point of his eye tooth. "Like I said, Diggs—we're not mixed up with fighting here. You'd almost think, coming over here with a member of the constabulary, you're trying to . . . what's it called? *Entrap* me."

Owe plucked a bag of potato chips off the wire rack and dropped it on the ground. Drinkwater watched him with bright birdlike eyes. Owe set the toe of his boot on the bag. The cellophane squealed thinly before the bag popped, spraying chips over Drinkwater's boots.

Pinching his jeans at the inseam, Drinkwater shook chips off his pant legs. "Now that," he said, small veins braiding under his shirt collar, "that *couldn't* have been an accident."

Owe pointed at the security camera above the counter. "You've got me. So don't say entrapment, okay? Not to mention which, I'm consorting with a known smuggler."

Drinkwater laughed. "Ain't my fault you don't pick friends with a finer pedigree."

"I'm talking about you, Lem."

Drinkwater batted his eyes. "Why, Officer, you of all people know I've never been convicted. As I recall, a great deal of your time and efforts have funnelled down that empty hole."

"You're clean," said Owe. "That doesn't stop a lot of people from thinking you're scum. Now that's a fact, Lem. It's the way you're seen."

Drinkwater's jaw went hard. He swallowed in one sinuous movement.

"You want to fight, uh?" he said to me.

When I told him I wanted to fight three men, Drinkwater's eyelids lifted from half-mast.

"One night," I explained. "Any three men you want."

"Think you're the first swinging dick with a death wish who's walked through these doors?" he said. "Anybody in particular?"

"Anyone'll do. Whites, blacks, Natives."

"No women and kids?" Drinkwater laughed softly. "I only ask because, well, I am talking to a man who cut another man's balls off with a carpet knife, am I not?"

I said, "That's not how it happened."

"No? That's the way everybody believes it went down around here. You snuck up behind poor Igor, slid a blade between his legs and slit him nuts to asshole. Were it not for the hard work of the police"—he turned to Owe, palms pressed together as if in prayer—"and bless you for that, Officer. *Bless you.* If not for the police you'd have gotten away clean."

"If that's the kind of guy you think I am, why not make it all Natives?"

Drinkwater said, "You're asking me to assemble a war party? You got it, Pontiac. Three stout Indians, of heart proud and true."

"I want to put a bet on myself, too."

"Yeah?" said Drinkwater. "Well, nobody put me on this earth to talk grown men out of being stupid."

The day before the fight I withdrew all but five bucks from my account at the Greater Niagara Credit Union. Edwina had sold our house while I was locked up and transferred my half into the account I'd opened as a ten-year-old to rathole the money I made mowing neighbourhood lawns.

The days leading up to the fight had passed quickly. I'd done plenty of running—I'd slacked off in prison, seeing as it made me feel like a hamster on a wheel. Now I ran at night. I'd wake up in the witching hours and drag myself to the bathroom. I'd open the cupboard and hunt out the bottle at the back with an old rag tented over it. *Tuf-Foot.* The tagline read: *A dog is only as good as his feet.*

I'd squeeze some goo into my hands and massage it into my joints. Afterwards my hands were stained brown and achy to the bones, but I needed them to stay together in the fights.

I'd yank on the heavy workboots I used to wear at the Bisk, a hooded sweatshirt, and enter the empty corridors of night.

The streets were pretty much deserted. The few guys I passed weren't dangerous so much as desperate, broken by pills or inhalants or strong drink or the unstoppable craving for all those things. Every so often a face would jump out of a dark alley asking for something, or offering it, and I'd think: *Jesus, I used to know you. We played baseball at Reservoir Park.*

I'd run down Stanley Ave. as the bars emptied out, juking around drunk kids laughing their batshit laughter, finding myself a little terrified by that sound—it was the laughter of people who felt invincible because of their youth and promise and the wide-open future. Guys in prison didn't laugh like that.

I'd run further down the block where other bars were letting out, the ones with dark windows and no signs where the hospital orderlies and tollbooth operators drank. Men would shoulder through black presswood doors with fixed expressions on their faces and cigs fixed between their chalky lips. I'd watch the fresh air smack them in the face, their pupils constricting as the realization dawned: *Sweet Jesus, I'm not anywhere near drunk enough!* Some of them gave me a slit-eyed look before nodding, but not chummily. These guys weren't a lot older than me, their faces wrecked from drink or just the years piling up with brutal math.

A lot of nights I'd end up at the Falls, leaning on the observatory railing. There was always light by the Falls. It made no difference if there was a full moon or a sliver no thicker than a bone fish hook: moonlight hit the spray at the base of the Falls and the mist projected it back, an upside-down bowl of light. Baby birds peeped from their cliffside nests, a sound I found mysteriously comforting.

The night of the fight I packed my duffel, tucked the money order into my pocket and headed to a convenience store near my folks' place. Owe pulled up. I tossed my duffel in the footwell. We drove along the river past the hydro station. Owe cracked the window and hung a cigarette off his bottom lip. "You mind?"

"We all got to die someday."

He pulled up in front of a bar. Bovine slid into the back seat smelling like he'd spent the afternoon marinating in a vat of Famous Grouse.

"Just a few hand-steadiers," he said as we drove away.

Trucks were parked ten deep at the warehouse behind Smokin' Joes. A knot of seamed faces clustered round the door.

"You'll be heading home with your scalp hanging out of your fucking mouth," one of them said.

"That wig's getting split straight down the middle," said another.

The air hung hot and close inside the warehouse. Pigeons cooed in the rafters. When we entered the fighting area, a heavy silence fell. The Antichrist himself may as well have entered the building.

The fight box was the same as I remembered: a ring of sawhorses from a roadside construction site. Spectators ranged down them, the toes of their boots edging onto the fighting surface. They were drinking but nobody seemed drunk; they wanted to be sober to better witness the destruction.

Drinkwater stepped out of the crowd, laughing over his shoulder with someone. He eyed me up and down, and untucked a cigarette and a wooden match from behind his ear.

"What ya done brung me, son?"

I gave him the money order: as good as cash but easier to get past the border guards. Drinkwater struck the match on the tight denim draping his thigh, then lit the cigarette.

"That's a significant wager" was all he said.

"If you can't handle it . . ."

"Save your energy," Drinkwater told me, oh so softly. "I don't want anyone going home without their fill of blood."

"Add this to it," said Owe, pulling an envelope out of his pocket.

"How much?"

"Why don't you count it, Lem?"

"I never learned how. I went to a residential school run by the white man."

"Ten."

Drinkwater tucked it into his pocket. "Three-to-one odds."

"Bullshit," said Bovine. "Seven-to-one."

Drinkwater stared at him. "Who knew shit could talk?" he said mildly. "Four-to-one."

"Six," said Owe.

"Five. And you can only throw the towel once per fight."

Nobody bothered to shake on it. It wasn't a gentleman's agreement.

"Get your ass ready," Drinkwater said to me. "We Natives are getting restless."

I snapped my head sharply to one side to drain the sinus cavities, rolled my shoulders loose and said: "Pitter patter, let's get at 'er."

First up was the big sidekick I'd seen weeks back at Smokin' Joes. Igor Bearfoot II. He was a skyscraper with legs, three hundred pounds, easy. Drinkwater wanted to tenderize me, so he'd brought in his biggest mallet. Once I made it past this one, I thought, Lem probably had a fillet knife lined up, ready to slice me to ribbons. A dandy plan, I had to admit.

Still, I was okay with facing this monster out of the gate. Stick and move, chop the guy down Giant Kichi-style. Hopefully I wouldn't be breathing through a mask of blood by the end.

"Jesus," said Bovine, watching the guy warm up.

We came out of our corners, me stepping lightly on the balls of my feet, keeping my shoulders rolling—a move I'd picked up in jail—staring at the big man out of the tops of my eyes.

My opponent fought stripped to the waist. His nipples sat in sunken wells of flesh. The skin above and below his bellybutton funnelled into a cleft in the centre of his belly, lapping over in delicate folds like the skin of a half-deflated balloon. At some point he must've lost a ton of weight, which left him with those Shar-Pei folds. A weird surge of compassion rolled through me.

The guy's right shoulder dipped as his fist came around. I ducked it easily but I heard his arm rip the air above my head in a wide sweep, like a sailboat's boom swung free. Pivoting on my heel, switching the power to my hips, I hammered my own right into the man's ribs. His flesh rippled in a wave and he stepped off, his body buckling before righting itself.

I backed away, throwing yippy rights and lefts. A flash jab tore the skin over his left eye, and the blood flowed round his socket and down the angle of his jaw. He pawed at the blood, smearing it down his neck, and swung. It caught me on the shoulder—more of a slap than a punch, but it still rocked me sideways. I righted myself and tagged his nose with a smart shot. The crunch of cartilage sounded like the top snapping off an unripe banana.

A cigarette hit my chest and hissed in the sheen of sweat. I stomped on it while stepping forward, blitzing the big guy with jabs he caught with his elbows and forearms as he peered hesitantly at me through his upraised arms. His face was a horror show and the fight wasn't even a minute old. Did this guy know *how* to fight? Would Drinkwater tilt me against a big cream puff with sixty thousand dollars on the table—

Bullrushing with surprising speed, the guy ducked his head and rose up with his hands hooked under my armpits. I had a crazy weightless moment, my legs kicking at nothing. Then I brought one fist down on the big man's skull; it sounded like a coconut hitting a softwood floor. He hurled me at a sawhorse. Hungry faces hunched in at the edge of my vision and something sharp—a razor blade? an untrimmed fingernail?—sizzled along my hip bone. The guy bridged a forearm across my chest, cheating the air out of my lungs and bearing down with his claustrophobic bulk. His breath was equal parts Wintergreen Skoal and camphor. I noted the fine grey edge of lead around his dead canine tooth.

The man brought one world-eating fist down into my face and everything exploded in starlight riots, hollowness threading down my jaw as if nothing anchored it anymore: my face was only a mask, the contents of my skull obliterated.

I staggered forward as he swung again, reeling into the middle of the ring and punching instinctively, not at a face or even a shape but just at that onrushing warmth. My fist collided with something hard again—*snap!*—and that hardness split, becoming two separate things under a tight stretch of skin.

I got knocked down again, my knees mashed to jelly and the air whoofing out of my guts in a helpless gust. The big guy was on top now. Fear chewed into the wires of my brain, the insane lung-chaining fear you feel when trapped under a bigger man's bulk while your life is slowly choked out of you. Four bloody knuckles dropped from a great height, a cloud-splitting Hand of God. There was a loud crunch inside my head as the back of my skull rang off the concrete, a shockwave juddering me spine-deep.

Then, miraculously, the weight lifted. A racking gasp tore out of me. My head lolled to one side and I spotted the towel on the floor. Bovine must have thrown it.

At Drinkwater's, the white towel didn't mean the end. A cornerman threw it as a time-out and the injured fighter could get his wounds licked before wading back in.

I dragged myself up and hauled my ass to the corner amidst catcalls and hoots.

"He took you out behind the woodshed, whitey!"

Owe and Bovine sat me in a bright orange cafeteria chair. Bovine held my face, scrutinizing the damage. I let my skull rest against his hands. He slapped a bag of ice on the back of my neck and had Owe hold it there while he worked.

"He lumped your forehead but bad, Dunk. Burst a blood vessel?"

The skin of my forehead was tight, an odd shadow looming at the upper edge of my sight. I was cut over my left eye. Bovine swabbed the cut with a Q-tip saturated with Adrenalin. The raw burn rode the nerve endings down the side of my face, cabling the tendons in my neck.

Glancing to the opposite corner, I saw the big guy's nose was badly bust: cartilage crushed on one side, leaving the other side jutting straight and strange like a shark's fin. Bright blood streamed from both nostrils but the man sat with an easygoing expression, taking dainty sips from a Hamm's tallboy. His cutman hovered over him with a packet of Monsel's solution—the filthiest trick in a cutman's bag. Of course it was illegal—just not at Drinkwater's fights.

The cutman applied solution to the big man's cracked-open beak, *shaking* it on like he was salting popcorn. I smelled it—a cooked smell like a skirt steak drenched in battery acid.

"His ponytail," Owe said. "The *ponytail*, Dunk."

"That's time!" Drinkwater called.

The crowd stirred as we surged out of our corners. The guy's nose was predictably hideous: lips of bubbly flesh opened down to the gleam of buckled cartilage. He'd have to find a doctor to dig out that pavement of scar tissue with a scalpel—otherwise he'd be left with a second pair of deformed lips running vertically down his schnozz.

He came out like a grizzly awoken from hibernation. I came out nimbly this round, my attitude set in the register of give-a-fuck, moving side to side with my hands hipped like cocked pistols. The fight was in my blood now, and it was an ecstatic feeling; my senses had jacked in at last, operating on some dog-whistle frequency only I could hear.

The big guy clipped me with a looping cross, opening the cut Bovine had just closed. I shook my head, droplets spraying, and cuffed him with a clumsy left as the crowd rose to a quick roar. We circled out of a sloppy clinch where I caught a heat-seeking whiff of raw adrenaline coming out of his pores.

We clashed in the rough centre of the ring. The guy hauled in bulldog breaths, blood burping out his nose. His sweat-heavy trousers had slipped around his waist to expose his BVDs, which were a cheery shade of robin's egg blue. He dipped his head and came on but this time I timed it and stepped aside, letting him rumble past like a subway on fixed rails. Next, I was able to make two small adjustments that pretty much put the fight to bed, and I was lucky enough to do them in one fluid motion—watching it happen, I guess you might think we'd choreographed the damn thing.

What I did was snatch the guy's ponytail with my left hand, doubling it over in my fist and yanking back hard like I was bringing a big dog to heel, which forced his chin to tilt up. Then I torqued my hips and came round with the dynamite right, whipping my torso to propel my fist with all the juice my body could generate.

The punch struck the big man dead in the middle of his face. The sound was like two flat rocks spanked together. Everyone in that warehouse leaned back—it was like an explosion had gone *bang* in the ring.

For a second the whole world sat still: me with that grimy handful of hair, my fist flattened against the big man's face. If you could have frozen that image, you would have seen my curled fingers resting flush with the poor guy's eye sockets, his nose having turned into mash.

The big man let out a muffled moan, spraying red spittle. His hands came up in search of blood or pity, I couldn't tell. And I reached down inside, crushed that tiny voice in my chest pleading for mercy, cocked my fist and drove it into the guy's face again.

That was it. The man's body hung slack, back bowed, held up by my hand in his hair—he looked like a dead shark on a dock with a gaffing hook sunk into his snout. I lowered him to the floor gently as I could, then found my chair and sat. The ice bag hit the back of my neck. Blissful cold washed down my spine like water trickling in a downspout.

"You got lucky," a voice hissed somewhere to my left.

I blew at the fringe of blood-grimed hair plastered to my rapidly ballooning hematoma and thought, *You got that right, buddy. I'm the luckiest man in all Creation.*

Two men dragged the big fellow away by his heels like hunters lugging a dead bear out of the woods. My next opponent warmed up across the ring. As predicted, he was young and thin, with whiplike arms and legs that, if they were attached to a woman, you'd say went on for days, took a break at the knee and went a few days more. He had the empty, edgeless gaze of a psychopath.

Bovine took my right hand in his own. "Is it . . .?"

"Broke? Yeah."

"I've got some cortisone."

"Just leave it be."

Before we got to it the kid stuck his hand out, wanting to shake. Bad sign: it meant he saw this as pure business, which meant he wasn't any kind of dick-swinger. Drinkwater had found a pro. For him this was punching a clock. This particular shift, his job was to put me to bed. Thankfully I got the sense he'd do no more than was needed to reach that goal—but he *would* finish me.

The first shot impacted the mouse on my forehead with the mathematical precision of a laser-guided missile. The kid followed it up with a smart jab to my nose and another to my mouth. I reeled. My nose was so packed with blood I couldn't breathe; my lungs emptied through my mouth in a ragged hiss, air singing over my newly chipped tooth.

The kid slipped in blood falling from my face. Lowering my chin, I threw a punch that came up over my shoulder and tabbed the kid where his collarbone met his neck. The concussive *smack* travelled up to the rafters, making the pigeons take flight.

The kid's knees buckled and he backed off shaking his head, the glazed look in his pale brown eyes turning into something far more feral and crafty.

I shook my head too, droplets flying off the tips of my blood-quilled hair. How many pints did a man have in him? It felt like I'd bled out a few pints and swallowed another: my gut was heavy with the iron-tasting stuff that flowed down the back of my throat.

Our heads clashed with accidental violence. The shockwave of bone on bone telescoped around my skull, a high ringing note like an air-raid siren. Rocking on my heels, I threw a hopeful uppercut but nobody was home to receive it. A left cross stung in reply. Next a body blow landed like a mule kick and once again siphoned the air from my lungs.

I pressed forward on instinct. A brutal shot sheered off my jaw. The kid's fist slammed the hematoma, again, again—he kept tagging it like some asshole pressing an elevator button. The mouse had swollen ridiculously: its Cro-Magnon curve dominated the crest of my sight.

I closed in and hit him twice to the body, intending to crush his liver and rupture his kidneys, bear-maul this kid and put him *down*. I cornered him against the sawhorses but my punch swung through clean air, missing horribly, and next I was face to face with a jeering man in the crowd. A fist slammed into my ribs and sent bile burning up my throat. Turning, I was met with a right that tabbed me flush. Black lights flash-popped before my eyes and I was falling backwards into a wonderful coolness that felt like ever-tumbling water, so cold, so sweet and—

I was in a cave. The ground was black and granular. A tree. No top, no bottom, roots braiding in both directions. A slit in the tree's bark. A man's face appeared in it. He unfolded himself from the tree with great care, like a contortionist from a glass box. Small, so goddamn small, his skin a pale translucence. He was incredibly old; just looking at him, I felt my eyes dry in their sockets. The man dug a hole. Sometimes his shovel blade made a sound like hissing snakes as it bit into the ground; other times, it sounded like raindrops. When the hole was finished the man cocked his head calmly as if to say: Well, son, it's your choice. *I climbed into the hole headfirst. Wonderful, warm and comforting. A ball of light bloomed, becoming larger, larger . . .*

I was slumped on the chair with Owe snapping a towel at my face. My skull felt like it had been cracked open and blowtorched. My ears were plugged as if I'd been swimming and water had packed into my ear canals. The kid stared at me from across the ring with a look of mingled respect and pity. *You dragged yourself up after being knocked down,* that look said. *But what's the use when I'm just going to plant you again?*

Bovine edged in on my right, a razor blade pinched between his fingers. "We've got to cut that thing," he said.

He drew the blade along my forehead, slitting the bulging mouse. Blood sheeted down my face, blinding me. Owe mopped it, and Bovine swabbed the cut with Adrenalin—I could feel the Q-tip moving inside the pocket of swollen flesh—and painted it with Hemostop.

Owe leaned in. "Keep going, Dunk? You sure? You've fought like an animal, but this guy . . . this *guy.* It's only money, man."

Acid curdled in my gut. *Only money.* It's always only money if you've always had it. I heaved myself up to meet the kid.

What happened next happened quickly, as things often do in fights. It was an accident, pure and simple: I stepped on the kid's foot.

I was rabbiting in, trying to close the distance. The kid side-stepped deftly, his left hand coming around with awful intent. My right fist was fixed on a similar orbit, moving slower but with a lot more *oomph.* Coming forward, I stepped on the kid's right foot. It was nothing purposeful or planned. The kid's fist collided with my ear, pinching a vessel threaded through the cartilage. My own punch landed solidly enough to knock him off balance. As he went back his left foot slipped on a patch of sweat, pulling him into an awkward splits.

His Achilles tendon tore. His left leg crumpled. The kid tried to stand. Instinctively, I offered my hand to help him up. I squinted down, wobbly on my feet—then withdrew my hand sadly and said, "You ought to stay down." The kid followed my eyes. The tendon had ripped off the bone, wadding up around his ankle like a loose tube sock. He nodded.

A few of the kid's buddies stepped from the crowd. They picked him up and carried him past Drinkwater, who stood with a painful, pursed grin on his face.

I didn't dare sit down; my legs would seize with scalding lactic acid. My broken right hand had mushroomed to double its size. I shuffled my feet like a man near the end of an epic dance marathon and waited for the next fighter. When he appeared, I smiled—not that anyone would have noticed since my lips were fat as sausages.

"Holy shit," Silas Garrow said to Drinkwater. "You sure you want me to hit this guy? Why not give me a feather—that'll knock him over just as well."

It had all started with a letter. It had arrived at the Kingston Pen in an envelope with a stamp of Chief Big Bear in full headdress—treaty stamps, they were called, dispensed only on reservations to card-holding band members. The envelope had been slit, its contents inspected by the mailroom guard. The return address had been scribbled over with a black felt-tip; all I could read was the band number, 159. The Mohawks of Akwesasne First Nation.

Greetings, White Devil! I trust you are keeping up with your
daily beatings, and I hope you have found a sparring partner
who is as happy to administer them as I was. As I am aware
that other eyes than yours will read this, I will only say that
rockin' is my business, and business is GOOD. I hear that one
of our mutual friends—Mr. Guzzlesoda, let's call him—has had
troubles as of late. Some sticky-fingered thieves took advantage
of him. What a shame! When you get out, make sure you look
me up. I'm always looking for spare punching bags. Until then,
I offer a thousand hosannas in your name.

> *Yours in Christ,*
> *Silas Garrow*

The day after my release I'd walked up the street to the motel
pay phone, fed coins into the box and dialled.

"Akwesasne Import–Export Holdings," said a female voice.
"How may I help you?"

"Silas Garrow, please."

After a snatch of elevator muzak, Garrow picked up.

"Import–Export, huh?" I said.

"We import lots," Garrow said. "Teddy bears, Japanese soda pop.
Why must you think so poorly of me, white man?"

"The big house hardened me."

I sketched my idea for him. Garrow listened silently, then said:
"It's Diggstown, baby. It's also just about the longest long shot I've
ever heard."

"Could you get yourself in?"

"Maybe. He generally invites tomato cans, doesn't he? Hell, he
invited you."

"You're a peach, Silas."

"If I did this, I'd have to set this up so there's no suspicion—that man's a lot of things, but a fool he ain't. And anyway, what makes you figure you'll make it past the first two?"

"That's on me. If not, it's an easy night for you."

Silas considered it. "On the one hand, it would be shit for my boxing cred—losing to a banana-footed white devil. On the other hand, it's not like Don King's knocking on my door, right?"

So Silas made the call, asking Drinkwater to set up a fight. Drinkwater said he'd keep Silas in mind. A few weeks later I'd laid the trap—"*If that's the kind of guy you think I am, why not make it all Natives?*" And Drinkwater walked into it.

"I'll have to hit you," Silas had warned me. "Not just to salvage a shred of dignity, but because we can't give Drinkwater a sniff of this being a tank job."

Silas skipped out of his corner lightly, crossing his legs over, making a full circuit around me where I stood rooted in the centre of the ring. Silas shook his head at Drinkwater, said, "Shouldn't I be wearing an executioner's hood?"

Drinkwater's lips were pressed into a whitened line. "Just get it over with."

Silas pumped out a few air-jabs, showing off his speed. I could barely raise my hands to parry them. Silas stepped back, scoffing, playing up his role, then hit me four times: right to the body, left to the body, right to the body, left to the forehead as he was backing away. The violence was sudden and the blows stung like bullets— either my body had stopped pumping adrenaline or I was too hurt for it to have much benefit. But Silas knew where to hit: the guts, the forehead. He avoided my knockout buttons—a liver shot might put me down for good, but anywhere else I'd survive.

I reeled from the volley, only selling it a little—it hurt like hell, no faking needed. The air-raid siren kicked up in my head; I took a knee. Silas backed off. Drinkwater nearly stormed into the ring.

"Hit him," I heard him cry. "Go on, quick! Keep at it!"

"Come on, Lem. He's down. Standing eight-count."

"This isn't goddamn Vegas! Hit him and keep on hitting him!"

I gathered my feet but couldn't quite find my balance: it was as if I was struggling in a fierce riptide. My body was approaching a cliff that my will couldn't bridge—no amount of strength would salvage me, no guts or heart. I'd simply topple over. No shame in that, I guess.

Silas punched me in the belly the way a loanshark punches a deadbeat—straight on, no grace. I hinged at the waist, a long runner of bloody drool between my lips. When Silas pulled his fist away I was almost sad to feel it go. At least it had anchored me in a standing position.

The simple act of straightening my spine drained me. Silas slipped a punch past my skull, bringing our heads together.

"Make it real," he whispered.

I did.

My left hand lashed into Silas's ribs, then I tightened my right hand and brought it up into his chin. The impact was genuine. Silas's eyes rolled back in their sockets. I broke another bone in my hand but that pain was no more than a sorrowful hum inside my flesh.

Silas went down on both knees like a man who'd been stabbed in the back, his hands clutching for the blade, then he fell face first onto the cement. His liquid snuffles filled the warehouse.

Drinkwater stared blankly at Silas Garrow, KO'd on the floor. He threw the white towel. It fluttered down on Silas's back and I couldn't tell if he was unconscious or selling it.

Ten seconds later, he hadn't moved. The towel rose and fell with his deep breaths. The crowd stood dumbstruck. This was just the freshest in a long line of soul-sapping injustices.

I fingered Drinkwater as he shrunk into the crowd.

"My money, Lem." I smiled, thinking it must be a sight to inspire nightmares. "Don't make me get rough with you."

I thought about the past eight years, the nights without sleep and the constant formless terror; I thought about Edwina because my mind was never far from Edwina; and I thought about cosmic fairness, how it is a mysterious commodity, but sometimes that great wheel really does come around.

I woke up blind.

My mattress was dented with the impressions of the bodies that had lain in it before me. My nose was swollen with crusted blood, but I could still smell industrial bleach on the sheets.

What had happened after the fight? I remember Drinkwater had balked at paying—as I was sure he would—shrugging his scarecrow shoulders and calling the second fight a draw because the kid hadn't gone down under my fists. He offered our money back, plus a few extra bucks for my pain and suffering.

Owe and Bovine called bullshit. Drinkwater smiled his way-off smile and played his fingers along the knife sheathed at his waist. But then Silas peeled himself off the floor, rubbing the nasty lump on his jaw.

"You pay these men," he told Drinkwater. "Every penny they're owed."

"That's not your call," Drinkwater said.

"It's not," Silas agreed, "but if you don't I'll make sure everyone on the Akwesasne knows about it."

A wretched cornered-rat look darkened Drinkwater's face. I held out my hand with dry insistence.

"Pay me, Drinkwater."

"I'll pay, god damn you. I'll pay."

I half remembered being carried out by Owe and Bovine, laid in the back seat of Owe's car. Now here I was, blind in a strange bed. My hands rose instinctively to my eyes, but someone held them back.

"Don't touch them." It was Bovine. "They're swollen shut. You're swollen all over."

I tried to say something but my lips were fused with a glaze of blood. Bovine wet his fingertips with water and ran them over my lips.

"Where are we?" I asked.

"Red Coach Inn. Jeez, what a dive. Red Roach Inn paints the better picture. But we couldn't get you across the border looking like this."

"Owe?"

"He left last night. You've been passed out almost two days. Your face is . . . Dunk, I've never seen anything like it."

My body was levelled with pain: the sharp variety from the broken bones in my hand, the throbbing variety sunk deep into my face and the bone-deep kind every other place.

For the next three days I barely moved. Bovine was there for most of it, and Owen checked in. They smeared Polysporin on my wounds and made me drink litres of Pedialyte. I lay in a half-waking, half-resting state where nothing was entirely real. The hum of the ceiling fan, the murmur of daytime talk shows.

On the fourth day I gathered my legs and stood. The room was quiet; Bovine was down at the motel bar. I fumbled my way around the bed, barking my shin on the bedpost. Teetering into the bathroom, I ran one blind hand along the wall until my fingers brushed the switch.

My eyes were black balls in the bathroom mirror, nose a mangled knob, shattered capillaries threading over both cheeks. Bovine had stitched the mouse shut; the half-moon curve of the incision bristled with catgut, my forehead dark as an eggplant.

I trailed the fingers of my left hand down my chest and stomach, let them linger on the softball-sized contusions on either side of my ribs: dark purple at their centres, sickly yellow at their edges. My right hand was swaddled in bandages; if I so much as grazed it on a solid surface, a serrated edge of agony would rip all the way to my elbow.

"Fuck it, Duncan Diggs," I told my reflection. "Were you ever really a handsome man?"

I rented the room indefinitely. Bovine returned to the mortuary. My days were spent reading, watching junk TV, taking epic showers. I sat on the balcony while the housekeeper changed the sheets, listening to the rumble of the Falls over the traffic surging down Buffalo Avenue. My bruises lightened. I could breathe through my nose again and no longer sounded like a tickhound with sinusitis.

One afternoon, there was a knock at the door. I opened it to find a Native teenager holding a duffel bag. The kid shoved it into my chest, spat on the cement near my feet and left.

Inside were stacks of fifties and twenties bound with elastic bands: $398,000, plus a single penny rattling at the bottom. Drinkwater had shorted us two grand. The note he'd slid in with the cash read: *It will never buy back the years you lost.*

"You're right about that, Lemmy," I said, with a laugh that hurt my sides. "But it'll make the years I've got left a little sweeter."

I slept soundly and awoke to a ringing phone.

"You bastard," Silas said. "We said make it look real, for the love of fuck, not knock me into a coma!"

"I could barely stand," I said. "Didn't think—"

"I couldn't think straight for a week! Still can't remember where I left my car keys."

"I'm sorry."

Silas broke the lingering silence. "You were something up from the grave, Diggs. Remorseless—a zombie! A relentless killing machine! How's your cabeza?"

Peering into the duffel, I said, "I'll live."

Silas grunted, unconvinced. "Get your ass back over here where the health care's free."

"Thanks, Silas. For everything."

"My tenderfeet tell me that big payoff left ol' Lemmy just about bust. You ought to talk to your cop friend—Drinkwater's in a desperate frame of mind."

I hung up and stared again at the money. It was more than I'd ever seen. For some it was nothing of consequence—a decent Christmas bonus for a Fortune 500 CEO—but to me it meant freedom. I just wasn't sure yet what that freedom would look like. I felt an urge to spread the bills on the bed and roll around like bank robbers do in the movies.

I walked to the window, threw the curtains open. Late-afternoon sunlight bathed the treetops overlooking the cataract basin.

Owe stopped by with a sack of bearclaws and coffee in Styrofoam cups.

"How you feeling?"

"Can't complain," I said, tearing into a bearclaw. I was feeling like a bear myself, just stirred from hibernation—devouring everything I could lay my paws on, the sweeter the better.

Owe watched me dump six sugar packets into my coffee. His cop's eyes were probably lingering over the skin that sat loose upon my frame, the muscle I'd earned in prison now melted away. I unzipped the duffel, tossed him a roll of bills.

"You go ahead, count it."

"I don't need to."

"I'd like it if you did."

Instead Owe snapped the elastic band off the roll, split the bills roughly in half, snapped the elastic band on one half and flipped it back. "I wasn't looking at it as a money-making opportunity," he said. "I just wanted to fuck with Drinkwater."

I wasn't about to argue. I nodded and dropped the roll back in the duffel.

"That last guy," Owe said, one eyebrow raised. "He was looking like a world-destroyer . . . until you caught him."

"Even the blind squirrel finds a nut, Owe."

"I thought you might be interested to know—Drinkwater may be making a move."

I watched him closely over the rim of my Styrofoam cup. "Yeah?"

Owen had heard the news from one of his fellow boys in blue, a district sergeant with the Niagara PD. The word through the grapevine was that Drinkwater wanted to get out of the cigarette-smuggling business.

"They say he's trying to sell off his entire apparatus. Cig makers, packagers, labellers, whole shebang."

"Who's the buyer?"

"It'll be a larger smuggling operation, which means either the Akwesasne or Kahnawake tribe."

"You're involved in the investigation?"

There was a moment of pent-up tension as the unspoken question lay between us: *Would you tell me if you were involved, Owe, seeing as you didn't the last time?*

"No investigation," he said, "just suppositions and scuttlebutt. My chief wouldn't detach me, anyway. Drinkwater's pretty much a dead issue around the precinct."

"But not for you."

Owe's heavy-lidded gaze oriented on the window. "I buried that fucker's dog, man."

A week later I was back at my folks' place, still thinking about what I'd do next. My nose was skewed at a fresh angle and a mottled scar was scrawled across my forehead. But Cataract City was a hockey player's town; bust-up noses were commonplace, and I could always grow my bangs out.

Guilt settled over the dinner table and Mom's bruised eyes avoided mine. She must be so ashamed, I thought. I wondered if my name came up at the Bisk, or during her bowling league night with her girlfriends—or had her friends learned to avoid the subject?

By this time, my post-fight euphoria had soured. I toted up the facts of my life: I was jobless, wifeless, childless, living with my parents, sleeping in the bed I'd slept in as a boy. I was an ex-con with a busted face whose joints ached on humid days.

One evening I sat with my dad at the Tannery on Stanley Avenue. We could pass hours in a silence that wasn't uncomfortable. Every so often one of us might sit up on our elbows and lean forward in a way that invited conversation, only to signal the bartender for another draft.

"Dade Rathburn," Dad said, frowning at the foam in his beer glass. "That time he took you and little Owen."

His shoulders rose almost imperceptibly. I was struck by just how sharp his shoulder bones were, by the chip in his canine tooth he'd never bothered to fix. I thought back to that night in the parking lot when Dad fought Dean Hillicker—he'd been pure *electric* back then. But the electricity had mostly bled out of him now.

"We got in the car," Dad said, "Cal Stuckey and me. Cal's car, remember? The flashy Fifth Avenue he got after his promotion. We'd been sitting in the precinct with officers buzzing around, asking a lot of questions but not taking any action. We both knew it . . . if you weren't found, it would have been over. I mean all of it. Don't want to sound dramatic, but . . . how can you be overdramatic, talking about your twelve-year-old boy? We couldn't have lived with ourselves, y'know? Our wives, your mothers, we couldn't have looked them in the eye, or they ours. The most important thing on earth ripped away—*on our watch.*

"Anyway, we got in the car. Drove. *Hoping,* was all. Guess we figured we'd find you on the side of the road somewhere, lost, hugging onto each other, but safe and in one piece. Cal kept whispering this little prayer to himself, I remember, telling God he could take away everything else he'd ever given but just give Cal his kid back . . . You forget the details of these things. It's a trick your mind plays. All you remember is that *fear*— that's all you ever need to remember to make sure it never happens again."

It was the longest speech he'd given in my presence since junior high, when he'd come to my room at Mom's insistence, hands squeezed into white knots to fumblingly explain the birds and the bees.

"You never found us," I said.

Dad laughed. "We ran out of gas. Neither of us was watching the needle. Cal had to call CAA."

The Sabres were getting clocked by the Wings in an early-season game on the bar's TV. Dead leaves skated up and down the eavestrough outside, a haunting sound.

"Some people say you make your own luck," Dad said. "I've never believed in that. Luck is just something that happens. It's nothing you can pull towards you. But I think if you get some, you do your best to make the most of it."

"What luck have you ever had?"

Dad flinched as if I'd reached over and slapped him.

"I've had plenty," he said hoarsely. "What kind of question is that? Jesus, wasn't I just saying . . .?"

"I'm sorry."

"Son, you're *out*. That's lucky. You're in one piece. That's lucky, too. You disappear a few weeks, come back with a busted face and a limp—you don't need to explain nothing—and maybe that's good luck or bad luck, I dunno. But your mom and me, we don't want to see you go back where you've been. So take your luck and make something of it. A small something. Start with that."

Eventually we walked home, Dad swaying ever so slightly. He tripped on the cracked tarmac leading up to the house, leaned into me and held that position, his head resting lightly on my shoulder.

The next night I returned to Bender Street and used the pay phone outside the Sleep Easy Motor Inn. Late-autumn midges clustered around the street lamps. Winter was threaded into the wind that wicked up from the Falls. A roll of quarters sat heavy in my pocket— I had taken some money from where I'd stashed it under the closet floorboards of my childhood bedroom—because who knew? Maybe we'd talk a while longer this time.

"You again."

"Yeah. Me."

I wanted to ask Ed why she'd kept this number, after all these years. I wanted to know how close she was; I knew she wasn't in Cataract City, but maybe she wasn't so far away. I wanted to know if she was happy and in love with someone else. I wanted to know if Dolly was lying beside her as she listened to me breathing down the line.

"It's weird without you" is all I said.

She almost laughed, but caught herself. "Is that your idea of a charming pickup line?"

Ed knew I'd never had anything in the way of pickup lines, charming or otherwise. "I'm just telling you how I feel."

"Well, you've had some practice of being without me by now. You should be used to it."

"How could I get used to it, Ed? It'll always be the worst."

"You'll live."

Yeah, I would. But I wished she weren't so hard—I wished she'd *give*, just the tiniest bit. Then again, I didn't deserve her softness.

"I'd like to come find you."

After a silence, she said, "I can't stop you from trying."

She knew differently, though. All she had to do was tell me to stop. But she didn't.

LIONS IN WINTER: OWEN STUCKEY

I thought about it a lot during those years when Duncan was in jail. "The Point," I guess you could call it.

What was the Point? That place in time where you'd been led, ceaselessly and unerringly, since the day you could first remember. The place you'll see sometimes in dreams, as familiar as if it belonged to your everyday life, that disappears the moment you rise into waking, its imprint washed away like footprints in the advancing tide. Then one day you'll see some aspect of it in the filigree of a leaf or the knitted steel of a suspension bridge, and that old dream will collide with reality so perfectly that it creates the whiplash we know as déjà vu.

In dreams I often found myself in the middle of what, in my waking hours, I knew to be the Niagara River. But this was a different river, I understood—a river of dreams, and it acted according to its own logic. When I kicked for shore a ripcurl would run under my feet, pulling me back to where I'd started. So I just drifted, treading water, but the shore drew no closer and pulled no further away. My sightline never changed: a hawk sat stunned above me, pinned to the blue sky like a butterfly in an entomologist's book.

In this dream, it dawned on me that nothing I did made any difference. As hard as I'd kick, that sly ripcurl always drew me back. When I treaded water, the current anchored me in place. My position was fixed—the river muscled and shoved and buffeted me into the exact spot where I was always supposed to end up—and nothing I did could ever alter that.

The Point is your specific place in the world. And not just your place: your moment. An instant in time, measurable in seconds, that acts as the hinge for everything you've ever done. Everything feeds into that moment: your backlog of experience and behaviours determine how you enter that moment and how you'll walk away from it afterwards. Every way you've ever been hurt, every grievance nursed, every secret fear, those moments where you've stood up or stepped down and all the love in your body—it all matters when you reach the Point. It is all brought to bear.

And you'll look back in the aftermath, trying to piece together how A met B, but you know what? The threads are tangled, yet the links exist in ways you can't even imagine. And whatever you owe, you pay.

The Point. It's in the water; it's in the sky. Things collapse into it, things spring from it. We're all either moving towards it or walking away from it.

———

THE DOG, A PIT BULL NAMED BANDIT, had been owned—much as anyone can own such an animal—by Igor Bearfoot, presently deceased. It nearly tore my hand off.

I'd trailed Bearfoot's Taurus down a side road and pulled into the cut-off a minute after its tail lights dimmed. The car was parked under a naked maple. I'd watched Bearfoot step out with Duncan. I'd been easing down a hill carpeted in dead leaves, pursuing them, when the dog attacked.

I felt it coming: a swift-moving *something* springing forward on my right side. It came low, submarine-style, hitting me at the hips in a frenzy of teeth and muscle. For an instant I thought it was a wolverine but then I saw the metal studs glinting on its collar.

It slammed me broadside and we tumbled down the slope, the dog angling for my windpipe. I'd thrust one arm between its fore-legs as its jaws sank into my wrist through the thin fabric of my jacket. I kicked it away but its paws dug into the ground, yanking me flat. I scrambled to my knees, slipping on the mouldy layer of leaves, and the dog let go of my arm and went for my skull. There came a fibrous tearing on the top of my scalp, then the piss of blood as warmth trickled down my temples.

My un-mauled hand scrabbled for the revolver in its holster—by then I was turtled on the ground with the dog tearing at my shoulder, trying to worm underneath to rip at my face.

I drew the gun from its holster and reared back; the dog's body glowed in the moonlight falling through the branches. I levelled the barrel at the centre of that perfect mass and pulled the trigger.

The dog jerked backwards. A mist of blood hung in the air for an instant before dissolving.

The ER doc had taken one look at my mitt and sent me up to the ORs. They called in a big-city blade to do the microsurgery—finger reattachment, skin grafts, nerve pathway and blood vessel reconstruction. My pinkie and ring fingers have a little feeling—the skin permanently prickling with pins and needles, like I've slept on them funny—and the skin is vaguely purple, but I can still make a fist.

I'd stayed at the hospital for two weeks; my folks visited often. Mom was retired by then but she knew most of the docs, and one of them, a myopic thoracic surgeon, flirted with her shamelessly until Dad caught on, *finally*, and told him to knock it off.

One afternoon Dad visited with a pair of hoagies in a sack. "Thought you'd like something other than hospital chow."

My right was heavily bandaged so I ate with my left, non-dominant hand; a tomato slid out the ass-end of the sandwich, dropping in my lap.

"Hey," Dad said, as if the fact had just slapped him. "You were born here. Two floors up, in Labour and Delivery. Such a little peanut. Six pounds, three ounces. You came three weeks early and your umbilical cord was wrapped round your waist. You got stuck in the birth canal. One minute everything was tickety-boo and the next machines were beeping and flashing, the room was full of doctors and your mom was whisked to the operating room. Emergency C-section. Back then they didn't usually let the fathers in, but your mother was known in these halls.

"They had this sheet up, y'know? Mom's head on one side, delivery docs on the other. I was on your mom's side and told myself: *don't look on the other side of that sheet.* They got you out and slapped your butt and put you in my arms so Mom could kiss you. That's the unfair part. Your mom goes through sixteen hours of agony and they won't let her hold you first. What had I done to deserve that gift?

"They told me to wait outside and as I'm leaving, my eyes drift over the sheet. Your mom was open, Owen, wide open. I'm sorry, but if I needed any more proof that your mom was the toughest person I'd ever met—tougher than I'll ever be—well, I had it then."

We'd finished the sandwiches and balled the waxed paper, flipping them into the trashcan. Dad made his shot, then retrieved my miss and dropped it in. Stepping into the hall, he glanced left and said, "Three doors down . . . four? That's where you stayed after that whole thing in the woods." He shook his head, eyes on the floor.

"Lord, those days. Jerry and me driving around scared out of our skins, hoping to Christ we'd find you. Never again have I felt so purely helpless, and thank God for that."

He'd returned to the room, sat again and patted my knee under the bedcovers. "After all that, Jerry and I basically stopped talking. I'd pass him in the parking lot—but we were on different levels at work, so it was easy to ignore each other. We kept you and Duncan apart, too—you were still young enough that we could dictate your friends. Maybe everything would have happened the way it did anyway, but I carry the guilt with me. Jerry too, I'm sure. You two kids were tight, and maybe that's not such a rare thing in boy-hood—but it's an exceptionally rare thing in life."

He gripped the sheet, fretting with threads frayed from much washing. "This thing that happened on the river with the ciga-rettes . . . you talked to Duncan about it?"

I'd wondered: *Had* I warned Dunk? That was Dad's real ques-tion. The answer was twisted. I had and I hadn't. Yes, I'd seen him at Smokin' Joes from the jumpseat of a helicopter, then later I'd spotted him on the Niagara through a pair of high-powered bin-oculars: Dunk and Drinkwater and Igor Bearfoot on a puntboat, me watching from the bluffs. I'd thought: *How much is he paying you, Dunk? A few thousand bucks? There are a million other ways to escape, man. Don't thin your chances until you've only got one.*

But Dunk had gone ahead and I'd caught him—my oldest friend. And for what? The cigarettes would keep coming anyway. A man was dead. Dunk would end up going to prison for it. And I'd be the one who sent him.

Had it been my duty to stop him? Maybe Dad thought so. Maybe it was Cataract City Code, Man Code, some bullshit code.

The thing is, I'd *wanted* to talk to Dunk. About what he was doing, yeah, but about so much more. I wanted to tell him about how the digitized shriek of the precinct phone killed something inside me, as did the fire sprinklers cowled in old spider's webs. It all made me sick deep into my guts; I see-sawed between wanting to wreck everything and wanting to curl into a ball under my desk and flinch at the hard-soled shoes stomping past. I wanted to tell him how damn little I'd learned in the years since we were boys. It boiled down to this: it's a lot harder to love than to hate. Harder to be there for those you love—to see them get older, get sick, be taken from you in sudden awful ways. Hate's dead simple. You can hate an utter stranger from a thousand miles away. It asks nothing of you. It eats you from the inside out but it takes no effort or thought at all.

When the hospital released me, I hadn't returned to my apartment. What was waiting for me there? One toothbrush in a plastic cup on the sink. A telephone that I'd stare at as if my slit-eyed gaze might cause it to ring.

Instead I went to Clancy's on Stanley, ordered a shot of rye and a Hed. The man sitting across from me had a scar on his neck: thick and bunched up, the skin as smooth and pink as carnival taffy. His hands trembled as if he was forcing them to do so. A layer of sweat shimmered to the surface of my skin. Why was something always *wrong* with the men around here? I'd never noticed it as a kid. Why so many missing fingers? The men around here put their hands at the service of a mean utility. Those hands got crushed between rollers at the Bisk, melted to stumps by arc-welding torches at the shipworks. I wanted none of it, was humiliated by it in some untranslatable way. But here I was—part of the fabric again.

Later, when I staggered home, I saw that a fire had been stoked in front of my apartment door. Twigs and random trash remained, plus the stink of kerosene. The fuel had burned off without igniting much else; there was nothing but a twisting scorch mark up the door. Bovine? It seemed like the kind of half-assed statement he'd make.

The landlord charged me for a new door. His reasoning: the damage had been perpetrated by my enemies, whom I'd rightly earned and whose reprisals were both unsurprising and—in his unvoiced but palpable view—completely justified.

Eight years went by, the passage of time conspicuous only by the sly pressures it exerted—the lines carving around my eyes and the yellow tinge to my teeth most noticeable when I shaved, my cheeks silked in white foam. One morning while flossing I'd caught a carbolic stink off the waxed floss and wondered: was this how you became acquainted with the smell of your sick, aging self?

I often woke from nightmares that drained from my brainpan like glue, scratching the undersides of my eyelids like motes of fibreglass. The most common one involved dogs flying out of an unending greyness, same way sharks appear out of silty water. Sometimes every one of those dogs was Fragrant Meat, his head bashed in from a truck's grille.

Sometimes I hated this damn city. The sense of omnipresent failure triggered a breed of nausea in me. With it came that feeling of being inside a prison cell with elasticized walls. If I wanted to leave again, Cataract City would let me go—happily, in all likelihood—but if I stayed, it would constrict: an anaconda squeezing me until I couldn't draw breath.

I came to sense a sinisterness about the city, too. It wasn't anything you could pinpoint—how could a city be *evil*? A city was just concrete and steel and glass, feeling no pain, retaining no memories. But then houses are made of the same stuff, and people go around claiming they're haunted all the time.

At first I'd told myself it was just me. I'd been away too long, returning under a dark cloud. But as the days bled past I recognized that it wasn't me—or *was* me, partially at least, because I'd inhabited these streets before, bearing the infection I'd harboured since birth.

I'd stay up at night, imagining a vast sea of poison underneath the city. A churning sea of lampblack-coloured ichor burbling, leaching into the soil as it spread the infection.

Part of that was the job. Want to see the ugly side of any city? Start carrying a badge. I would cruise ours at night, an embalmed moon throwing its light upon weed-strewn lots and sagging rowhouses long vacant of human habitation. I'd listen to the wind whistle through those empty skeletons, singing off exposed nailheads and around flame-thinned beams with a low mournful sound. Empty houses have this look to them, or at least they do in Cataract City: like faces ravaged by leprosy. Shattered bay windows resemble leering mouths; punched-out second-storey windows look like avulsed eyeballs. Darkness had a way of transforming everyday sights into nightmarish apparitions. It did the same when Dunk and I spent those nights in the woods.

Sometimes I'd drive into the farmland on the outskirts of town. A rot-toppled silo lay in the fields to the north, isolated beside a decaying granary. A long, dark tube softening into the earth like a giant earthworm half smashed under a boot. It had torn up rags of fibrous earth when it fell; the rags, still attached to the silo's hull, fluttered like curtains as the wind blew over a carpet of withered seeds: a sound like the pattering of tiny feet.

If I squinted, sometimes I'd see odd movement in the silo, deep in that brooding darkness. I'd *think* so, anyway. Who—*what*? It's not something I've investigated. Or ever will.

Something's the matter with Cataract City. To live here is to be infected with it. And you don't even know how sick you are. How can you, when we all share the same poison?

For eight years my life was locked in stasis—I may as well have been frozen in a cryo-chamber. I became jaded, a stranger to myself: a desk sergeant with the Niagara Regional Police, tracking down child welfare beefs with a rotating cast of pantsuited social workers. Putting bad men in jail only to see them sprung by a showboating defence lawyer or some give-a-fuck judge. The system was broke— most systems were—and I was just one gear spinning imperfectly within it.

After work I'd hit one of the bars along Stanley Road, prop myself up on a stool with the rubadubs, listen to country music on the jukebox and inhale the sour whiff of spilled beer. Then I'd go home to the shoebox apartment, the unmade bed, empty bottles queued along the windowsill like giant bullets in want of a revolver, and the dripping faucet that I couldn't quite rouse myself to fix.

Every so often I'd pick a convenient start point—New Year's Day was popular—and say: *Time for a change, Stuckey!* Get a membership at the Y, show up for pickup basketball with the old men and high-school dropouts, can a few jumpers and get a little groove going. But soon the six pins and quartet of screws holding my knee together started to burn with smokeless heat; I'd gimp to the bench, my resolve already eroding.

I'd see old faces around. Duncan's mother, Celia, waiting at the bus stop after her shift. Wearing a pencil skirt and support hose— hot date with the mister?—varicose veins bulging up the backs of her calves. I drove past without stopping, feeling the weight of her gaze on me. Sam Bovine would wash up in the drunk tank as reliably as the tide, usually around the holidays. He'd pass out in the holding cell, tinselly Christmas garlands noosed around his neck. One night he showed up outside my apartment screaming incoherently, although the gist was clear: *you're a turncoat, Stuckey, a scummer and a snake*. I rang Dispatch and when the cruiser arrived Bovine stared at my window, wounded and pissy. I had the officers drive his drunk ass home.

I saw Edwina once, a few months after Duncan's arrest. Driving past their old house, ostensibly on a neighbourhood sweep, I'd spotted a FOR SALE sign on the lawn and a U-Haul trailer stacked with boxes. I slowed down, knuckles whitening on the wheel. Ed walked out the front door with a gooseneck lamp, Dolly padding at her heels. She'd held on to her wintry beauty—although it was flintier now—retaining that bodily wildness both Duncan and I had surrendered to.

A moment came back, plucked free of time. Ed and me in the coatroom at Derby Lane, the usual dog track smells—wet greyhound, cigar smoke and the alkaline tang of dog drool—overmastered by the smell of her: clean and electric and somehow witchy, the taste in your mouth as a thunderstorm darkens the horizon. Her body was dewy and obliging, which was odd seeing as she was so often distant, untouchable. But back then she had softened as I braced her against the wall, coat hangers jangling round our ears with a musical note. It was not at all how I'd imagined it but still good, so very good, the youth in our bodies electric—I thrummed with it, fumbling but sincere, nervous lightning popping off the tips of my fingers—as she socked her head into the crook of my neck, smelling of Noxzema and Export A cigarettes, of sweat and the dust of the track, biting my throat with her small, even teeth. Laughter bubbled up inside me—the hysterical, uncontrolled giggles that had plagued me as a boy, concentrating first in my belly and fluttering up my throat like antic butterflies. The more I tried to tamp them down the worse they got—like when Bruiser Mahoney signed that Polaroid *BM* and that sick, insulting laughter had boiled up in me. I'd felt that same fear in the coatroom. You weren't supposed to *laugh* when a woman nuzzled your neck, so I'd stifled it—*Shhht-SHHHT!*—the snort of a horse. Ed stared at me cockeyed for a second before we kissed—and it had been warm and spitty and sloppy like a first kiss ought to be.

She stopped halfway down the driveway, lamp in hand, gazing at me as I passed. There was no quiver in her eyes. She was stronger than fate—by which I mean she hadn't imbibed the defeatism at the core of this city, the sense that each step of our lives had been plotted and our role was to follow those footfalls. Her lips moved but I couldn't make out the words.

It could have been "Bye, Owe." Or it could've been "You owe."

I did owe and I did pay, after a fashion. For eight years I drank too much, nursed a sullen emptiness and waited for something to change, all the while knowing this was the single biggest lie people told themselves: that change will eventually come on its own if you wait patiently enough for it.

I told myself: *When Duncan gets out, you make it right. However you can, in whatever way necessary. Make it right.*

And then, three months after Dunk was released from prison, and three months after his fight at Drinkwater's, I was given the chance.

———

"NEVER FIGURED I'D SEE THE DAY where I was rigged to a wire . . . by a white man, no less."

"It's not a wire," I said. "It's all wireless nowadays. Welcome to the twenty-first century."

Silas Garrow made a face. "Explain again how I let you talk me into this."

We sat in an unmarked cruiser in the Niagara River spillway. I was in the back seat with Silas, affixing a tiny microphone to the furred hood of his parka. Duncan sat silently up front.

Silas was set to meet Lemuel Drinkwater on the frozen Niagara to negotiate a deal for Drinkwater's Molins Mark 9 cigarette machines. After talking with his band elders, Silas had agreed to co-operate with the police.

Silas and Drinkwater would meet alone. A recent rash of thieveries and his bad luck at the fights had sown a seed of distrust deep inside Drinkwater—and apparently that seed had since flowered into a vine of runaway paranoia. He no longer spoke on cell phones, preferring to dispatch his orders via an ever-shrinking network of impressionable Native teens.

"This is just preliminary evidence gathering," I told Silas. "Once we've got him on record, I'll go to my chief and requisition manpower for when the actual deal goes down."

Nobody knew about tonight's activities. I'd signed out the surveillance equipment from the tactical ordnance officer, who handed it over no questions asked. It wasn't uncommon for officers to pursue their own investigations—some even did freelance PI work, bugging the no-tell motels on Lundy's Lane, ratting out philandering hubbies to their suspicious wives.

Silas said, "So what do you need?"

"Time, place, price," I told him. "Most of all, intent. Just talk naturally. The information will come."

The Niagara Peninsula was clad in sparkling snow. The crescent moon fell upon the iced-over river, its expanse like a polished razor. Silas straddled the skidoo he'd trucked up from the Akwesasne: a tricked-out model with a silenced exhaust that was built to ferry sleds of cigarettes across the Saint Lawrence Seaway.

"Should I have a gun?" he wondered.

"Do you foresee any need for one?" I asked.

"It's Drinkwater," Silas said simply.

I grabbed the police-issue Mossberg pump-action shotgun from the cruiser. Silas strapped it to the skidoo.

The rusty burr of a motor carried across the night-stilled air, climbing to a keen. Drinkwater was coming. Silas started his own skidoo and gunned the engine.

"Make it short," I said. "Just the essentials."

Silas nodded, the trace of consternation never leaving his face. He tore out of the spillway, down the alluvial slope of the riverbank into the river basin, accelerating now, his tail lights flaring bright red—the eyes of some predatory animal—then dimming as he navigated a rim of crested ice.

Duncan and I sequestered ourselves in the cruiser, listening to the microphone feed. At first we heard nothing but the hornet-drone of the skidoo motor and the wind raking the mic.

"Cold as a witch's tit," we heard Silas say.

The motor decelerated; there came the *tink-tink-tink* of metal treads crawling across the ice. From our vantage we could see a brief flare of the tail lights as Silas came to a stop about four hundred yards from shore. The moon cut a rift across the frozen river, glossing the torsional shapes of both skidoos. The crunch of boots on winter snowpack was punctuated by Silas's ragged exhales.

SILAS: "You okay?"

DRINKWATER: "Why shouldn't I be?"

"No reason. Look a little troubled, is all."

"Meeting out on a goddamn winter river—why shouldn't I be? Cloak-and-dagger shit. But you want something done right, do it yourself. I'd be a damn sight better if you hadn't gotten your ass handed to you by some over-the-hill pug. Where the hell'd you get those boxing titles? Out of a Cracker Jack box?"

"That guy had stones in his hands. What can I say? Wasn't my night."

"*Your* night?"

"Lemmy, listen—I didn't come out here to cry over spilt milk."

Lingering pause.

DRINKWATER: "What's *that*?"

SILAS: "What's what, Lem?"

"*That*, you goddamn shitbird! That . . . *that!*"

A finger of light bloomed on the night river, followed by the report of gunfire.

Dunk and I put boots to snow, racing down the slope, slipping on the ice-slick stones. We found Silas laid out on the ice, staring up at the sky with a serene look on his face.

"He shot me," he managed. "He saw the shotgun. Police issue, isn't it?"

I unzipped his parka. The bullet had sheared through his shirt and the meat of his biceps. "Clean through."

Wincing, Silas said, "So that's what—*good*?"

I said, "The bullet's not stuck inside of you. Didn't ricochet off your bone, otherwise it would have snapped. Let's get you back to the cruiser."

"No way," Silas told me. "No police, no doctors."

"You've been shot," said Duncan.

"Thanks for the update. I've been *grazed*, right? I got you all the evidence you need, right?"

I said, "We've got him on attempted murder now."

"So go *get him*. Another five minutes, that man will be nothing but a vapour trail. You'll never find him."

I exchanged a look with Duncan. A profound, impossible worry sparked in his eyes.

"You'll be okay?" Duncan asked Silas.

"I have people nearby. We Injuns have people *everywhere*."

Duncan drove. Silas's skidoo shot across the river so fast that the speed squeezed tears from my eyes, all of which vaporized before reaching my ears.

Drinkwater's sled tracks cut south, back towards the States, until the ice began to groan ominously—I spotted a black lapping edge where the river wasn't yet frozen. Then the tracks cut back north.

The skidoo engine buzzed like honeybees trapped in a tin can. Now Drinkwater's tracks veered sharply towards the northern shore. I squinted at the banks, dark beneath the pines. No street lamps or bridge lights or car headlights flashed through the trees. The only man-made light came from Clifton Hill: a gauzy bowl of whiteness that was dimming by the second.

Duncan angled his body into a turn, following the line Drinkwater had carved. The night was clean and clear. No snow to cover up the tracks. He was driving too fast, amped up on adrenaline.

"Throttle down, Dunk."

He drove parallel to the riverbank, bloodhounding Drinkwater's tracks. They zagged towards the shore as if Drinkwater had been debating whether to enter the woods. Winter-naked trees and snow-draped shrubs blurred into a thick wall of foliage.

At last the tracks rose up an incline into the forest. Why had Drinkwater chosen this entry? Had he heard us coming and panicked? Or was he lying in wait a few hundred yards past the treeline?

I pointed to an orange trail marker spiked atop a rusted pole. "He followed a trail. Hiking path, maybe an old surveyor's line."

"You figure he knows where he's going?"

"He's done plenty of business on this river."

Pins and needles shot up my spine. We'd been searching for forty-five minutes. The river snaked eastward, its whiteness dissolving into the remote darkness of the horizon. Moonlight ghosted the trees, shining on their ice-encased branches—but the light didn't touch the forest floor, which was carpeted in smooth-running shadows. Apart from the hum of the muffler, the silence was enveloping.

I thought about how we forget there are still places on earth where you can move so easily from the safety of known roads to the solitude of nature. If you're not paying attention, you might not even know you've crossed that line.

"Go on," I said. "He's running, not waiting."

"He's still Drinkwater."

"You'd rather turn back?"

Dunk opened the throttle, carrying us over the river's lip and into the woods. Drinkwater's tracks veered wildly through the snowpack. These trails hadn't seen use in years. Trees here rose high into the night, oaks and birches nourished by the alluvial silt kicked up from the river. Their trunks were furred with old man's beard that shone with hoarfrost.

We nosed into a tributary. Skeins of ice shattered under the treads with the sound of busted light bulbs. Drinkwater's tracks disappeared. Maybe he'd cut further down the inlet?

Duncan switched off the engine. The summer woods were host to many sounds, but in the winter woods, sounds were rare, and those that remained took on a haunting note: the hoot of snowy owls, the green-stick snap of a tree limb under the weight of snow, the booming crack of ice fissuring under tremendous pressure.

Faintly, the whine of a motor—to the north, further down the inlet.

Duncan forded the tributary, which branched eastward, narrowing, hemmed by shaggy spruces. Soft, hand-shaped spruce fronds lapped our shoulders.

We surged into a snowy chute that tapered to a flat expanse. Drinkwater's tracks cut straight ahead, aiming for the thick forest looming against a scrim of winter sky. Duncan charged full-bore, the muffler's silencer failing, the motor issuing a band-saw buzz. The night moved as winter nights so often do: in soft crests and eddies, plays of moonlight and starlight. Soon Drinkwater's tracks bent sharply—so sharply that they seemed to disappear. The snow was abruptly trackless.

I barely sensed the threat.

Years later I'd return to this spot, a steep decline that lay some four hundred yards shy of the forest. It fell sheer, almost twenty feet straight down. It would take me some time to locate, even in daylight. But then, at night, running flat out, it was nearly impossible to see: the snow and shadows made it look as if the land continued on an even plane.

Too late, I sensed the outcropping where the snow crusted in a ragged edge. Dunk squeezed the brake levers instinctively but our momentum was unstoppable. We went over the crest at thirty-five miles per hour. A giddy weightlessness gripped my guts, the kind you feel on a roller coaster the instant before the tracks drop from under you.

The skidoo free-fell, then slammed into a powdery drift. One tread bit, differentials howling, metal shearing apart and spitting off in sharp spears. What I remember of the impact exists in polar flashes. My chin slammed into Duncan's shoulder, teeth colliding with a brittle *snap*. My knees popped as I was jolted off, following a broken flight path. With dreamlike clarity I saw Duncan's chest crush the handlebars; his neck snapped forward, face bashing the hood. His body kicked over the bars and he was sailing free, his arms pinned to his sides like a man kicking furiously towards the water's surface.

I came to with pain singing down my arm: an aria, the type sung by sopranos with voices capable of shattering crystal stemware.

I lay in a drift. I blinked away the flaming birds that flocked before my eyes, focusing on a pine tree to my left. Had I hit it, my skull would've been crushed. Pulling my knees in, I struggled to stand. At this I failed.

I held my arms out. The right was heavy. I let it fall a few inches. A rivulet of blood ran out of my parka sleeve. The pain was duller now, its knife edge gone.

What had happened? I remembered the headlights falling off the cliff, remembered clinging to Duncan tightly, figuring—with that childlike hope that attaches itself to fearful moments—that if I held on to him the way I had as a boy, everything would work out.

"Dunk? Man, you okay?"

Silence. Running the fingers of my left hand over my right arm, I could feel a small surgical incision in the fabric above the elbow. I prodded two fingers through the slit until they met something soft, warm, pulpy. Hinging my arm at the elbow, I felt something stuck in my flesh near the bone.

Shock: this, too, came from far away. I must be in shock. When I pulled my fingers out they were chalk-white to the second joint, after which they turned red.

"Dunk?"

Fear seeped into my chest when this second call went unanswered. I noticed that a fingernail was ripped off my right hand. My phone! Patting my pocket, I felt its comforting shape. But when I dug it out, its face was spidered. The liquid crystal leaked through the cracks like oil.

A fingernail-slice of moon hung over the pines. The only light came where it reflected off veins of quartz in the cliff face: these shone like rivers on a map. The skidoo lay twenty yards off. One tread had shredded off; shards of metal winked in the snow.

That's when I saw him. Duncan lay thirty-odd feet beyond the wrecked skidoo. His body was heaped near a rocky outcropping. Fear thrummed down my neck.

Be okay—god damn it, you be okay, Dunk.

I staggered around the skidoo and drew near to Duncan. Now I saw that it wasn't rocks he was sprawled across: it was bare bracken, as black as obsidian. He rolled over, groaning weakly. His face appeared to be covered in molasses. His nose had exploded. The cartilage was shoved off to the right and blood bubbled out of his nostrils.

"Breathe through your mouth," I said. "Your nose is . . . bad."

Duncan must've heard me; he quit bubbling. His limbs jutted at the proper angles: no green-sticks or feet facing the wrong direction. His hands were a mess, skin rasped off the remaining knuckles. One of those hands rose instinctively towards my face, moved over my chin, the pits of my eyes. Satisfied, Dunk let it drop back into the bracken.

"Jesus, Owe. I'm sorry."

"It's okay. I didn't see it either. Your nose . . ."

"Bad. You said that already." He pawed at his face and said, "Yeah, it's bust . . . it's been bust worse."

I had a hard time believing that. "We got lucky. The good Lord watches over drunks, fools and skidooers."

Duncan rose to his knees, then stopped abruptly, clutching at his chest.

"What's the matter?"

His fingers crawled over the front of his parka. "I don't know . . . That hurt, though."

I couldn't recall a time Duncan admitted that *anything* hurt.

"Can you stand?"

Duncan did. "You said something about your arm?"

"It's fine for now. Do you have a phone?"

He shook his head. "I was meaning to get one, but . . ."

We hobbled to the skidoo and hunted through the emergency satchel: two flares, a Leatherman tool, protein bars, duct tape and a medical kit. No phone.

Duncan unzipped his parka. His fingers roamed under his sweater, investigating his chest. "Sorta like heartburn. Worst case ever."

Starlight reflected off the curved metal jutting from his waistband.

I said, "What's that? Tucked into your pants."

His gaze met mine, the momentary quiver in his eyes hardening. He lifted his sweater to show me Bruiser Mahoney's gun.

"Mind telling me why you're carrying that?"

"I wasn't planning to shoot Drinkwater, if that's what you're asking."

"You carry a gun, Diggs, you ought to have a reason."

"Gee, thanks, pops."

We stared at each other evenly. The blood on Duncan's face was freezing to a shiny glaze.

"I'm not asking that you hand it over . . ."

"But you'd highly recommend it?"

"This is still a police investigation, Diggs."

Duncan pulled the sweater over the gun and zipped his parka up.

We stripped the skidoo. Duncan detached the oil reservoir and dumped the oil. Next he used the Leatherman to cut the length of rubber hose connecting the air intake to the carburetor, unscrewed the gas cap and slid the hose down. He sucked until his mouth flooded with gasoline, retched, and siphoned gas into the reservoir.

I unscrewed the mounts and tore out the twelve-volt battery, along with a few connecting wires. I slit the nylon straps mooring the shotgun to the frame and pulled it free.

Drinkwater's tracks were gone. He must have edged his way down west of here, where the incline descended more gently. He'd be miles away by now. Back over the river, maybe, in his truck driving towards some sleepy border crossing.

We weren't far from the river—fifteen miles, tops. But the incline was too steep to retrace our path. Possibly our best bet was to stay put. If a search helicopter swept past, it might spot our fire—providing we'd retained enough of our Boy Scouts fire-craft skills to build one.

Standing shoulder to shoulder, we peered into the forest. My eyes had become accustomed somewhat, but human eyes were not built for this kind of dark. Here and there I caught—sensed?—sly shiftings and shadings, movement tracing over the rocks and trees. I squinted at the luminescent hands on my watch. It was past 2 a.m. On a typical Friday night I'd be . . . drunk, probably. Passed out in bed. My warm, soft bed.

I gestured into the heart of the woods. "Got to be something. A road, a logging route, an old trapper's shack."

"Something. Sure."

Duncan hitched the satchel up on his back. I slung the shotgun over my shoulder. We entered the blackness of the woods.

A winter forest is pure whiteness rolled flat. Austere endless white that dissolves every landmark. Imagine trying to find your bearings on the moon.

It's tough going, especially without snowshoes. Each footstep breaks through the snow crust, miring your boots in the soft powder. Before long the eyelets and uppers are iced over and heavy.

Envy of chipmunks and dormice sets in: weightless creatures who skitter across the crust.

Cold radiates from that whiteness, borne on slinking winds that curl under pant-legs and down collars. Coldness wraps around your skull, encasing the brainstem in ice. You get foggy-headed with it, and it dawns on you that all you want to do is sit. Your boots are so heavy it's like hauling anvils. The snow is soft and inviting. People who freeze to death are often found with faint smiles on their faces: during those last moments they occupy a different geography in their minds. You have to fight the urge to just . . . sit . . . *down.*

We trod lightly, bodies tilted against the wind, carving a path between the poplars. The naked branches knit together, a lattice-work of angles shielding the winter sky. We were tired and achy but the adrenaline hadn't yet burned off. A snowy owl watched from a low branch, eyes shining in the ruffled oval of its face. It hooted—a trilling, melancholy note—and took flight, white wing-tips trailing into the darkness.

We'd barely covered a mile before we came across Drinkwater's skidoo. Its hood had crumpled against a lightning-felled oak, and one ski had snapped off and stuck in the bark. The right tread had sheared off its runner.

I set a gloved hand on the muffler. "Still warm."

Fifteen feet past the fallen tree we could make out the spot where Drinkwater's body had hit. There was a dark stain on the snow the size of a dinner plate. I inspected the skidoo's empty webbing and untied straps, figuring Drinkwater must have scavenged it. Dark coins dotted the snow around the machine. From there, Drinkwater's footsteps advanced into the woods in a determined line.

I pulled Duncan down behind the skidoo. "He could be out there. He's got a gun."

I imagined Drinkwater hunched a hundred yards off, eyeing us down a rifle's sights. Worse, I pictured Drinkwater bleeding out somewhere in the dark, stubbornly refusing to call for help.

"Lemmy!" Dunk shouted, as if channelling my thoughts. "You all right?"

"*Shut it,*" I hissed. "What's the sense of that?"

Duncan didn't answer. The effort it took to shout doubled him over. "He's running," he managed to say through gritted teeth.

"You don't know that."

"He's hurt and he's running, Owe. He could die out here."

"We could, too."

We sat with the possibility until I said, "Twenty years later . . . Finnegan, begin again."

Duncan smiled. "Same shit, different day."

We shared a gravedigger's laugh. The cold locked around our joints, crimping our nostrils shut with each inhale.

"We should make a fire," Dunk said.

"He could see us."

"If he doesn't make one himself he'll freeze to death, anyway."

We cleared a spot next to the skidoo, scraping with our boots until we hit the frozen earth. We snapped twigs off the fallen oak. Duncan doused the heap with gasoline and pulled a flare from the satchel.

"Not that," I said. "We may need it later."

I sat the twelve-volt battery on my lap, stripped the plastic coating off two wires and twisted one around the negative coil and the other around the positive coil. When I touched the wire-tips, they glowed. I rubbed them over the kindling pile until a spark caught the gasoline.

We sat on the skidoo seat, hands held to the licking flames. The twigs crackled and glowed, sending up a grey coil of smoke. I thought about how making this fire didn't have the same life-or-death quality it had when we were kids down to one paper match with the darkness chewing at our backs. But it still felt like a distinctly human act that set us apart from the surrounding wilderness.

I peered across the flames, following Drinkwater's footsteps into the gloom. Was there a faint flicker out there? A wavering orange dot? It could have been a few hundred yards off, a mile, or a trick of my fatigued mind.

"You think he's out there?" Dunk asked.

"He's a survivor. I heard Native boys used to get sent out into the woods for a week, no food, no nothing—a quest, to find their spirit animal. A raven, a wolf, a bear. Once they'd found it, they returned to the tribe and were accepted as warriors. I'm not saying that happens anymore. It's a survivor culture is all I'm thinking. Hey, what if you found out your spirit animal was a weasel?" I laughed. "What if a worm came to you in your dreams?" Laughing even harder. "I'd lie my ass off. Tell the chief, *Oh, yeah, I saw a moose. Big mean bastard.*"

Dunk found a shard of clear ice and bit into it as if it was peanut brittle. We both ate a protein bar. We had three guns between us, but no rifle. I wondered if Dunk would try to shoot something with Bruiser Mahoney's old pistol, just like Mahoney had shot that poor raccoon.

Warmth prickled my skin, bringing the pain roaring back down my arm. It was sharper now, an edge of glass raked across raw bone.

"What's the matter?"

"This arm . . . something must be in it."

"If something's in there, Owe, we ought to get it out."

Gingerly, I unzipped my parka. The right side of my shirt was dark and heavy red. Duncan helped me peel it off. My right sleeve was stuck to my wrist with a gummy collar of blood. Duncan used the Leatherman to cut the sleeve near my shoulder. He slit it down my biceps and wrist, and the material fell off my arm like a shed snakeskin.

"It's deep," Duncan said, "but clean. Not wide . . . but yeah, *deep*."

"See anything inside?"

"Just a sec . . . uh."

"What?"

"Just a glint. I can get it."

"How?"

Duncan unfolded the Leatherman, brought the prongs of the needlenose pliers together: *snick-snick*. "Meatball medicine." He cut a length of canvas rigging off the skidoo and tied it around my arm. With the tourniquet in place he held the pliers over the flame.

"Not too long," I said. "I don't want to be cauterized."

Duncan plunged the pliers into the snow. The hot metal hissed. "Just sterilizing them, man." He angled the wound into the firelight, debating. "How about I get hold of it and just, uh, wiggle a little?"

"Sounds magical."

He worked the tip of the pliers into the slit. My arm jerked involuntarily, but Duncan gripped my wrist to keep me steady, nosing the pliers deeper. The coagulated blood at the edges of the cut gave way; fresh blood dripped into the snow. Then the pliers brushed against something hard, too shallow to be bone.

Dunk closed the pliers' jaws around whatever it was and squeezed them together—then came a sharp *click* as the pliers slipped off a metallic edge and snapped shut.

"F̶̶̶̶̶̶̶̶̶̶̶̶̶—!"

"Sorry," Dunk said. "Got to get a good grip." He handed me a thumb-width piece of kindling. "Bite."

I jammed the stick between my teeth and bit down so hard that my jaw trembled. Duncan wiped away the blood and probed again. The pliers gritted against whatever was embedded in my flesh, a metal-on-metal rasp. The pain was monstrous. My entire skeletal system lit up like a Christmas tree. The stick went *snap* between my jaws. I spat out the splinters and said, "Just go. Just keep . . . keep oh oh god keep going."

Steadying his free hand on my wrist, Dunk pulled carefully. "Got it."

He held it up to the firelight: a shard of metal in the shape of a diamond—one of the interlocking diamonds that made up a ski-doo tread. He dropped it into the fire. The stink of fried blood rose off the coals.

The bleeding slowed to a trickle. Duncan found the med kit, slathered some gauze with Polysporin and told me to poke it as far into the wound as I could bear. He stuck a Band-Aid over the gauze, then wrapped surgical tape around my elbow to keep everything in place.

"Good enough?"

I said, "Yeah, good. Thanks."

He settled back against the skidoo. His exhales were syrupy and bubbly, as if he was forcing each breath through an inch of pancake batter. I hoped it was just the busted nose, which would make breathing hard. He'd probably swallowed a lot of blood, too. I stared skywards, flakes of snow scrolling above the flames.

I drifted into a half sleep, snapping awake to spot mouselike shapes racing round the edge of the fire's light, too fast to track. A thicker dark fell around us, airless and isolating. We fed the flames and pulled our collars tight and got used to the phantom movements beyond the fire. I told myself they were nothing but the play of starlight on wind-sculpted snow.

Before dawn those movements coalesced into permanence—a group of shapes all roughly the same size and moving with the same low-slung lope. Thirty yards from the fire, circling clockwise.

"Dunk . . . hey, Dunk."

Duncan cracked one eye, followed my pointing finger. Sight wasn't needed—you could smell them: like wet dogs, only more primal.

I said, "Coyotes."

One of them let loose a high mocking gibber. This was answered by a series of excited yips.

I rooted a flare out of the satchel and tore the igniting strip. An umbrella of red light draped us both, flecks of molten phosphorus spitting in elegant arcs. We saw them clearly: a pack of coyotes ringing the fire, hackles raised, fur running down their spines on a band-saw edge.

I tossed the flare to scatter the pack. It sailed end over end to land on a patch of black ice behind them.

"Jesus," Duncan said.

Three timberwolves stood illuminated in the fan of flare-light. Bone-white, almost indistinguishable from the snow. Only their black snouts gave them away. They stood in a casual threesome—the largest wolf standing, the other two hunched on either side. Their legs were shockingly long, strangely thin: a herbivore's legs, almost, carrying their torsos high off the ground. The biggest wolf opened its mouth—its jaws enormous—and licked its chops.

The coyotes scattered, baying plaintively. I picked up the shotgun. Duncan laid Bruiser's pistol across his lap. Was there enough wood to last through to daylight? The flare guttered, guttered. The wolves stayed in place, watching.

Dawn took forever to come.

A light snow had fallen overnight. The temperature rose slightly as the sun crawled above the horizon. It remained sub-zero, though, and neither of us was properly outfitted. I wore uninsulated police-issue brogans, the leather cracked along the soles. Amazingly, my knee didn't hurt that much. Sure, I could feel the pins and screws—fine needles like icy worms knitted with the flesh and bone—but the physical sensation wasn't that painful. It felt *good*, almost: a dull throb that drew attention away from sharper pain in other parts of my body.

I'd chosen wool pants—a stroke of luck—but my shirt was now missing its sleeve and there was a rip in my parka where the metal diamond had pierced. Duncan had on warm boots, jeans with a rip in the knee, a heavy sweater and coat. He'd also found a flimsy pair of Magic Gloves in his coat pocket—I pictured his mom stuffing them in there, one of those protective things mothers do.

We set off at daybreak. Blood from Duncan's broken nose was crusted like rust in the seams of his face. I'd patched my parka with a strip of tape from the medical kit. Duncan hacked the upholstery off the skidoo's seat with the Leatherman, rolled up the padded material and stuffed it into the satchel.

Drinkwater's bootprints were faint traces in the snow.

"Follow them?" said Duncan.

"What makes you think he knows where he's going?"

Duncan shrugged.

"Maybe he's got a phone." I said. "He could call someone. A bunch of guys. What if he's looking for *us*?"

"Doubt it."

I held my arms out. "What better place? We're miles from anywhere. Put us down, one shot in the back of the head. Boom. Easy. The coyotes will eat most of us, the birds will take what's left. By spring thaw there'll be nothing to know us by."

"So what's your idea?"

I puffed breath into my cupped palms. "Follow his tracks, not him. We're not after Drinkwater anymore, okay? Let's just get out of this."

Before setting off I cut four sheets out of the silver Mylar emergency blanket. I flipped a hot ember out of the fire into each sheet and crimped them into balls, placing two in my coat pockets and giving two to Duncan.

We followed Drinkwater's bootprints, our hands sunk into our warm pockets, walking directly into the sun as it bathed the snow in a reddish glare. I took the lead, feet sinking deeper into where Drinkwater's had been. Duncan followed, breathing heavily.

We found Drinkwater's fire, its embers still flaring with the wind. He'd fashioned a lean-to, the ends of which he'd whittled and slotted flush. He must have draped it with an emergency blanket and hunkered inside—he may have even gotten an hour or two of sleep. It was the campsite of a seasoned outdoorsman, assembled with ease, abandoned quickly.

A frozen pool of blood lay next to the fire. The blood had a matte look, platelets frozen to a dull gloss. I chipped at it with my thumbnail. It wasn't frozen solid, the way water freezes; it was softer, the consistency of a Fudgsicle. I tweezed a needle out of the blood, attached to a hank of black thread. Had Drinkwater stitched himself up?

"He knows we're following him," Dunk said.

"How do you figure?"

He pointed ten yards past the fire. Drinkwater had unzipped and relieved his bladder, scrawling a message in the snow.

F.U.

"He even got the periods in there between the letters," Duncan marvelled.

The sun climbed a cloudless sky, lacking the wavering edge it held on summer days: looking at it was like staring into a blast furnace through a hole cut in blue Bristol board. Still, it was better to look into the sky or straight ahead. Staring down brought on the oddest vertigo, the snow sizzling like a lake of fire.

Duncan began to cough. He pressed a fist to his chest as it built to a rumbling thunder rolling through his lungs. I could tell he was in serious pain, his face wrenched into a tortured expression—he looked as if a thousand fish hooks were tugging inside his chest. He doubled over, palms braced on his knees. He coughed until tears rolled down his cheeks. When the coughing finally tapered he tried to stand up, but his boots skidded in the snow and he fell to his knees, then forward onto his hands. He spat. A red splotch hit the snow. He tried to cover it up so I wouldn't see but the blood just churned into the snow, making it pink.

After a while I said, "Need a hand up?"

"If I can't get up on my own, we've got trouble." He rose unsteadily, and we carried on.

Drinkwater's tracks cut through the snow on a determined line—looking at them, you'd think they'd been made by a man who knew exactly where he was going, or at least had no fear of what lay ahead. In my mind I imagined an animal travelling on four legs rather than two. Drinkwater's nose was the black of a dog's nose. One of his eyes was milky, the result of some past scrap. We were following a cunning old lion—and he *knew* he was being followed.

The land unfurled in terrifying swathes of arctic whiteness to every point on the compass. My toes had gone numb without my realizing. Idly, I wondered how long it would take for frostbite to set in. I'd seen a TV show about mountain climbers trapped on a cliff during a snowstorm. One of them, a smiling blond Swede, lost eight toes and seven fingers to frostbite. He kept them in a mason jar. The amputated digits were black, as if they'd been spray-painted. The sunny Swede said they'd just snapped off, especially the toes. He'd taken his boot off to find them rolling around in the heel like black licorice jujubes. He was incredibly well adjusted to his loss.

As we walked, I sang old camp songs. It wasn't wise to announce our whereabouts, but the tunes kept the oppressive silence at bay.

"Land of the silver birch,
home of the weasel,
Where still the mighty moose
wanders at will.
Blue lake and rocky shore,
I will return once more.
Boom diddy-yaa daa, boom diddy-yaa daa,
Boo-hoo-ooo-hooo-oom."

Duncan said: "Pretty sure it's 'Land of the silver birch, home of the *beaver.*'"

"Really? I like weasel better."

Drinkwater's tracks stopped, went forward again, seemed to hesitate (judging from the depth of the imprint), then backtracked fifty yards to veer into a dense thicket. The shrubs were bare where Drinkwater had picked his way through; snow sifted off their limbs. I wondered what had caused him to change course.

The snow ran deep between the shrubs, almost knee high. We hit a natural laneway between the foliage, about two yards wide. There were animal tracks in the snow, roughly the size of a dog's paw prints. Drinkwater's bootprints were not as deeply impressed here: for a few steps they were barely visible at all before re-establishing themselves on the far side of the laneway. I stepped forward and—

"Stop!"

Duncan's hand was hooked in my collar.

"It's a fox run," he said. "Silver foxes, probably."

"So?"

"Don't move."

He dug in the satchel for the battery and lobbed it at the faintest of Drinkwater's bootprints. The trap sprang out of the snow, teeth colliding with a metallic *schnik*.

Duncan pointed at a ring of dull yellow spray-painted around the trunk of a poplar tree. "A trapper's marker. Drinkwater must have seen that, found the baited trap, sprung it, reset it, covered it with snow. Then he stepped past the fox run, walked back down his own bootprints—he probably walked backwards, looking over his shoulder to make sure his boots came down exactly where they'd been—then took off one of his boots and made a print in the snow right over the trap."

I could picture it perfectly: Drinkwater balanced on one leg with his socked foot outstretched.

Duncan said, "Christ, he's crafty."

"It didn't work, you prick!" My voice rose into the icy altar of sky, going out and out. The sound settled into silence—at which point another voice may have come back, a soft, wavering note.

It will – ill – ill – ill . . .

It was that point in winter where afternoons were non-existent. First there was morning, sun twinkling off the snow. Next came a terminal grey interregnum, after which twilight swiftly fell.

The sun began to set, very red and cold. The twilight was growing teeth by the time we came upon a steep ridge. Our shadows stretched across the snow, outlines liquefying into the dusk. Wind scrawled the ridge's whitened edge, helixes of snow spiralling. Darkness locked the cold into our bones; the Mylar-wrapped coals in our pockets were long dead. Drinkwater's footprints picked a cautious path down the ridge. At a depth of twenty yards they, too, softened into the encroaching dusk.

Duncan's breaths were ragged and phlegmy; he'd been stopping often to hack up blood. Twice in the last hour he'd collapsed, coughing helplessly. Not one familiar signpost had carved itself out of the terrain. I found it remarkable that two men could live nearly their whole lives in one place and still be completely disoriented by the wilderness that surrounded it. A band of fear tightened round my heart.

Clouds scudded the horizon. A snowflake touched the nape of my neck. We didn't want to be stuck atop this bluff when night came down.

"Lower ground's better, Dunk. Even if we manage to make a fire up here, it could blow out."

"Long way down," Duncan said, his body angled against the wind as it howled up the ridge.

"Not from where I'm looking."

The decline was clad in shadows, the basin nothing but a grey gulf—it wasn't a long way down so much as an *indeterminate* way down. Our heels dug into the ridge. In the summer it'd be treacherous, but now, the rocks encased in ice, it was deadly. Saplings clung to the snow-clad shale. I grabbed one and stumbled back as it tore out of the ground, its roots as flimsy as threads.

Snow fell with sudden aggression, filling in the prints we were desperately following. A rough path presented itself: a series of rocky shelves switchbacking down and down. One misstep would send us tumbling over the edge. We inched down with hesitant stutter-steps. Sheaves of snow threw crystalline lancets at my eyes. I squeezed my eyelids shut and opened them as another gust raced away with my breath. Blood beat hotly at my temples yet I was colder than I could ever recall. It was no surprise to discover frost crystallizing on my face.

Drinkwater's tracks became two solid rails in the snow. The cold had locked itself so deeply around my brain that it took a while to realize what Drinkwater must've done.

"He started *crawling*, Dunk."

We got down on all fours, too. Rocks dug into my kneecaps and the butt of the shotgun banged my tailbone. The sky was only slightly lighter than the rocky scrim. Halfway down yet? No, but still far enough to seal the decision. Here and there shrubs protruded from the snow, their branches clad with frozen berries as pretty as Christmas tree ornaments.

We found a rock carved into a recessed pocket with an overhang to keep out the snow. We stopped and huddled inside, bodies pressed tight, legs drawn into our stomachs. Duncan heaved like a sheepdog with a busted septum and we both shivered uncontrollably: the cold had sunk so deep into our chests that we couldn't stop our teeth from rattling.

My fingers were waxy looking, the swollen skin stretched tight. Cold ulcers. Next came frostbite. The sunny Swede . . . what had he said happened when a body froze? On TV or in the movies, a body found in a meat locker was usually pasty-white, little icicles dangling from its chin. But in real life the skin would be black, wouldn't it? Frostbite bursts the surface blood vessels. Your blood freezes black.

"Are you g-good to g-go?" I asked.

Duncan wiped the blood off his lips and nodded.

We set off at a tormented crawl. Full darkness had fallen, which was a relief in its way: as we could no longer see the basin, we weren't dispirited by how far away it remained. A blade-edged wind tore down the rock face; I curled my hands into fists, plodding like a mule. My equilibrium was shot; half the time it felt like I must be climbing uphill. I stared skywards at a freak meteor shower: thousands of streaks through the air. I blinked. The meteors vanished.

The next time I put a hand down, the earth wasn't there. The path had hit an unseen edge. I lurched forward with a squawk, outflung arms grabbing for something, *anything*, closing around a sapling

growing at the lip; the sapling stripped through my hand like burning rope, flaying skin. Something clutched at my hips—Duncan's
hand clawing for my belt—but his fingers tore free and I was falling,
too startled to scream, shocked that it could happen like this, no
chance to say goodbye.

I came to in a deep drift, snow swirling above me like lunar
moths in a dark vault. I patted my body down to check if anything was obviously broken or leaking. My fingers were so numb
it was hard to tell what, if anything, was wrong. Running my
hands over my own body felt no different than running them
over the hood of a car.

Duncan elbowed through straggly pines, his face plastered with
blood.

"Stay st-still," he said. "Can you f-feel your feet? W-wiggle your
t-toes."

I almost laughed. For all I knew my feet had snapped off at the
heels. Duncan offered his hand. The fact I could stand stunned me.
Something may have been ruptured inside but the cold acted as
a natural novocaine.

The snow blew nearly sideways, pinging off my skin as if off
glass. The eyelashes of Duncan's left eye were frozen. He wet his
fingers with the blood pooling in his mouth and massaged his lashes
until they unstuck. Then he pulled the final flare from the satchel,
popped it alight.

Had anything been watching from a godlike vantage, hovering
miles above, it would've seen a wavering ball of red light moving
with agonizing slowness through the night. That ball was surely the
only light to be seen for many miles.

Trees filled in around us; soon we were sidestepping them, stumbling over buried sticks and branches: should we collect them, build

a fire and hunker down? The very idea of shelter was silly—what would we build, an igloo? You couldn't hide from this cold.

My worldview winnowed to a pinprick of intent: keep . . . moving . . . *forward*. My breath came in shallow gulps but miraculously I'd stopped shivering; a calm had settled into my bones. I felt like sitting down. A cheery, sensibly gruff voice in my head told me to do whatever I felt like.

Take a load off, son. . . . sit your ragged ass down.

We struck it in unison: a ringing metallic wall. Duncan tripped back as the hollow reverberation trailed into silence, and squinted at the boxy obstacle in our path. Was this it—had we reached the edge of the universe?

My mind was so numb that I couldn't puzzle out how to get around it, whatever it was. Maybe we would have kept bashing into it like flies into a window had Dunk not given it a half-hearted kick. A sheet of snow dislodged from the underlying metal.

A van. A very old van.

A very old brown van.

Bruiser Mahoney's old brown van.

We burned the seats first.

The upholstery had been picked at by animals, the stuffing stolen by birds. We tore out what was left in spongy handfuls, hacked the leatherette upholstery with hands now trembling not from the cold but in anticipation. We piled it outside the van's rear doors, doused it in gasoline and lit it with the flare.

It ignited with a hugely satisfying *whoomph*. Duncan's hands were nearly *in* the fire: neither of us could properly feel the heat. I wanted to cup the fire like water, splash it on my face and up my arms.

By the time my fingertips were prickling with sensation the flames had burned dangerously low. It took the greatest effort to haul ourselves away and scavenge in the van for anything else that would burn.

We hacked ragged Xs into the passenger seat and harvested every scrap of foam. We tossed water-fattened bodybuilding magazines on the guttering fire, laughing like children as the flames devoured the veiny beefcakes.

Duncan tore hunks of radial tire off rusted rims: they peeled in long curls like monstrous black fingernails. They hit the flames and smouldered, sending up a noxious stink. I found the emergency spare under the bench seat and heaved that on, too.

The temperature inched upwards. Our faces were swollen and windburnt. Cold blisters burst on my fingers and oozed down my palms. My mind started to tick again, but the flames were already dipping. I crawled to the front of the van and tore the stuffing out of the driver's seat. A small wooden box hidden within the seat coils fell to the floor. Curious, I dumped the box's contents—ancient vials filled with piss-yellow liquid and a reusable syringe—then returned to the fire. The box was made of cheap presswood; the flames devoured it greedily.

I crawled under the van and found a log big enough to burn through the night. Once its icy encasement melted, the fire crept along the wood with grasping orange fingers.

Duncan lay with his legs dangling over the bumper. His hitching, shallow breaths sounded a lot like hiccups. He looked helpless, a fish asphyxiating to death on the beach.

"It's your lungs," I said. "Blood in them. Can I take a look?"

Dunk gave a vague shrug. I unzipped his parka, rucked his sweater up. His chest was nearly black from nipple to nipple, the skin tight-swollen. There was a horrible dent on the heart side of his chest near his abdominals.

"Broken rib . . . punched into your lung? Jesus, Dunk. How did you make it this far?"

Duncan closed his eyes. Blood dripped out the side of his mouth. If we couldn't get the blood out of his lungs, he'd choke to death on it.

I crawled to the front of the van, searching for the contents of that wooden box. I found the vials first. Their labels were faded, but one I could make out: *Testosterone ethanate.* The other read: *Equipoise.* Bruiser's travelling 'roids case? I rooted under the seat until my hand closed on the syringe. Old, Victorian-looking; I envisioned genteel addicts in deerstalker hats funnelling opium into their veins with the thing.

It *could* be done: slide a needle into Dunk's lungs, drain the blood. The needle looked up to the task: long, with a wide gauge. A hog-sticker. The tip didn't look especially sharp. Would it pierce the chest plate? Was there an actual plate of bone behind the rib cage, or just durable cartilage? The needle could pierce cartilage, surely. But I'd have to drive it hard into Duncan's chest.

A foolproof plan? Hardly. The needle could break. There was that. Or not quite reach his lungs. Or Dunk's blood might be too coagulated to flow, and it would be like sucking wet sand through a cocktail straw. Those problems didn't seem important when I considered that Dunk would surely die if I did nothing at all.

"I could try to drain the blood."

Duncan cracked one eye and saw the needle. "With that?"

I nodded. "I've seen it done."

"Where?"

"Can I be straight with you? I saw it in a movie."

Duncan smiled. Blood shone on his teeth. "Which one?"

"Don't remember. It had Mark Wahlberg in it."

"Marky Mark?"

"I don't even know if it'll work, Dunk. Plus I guess it could snap. Infection's a possibility—who knows what Mahoney used this thing

for. Worst-case scenario is, you end up with a needle sticking out of
your chest."

Duncan shook his head. "W-worst-case scenario is . . ."

"We know the worst-case scenario, don't we?"

Dunk let his eye slip closed. "So try."

I dipped the needle in gasoline, shook off the excess and held it
to the flames. A tongue of fire lapped the metal. I held it until the
heat blistered my fingertips, then doused it in the snow.

I screwed the needle back onto the hull, debating. Ultimately I
elected to straddle Duncan's hips so I could bear down with my
full weight. Running my fingers across his chest, I hunted for the
separation between his ribs. The skin was too swollen to make it
a certainty. I found the spot where Duncan's heartbeat was stron-
gest; I guess I'd aim someplace to the right of that? Couldn't push
too hard—if the needle hit bone and snapped, there went our
chance. I'd have to slide it in real nice and slow.

"Ready?"

"Go."

I positioned the needle on the perimeter of blackened skin.
Shoulders hunched, I bore down with even pressure. Duncan's skin
dimpled slightly before the tip pierced; he grunted as the needle slid
through layers of tissue into pectoral muscle. It hit an unflexing
hardness. Bone? I let go of the needle, left it jutting from Duncan's
chest. I felt my own chest. My ribs were closer to the surface, I was
sure of it—I must've hit Duncan's chest plate.

I gripped the hull again and pushed. The cartilage buckled like a
sheet of plastic. A burbling noise came out of Duncan like a sewer
backing up. A bubble of blood formed between his lips, bursting
wetly. My arms flexed. My elbow wound tore open, and blood
streamed down my forearm.

The noise the needle made punching through Dunk's chest plate would have been familiar to any schoolchild: a three-hole punch crunching through a sheaf of construction paper. The shaft sank into the softness of Duncan's lungs. Blood geysered out.

Dunk inhaled a huge lungful, then his breathing rapidly settled into a normal rhythm. After the initial eruption the blood settled to a steady trickle that ran down and around his hip bones. We lay together listening to his lungs drain.

"Turn on your side," I said. "That could help."

In time he sat up. Blood lay dark on his chest. It had soaked into his jeans, and it dribbled out of the syringe like a drippy faucet. He unscrewed the glass hull so just the needle protruded from his chest.

We sat with our legs dangling off the bumper, feet kicking as if we were kids perched on a railing. The wind had tailed off now, and the snow fell in big soft flakes.

A wolf sat beyond the firelight, nearly invisible in the snow. In the night stillness I heard it breathing, smelled the gamy oil of its coat.

"Go on," I said. "Scat. Skedaddle."

The wolf stayed, but I didn't mind. It wasn't aggressive—just curiously opportunistic, like any wild animal.

"Tell me a story," Dunk said.

"What?"

"The last time we were out here—remember? The . . . the dogs living on that giant meatball. Or the one about the man who lives behind the Falls."

I could barely remember telling those tales. "I haven't told a story in years."

I found two Coke cans, cut the tops off, packed them with snow and set them near the embers. Once the snow had melted I handed one to Duncan. The water was icy-cold, clean and sweet. We drank, burped, repacked the cans.

Duncan said, "I have a story."

"Yeah?"

"Well, not so much a story as this dream I'd have in prison. It always started at the end. Ed would be standing there and I'd be going away from her . . . being pulled, more like. And I'd say, 'I'm coming back. To you, to everyone—Mom, Dad, Owe, everyone. I'm not gone long. This is just the wandering time.'" His expression was perplexed. "*The wandering time?* And Ed, she's not upset or angry. All she says is, 'I won't be here when you get back.' Which crushes the hell out of me, y'know? And what I say is: 'I'll find you.' After that it's nothing . . . it's whiteness. Ongoing white, like out there." He pointed into the snow. "And I'm gone in it, right? For how long I really can't say. I wake up staring through white, like someone has poured milk on my eyes. But I always think I'm almost back where I belong. Just before I wake, I believe I'm almost out of the white."

The first edge of dawn broke along the bottom of the eastern sky and the wind picked up out of the trees.

We'd dozed fitfully. In the witching hour something settled softly upon the roof. It bore a musty smell, like hay in a barn. I stared up at it through the heavy grey. A metallic *scriiiitch*. A trio of dark sickles—talons, I realized, likely belonging to an owl—hooked through rust holes in the roof. Perhaps this was something this particular owl did often—a nightly observance? It took flight again, its heavy wing-beat carrying over the night's tranquility.

There is a silence particular to the wilderness at dawn: every creature still sleeping, the earth resting, too. The rising sun reflected off the fresh-fallen snow, postcard-pretty. I sat on the bumper, staring bleary-eyed across the grey light of the clearing. The wolves were gone. My feet were swollen inside my brogans.

I pulled the shoes off, wincing. My socks were tacky and crusted—they appeared to be fused to my feet. I rolled the left one down to my ankle, noting how the skin beneath was fish-belly pale. Then I gritted my teeth and peeled it all the way off.

The sock made a gluey sound, like a strip of ancient duct tape coming off cheap upholstery. Translucent webs of fluid pulled away from the pink blister on my heel; it was as big around as the mouth of a teacup, peeled down through several layers of skin, edges curled up like the caldera of a volcano. A puck of milky skin was stuck to the inside of my sock. There was another deep blister on the pad of my foot, but the worst were my toes. The skin over the phalanges was an ulcerated, shiny red; higher up, the flesh had sloughed away to disclose my nail beds. The skin near the tips had a crystallized, wooden look, like a slab of steak forgotten in a deep-freeze. The end of each toe was black—not blood-blister black, but a terrifying withered black that indicated the flesh was past the point of regenerating.

Four toenails had fallen off. I touched the one that remained on my big toe. The nail sank into the flesh. A substance resembling blood-strung Vaseline oozed around the nail, which slid easily out of its bed—no less shocking than if I'd reached into my mouth and effortlessly pulled a tooth out. I brought the toenail to eye level, stuck to my fingertip, studying it with horrified wonder.

"Don't bother looking at the other foot," said Duncan, propped up on his elbow.

After shaking the toenails out, I put the sock back on, which was far more painful than pulling it off. Duncan cut vents in the sides of my brogans so I could slip my swollen foot inside. He cut swathes from the skidoo upholstery and lashed them round my shoes with duct tape. When he was done my feet looked as if they'd been dipped in pewter.

"You look cheery," I said.

"I feel a hell of a lot better. Sure, it's weird—a spike of metal skewering me like a moth on a pin, but I can breathe almost full."

"Should we risk it?" I said. "We could stay here, keep the fire going. We've got all day to gather wood. You have to assume someone's looking for us by now, right? A search helicopter's sure to spot the smoke."

"What about food?"

"We might be able to kill something. Anyway, I heard a body can go awhile without food. A week at least."

Duncan didn't disagree in words. He simply packed up our meagre supplies and crossed beyond the guttering fire.

"It can't be that way," he said, pointing towards the steep incline we'd crawled down the night before. "And it can't be anywhere that way, either," he said, gesturing to where the van's hood was pointing. Eventually he pointed east, where the whitened crest of escarpment merged into the cloud-strung horizon. "That way."

"Okay, Dunk. But how far?"

"Four hours? Six? We can make it out before night falls."

"You're sure?"

"Pretty sure."

"Such confidence! You're an odd one, Duncan Diggs."

"Odd as a cod, Owen Stuckey."

We set off through the morning silence, boots crunching through the hardpack. The wind pushed gently at our backs. Our bodies were damaged, but the pain was manageable. We walked for half an hour before stumbling upon Drinkwater's bivouac.

At some point in the night, with darkness falling and the snow swirling, he'd found a huge oak snapped in half. Its insides had been eaten away by termites and dry rot, leaving a hollowed-out bowl. The wood inside the bowl was scorched in spots. We sniffed the mingled smells of charcoal and urine.

"He . . . he *slept* in here?" Dunk said. "Holy shit."

I doubted Drinkwater had slept. He'd probably scooped out the snow, hunkered down and capped himself in. He'd waited out the storm inside a *tree trunk*. He must be carrying a butane torch; he'd obviously set fire to the termite-softened wood.

"Look at this," Dunk said.

A firepit lay ten feet from the tree, its coals still warm. A gutted carcass lay nearby. The smell gave it away.

Duncan said, "You ever hear the phrase 'I'm so hungry I could eat a skunk's asshole'? Drinkwater actually did."

One of the skunk's back legs was snapped and gored. Had Drinkwater found it in the fox trap he'd set for us? If so, that meant he'd carried it around for hours, trudging through the snow with a dead skunk strapped to his back.

Drinkwater's tracks set off in a direction opposite to where we were headed. I considered: Drinkwater was exhausted, cold, probably injured. Depending on the freshness of that skunk, he might have food poisoning. Was he delirious? Did he even want to escape the woods? Maybe he wanted us to follow him like dogs chasing a coyote, running us in maddening circles. Was he happy enough to die if it meant killing us, too?

"We stick to our line," I said.

The sun charted a course behind banks of iron-grey clouds. Though not especially bright, the day was unseasonably warm. The snow lost its glitter and took on a gleaming quality: long bands of light ran across its surface the way light fills the slack water between ocean waves. A booming *crack* rolled across the earth as dead timber split under a weight of heavy snow. A low pattering filled the air as clumps melted and dripped off branches.

I craned my ear over that pattering, searching for the *thucka-thucka* of helicopter blades. I desperately wanted to believe a search party had been dispatched. At the very least, surely Silas Garrow would have wondered about us by now? Or Dunk's parents, when he hadn't come home?

Quicksilver shapes fled along the periphery of my vision. At first I figured they were chimeras born of sleeplessness and frayed nerves, but I focused and saw the wolves were back. Had they ever left? Loping a few hundred yards to either side—the two smaller ones, probably females, on the left, the big male on the right. *Ghost wolves*, I thought.

We reached a meandering creek. The snow had melted along its banks to expose dark brown mud. I wondered if it was the same stretch of water where Dunk had held a thrashing mudpuppy in his palm years ago. We navigated the frozen creek bed, boots whispering over the ice. I scanned for signs of human intervention: fence posts, trail markers, a moonshiner's still. Nothing. Even the rusted pop cans and plastic bags—tumbleweeds of the modern world—were buried under the snow.

As the day entered afternoon, a rifle crack carried out of the woods. Both of us ducked instinctively, but my heart leapt. Could it be a hunter or trapper who knew how to get to a road? Next a hollow scream rose above the trees. It wasn't a human scream but the sound of a creature dying in agony or fear.

"What the hell was that?" Duncan said.

This was followed by a wild sobbing howl: a sound made by a human, yes, although the voice box must've been nearly torn apart from the strain. The howl fled into the icy sky, climbing steadily before dropping, only to climb again: the vocal equivalent of an air-raid whoop. It was the howl of a madman, and it belonged to Drinkwater.

"You figure he's following *us* now?" I said.

"Could be."

A gassy, fetid stink rose out of the earth. The ice took on a sickly yellow tinge. Duncan put his foot down. The ice cracked; water surged through glassy fissures. It was the hue of an alcoholic's piss with webs of blackly rotted matter suspended within it. My mind made a terrifying leap: could this be the same miserable grey muskeg we'd walked through as kids, the one that sucked the sneakers off our feet?

There are plenty of muskegs out here, I told myself. *It's low country. Water collects at the bottom of the escarpment.*

And I believed this, at least partially. That is the greatest trick of survival: making yourself believe the best-case scenario. It was when you started to believe the worst-case scenario that you were doomed. I breathed shallowly, trying not to vomit. The stink rising off the ice was nauseating. I couldn't afford to lose whatever precious nutrients remained in my stomach.

"Hold up a minute," I said, leaning heavily on a tree. My gorge throbbed against my Adam's apple. The tree snapped, and I clutched desperately at the rotted trunk as I fell, splinters driving under my fingernails. My knees hit the ice, which spiderwebbed under my kneecaps. Rancid water seeped through to soak my trousers. A gas pocket ruptured, bubbles popping lazily through the ice. The stink was indescribable. Black dots swam before my eyes. I vomited helplessly into my mouth. It took every ounce of self-control to breathe deeply through my nose and swallow it.

"You okay?" Duncan asked.

Dark slivers lay under my fingernails. My knees were soaked with reeking water. I'd thrown up and swallowed stomach acid.

"Let's just go."

We left the muskeg and its sad shattered trees. The sunlight was fading and the snow took on a granular, slate hue. The chill crawled back into our bones.

The outline of a radio tower carved against the horizon. We progressed towards its lacework of man-made angles. Maybe it'd have a telephone or at least an emergency switch to pull . . . but no. It was only criss-crossed metal escalating to a cell-phone dish. Why *would* it have an emergency phone?

I slumped at the base of the tower, racked with an exhaustion that was almost comical. Maybe Duncan could roll me up like an old carpet and carry me over his shoulder.

"We could chuck rocks at the dish," I said at last. "Maybe there's a sensor that trips an alarm when it's wrecked."

The dish was over a hundred feet up. Could either of us heave a rock even halfway? Duncan hacked wetly; blood burped out of the needle. "Come on, Owe," he said.

I barely heard him. I was thinking about the plastic vent on the side of my childhood house, the one that connected to the clothes dryer. In the winter, I'd come home after tobogganing and see white plumes coming from the vent. Crouching beside it, I'd rub my hands in the warm air. It smelled the way my mother did in dreams: of fabric softener and dryer sheets. The basement window sat next to the vent. One time I'd seen Mom hiding Christmas presents above the heating ducts, something that had made me sad: I hadn't believed in Santa—Bovine had spilled the beans about the jolly fat man on the playground, ruining everything—but still, I *wanted* to believe.

"Get up," Duncan said roughly. "We got to keep going."

"In a minute."

"No minute, man. *Now.*"

"Jesus Christ, Dunk." I hated the timorous, whiny sound of my voice. It reminded me of when we were younger, how I'd always buckle to Duncan's subtle commands. "I'm not fucking ready, okay?"

"If we don't keep moving we're going to seize up. Do you want to make it out of here today or not?"

"Where the hell *are* we? You said we'd be out of here in a few hours."

"I said four, maybe five."

"You see that *swamp*? Pretty sure it's the same one we dragged our asses through as kids! Weren't you thinking the same thing?"

"It could be a different one."

"Oh *bullshit*, man. Bullshit. Look, I'm not putting this on you—"

"Really? 'Cause it's sorta sounding that way."

I stood. If this was going to happen, I needed to be squared up, looking my old pal full in the eye.

"I'm not putting this *specifically* on you," I said. "The decision to leave the van, I mean. If we're miles from safety—and yeah, I think we are—well, hey, that's on me, too. I made that decision with you. But the fact that we're here in the first place . . ."

"What are you saying?"

"Don't give me the fucking thickhead routine, Dunk. I've sweated out smarter guys than you. I'm saying this whole thing with Drinkwater. This vendetta you've got against him."

"I'm sorry? Weren't you raging about having to bury his dog?"

"I want him, yeah. But you'll chase him to Siberia."

Duncan held his hands out as if presenting me with a fragile gift. "Don't I have good reason, Owe? Eight *years*, man. I'm not saying I didn't deserve it. And this whole thing—you helped set it up!" He fixed me with a baffled, pleading expression. "How is this not both of us?"

"Because it wasn't both of us, was it?" I said, my eyes feeling hard as stones. "Never has been. You make it out like there's some kind of equality between us. Maybe you even halfway believe it. But the order's always been pretty clear: first you, then me."

I knew I was charting dark territory here—old resentments burbling up. "What was your big idea, Dunk? Hop on the skidoo, chase Drinkwater down and what, drag him back to the sheriff? We fly off into the night, driven by your all-consuming need for . . . for *what? Justice?*"

Duncan ran his hand through hair that was oily-slick, matted with the residue of burnt radial tires. "Just . . . fairness, man. That's it."

"Fairness? Oh, for fuck's sake. *Fairness?* What world do you live in? Doesn't the situation we're in right now—doesn't the sum total of your *life*—hasn't it taught you that there's no such thing? Fairness and luck are for other people, man."

"You're wrong, Owe. I've been very lucky in my life."

I could only stare at him, gape-jawed. "Oh, really?"

"Not as lucky as some, but . . . we got lucky the last time we were out here, didn't we? We'll get out this time, too."

"And that's just it, isn't it?" A terrible calm settled over me. "You're always just so . . . so fucking *sure* of yourself."

Duncan said, "You didn't have to come, man. You could've stayed put. I wouldn't have blamed you. So why come?"

My pulse beat in every broken inch of me. This was the deepest part, wasn't it? The part I could hardly bring myself to contemplate, let alone voice.

"Maybe because of . . . I don't know, my anger at you all these years, that I thought was buried . . . Maybe I let you hang yourself that night on the river." It was my turn to hold my hands out, a wretched, out-of-place smile on my face. "I can't say for sure, Dunk. I mean, how well do any of us know ourselves? You paint a picture of the man you hope you are and pray that circumstances never challenge it. And I mean, if I *did*, if I let you walk right into it and did nothing . . . what does that make me? You're my best friend."

"It wasn't on you," Duncan said after a long pause. "Over the years I thought about it and I followed it back, too. You gave me fair warning. You painted the picture. I just didn't see it, or didn't want to."

"If your friend's got his neck in a noose, you don't kick the chair from under his feet."

"I kicked it myself."

Suddenly I was flooded with immense gratitude. I wanted to reach out and touch Dunk's face. But it was impossible—impossible now to find the effortless touch of our twelve-year-old selves who'd slept with our bodies pressed tightly together, spooning like young lovers, perhaps on this very spot.

"Want to know what I was thinking about?" I said. "The dryer vent at my old house. I used to crouch beside it on winter nights. It was warm, smelled nice. This one time I saw my father smoking in the basement. He'd promised Mom he'd quit, right? He smoked with quick little puffs, waving madly at the smoke, then dropped the butt down the flood drain. It was strange seeing him so worried, so rabbity. It was my *dad*, y'know? The toughest man in my little universe. But now every time I see him he looks older, frailer.

"There'll come a day when he slips in the shower and won't be able to get up. He'll be ninety, I hope to God, but it'll happen. And it will shock me, because I'll remember him in times when he was so strong. And all that strength will be gone, and he'll probably be angry and confused about it. So I'll need to be there for him. I owe him that. Mom, too. I've got to be there to pick them up when they're too weak to do it themselves, like they did for me all those years ago when I fell on my butt as a baby."

I shouldered the shotgun. "We've got to get ourselves out of this, you get me?"

"I get you," Dunk said.

The daylight held out longer that evening. The sky was low with a hazy sheen, the sun buoyed by heavy clouds. It hung above the horizon, a diffuse orange ball, edging the trees with a persistent mellow light. Every so often a noise bubbled up from behind us: the stealthy crack of a stick or a distant crazed holler. Drinkwater was back there somewhere, tracking us.

Just before dusk the heavy throb of helicopter blades washed over the landscape. The sound swelled, swelled . . . then steadily receded. It was probably the sightseeing helicopter that lifted off from the roof of the downtown Hilton; the Falls were especially beautiful at dusk, although I'd never seen them from the air.

The forest thickened. The land sloped upwards and narrowed to a natural bridge of sorts, thirty yards wide. The trees below were thin and bone-white, the tusks of enormous buried mammoths. We charted the incline and came upon a massive deadfall: a fallen oak with the smaller tusklike trees piled over and around it. The oak had fallen directly across the path; the rock drew steeply down on either side into a forest of those bony trees; if we fell, chances were we'd impale ourselves on them.

Small saplings grew out of the oak. It was a nurse tree: as it rotted, it provided nourishment for smaller trees. But it was a poor nurse: the tusks grew up from the dead oak only to topple over, dead. Their limbs lay at splintered angles, making the deadfall all but impassable.

Duncan said, "Turn back?"

I chided him. "You of all people."

Duncan clambered onto the oak. The bark collapsed under his boot and his leg punched into the rotted tree. He clutched his chest. I wondered if the impact had jarred the needle loose. He pulled his leg out, brushed petrified wood off his thigh and peered into the hole. "Huh. Could be easier to just go *through*."

A solid few kicks broke a hole. The insides were hollow, wood pulp glittery with frost. I pushed my shoulders inside the tree, inhaling a fusty sawmill smell. Chains of fibrous wood hung down, clung with insect chrysalises that looked like translucent seeds; it felt like being inside a pumpkin. My skull brushed those fibrous chains; a few snapped and fell down my neck, cold as icicles. I reminded myself it'd be far worse in the summer, the tree alive with squirming insects. I pushed at the far side of the dead tree. My palm broke through with ease. I cracked the bark away in jigsaw sections, opening a hole big enough to crawl through.

Dunk spied an overhang to our left, carved into the base of a steep cliff that spilled into an alluvial floodplain. There was room under the rocky shelf for both of us.

We gathered wood from the deadfall and kindled a fire with the last drops of gasoline, sitting on the stony wash as night rolled in. Dunk's face had a loose, distant quality born of physical exhaustion and mental fatigue. I'm sure my face looked much the same.

"A village once sat at the high side of the Falls," I said, beginning the story I'd been thinking about all day. "Did you know that?"

Duncan smiled wanly. "I did not."

"Centuries ago, okay? An unknown plague struck the village. At night, the graveyard was dug up and the bodies devoured—no, not devoured but sucked dry. The villagefolk—"

"Villagefolk," Duncan said dreamily, rolling the word around in his mouth like hard candy. "I like that."

"Yeah, so they believed something evil must live in the caves under the Falls. It must creep up the cliffs while they slept to feed on the dead. So they loaded up a canoe with succulent fruits and sailed it over the Falls. But the next night the graves were cracked open again, bones strewn across the ground. The village elders decided to send a virgin over the Falls."

"Those elders always figure a virgin will do the trick, don't they?"

"So they grab this poor girl and plunk her in a canoe. But once she's sailed over the Falls the elders get a bit of buyer's remorse. They go to the best warrior in the village and say, 'Hey man, will you go down and get her?' And he gives them a long look and says, 'Nah, fuck it.'"

"Really?" Duncan said. "*Nah, fuck it?*"

"I'm paraphrasing, but yeah, that's the gist. But the youngest warrior, he's always had a crush on the sacrificial maiden. He volunteers to go. The elders shrug and say, 'Fill your boots, kid.' So he clambers down the cliffs and finds a seam in the rock leading behind the Falls. It's dark in there. He hears the trickle of water on rock. And just underneath that trickle is another sound, soft—a whimper.

"The young warrior creeps into a honeycombed cave under the Falls and he sees . . . *it*. His heart quivers. It's huge. It's revolting. It's . . . a spider. The virgin is cradled in its eight furry legs, each as big as a fence post. Its fangs are dark elephant tusks. Its eyes are black boiled eggs, hundreds of them crammed into the nightmare of its face."

"Oh, jeez. That's so *gross.*"

"What could the young warrior do? A buffalo he could handle. A bear, even a moose. But this? He has to *out-think* it. So he backtracks out of the cave. He sees the spider's tracks going up the Falls—strands of gossamer as thick around as ropes swung from the rock face. He notices the spider's path scrupulously avoided the water. Is it scared of water?"

"Then why's it living under the Falls?"

"Maybe," I said, fixing Duncan with a sidelong look, "the spider was born there. Maybe it doesn't know any better. Or maybe it was rent-controlled and he was a penny-pinching, miser spider. Fact is, this particular spider didn't care for water."

"Ah."

"The warrior gathers strands of sticky gossamer and lashes them to an outcropping above the spider's exit hole, high enough that he'd have to jump to reach them. The rocks around the exit he coats with bear grease to make them slippery . . . except he leaves a few patches dry. Then he creeps back into the cave and yells, 'Hey, bug!'"

"Is that so?"

"It is so. Spiders hate being called bugs seeing as, technically, they are not. The spider flings the maiden aside and pursues the warrior. They scramble up the cave, the warrior a mere half-step ahead. Venom drips from the spider's fangs. A drop strikes the warrior's skin and burns painfully.

"He races out of the cave, steps nimbly on the ungreased rocks and leaps, grabbing a gossamer rope. The spider races out over the cliff, slips and falls. It hits the bottom of the Falls with a splash. The young warrior returns to the cave and finds the maiden. They marry—such was the custom at the time—and have many children."

"What happened to the spider? Did it drown or what?"

"Probably. Let's assume so."

"What do you mean, probably?"

"You're never satisfied, are you? Every 'i' needs to be dotted."

"That's right."

"Fine . . . know what? The spider was fine. It floated down the river and found another village and sucked everybody dry as a bone. Then it laid eggs in their mummified skulls, which hatched into a brood of huge pissed-off super-spiders who laid siege to the land. Many, many innocents were senselessly slaughtered. An epic bloodbath."

"Jesus, Owe!"

"Next time don't ask."

"How smooth is the language of the whites," a new voice said, "when they can make right look like wrong and wrong like right."

We reached for our weapons.

A guttural, mocking laugh creased the air. "I could've shot you both if that had been my aim."

A sickle of light bloomed on the far side of the deadfall. Drinkwater's face hovered in a flashlight's beam. Stubble glittered in the sunken pockets of his cheeks and dark matter was caked around his mouth. His eyes were deep holes in his face.

I said, "Why follow us?"

"Why not? You've been following me. Turnabout is fair play."

"You tried to kill us."

"When?" Drinkwater said, confused.

"The trap."

"The what?"

"The fox trap. Remember?"

Drinkwater waved his hand. "*Kill?* You were hunting me like a dog. Dogs bite when they're pursued, don't they? Nothing evil to that."

Duncan came around the fire until he was facing Drinkwater.

"You have a gun?"

Drinkwater nodded. "You, too?"

Duncan nodded. "Are you cold?"

The flashlight beam shifted, providing a momentary glimpse of Drinkwater's eyes. Bloodshot, jittery. Those eyes painted a picture of a man barely holding on to his life and sanity.

"My butane torch ran out," he said, "and the dark . . . the dark is *hungry.*"

Duncan pulled a burning stick from the fire. I watched, not saying anything, as he handed it through the deadfall. Drinkwater's face registered pathetic gratefulness. He lit a small fire. Soon there arose the smell of cooking meat.

"Want any?" Drinkwater asked.

"No," we said in unison, thinking about the skunk.

We listened as Drinkwater tore into leathery meat. Almost immediately afterwards came the sound of agonized heaving, followed by the stink of bile.

"Can't keep it down," Drinkwater said. "Full of worms. First the meat, now me."

All three of us sat in silence for a while, laying our grievances aside for tonight.

Finally Drinkwater said, "I have a story. A traditional tale my father used to tell."

"Knock yourself out," Dunk said.

"Once there were two brothers. Wolf, the elder, and Horse, the younger. Wolf was married to an evil woman. A real bitch! She lusted for Horse and wanted to see the younger brother ruined. She made seductive advances towards Horse, who always told her to bugger off out of love for his brother.

"One day Wolf came home and found his wife's clothing ripped and her hair in a tangle. The salmon-jawed witch told him Horse tried to have his way with her. Wolf was livid and sickened to hear it. But Wolf was also a snake—he resolved to kill his brother by stealth." Drinkwater paused. "You two ever fight over a woman?"

Duncan hesitated before saying, "No."

"Huh. You sure?"

"Why do you care?"

"No reason. Anyway, every summer the waterfowl would moult. They left feathers on the surface of the lake Wolf lived beside. The two brothers got into a buffalo-hide boat and paddled to an island in the middle of the lake to collect feathers to fashion fletching for their arrows. That summer, while Horse gathered feathers, Wolf paddled away, leaving his brother to die alone on the island.

"The lake was deep, prone to sudden storms. Flight from the island was impossible. Deeply hurt, Horse looked into the water and began to cry. He prayed to the nature spirits for help. He called on the Moon and Planets to vindicate him. Along came a friendly Beaver. Beaver said, 'Why the long face?' *Hah!*" Drinkwater slapped his knee. "Get it? When Horse told Beaver his sad tale, Beaver was outraged. He invited Horse to live in his dam. They lived happily together through the winter and spring.

"In the summer Wolf returned, expecting to find his brother's bones. While Wolf was looking around, Horse crept down the shore, stole his boat and paddled off. Wolf grovelled, 'Come back, bro! A misunderstanding!' But Horse smelled his brother's bullshit a mile away. When Wolf's wife saw the boat returning with Horse in it she fled into the forest, never to be seen again. The end."

Duncan said, "Kind of anticlimactic, Lem."

"A traditional Native tale," Drinkwater said stiffly. "We don't give a fuck about your Hollywood endings."

After a while I said, "You know we're going to take you in, Drinkwater. You may have killed a man."

"Just one? Can't you let me off with a warning?"

"It's all over, Lem."

Drinkwater's laughter held a wavering edge of spite. "Okay, mistuh officer. Whateva you say, mistuh officer."

Duncan said, "Good night, Lem."

Drinkwater spoke no more. We tended our fires, sleeping a little but none very well.

I rose with the drowsy half-light of dawn. The sun hummed against the horizon while the moon hung in its western altar like the last melancholy guest at a dinner party, too lonely to leave.

Varied parts of my body cracked, popped or crunched as I shuffled past the fire's embers. My skin was rubbed raw around my waist, which had shrunk significantly over the past two days. *The ultimate diet plan*, I thought grimly.

Drinkwater lay on the other side of the deadfall, curled in fetal position. The heel was broken off one of his cowboy boots, his coat was torn and bloodstained, his hair crowned his head in a messy bird's nest. I caught a smell, rank and rotten, and figured it was him—though who knew? Could have been me. All three of us were filthy and sick.

I walked a little way into the bush and unzipped. The morning was warm, even springlike. I squinted across the clearing as I unburdened my bladder, a small pleasure. The purple stole out of the sky as noiselessly as it had set in the night before. As my urine splashed the snow I scanned to my right and saw a deer standing fifteen yards away.

A doe. Her head was cocked at an inquisitive angle, her expression one of two that deer always wore: blithe or shit-scared. She seemed supremely unconcerned—why shouldn't she be, facing this human shipwreck in a tattered parka? Yet I felt the weight of my pistol in its holster and realized: I *was* dangerous.

Its eyes were the colour of a wet branch, its ears pricked up to the breeze stirring through the trees. Suddenly, the doe's ears pinned back. Her hind end went down and she sprang across the clearing with gangling pogo-stick strides.

The wolf passed by so close that I smelled the adrenal stink of it and saw the dark tufts of fur on its pistoning shoulders. It was the biggest one, the male. It dropped into a running stance that reminded me for a moment of Dolly. But the wolf ran with predatory zeal, covering the snow in reckless lunges that lacked a greyhound's grace.

There were flashes of movement in the trees on either side of the clearing. The other two wolves had appeared soundlessly, as hunters do. They were closing in from both sides: a classic scissoring move, a tactic as old as predator and prey.

The deer sprang forward, head darting from side to side, sensing the threat but not *seeing* it yet. The big male closed in, hackles bristling in the deer's blind side, ropes of saliva whipping back from his open jaws.

I drew my pistol. I'd fire into the air, scatter the hunting party. Thwarting the natural laws of nature? Sure, but I couldn't bear to witness it. I raised the pistol and—

The sound came from behind me: a whistling gasp, like the final breath of a dying dog. I slanted my chin over my shoulder, not wanting to take my eyes off the deer. Drinkwater was on top of Duncan, knees pinned to his hips. I caught the blade in Drinkwater's hand: the same bone-handled knife he always carried. Duncan's arms were up, forearms crossed in front of his face: that intuitive defensive posture a person takes just before a car hits them.

The knife slashed. Blood leapt into the still morning air. I lowered the pistol and fired. The bullet whined off the rocky outcropping. Drinkwater rolled off Duncan and fled into the brush before I could squeeze off another round. My gaze flashed briefly to the deer. The big male had his jaws locked round her shoulder, bearing her down under his weight.

I rushed to Duncan, who'd rolled onto his knees. Blood spilled between his tightly clenched fingers, shockingly red.

"Must've crawled through the deadfall," he said. "Suddenly he was on me."

He pulled his hand away from the wound. The slash went up his forearm, connecting his elbow to his wrist. It was near-surgical—layers of severed flesh, each with their own distinct banding like age rings in a tree.

"God damn that man," Duncan said. "God *damn* him." He stood.

Blood flowed down his hand, split into four streams and dripped off each finger. "I'm going to kill him," he said simply.

Next he was running—*fast*—through the glittery dawn world, the air cool and fresh. I realized this was all Duncan had been waiting for: an overt display of aggression. Drinkwater had finally assaulted him directly—with a knife, tried to slit his throat. *Thank God!* Duncan must've figured. *Now I can kill him.* He'd let his rage and pain carry him over. It'd be as easy as breathing.

No. I would not let it happen.

I pursued, losing ground. My boots were still covered in duct tape, making running difficult. Drinkwater appeared suddenly, dashing through the trees. Duncan clawed for Bruiser Mahoney's old pistol, freeing it, digging his heels into the snow and accelerating.

Drinkwater wheeled clumsily. His hand exploded with light. A slug drilled a tree five feet to Duncan's left. Duncan raised his own gun, but didn't fire. Was it jammed? I saw him stare at it, still running. Was the safety on? He fiddled with it, then fired. The pistol bucked in his hand, throwing his arm up. The bullet snapped a twig off a branch directly above Drinkwater's head. A little lower and the slug would have put a permanent crease in his forehead.

Drinkwater turned and fled again.

I ran, too, but after a few minutes, Duncan was so far ahead that he'd become part of the woods. The trees peeled away abruptly, spitting me out onto a smooth expanse. My boots hit it and skidded. An unbending flatness, with enormous firs edging the northern shore. We had reached the river. We actually *had* looped around and hit it again, further downstream.

I cocked my ear to the rush of the Falls . . . yes, yes, it was there. We only had to follow the river towards the sound, hug the shoreline, and soon we'd see signs of human industry: rolls of red-painted snow fencing, a slick strip of bare road, maybe a solitary truck ferrying a couple of ice-fishermen to their shack. We could hitch a ride. Might take a while to convince someone to pick us up, wrecked as we were, but the heart of Cataract City was huge. All we had to do was—

A bullet chipped the ice ten yards ahead, throwing shards into the air. Squinting against the sunlight flooding the frozen river, I saw Drinkwater toss his pistol aside. He and Duncan were thirty yards from shore, staggering like men nearing the end of a death march.

The shadow of a cloud slipped across the sun; in the fragmentary gloom I noted Drinkwater's knife was unsheathed and he was beckoning Duncan forward with it. Blood lay bright on Drinkwater's coat. Had Duncan winged him?

"Don't do it!"

Duncan mustn't have heard. He threw Bruiser Mahoney's pistol aside, lowered his head and charged at Drinkwater.

I saw it happening before it happened. It came as a premonition—something that, until then, I'd never believed possible. At the station, people showed up all the time who claimed to "know" they'd be involved in a car accident days or hours or minutes before it happened, or people who "knew" their loved one was missing because some harbinger, some dream, some dread instinct told them so.

I'd never believed those people until I pictured the ice cracking before it actually did. I heard the fault line split the surface—the sound of an aluminum can tearing in half—before it appeared. And I saw Duncan vanish as the plates of ice snapped beneath him, dropping him into the river as neatly as a sprung trap door, all a split second before it happened.

The next moments unfolded in brilliant slow motion, as if the world were a 78 rpm record played at a laid-back 33. I ran past the hole, steering wide, but the shatter lines radiated towards me, causing me to leap back with a yelp. Duncan was a spiderlike apparition under the ice—the white water ripcurled round his body, making it look as though he'd grown extra limbs.

Hot wires of fear twisted in my guts as I followed Duncan upriver, passing Drinkwater, who sat slumped on the ice. How to get at Duncan? May as well reach through aquarium glass and catch a swimming fish. I imagined the river crawling into Duncan's lungs with icy fingers, the familiar mineral taste of the Niagara filling him. The river flowed north from Lake Erie into Lake Ontario, passing through low country strung with willows whose branches drank from its fast-running flow, over a dolestone bottom and through the hydroelectric plant, which conferred its steely alkaline tang. I had a flash of how Dunk and I used to jump off the old train trestle upriver and the water would shoot straight up our noses; we'd surface with throbbing sinuses, spitting the water out, laughing like hell and kicking for shore.

A terrifying resonance carried across the frozen plate, the sound of a fist thumping a solid oak door. I believed it was Duncan, punching the ice. I had no real clue where he might pass—the Niagara's currents were notoriously tricky. My only choice was to guess and then hope. Racing twenty yards ahead of Duncan's shape, I pulled my revolver and shot a quartet of holes through the ice, which webbed as the bullets drilled through; gouts of freezing water spurted through dime-sized holes.

I stomped hard. The ice flexed and water spurted, but the surface didn't break. Duncan was ten yards off, on track but drifting right. I unloaded a fifth round and stomped hard enough that my boot cracked through, making a foot-wide hole. Brown water sucked the smallish plates of ice away.

I spread my arms and jumped in, dropping to my waist before hitting the rocky river bottom. Blistering cold twined round my legs.

I reached under the ice, grasping madly for Duncan as he passed by. The Niagara clutched greedily, buffeting my hips. My duct-taped boots skidded on the slick rocks.

C'mon, Dunk, be *there . . .*

It felt like being bitten by a big fish. Duncan's hands were so frozen and rigid that I nearly jerked away in fright, and in so doing I'd have lost him. But instead some instinct made them tighten spastically and I gripped back, as if to fuse our flesh together.

Duncan's body rolled with the water. For a long moment it was like a fishing line lying slack in the water. Then came a jerk as he passed further downriver, forcing me to anchor him against the current. My chest shuddered against the jagged crust of ice, knocking the air from my lungs. Digging my feet into the rocks, I realized that if I slipped I'd be under the ice too, both of us dragged into the depthless channels of the river to die amongst the brook trout and catfish locked in their winter stupor. Duncan's hands gripped mine tightly—was it just nerves now? Did fingers keep gripping after life had fled the body, the same way hair and nails kept growing? Bovine had once said that a corpse's hair kept growing up to four months after death. *It's true, man. You could dig up a grave and find an old businessman with a mullet.*

I managed to grab Dunk's elbow and gave a convulsive jerk, not caring if I broke the bone. Bones healed. Brains stayed dead. Gripping his collar, I drew him to me. His hands appeared over the icy lip. They remained outstretched for an instant, livid . . . then they tightened.

Duncan's head appeared, his eyes wide open. For a long moment he did not breathe. Then his mouth flew wide and he drew in a massive choking inhale. I dragged him up, laid him on the ice. Blue veins stood out on his forehead, like on a baby's head.

My gun was where I'd dropped it. One round left. I staggered downriver, the water already crackling on my trousers, and found Drinkwater in a spreading pool of blood.

"Give me your coat, Lemmy."

"No," Drinkwater said.

"Now."

"No," he repeated.

I grabbed his coat, aiming to take it from him as you would from a truculent child. He fought back fiercely. Something fell out of his pocket. It lay on the ice, its shiny casing winking in the sun.

I blinked, disbelieving my own eyes. A cell phone.

I picked it up. It worked. The signal displayed five full bars.

Drinkwater pulled his legs to his chest, encircling them with trembling arms. "You can't trust anyone," he said.

THE CITY

OWEN STUCKEY

⸺

T he city holds you.

And not just this one. Every city has that potential. A city holds you inside itself. The feeling is as comfortable as nesting in a warm cupped palm. And if that hand should tighten into a fist—hell, most times you'll barely feel it.

A city knows the shape of things and it shapes itself around you—or perhaps you shape yourself around it. The result is the same. The city doesn't really change. The city changes you. In my city, you come through hard if you come through at all. But I think people can be more beautiful for being broken.

We all occupy our own square of space and time. We have our memories and no one else's. We live one life, accumulating it in our minds as we go along. The city is part of that, too. The city is networked into the memories of everyone who walks those same streets, who works at the same factories, who plays baseball on the same diamonds where the dust still hangs along the base-paths minutes after a player's passage.

We city dwellers know the same things about our home, even

though we each see them from our own vantage. I know the
worn earth along the river's edge, tromped smooth by adventur-
ous children. I know small lawns fenced with green chain-link. I
know backyard pools with empty cans of Laker floating on the
surface. I know plastic drinking glasses beaded with sweat from
the Kool-Aid inside. I know two boys walking down a secret path
to fish rock bass out of the basin, fishing poles slung over their
shoulders like carbines. I know the forever surge of the Falls that
roars with the blood in my veins. I know of night woods that run
thick with white wolves. I know the slow sweet nectar of a Sunday
afternoon as it shades into evening, twilight braiding down the
streets and across a still river whose waters run deep, street lamps
popping alight to hold back the swallowing night.

Still, you can come to resent your own home. You can fill yourself
with the need to escape it. I remember feeling that way, then looking across Lake Ontario at the steel spires and reflective glass of the
bigger city in the distance, unable to fathom the industry taking
place there. But my smaller city, Cataract City, made sense in an
elemental way, the same way wrestling did back when I was a boy.

These days I drive the city sometimes, alone at night. I drive past
the places that built me, remembering. Past Derby Lane at post
time, the air crackling with electricity as Harry sends the hare zip-
ping down the rail. Past the weed-scudded lot where the Memorial
Arena once stood and where my childhood idol had flown in the
ring, unfettered by gravity.

Those places created me. Time shifts and passes more quickly
now, and I sense things will never seem as real as they did in those
days. Still, there's a vital current that runs through the heart of
Cataract City, too. That current twists and bends and flows into still
pools from which there is no exit. And there is a shadow side to that
current, an undertow that flows towards the Falls. In it you can see

things toiling, things shifting. And there are always hands to beckon you over.

Often I find myself at the Falls early in the morning when the tourists are gone. I picture the old man behind the falling water, he of the translucent skin. I think of the men and animals who've passed through his swallowing garden—Bruiser Mahoney, Igor Bearfoot, my dog Frag—and gone on into everlasting light. It no longer embarrasses me to think these things.

We all survived—me and Dunk and Drinkwater. I guess that much is obvious. I made the call on Drinkwater's phone; ten minutes later the medevac chopper was buzzing overhead.

It was a near call for Duncan. Stage 3 hypothermia with severe ataxia. Minor brain damage due to oxygen loss. The medics pumped his lungs, flooded his system with Adrenalin and glucosamine.

He pulled through. Of course he did.

Drinkwater was in rough shape, but he's a tough bastard, too. He'd lost three pints of blood from where Duncan plugged him and was bleeding out fast. They slapped on a tourniquet, pumped him full of coagulant and transfused him at the Niagara Gen—where, in one of life's little ironies, my own mother performed the blood transfusion.

He went into a five-day coma and came out in time to face charges of attempted murder. Silas Garrow had survived, too, and was more than pleased to point a finger at Drinkwater.

As for myself: I lost two toes to frostbite, plus the tips of three more. It messed with my balance for a while—you'd be amazed how accustomed you get to distributing your weight across all ten toes—but I got used to it. The surgeons opened up my elbow, pumped me full of anti-infection meds and stitched me up proper.

The captain has me riding a desk pending further evaluation. That's fine. I've been thinking about quitting the force anyhow.

There's a saying around Cataract City: *The sun'll even shine on a dog's ass some days.* I'd never really understood that turn of phrase before, but now I know what it means: Sometimes you fall ass-backwards into good luck. And, yeah, the sun was shining bright that day.

Duncan left Cataract City shortly after he recovered. He hugged his parents, said goodbye to the rest of us. He's off to find Ed. And I'm sure he will. He'll go to the ends of the earth, just like he said. And I'm sure that when he does find her, she'll take him back. If ever a pair were meant for each other it's those two.

A month after he left I got a postcard in the mail. It had the portrait of a bosomy lass in a red bikini on the front, with the words: *Wish You Were Her.* On the back was a note written in Dunk's clumsy all-caps scrawl:

OWE,
HEY MAN WHAT'S SHAKING? I'M SITTING IN
THIS MOTEL ROOM, FLIPPING CHANNELS.
WRESTLING'S ON. GOT ME THINKING OF
YOU . . . TO BE HONEST I DON'T KNOW WHY.
THE DOCTORS SAID THAT, YOU KNOW . . . THEY
SAID WHEN A BRAIN IS STARVED FOR OXYGEN,
IT'S LIKE BLACK HOLES CHEWING INTO IT.
THEY SAID YOU COULD EVEN FORGET YOUR
OWN MOTHER! ANYWAY, I SAW IT ON AND
THOUGHT OF YOU. AND IT WAS A GOOD FEELING.
SO IT MUST HAVE BEEN SOMETHING SPECIAL
EVEN IF I CAN'T REMEMBER ANYMORE.
I HAVEN'T FOUND HER YET. I WILL.

That note filled me with ineffable sadness, but I know all minds hold on to what is necessary and jettison the rest. I'd just have to carry those memories for both of us.

Dunk gave Drinkwater fire when I would've happily let him freeze to death. He's a better man than me. The admission bears with it no shame. If you encounter one of the world's exceptional specimens and happen to fall short of that standard, where's the shame in that?

I'm still kicking around. Sam Bovine and I go to the Cairncroft Lounge, which sits beside the Food Terminal on Lundy's Lane. It's a middle-aged meat market, to be frank—but what am I if not middle-aged meat?

I met a nice girl there, Gayle. She works at the Bisk. Nilla Wafers line. Skin sweetly perfumed of vanilla. Divorced, one child. I like them both a whole lot. We're talking about me moving in, and I'll do it if she'll have me.

The other day I drove across the river to the Attica prison just east of Buffalo. The day was clear and clean. White ribbons of smoke pumped out of the smokestacks at OxyChem.

I parked in the prison lot, sat on the hood of my car. The yard lay behind a maze of reinforced chain-link banded with razor-wire. The inmates milled in the yard, playing pickup ball or lifting free weights.

Drinkwater looked like the world's oldest scarecrow in his orange jumper. His hair was shaved down to a half-inch. He walked down the fence, then turned his eyes fearfully to the sky as if he thought something would plummet down on him.

He hooked his fingers into the chain-link. His lips were moving but I couldn't make out the words. I wondered if he'd gone soft. Then his eyes locked with mine across the fifty yards separating us.

I saw that old calculating clarity, the gears still winding true, and was relieved.

Some places you just can't leave, y'know? The specific gravity's too strong, keeps you locked in orbit. You've got to be *launched* out, like a circus performer from a cannon. If you manage to find that separation, it's all care free horizons. And if you never find the separation . . . well, maybe it was nothing you really wanted.

I'm glad Dunk's gone. Not *happy*, but glad. It's a big world out there. And I think Duncan Diggs was always meant to gobble it up in great big bites.

Drinkwater spread his arms wide, a crucifixion pose, and gave me a smile as big as the sky. This time, I could make out the words he spoke just fine.

"I'm still here, baby."

Spreading my own arms, I gave him that smile right back.

So am I, baby. So am I.

ACKNOWLEDGEMENTS

I figured I'd ladle out my thanks in the simplest order: the order of those who read the manuscript as it slowly turned itself into a book, offering their help and guidance.

So first, thanks to my father—always my first reader—for consuming and commenting on each part of *Cataract City* as I wrote them. For a retired banker, he makes a great first reader. "Well, son of mine," he said, "this is something different out of you. The same in some ways, sure, but different. In a good way, in case you were wondering."

Thanks to Neil Paris and Erin Tigchchelaar, who read an early draft of Part One, "Dogs in Space," and offered keen suggestions.

A huge thanks to my agent, Kirby Kim, who picked me up off the scrapheap in many ways, tuned me up, and got me back into the race. He worked the manuscript over, proposing changes that put the book in its best possible shape before sending it out for submission. Thanks to Ian Dalrymple for his comments as well.

An equally huge thanks to Lynn Henry, my editor. A more sensitive, writer-friendly editor you will not find. Under her guidance I molded the book into something different, and better, than what it was originally. You have to trust someone pretty deeply to embark on such a process, and I trusted Lynn completely. That trust was well-placed. Thanks as well to Kiara Kent, who made some very wise and helpful edits. Also to Francis Geffard, Ravi Mirchandani and Steve Woodward for their suggestions for improvement.

Thanks, finally, to the love of my life (corny, sure; but true), Colleen. She read the book at its final stage, fine-tooth-combing it for the tiny, maddening mistakes that can plague any first-edition book. I'm not saying they're all gone, but it's not for her lack of scrupulousness. Love you, baby.

Finally, thanks—and perhaps an apology—to Niagara Falls. Lest anyone get the impression it's *exactly* as I describe, I fully acknowledge it's not. The geography of the book doesn't always follow reality. And sure, it's got its share of demons and ghosts, but that's the same for any place. Any Cataract City residents who read this and feel a little sore, or believe that I've done their city a disservice, please understand that I hold a spot of profound affection for your hometown.

CRAIG DAVIDSON is the author of *Rust and Bone*, which was made into a critically acclaimed film; *Sarah Court*; and *The Fighter*. He is a graduate of the Iowa Writers' Workshop, and his work has appeared in *Esquire*, *GQ*, and the *Washington Post*. He lives in Toronto.

A NOTE ON THE TYPE

The body of *Cataract City* has been set in a digitized form of Caslon, a typeface based on the original 1734 designs of William Caslon. Caslon is generally regarded as the first British typefounder of consequence, and it is believed that these original fonts were used in the first edition of Adam Smith's *The Wealth of Nations*, a pioneering work in the field of systems thinking. Caslon is widely considered to be among the world's most "user-friendly" text faces.

The display heads, captions and table/figure texts are set in DIN ("Deutsche Industrie-Norm") Mittelschrift, a typeface originally designed for use on German road signs and licence plates. Two of the primary criteria for the DIN type family design are a facility for reproduction, and a clear readability in virtually any point size.

Text design by CS Richardson. Manufactured by Versa Press on 30 percent postconsumer wastepaper.